SAVAGE FURY
Wanda Owen

ZEBRA BOOKS
KENSINGTON PUBLISHING CORP.

ZEBRA BOOKS

are published by

Kensington Publishing Corp.
475 Park Avenue South
New York, NY 10016

First printing: June, 1989

Printed in the United States of America

I dedicate this book to my four constant companions, who give to me their love and devotion. Always, there is my husband, Bob. Sharing every minute with me as I type are my tiny poodle, Fancy, and my parakeet, Pepe. For those special times to relax, there is my Spitz-Samoyed, Gypsy.

Author's Note

My story and my characters are fiction but the arduous feat of laying the tracks of the Southern Pacific Railroad in the Arizona Territory in the 1880's is based on historical fact.

I did take the liberty of having the mighty Chiricahua chieftain, Cochise, die at a later date than history records his death. It was in 1874, at the age of fifty-one, that Cochise died, as he predicted he would when he last spoke with Thomas Jeffords, Reservation Agent of the Interior Department. Had Cochise not died when he did and had Geronimo not taken over to lead the renegade Apaches to raid and kill, many lives would have been spared—both the white man and the Apaches.

Part One

A Fury of Passion

A rescue of love,
in his eyes it had shown.
Unleashing a passion
she never had known.
—Sheila Northcott

Chapter One

How peaceful it seemed to Gillian Browne as she sat on the lofty plateau in the stillness of the afternoon to gaze down into the deep canyon below. The majestic Maricopa Mountains were there for her to enjoy and the winding Gila River intrigued her: where did it begin and where did it end?

Now that she'd celebrated her sixteenth birthday, it seemed she had an insatiable curiosity about everything around her. She could not explain it to herself so she didn't expect anyone else to understand it, either.

When she was fourteen she'd been taken into the family of John and Nancy Foster after a band of renegade Apaches attacked her parents' wagon train. How she had escaped death or being taken captive by those savages had been a miracle, she'd been told by the Fosters. When the Fosters had found her in the smoldering ruins of the burning wagons, with death all around her, she was in such a state of shock she could not remember what had happened. Now, some two years later, she realized that it was probably so horrible that she had not wished to remember it.

Gillian was thankful that she'd been taken in by such kind, good people as Nancy and John Foster. She tried to be the dutiful daughter they deserved because they'd given so generously of their love to her.

The fact that they were about her parents' age and were hardworking people of the land made it easy for Gillian to fit into their way of life. Gillian was old enough to remember why her father, Edward, had wanted to come to Arizona to seek a new life. Her mother, Amy, was eager and willing to accompany her husband on this adventure into a strange new territory she knew nothing about. She trusted his judgment and was certainly not afraid of hard work.

Gillian remembered her mother's delicate beauty. To gaze upon that fragile English loveliness, one would hardly believe she could endure what Gillian knew she had. And then to die so young! It seemed terrible to Gillian when she allowed herself to dwell on that horrible day.

Gillian tried to remember her father. She recalled the gray-streaked bushy hair and his heavy-bearded face. He had been much older than her mother. She wondered why he had brought such a delicate flower as her mother to this rugged countryside. She should have led a pampered, comfortable life, Gillian thought. Lately, she'd found herself feeling a deep resentment of her father for being so thoughtless of her dainty mother's welfare. She placed the blame for her untimely death on her father.

Somehow, it seemed different with the Fosters. Nancy Foster was a big-framed woman who could lift a sack of grain with as much ease as her husband, John, could. There was no beauty in her plain face or her stout figure. She could put in long hours without being exhausted. She had been born and reared in this rugged countryside of canyons, deserts, and mountains.

What a strange, magnificent place it was, with the snow up in the mountains and the unbearable heat of the desolate desert only a few miles below. Gillian loved to ride her little mare along the plateau and look down on the arroyo below, which seemed to be bottomless.

Her favorite peak on one of the plateaus was called the Eagle's Nest. It was here she sat this late summer's day to enjoy a few moments of serenity before going back to the Fosters' ranch.

Suddenly every fiber in her young body came alive when she saw the pinto pony gallop into the canyon below. Its rider made Gillian's bright blue eyes flash with excitement, and she brushed aside a wisp of her deep auburn hair that was distracting her view.

She found herself gasping, "God, he is magnificent!" It was true that the man she viewed was a most impressive figure in his buckskin pants, molded to his firm muscled body, his chest bare and bronzed. His jet black hair flowed around his back and to his shoulders. The classic features of his face were enough to draw admiration with the high cheekbones and black piercing eyes. As far away as she was, Gillian could make out the expression on his handsome face and the way his fierce eyes flashed.

She watched as he leaped off his pinto and walked down to the water's edge to help himself to a cooling drink from the stream coming down from the mountains.

He drank his fill greedily and eagerly as Gillian watched, spellbound. Her heart was pounding wildly and she realized she was breathing heavily. Why was the sight of him doing this crazy thing to her, she wondered?

As she sat there pondering this, she was dealt a more startling surprise. The bronzed god rose up from the small gully to look directly up at the plateau where Gillian sat, as if he had known she was there all the time. He stood there with the majestic presence of a king, giving her a lazy broad grin. Never had she seen a more handsome face.

She sat there, frozen. What she couldn't know was that this man knew her well. He'd seen her on the day her parents were killed and he'd witnessed the killing. From that day, Gillian Browne had been his obsession. As a young man of eighteen and a half-breed, he had been grateful that his tribe had not taken the lovely girl as their captive. He'd watched over her until the Fosters had rescued her. Only then had he ridden away to return to his mother's shack.

They called him Hawk, and his mother was a white woman. She had told him he was the son of an Indian chief who had taken her captive when she was a young woman. She never told him who the Indian chief was, nor had he asked as he grew up. He was just grateful to the man who'd rescued his mother from captivity and taken her as his wife, along with the infant boy she'd borne.

Hawk was always sorry that he'd never really known this fine gentleman who'd taken care of his mother and him for the next four years. But he understood why he was different from the Indian chief who'd sired him. His features were mellowed by the fair features of his Anglo-American mother, Solange. She was of French descent.

On the day of the raid that rained death and destruction on the wagon train Gillian's parents were traveling with, this fierce Indian chief had come to his mother's shack, demanding that his son accompany him. It had been futile for his mother to protest. Hawk recalled the man's words, "He is my son, too. I wish him to know his father's ways."

She'd pleaded, "Oh, please—please don't do this!"

"It is our way, Solange. It is the way of an Apache. Are we not called the nomad? Hawk is part Apache, whether you like it or not! You took yourself another man, but he is my son." His black eyes had savored the loveliness of her fair face for a moment before he spoke again. "Never have I adored a woman as I did you, but I could never have made you happy no matter how much I loved you. We are of two different worlds. But you gave me a very fine son, a far better son than I have from my other wives! I have my reasons for taking Hawk on this raid, Solange. There is a man in this group who must be destroyed because he wishes to destroy my people. I must kill him and all who follow him."

Hawk had allowed the tall chief to lead him from his mother's cottage in the woods. Awkward and ill at ease, he had sat on his horse as his father had rallied his impressive braves

12

around him to ride down into the Arizona canyon where the circled wagon train had camped for the night. But when the dawn broke and the fierce warriors had spurred their horses into action to ride down the canyon to kill, as his father had ordered them to do, he shied back in the wooded grove where they'd camped the night before.

Only a part of him was Apache; the real force in his life was his white mother. He adored her, and he loved the mountain man from Tennessee who'd married his mother.

He felt a bond of responsibility toward the lovely young maid who'd survived that raid, Gillian Browne. She'd never suspected it, but he had been her shadow for the last two years, watching and protecting her from afar. As a virile young man, Hawk had confessed to himself that he was in love with the lovely young maiden with her hair of fire.

It mattered not that he'd never spoken to her, nor kissed her. He loved her! She was everything he'd ever dreamed of falling in love with. Someday, they would meet, he knew this! Someday, he would kiss those luscious lips and heaven's doors would open. Paradise would be his! He was a patient man.

The young carefree Solange Touraine had never suspected the horrible fate awaiting her as she'd traveled with friends on the journey that was supposed to be a wild adventure. So lighthearted and gay had been their mood when they'd started out on their trip! None of them had been spared by the vicious Apache band who'd attacked their party.

It had been Solange's breathtaking beauty that had enchanted the leader of the band of savages. Solange did not know then that he was the fierce warrior, Cochise. Neither did she realize that her expensive French cologne intoxicated him more than his peyote pipe or the mescaline juices of the cacti. He claimed her as his woman and took her to his camp. He gave her more privileges than he had ever given any of his wives or women, but Solange found him repulsive. Her life was a living

13

hell, but she was determined to survive.

However, after a few months in his camp, Solange knew she carried his child. This would forever taint her. She was an Indian's squaw and society would never accept her again.

Being a woman full of life and spirit, she sought to live with the hope that she could somehow escape the Indian village. A lesser woman would have given up and not pursued that impossible dream, but she knew that was all that kept her from going mad during those next months.

Her son, Hawk, was only three weeks old when she found the golden opportunity to escape Cochise's camp. Fate was generous to Solange Touraine the day she fled from the camp and her path crossed with a kind-hearted, compassionate woodsman by the name of Tim McGrath who took her and her infant son to his secluded cabin in the dense woods.

This was where she still lived. The husky McGrath had married her, and they'd shared a happy life, raising Solange's son. Never again was she to bear a child so Hawk was very special to her and Tim. But five years ago, she lost her beloved Tim when a mountain lion mauled him to death. A deep void was left in her life and Solange found herself doting more and more on her son. More than ever, she worried about what the future held for Hawk. She knew the obstacles her half-breed son would face.

No one could have been more stunned than Solange when she watched her peaceful cottage being invaded by Cochise two years ago. Finally, he had tracked her down. When he and his five braves took Hawk away from the cabin, she never expected to see her son again.

What joy filled her heart when a few hours later Hawk was allowed to return! As Cochise marched out of the door he barked disgustedly at her, "Here, woman—keep this son. I want no part of him. Only your blood flows in his veins."

Solange didn't know what he meant, but Hawk did. He had taken no part in the raid into the sleeping wagon train. He had been horrified by the other braves, screaming and yelling like

14

wild things, raining their evil destruction and death on those poor people. No, he wanted no part of that!

Solange was not to know about the shame that filled his soul each time he recalled that horrible time. She was not to know about him riding back to the site to watch in secret as the rancher and his wife rescued the lovely, weeping maiden. She was not to know that for the last two years, he'd kept a constant vigil, watching this lovely girl anytime he chanced to see her riding her pony or strolling around the ranch. There was a very strong and deep feeling within him when he gazed upon her breathtaking beauty. It was a strange feeling for Hawk, because he'd never felt that way before.

This day, as he'd ridden into the canyon, he'd known she was sitting there on the lofty peak. Dear God, his heart pounded wildly in his broad, bronzed chest as he beheld her. She was everything a young hot-blooded man like himself dreamed about.

After he had quenched his thirst from the waters of the stream and had risen up to look at her, there on the plateau, he wondered what her response would be if he smiled or called to her.

When her dainty hand returned his wave and he saw the lovely smile on her face, he felt his spirit soar to those heights to join her. If he could have, he would have delighted in doing just that! Instead, he murmured softly to the winds blowing through the canyon, "I love you, Gillian Browne. I love you now and forever!"

It seemed his message of love ascended the vast space that divided them. A strange feeling engulfed Gillian as she waved back to the handsome bronze god standing there below her. Was he human or was he a god? Was she dreaming? Gillian's romantic heart prayed she was not just imagining all this.

15

Chapter Two

Nancy Foster roamed leisurely through her flower garden gathering flowers to fill her treasured crystal vase on her parlor table. The Foster cottage did not have many luxuries and it certainly had no fine furnishings. The furniture was simple and sturdy, made from dark native timbers. Nancy's windows weren't draped with expensive velvet, but she liked the colorful curtains she'd made herself. Matching pillows rested at the back of her sofa and on John's favorite chair.

He constantly blamed her soft little pillows for making him feel so cozy after their evening meal that he was forced to take a nap. She always gave him a sly, knowing smile for she knew it was her good food that induced that evening nap.

Lord, it was a good life they had here in this beautiful country, she thought to herself as she wandered contentedly across her yard where she could view the panorama of the majestic mountains to the south and, across the way, the golden-red canyons. Over by the small front porch of their cottage, two huge saguaro cacti stood guard to her home. She could recall how small they were when she and John had first come here.

She swiped away a straying wisp of hair from her forehead and smoothed back her thick hair that was pulled into a large coil at the back of her head. Some motion caught her eyes as she glanced toward the east and a slow, pleased smile broke on her plain face. The sight of that glorious deep auburn hair blowing back as Gillian rode her horse swiftly toward the cottage was enough to delight Nancy.

She adored the young girl as much as if she'd given birth to her. Oh, how she wished she could have given John a son or a daughter! God knows, she didn't know why she had failed. Everything about her big-framed body would have made having a baby so much easier for her than it had been for her friend and neighbor, Molly Hart.

She consoled herself that Gillian had surely been sent to them by God to make up for the void. She'd enjoyed every minute she had played the role of mother to Gillian Browne. She had become the joy of her life, and John's.

Like this wonderful, enchanting land, Gillian was a most unusual young girl, Nancy Foster had learned. There was an entrancing quality about her. John Foster agreed with his wife about that.

"Granted she's a beautiful little miss, Nancy, but there's something about that girl that I can't find the words to describe. You know what I'm trying to say, don't you, Nancy?" he'd declared after Gillian had been with them for about a year.

Now another year had come and gone, and the little fourteen-year-old girl had blossomed into a breathtakingly lovely young lady.

Just recently Nancy had voiced a new concern to John about Gillian. "It almost frightens me, John, how beautiful she is. I know that may sound silly but I can't help it. To be too beautiful can cause all sorts of problems."

Her easygoing husband had calmed her fears. "Now, honey—Gillian has caused no problems yet, has she?"

"Not yet, John, but you may not be saying that by the time this year is over. You mark my words, some young man is going to spy Gillian when she's riding around the countryside and then you just watch what happens."

A broad grin came to John's weathered face, tanned by the

hot Arizona sun. He thought to himself what a shame it had been that his dear Nancy could not have had her own children. She would have been the perfect mother. He loved her even more for her deep concern for Gillian.

He wished to set her mind at rest, so he suggested to her, "I think it would be nice if you took Gillian when you go to visit your sister next month. It would make me feel much better to know you had her as a companion on your trip there. Think seriously about that, Nancy. I can manage fine here by myself as you know."

Nancy had been so busy that she'd completely forgotten about the visit to her sister's. It seemed, now that Gillian was with them, that the days passed so very fast. It was a splendid idea John had suggested to her and she felt Gillian would be delighted about the trip.

Watching her ride toward the corral, Nancy decided she would tell her the minute she joined her. She watched her ride by and admired the radiance on her face. If she had known what had caused that flush on Gillian's cheeks, Nancy would have been terribly disturbed.

She did not turn to enter her front door until she saw Gillian dismount. Nancy watched her leap off her horse and could not help envying her youth and vitality. Oh, how wonderful it would be to be so young again! She sighed, watching the girl by the corral.

Nancy moved on through the door with her basket of fresh-cut flowers, knowing Gillian would soon be bouncing through the door to join her.

It was always sweet music to Nancy Foster's ears to hear Gillian address her as Mother Foster. She felt herself swell with pride, for she had not asked Gillian to call her by this title. It was Gillian's choice when she'd come to live with them. Actually, those first few days after she and John had rescued the girl from the ravaged wagon train, Gillian had called her Mrs. Foster.

Then came that particular afternoon after Gillian had been

with them a couple of weeks that she'd burst into tears, mourning the loss of her mother and father. As Nancy had comforted her and embraced her lovingly as her own mother would have done, Gillian had sobbed, "Oh, Mother Foster, I'm so glad I have you. I'm so glad you found me!" So it had been from that day until now that Gillian addressed her as Mother Foster.

Nancy had just placed her basket of flowers on the kitchen table when Gillian burst through the door.

"Isn't it a beautiful day?" she said. Nancy turned with a smile to observe the girl standing before her. Such a rosy flush was on her face, and a radiance that Nancy had never seen before.

"No more beautiful than you are, my dear! I think the only thing I could compare to that lovely face of yours are these pretty flowers in my basket."

It seemed to Gillian that Nancy Foster was always telling her how pretty she was. To most people this dear, kind-hearted woman would have been considered plain or maybe even ugly, but Gillian saw a beauty in that plain face. In the two years that she had lived under Nancy's roof, she had come to love her and her husband most dearly.

It was not the same love she had felt for her own mother and father but it was a special kind of love. It would forever endear them to her she knew.

Since her encounter this afternoon with the handsome bronzed god she'd viewed in the canyon, she'd been wondering if she'd experienced a new kind of love. Was this what a man and a woman shared, what led to marriage? Was the attraction she had felt as she viewed that virile young man—was that how a young lady felt when she was courted?

Gillian had never been kissed. Only recently, she'd been pondering these things a lot. For now, she dwelled in fantasy and daydreams of the man who would steal her heart and possess her love. Her inquisitive nature and the changes in her figure had ignited new feelings within her. As yet, she'd shared

20

none of these thoughts with Nancy Foster for fear that she would not understand. She had kept her secret thoughts to herself.

As Nancy Foster stood observing this sweet-faced girl of sixteen, she reminded herself that she and Gillian must have a talk soon. With such glowing, maturing beauty as hers, it was time Gillian talked with an older woman, since her mother was not here to speak about such things. A young man would surely be entering her life soon. It was inevitable, the older lady knew.

"Gillian, dear—I've a visit to my sister's I'm going to pay shortly and I thought that you would like to accompany me. I'm sure you would enjoy our visits to the shops in the city where she lives and she has a daughter about your age. John swears he can do very nicely without us."

Gillian's lovely face sparkled with excitement and life. Her blue eyes twinkled like exquisite sapphires as she exclaimed, "Oh, Mother Foster, it sounds wonderful!"

"Then I shall tell John that we are going and he can just hold down this place all by himself for about a month, eh?"

Gillian giggled with delight. "Oh, yes—yes, I can't wait!"

"Well, I'm glad that's settled, for I will be a busy woman the next few weeks doing some sewing for us. A couple of frocks we can both use, don't you think, my dear?"

Eagerly, Gillian offered her services, "And I shall help you, Mother Foster!"

Nancy gave one of her infectious gales of laughter and moved to embrace the young girl in her strong arms. Once again, Nancy was made aware of what a tiny little thing Gillian was, compared to herself. No wonder everyone had considered her a tomboy when she was Gillian's age and oh, how she'd resented that!

She gave a delighted sigh as she held the girl there in her arms. "Oh, Gillian—you are such a sweet child!" As she spoke the words, she knew she had voiced her secret wish: that Gillian was only a mere child, so they could have her with them longer. A child she was not, and Nancy knew this. She was only wishing!

John Foster's friendly voice interrupted them, teasing them, "Well, you two women seem in a very gay mood." He'd heard enough of their conversation to know that Nancy had finally spoken to Gillian about the trip to her sister's. He was happy; it would be good for both of them. After all Gillian had experienced, she certainly deserved some lighthearted fun. This Arizona countryside did not offer much for young people like her. God knows, his Nancy was entitled to a little enjoyment, too, and a visit with her only sister, Jane.

The two women turned to see John standing there, his broad grin creasing his tanned face. Each of them gave him a smile. To Gillian Browne, John Foster was a hardworking, generous man she knew she could trust and depend upon when she needed his help. Nancy appreciated all the hard work John had done to provide for her all these many years of their marriage. But the thing that truly endeared John to her was his unselfish, devoted love for her. No one had to tell Nancy that John Foster was a far handsomer man than she was a pretty woman. But he had fallen in love with her and that was all that had mattered to Nancy.

She sought to tease him by saying, "We girls are plotting to leave you on your own, John Foster. Gillian is going to visit Helen with me. You'd best behave yourself while we're gone." There was a look of mischief in her eyes.

Gillian loved the lighthearted way these two could jest with one another. She knew their love had to be a grand one to permit it. This was what she wanted in the man she fell in love with. Such warmth glowed in their eyes still, after all these many years they'd been married, and she'd seen the tenderness of their touch when they strolled around the yard in the evening or held hands. She'd found it very inspiring and wonderful. She hoped she would be as lucky as Nancy Foster had been when she found her John.

John Foster played along with Nancy's teasing game. "Oh, pet—I'd dare not misbehave 'cause I know you'd take that cast-iron skillet and bust me over the head."

The three of them broke into roaring laughter. Gillian suddenly realized what was so special about this little cottage and the Fosters, as she stood there observing the two of them.

Happiness was theirs! Gillian had shared it during the last two years. Deep in her heart, Gillian felt that somehow her mother and father must know that their daughter was in good, loving hands. They had to be at peace about her.

This thought made Gillian happy!

Chapter Three

There were still hints of the beautiful young woman Solange Touraine had once been. Her dark hair was now lightly streaked with gray even though she was not yet forty. There was still that gleam occasionally in her entrancing emerald green eyes. Perhaps the gleam was different from what it had been when she was the flirtatious French coquette captured by the mighty Cochise.

For many years, she'd not given way to vanity to protect her fine, delicate features from the sun. Usually, she forgot to wear her wide-brimmed straw hat, as she would have done earlier in her life. Life with her good-hearted Tim had not been exactly like the pampered lifestyle she'd been accustomed to before she came to this rugged territory.

But this late afternoon, as she stood contentedly watching the sun set and its golden reflecting rays gleamed down on the reddish-brown earth of the canyon, Solange swore she had never seen a more glorious sight. She stood there with a silence surrounding her in her solitude, thinking to herself that perhaps her life had been far more fulfilling than it would have been had she pursued the frivolous, reckless ways she'd thought were so exciting when she was nineteen.

Maybe destiny had been good to her after all. That was what she would like to think. *Mon Dieu*, she had a most magnificent son whom she adored with all her heart. Hawk was a fine young man, far more handsome than any of the dashing young dandies courting her in France before she'd come to this country.

Ah, yes, she had to confess that there were things she regretted and things she wished had never happened, but never did she regret having Hawk. It mattered not to her that she had been raped by the Indian chief. Solange's salvation for that horrible savage's degrading and shaming her had been to pretend he was the handsome young man she'd met only once back in France. That one meeting was enough to convince her that she loved that magical man, but as suddenly as he'd come into her life, he had vanished, leaving her with a broken heart.

It was this happening that had led her to accept her ardent suitor, Monsieur Jean Louis Beaulois's, invitation to accompany him, his brother and his wife to the new world.

Shortly after she'd left France, Solange had sadly realized she'd made a horrible mistake; Monsieur Beaulois was not an honorable gentleman. But there was little she could do about it then. France was hundreds of miles away.

Although nearly twenty years had passed since that fateful day when the hand of brutal Apaches had attacked their caravan, Solange recalled vividly the horrible end the Beaulois brothers and Madame Beaulois had suffered. Only she had been spared.

She liked to think that it was God's will that she give to the world a wonderful son like Hawk. It stirred great joy in her heart to think this.

It was these musings she was dwelling upon when she caught sight of the pinto pony with her son astride galloping as wild as the winds howling through the canyons, coming home. She stood there with a smile on her face. A most striking-looking figure of a woman she was in her full-sleeved tunic and copper-colored full, gathered skirt. Around her trim waistline she wore a treasured hammered-silver belt Hawk had made for her when he was sixteen. The brown leather boots she wore were also a gift from Hawk, costing him the salary he'd earned as a scout, and she cleaned them daily, using her special oils on them to preserve the fine shine of the leather.

Hawk saw her standing there, looking so proud and regal, and he threw up his hand to wave to her with a broad grin on his tawny face.

Solange stood without moving as Hawk raced the pinto up to the hitching post just outside the fence surrounding her cottage. With a vigorous leap, he dismounted from the horse and jauntily dashed through the gate. His strong hands clasped her waist as he swung her around as though she were as light as a feather, declaring, "Ah, Mama—you're as beautiful as the sunset this evening!"

Breathlessly she laughed, "Ah, Hawk—you must have enjoyed a nice afternoon. I'm glad that you, too, noticed the lovely sunset."

"One would have to be blind not to see that wonderful sight, Mama. For one brief moment I thought to myself, the sun was surely going right down into the canyon over there. Such a pretty sight it was—all golden."

Solange smiled lovingly at her tall son, glad that he appreciated the wonders around him. Secretly, she thought to herself how blessed the young lady would be who would win his heart. He was such a loving young man. Ah, yes, whoever she would be, she would be a happy, contented lady. Solange knew that her son would make her happy.

She had no inkling that he had gazed upon the woman he'd loved from afar for the last two years just a short time ago. Hawk was not ready to tell his mother this just yet. As close as they were and had always been, he knew the moment was not right, so it would remain his secret for a while.

But Hawk knew that if his mother and Gillian Browne should meet, they would instantly like each other. He instinctively felt that!

It would happen, he was certain, when the time was right. Whether or not he sought to admit the heritage of his fierce, savage father, a part of him was there, flowing in Hawk's fine-muscled body.

27

Hawk wished not to accept that part of himself. He was Solange Tourmaine's son and he took a great pride in that. He was grateful that his skin was not as dark as the Indian chief who'd taken him on that raid two years ago, nor his face as coarse-featured.

Solange only had knowledge of the turmoil that churned within her son from time to time, as it had since that day Cochise and his braves had ridden up to her cottage to carry Hawk away with them. Hawk had never given her any reason to concern herself with the many things that troubled his soul. Yet, his concerns about his future as a half-breed were the same ones that gave Solange many a sleepless night. She knew the tremendous obstacles he would have to overcome. She knew the Anglo-Americans would never accept him into their society. This frightened her.

Hawk knew one job he could always fill, and this was what he planned to pursue for the immediate future. A half-breed Apache scout was always in demand. He had not told his mother yet that he'd taken such an assignment. He had procrastinated because he hated to see the sad look on her lovely face when he told her that he would be away for several months.

Hawk had felt it a great honor to be hired as a scout by the Southern Pacific Railroad. Southern Pacific was most eager to get their lines laid across New Mexico and Arizona. However, the treaty made on December 30, 1853 by a prominent Southern railroad man, James Gadsden, granting the right of way to the railroad, had not been easily won. There were still problems that the Gadsden Purchase had not achieved. Indian raids were still playing havoc in the Arizona territory and taking many American lives.

To take part in preventing these raids was very important to Hawk. Somehow, it eased the horrible nightmare he'd witnessed two years ago which would forever leave a terrible taste in his mouth. If he could help the Americans, then this was what he sought to do. It was one way to rid himself of the taint and soil of being the son of the Indian chief, Cochise.

Hawk did consider himself soiled by the man who'd sired him, and that is why he'd sought to apply as a scout by the name of Joe Hawk.

Solange did not know that her son had suddenly given himself a new name!

Hawk had picked the name of Joe because of an old miner who'd befriended him as a youth. He'd always remembered the old man for his gentle ways and kind heart. To announce that he was Joe Hawk sounded grand to Solange's half-breed son. It swept away the hint that he was any part of an Indian.

Many miles away from the territory of Arizona and across a vast ocean, there was a young man by the name of Stephen Lafferty. If you were considered one of his special friends, you could call him Steve or Captain Lucky. His seafaring pals knew him as Captain Lucky because he was the master of a fine, slick-lined schooner, *Lady Luck*. The numerous ladies who'd lost their hearts to him knew him as Steve.

Lafferty saw no reason to inform them of his last name, and it was not because he felt any shame about it. He just figured they did not need to know it. The elusive Lafferty had no intentions of having a lingering relationship with any woman. He was going to roam and wander this world for the next ten or fifteen years, so he wanted no woman hanging around his neck. A moment's pleasure was all he sought. Handsome he was, and he knew it! His firm, muscled male body was enough to make any woman sigh with delight.

His skin was deeply tanned due to the days spent on the deck of his schooner, sprayed by the salty sea. His sandy-colored hair was allowed to grow down his neck to tease the top of his broad shoulders. But it was his magnificent eyes which entranced the ladies. They were the shade of the seas he loved to sail, and they had a hypnotic effect on the ladies he courted and a strong but quite different effect on the crew of ruffians he mastered on his schooner.

As young as he was, he was effective as the captain of his

29

ship; that's why he was called Captain Lucky, a name that instantly demanded respect in England as well as the eastern coast of America.

All the harbor masters of the eastern coastline of America and along the Florida Keys knew of Captain Lucky. In the last few months, his name was becoming known along the Gulf of Mexico, too, since he had been commissioned by Southern Pacific Railroad to deliver materials they needed to complete their tracks to California. Their fee was enough to excite Steve Lafferty!

Steve could not believe the figure they'd taunted him with to take on the task they wanted him to do. He had to admit that he felt a heady giddiness at the figure they'd projected. It was a hell of a fee for four months' work. All he had to do was think of the luxuries he could give his mother to convince himself that he must do it.

The summer day he set sail for that strange country across the vast Atlantic, Steve Lafferty had no inkling that his whole life would change. Never would the randy sea captain have imagined that an encounter with a tiny miss with hair of fire and eyes of brilliant blue would change his life. But, it was written in the heavens above that these two young people must meet. This lovely miss by the name of Gillian Browne and this young man by the name of Stephen Lafferty were fated to cross paths. Entangled in their lives would be a young man by the name of Joe Hawk—a man who gave no quarter to any man.

Young and innocent Gillian Browne was hardly prepared to match the fierce, hot-blooded passions of Hawk, nor was she experienced enough to resist the charms and smooth tongue of the reckless Irishman, Stephen Lafferty.

But Gillian possessed a powerful weapon she was not aware of: her ravishing, bewitching loveliness. It could render men like Joe Hawk and Stephen Lafferty utterly helpless!

Neither of these two men would have believed he could be so bewitched by a woman. But neither had ever met a girl like Gillian!

Chapter Four

Never did the birds sing so sweetly as they did in the early morning hour. There was such peace in the countryside! A heavy dew covered the grasses of the woods as Gillian took her morning ride along the trail leading into the Maricopa Mountains. She wore a faded blue shirt and a pair of John's old pants which Nancy had cut down to fit her petite figure because Gillian did not like riding sidesaddle.

Her long flowing auburn hair cascaded down her back as she reined her feisty mare along the trail. Marvelous aromas teased her nose as she rode along, and her brilliant blue eyes were busy taking in everything around her. It was exciting to explore all the beauties of nature. The trees and the wildflowers interested her. The birds and the creatures of the forest intrigued her; they could hold her interest and her time for an hour or two.

But Gillian was not prepared for the abrupt blast of rifle fire echoing through the woods, nor was she holding the reins tightly on her mare, Dancer. The sudden shock caused Dancer to panic and rear up, tossing Gillian to the ground. She happened to fall on a huge boulder; her lovely head hit the side of it and she lay there inert, her long hair entangled with the wild ferns growing around the huge rock. Gillian felt herself sinking into a blackness.

31

When she fluttered her long-lashed eyes to gaze into the face of the handsome man holding her securely in his arms, she returned his smile. Hers was a very weak smile, for she was still dazed by the tremendous blow she had taken to her head, but it was enough to ease the concern Hawk was feeling when he had come along the trail to find Gillian lying there. Her horse was nowhere in sight. Hawk figured that it was probably making its way back to the Fosters' ranch. Something had panicked her.

To see her lying there, so helpless, had devastated Hawk. As he'd leaped off his pinto to rush to her and cradle her in his arms, his heart was pounding wildly until he assured himself that she was all right, just stunned. He held her in his muscled arms as he mounted up on his pinto and rode toward his mother's cottage.

Still dazed, Gillian did not recall the ride she shared with the bronze god she'd viewed the day before, down in the canyon.

When she was conscious and was aware of her surroundings, Gillian opened her eyes slowly to see a pleasant little room with the sweet smells of herbs and flowers. She sensed the feeling of warmth and love abiding within the walls of this humble cottage, so she was not afraid.

She lay there staring at the ceiling before allowing her eyes to dart to the right or the left. But when she did, she saw the loveliest lady she'd ever seen.

Such a warm smile was on her face as she inquired, "Ah, *ma petite*—are you all right?"

Gillian gave her an assuring nod of her head which seemed to satisfy the older woman. Being a woman of passion, Solange did not need to be told that her son's feelings went deep for this pretty lady he'd brought to their cottage. She could see why he would be so affected by one so beautiful as this lovely little mademoiselle. Gazing down at her, Solange was carried back to years long ago, when she was in Paris. Such beauty as this young maiden possessed reminded her of those gay, carefree days.

Ah, yes, she could understand why her son's eyes were

shining so brightly as he'd carried the lovely miss with her hair of fire into their cottage. She recognized the look on his handsome face, for many a young man had looked at her exactly the same way. Solange had realized, since Hawk was a youth of sixteen, that he would be a hot-blooded, passionate man.

She scrutinized the young lady carefully and a fear gripped her: Hawk would face a hopeless situation once her family met him. Oh, she was a lovely one and there was no disputing that! Her sensuous figure was obvious even though she wore a faded shirt and dark blue pants. Solange's eyes saw the tantalizing curves of her rounded hips and full breasts pressing against the shirt.

Gillian slowly tried to raise herself up from the bed, but she was forced to lie back down. She gave out a moan. Solange asked, "Are you all right? It was a sharp blow you took to the ground, my son tells me."

Gillian sensed the cool cloth draped around the top of her forehead. It had a soothing effect, but the throbbing was still there. Nevertheless, she assured the kind lady she was feeling better. "And I thank you for your care," Gillian told her as she offered her hand to Solange in a friendly gesture. "I am Gillian Browne."

"And I am Solange Touraine, dear, and it was my son, Hawk, who rescued you on the mountain trail," she told Gillian in that soft, gentle voice of hers. Something about the woman's charm and her accent instantly caught Gillian's attention. The name of her son fascinated Gillian. It was a most unusual name.

"Hawk?" she echoed, rising up to prop herself on the pillows.

Neither Solange nor Gillian had heard the tall, towering figure, shod in soft leather moccasins, reenter the room, but his deep voice caused both of them to turn to look at him when he declared, "My name is Joe Hawk, Gillian." His black eyes stared directly at her and a fire sparked in them like nothing

33

Gillian had ever seen before in any man's eyes.

"Then I thank you, Joe, for coming to my aid and bringing me to your home," she replied, praying that her voice wasn't cracking or the flush she was feeling was not showing on her face.

"It is my honor and my mother's pleasure to help you," he declared standing before her so captivating and majestic. The sight of him, and his nearness as he stood at the foot of the bed, made Gillian tremble. Those all-knowing eyes of Solange detected the nervous fluttering of her long lashes and she allowed herself to steal a glance at her son. Perhaps he didn't realize the impact he had on this lovely young maiden. But his mother did.

"Now that you are here to keep the young lady company, I think I shall fix a fresh pot of hot tea," she said. "Would you like that, Gillian?"

"Oh, yes, ma'am! That sounds wonderful." Only now did Gillian notice how petite she was as she rose from the chair to leave the room. Gillian could not help comparing her to the tall, stoutly built Nancy Foster. This lady was about the same size as her own natural mother, Amy.

Gillian's inquisitive nature was already pondering why the handsome, dark-skinned man had said his name was Joe Hawk when the lady had introduced herself as Solange Touraine. Yet, she said he was her son.

Slowly, he moved to take the seat where his mother had been sitting. His dark eyes were still devouring her as he moved. An easy, warm smile creased his tanned face.

"My mother's tea may not be like the tea you are used to drinking, Gillian. Her teas are brewed from the flowers she gathers in the woods and the plants she grows in her garden. There are clover flowers, chamomile, yellow and elderflower. Now, tell me if that sounds strange to you?"

Gillian gave a soft little gale of laughter. "I must confess that it does."

"Wait until you taste it," he said.

When his hand reached out toward her face, Gillian stiffened, not knowing what he was going to do, but he merely sought to check the cloth on her head. When he felt it, he declared, "Excuse me, Gillian, while I moisten this again in the spring water I just brought up. This has become warm." He rose up from the chair and left the room.

Swiftly, he returned to the room and his gentle hands placed the cool cloth in place around her head as it had been. "There, I'm sure that feels better, doesn't it?"

"Ah, yes," she sighed.

A short time later, after she'd enjoyed Solange's herb tea, she was pleasantly delighted to be rid of the throbbing in her head. She was also amazed how swiftly it had eased after drinking the tea.

"What magic potion does this tea contain?" she asked Hawk. "I'd like to know so I can brew a pot for myself."

"That I will have to let you discuss with my mother, Gillian. I don't really know, even though I've drunk it all my life. I'm— I'm glad that you have enjoyed it," Hawk said.

Gillian knew not what the magic ingredient of his mother's tea were, nor could she identify the mystic charms that Hawk possessed. Nevertheless, they were there, having a most pleasant, exciting effect on her.

So entranced was she by the magic surrounding her in this cottage Gillian had given no thought to the time or how long she'd been gone from home. Nancy and John must surely be concerned by her long overdue absence. Never did she linger this long when she took her early-morning ride over the countryside.

The sudden realization made her sit up straight in the bed and swing her legs over the side. "Oh, mercy—my family is surely frantic about me, Hawk. I—I just get back home. I really must!"

Her lovely eyes reminded Hawk of the blue wildflowers he'd seen growing in the woods. Her concern for her folks told him she was a caring person and this Hawk admired.

35

"Then we must see about getting you home, little Gillian—yes?" He spoke with such tenderness it was as if he were murmuring soft words of love. Gillian's young romantic heart wondered what it would be like to be held in his firm, muscled arms as he whispered those words of love. She had noticed his sensuous lips and she was curious about what it would feel like to be kissed by those lips.

He offered her his hand as she sought to stand by the side of the bed. It shocked Gillian when she realized how weak she was when she tried to stand up. The security of his strong hand steadied her. She gave out a nervous little laugh. "Good grief! I must have got the wind knocked out of me!"

"Come—let me lead you around the room very slowly, Gillian," he urged her. He continued to hold her hand but his strong body moved closer to her and she sensed the strength and power there. That force was overwhelming. He did not rush her, but followed her pace. All the time she felt his dark eyes looking down on her.

They had circled the room three times when he pointed out to her, "You're getting your legs back again now, Gillian. Am I not right?"

She looked up into his inquiring eyes and smiled warmly. "You are right, Hawk. I am feeling stronger—thanks to your supporting arm."

With his arm pressed against the side of her supple body, Hawk had to fight the urge to take her in his arms and seek a kiss from those tempting lips. Never had he endured such agony as he was now experiencing, denying himself the joy he would feel if he did give way to the savage desire pounding through his body. He would not have denied himself if he could have read the wild, impulsive thoughts in Gillian Browne's mind as she stared up at him, wanting him to enclose her in his arms and bend his head down to meet her eager lips in a kiss. Oh, yes, she wanted that just as anxiously as Hawk did!

In a faltering, hesitating voice, she mumbled, "Hawk—Hawk, I guess I should get my boots on and be on my way."

Hawk sensed her sudden ill-at-ease manner but never did he imagine that it was his effect on her that was causing it. If he had, he would have been the happiest man in the Arizona territory. He would have certainly become far bolder! But he dared not do anything to offend her, for he cared too much for Gillian Browne.

Solange had come to the doorway of the room as the two young people were making their promenade, and she stood silently observing them. She noticed how their bodies seemed to press so naturally one against the other and she saw her son's eyes gazing down adoringly on the tiny miss whose head just reached his broad shoulders.

Silently, she moved away from the door to allow them their private moment. How happy Hawk seemed in the company of this young woman and yet Solange feared he was opening the door to the most devastating heartbreak he would ever know. She knew not what she could do to prevent it. She did not know whether or not she wished to prevent whatever moments he could have with the lovely Gillian. Solange liked the bewitching auburn-haired beauty!

She knew full well that an all-consuming passion always caused pain as well as pleasure. Had she not found that out when she'd given her own heart to a young man so many years ago?

Where had he gone when he'd sailed away from the shores of France leaving her alone to wonder about him? Why had he not told her goodbye after that wonderful night of passion they'd shared? She still questioned that after all these years.

Never could she accept that he was not as much in love with her as she had been with him. But life had made her face reality and she knew she'd never have the answer to the mystery.

Her private musings were interrupted as her son, leading Gillian by the hand, came into her front room to announce that he was going to accompany Gillian to her home.

Solange was impressed by the young girl coming to her to give her a warm embrace as she expressed her appreciation for her generosity. "I hope we shall meet again, ma'am."

"Oh, we shall, Gillian. I feel sure of that," Solange declared.

She stood there, watching the two of them go out the front door. She returned her son's smile and waved farewell to them. Silently, she said a private prayer for her beloved Hawk.

"I wish I could spare you the hurt you'll have, but I know I can't," she whispered softly. Instinctively, she knew Gillian Browne was going to give her son the greatest joy he would ever know in his lifetime.

Solange Touraine also felt that this lovely girl would surely cause Hawk a torment he could not possibly deal with. And she would be innocently unaware of all the problems she would create.

Nothing could change the fact that Hawk was a half-breed!

Chapter Five

Hawk knew he could not accompany her all the way to the Foster Ranch, and as they rode along the trail he silently pondered what he would tell her, how he would excuse himself from being the considerate gentleman he would have liked to be. What Gillian thought about him was very important. But how could he bow out of escorting her through the gate of the fenced grounds of the Fosters' home and gallantly walking her up to the front door? Nancy and John Foster would know *what* he was the minute they saw him even though they wouldn't know *who* he was. If they were like most of the Americans here in the territory, they would hate him for being part Apache.

As they rode through the last canyon before the ranch would come in sight, Hawk knew he could no longer delay saying something to Gillian.

"I think it would be best that I leave you to ride into your home alone," he told her. "After all, I am a stranger to your people." He watched the blue eyes turn on him, reflecting surprise or disappointment. He could not be sure which it was.

"But I want John and Mother Foster to meet you, Hawk. They will be grateful for what you and your mother have done for me today." Gillian assumed that Hawk was being shy. Never did it enter her mind that it was the Indian blood flowing in his veins that caused him to worry about meeting her folks. Gillian was so entranced by the tall, dark stranger that she'd given no thought to that possibility.

He gave her a warm, tender smile as he tried to pacify her. "Oh, I'll meet them one day, Gillian, when they'll be in a more receptive mood. Today, they must be very concerned about you and your long overdue return back home. You see what I am saying?"

Slowly, she gave him a smile and nod of her pretty auburn head. How very wise he was, she thought to herself. She had not given that any thought, but Hawk had. He wanted their meeting to be a calm, pleasant one, she concluded.

"I see exactly, Hawk," she replied. By now the countryside was familiar and in another few minutes she and Hawk would go their separate ways. A feeling of sadness washed over her. She yearned to spend more time with this handsome man she'd met only a few hours ago, this magnificent bronzed god with coppery skin and jet black hair.

"Couldn't we stop for a moment, just to talk a while, Hawk, before we part company?" she asked, her deep blue eyes pleading as they darted in his direction.

He found it difficult to refuse her, but he also knew that John Foster and a party of men would surely be in search of this pretty miss. And if John Foster happened to be one of those hotheads who had a hatred for any half-breed, then he could be in trouble.

"I guess we can for a little while, Gillian—if that is what you wish," he said, with a slow easy grin on his dark face.

"Yes, Hawk—that is what I wish."

He pulled on the reins of his pinto and leaped down to the ground. His agile body swiftly moved around to help her down. A flame of passion consumed him as he felt her dainty hands clasp his neck and her fingers trail in his thick hair. As her petite body slid off the horse, slightly brushing against the front of him, he was tempted to steal one kiss from those luscious lips.

Gillian noticed the look in his eyes and the heat of his firm
★ male body. Like smoldering black coals, his eyes seemed to be
dancing over her face. Some instinct told the innocent Gillian
he was going to kiss her and she found herself wanting to be
kissed.

In one magic moment everything changed for both of them.
It mattered not that they'd just met. Hawk could not resist the
soft, half-parted lips inviting him to kiss them. As his lips met
hers, Hawk felt the exciting trembling of her body as she
lingered in the circle of his strong, muscled arms. But when his
arms released her and she breathlessly gasped to look up at him
with wide-eyed innocence he wondered if he'd been too bold.
Never would he have wanted to frighten her.

He looked down at her and smiled warmly. "Ah, little one—
we shall talk another time. For now, I think it best that you
walk on home to save your family worry and concern." What
he dared not tell her was that he didn't trust himself if she
lingered there with him any longer.

"Yes, I—I suppose you are right," she stammered.

As she began to make her way down the trail toward home,
she called back to Hawk, "I shall see you again, won't I,
Hawk?"

A broad grin lit up his bronze face and his chest swelled with
joy. "You'll see me again," he called out to her. "I promise you
that, Gillian!"

With a pleased nod of her head, she walked in the direction
of the Foster ranch, but the heat of his dark eyes were on her,
watching her all the way to her front gate. Only when he saw
her rush through the gate to the Fosters' front porch did he tug
on the reins of his pinto and ride back toward his mother's
cottage.

There was a horse tied up at the Fosters' hitching post, Hawk
noticed. Obviously, they had a guest at their house. But Hawk
didn't recognize the fine horse as one he'd observed before in

41

the two years he'd been watching the comings and goings of Gillian. No one but Hawk knew how much time he'd spent surveying that ranch.

As upset as she'd been the past three hours, the last thing Nancy Foster wanted this miserable morning was a stranger calling on them. John had gone out to search for Gillian but had returned home to give her the discouraging news that there was no sign of Gillian or the mare. "I'm going to have to call on our friends and neighbors, I guess. It is too much for just one man," he'd admitted.

But Nany had urged him to rest a while and refresh himself with her hot coffee before he struck out on the trail again. This was what John Foster was doing when they heard a rapping on the door and Nancy saw the silhouette of a young man who was a stranger to her. She muttered as she marched toward her front door, "Damn, don't need a visitor right now!"

She opened the door with a frown on her face, for she had no intention of inviting this wayfaring stranger in, as she would normally have done. But when she gazed into the emerald green eyes of the sandy-haired young man standing there giving her a broad, friendly smile, she mellowed. She saw a bit of the devil in those eyes even before he greeted her. "Morning, ma'am. I'm Stephen Lafferty and I assume you must be Mrs. John Foster?"

"You—you assume right, young man. Come in," she said as she shook her head in disbelief. "You don't have to tell me that you're Roger's son. You're the spittin' image of him."

Stephen laughed. "I've been told that a lot of times before, I can assure you. My mother told me I wouldn't fool you for one minute. She said she'd bet you'd recognize me immediately, even though you'd never seen me."

As they entered the small kitchen John did not have to be introduced to know that the young man was the son of his old friend, Roger Lafferty.

It had been a sad day when he and Nancy had received the letter from Roger's widow, telling them about his death some five years ago. Neither he nor Nancy had ever met Roger's English wife.

John Foster was already out of his chair with his hand extended to shake Stephen's hand. "I'm John Foster and it is a pleasure for me and Nancy to have Roger's son in our home." A broad grin was on his face as he added, "I happened to overhear you tell my wife who you were."

Lafferty hadn't been in this cozy, warm cottage five minutes before feeling that these two people were his own good friends as well as his father's. He sat there enjoying a steaming cup of Nancy's black, strong coffee while the three of them spoke briefly about his father's death. When they inquired about his mother, he told them that she still lived in Bristol in the same house where he'd been born.

They explained to him about their air of tenseness and concern about the young adopted daughter who was so late getting home that they were now truly worried.

Steve instantly offered his services to John Foster, and John quickly accepted. "Finish your coffee and I will do the same before we go searching for her," he said. "I guess you've figured out by now that Nancy and I look upon her as our own. She is very precious to us!"

"Then we must find her!" Steve declared, taking a quick sip of the coffee.

"Can't believe anything has happened to that little red-haired firebrand. She's quite a spunky gal. But Gillian would never be gone this long if she could help it, for fear she'd make me or Nancy worry. She's a thoughtful person and a caring one," John told him.

John's remarks reminded Steve about the gifts he'd brought for them but had left in his saddlebags. There were some spices from the Orient and a soft, light woolen shawl from Ireland for

Nancy. For John, he'd picked out some aromatic tobacco and good French brandy from his various cargoes.

With a fast final gulp of his coffee, he rose up from the chair to excuse himself. "I'll be back in just a minute and then we can go, sir, if you'd like." He gave both of them another of his winning smiles, which reminded them so much of Roger, and he swiped away an unruly wisp of hair falling down over his forehead. He hesitated long enough to declare, "We'll find her, sir!"

John and Nancy exchanged smiles. Each of them knew what the other one was thinking. Roger's son was as cocksure and arrogant as his father had been.

As his powerful, muscular body moved swiftly to go out the front door to get his gifts for the Fosters, he was blasted by the rushing little mite of a miss dashing through the front door. All Steve saw was the glorious, auburn hair that covered her shoulders, flowing free and loose as her tiny body hit his with a mighty impact. It was only when his hands reached out to steady the breathless beauty that he saw the breathtaking loveliness of the face staring up at him.

He was instantly smitten by her and he knew this must surely be Gillian!

Gillian was at a disadvantage, for she had no idea who this smiling gentleman was. She knew one thing though: his firm body must be made of iron as she'd slammed against him. As his strong hands clasped her shoulders, she also felt the force in them. But the thing that held a hypnotic effect on her were his green eyes which reminded her of a lavaliere her mother, Amy, had worn around her neck on a delicate gold chain. Hanging from the chain was a brilliant emerald. She knew how much her mother had always treasured it because it had been a gift to her when she had married Gillian's father.

Now, it was in Gillian's possession. No savage Indian had managed to yank that from her mother's neck. She heaved a deep sigh as though to catch her breath. "You are all right, I trust?" Steve asked.

She moved slightly away from him and gave her clothing a yank. "I am, thank you!" There was a curious look on her face, for she was questioning just who this stranger could be. But before either of them could say another word, Nancy came rushing out, overjoyed to see that thick mop of auburn hair which Steve's huge body did not overshadow.

"Oh, thank God! Thank God, you're home!" The tall, robust woman rushed to take Gillian in her arms and give her a loving hug. But as Nancy held Gillian in her arms she sensed the slight tremble of her body and she assumed the girl must have had a harrowing experience. She stared down at Gillian's flushed lovely face to inquire, "You all right, honey? You have nothing to fear now, dear." Turning to look at John, Nancy informed her husband, "Our Gillian is upset. Why, I could feel her shaking."

Motherly concern was written all over Nancy Foster's face as she urged Gillian to accompany her into her kitchen. "Come on, honey—come and just sit down. You can tell us about it later. Right now you need a cup of coffee. And John, put just a little drop of your whiskey in it to calm the child down. Now, mind you, John Foster—just a wee drop!"

Steve suggested that he fetch their gifts, as he'd started to do when he had his surprised encounter with Gillian. "I've just the ingredient to lace in the young lady's coffee—a fine French brandy. I'd brought it for you, Mr. Foster."

He quickly left the three of them as Nancy guided Gillian into the kitchen. Feebly, Gillian tried to protest to Nancy that she was all right. She could hardly explain to Mother Foster that her trembling had nothing to do with fright. She had been in the lightest spirits as she'd bounced up the pathway to the front steps of her home.

The overwhelming impact with Steve Lafferty and the feel of his powerful male body was what had affected her. His sparkling green eyes piercing her in such an intimate way, was what made her tremble with a strange excitement.

To meet one fascinating man was enough to stir up any young miss like Gillian Browne, who'd lived only with girlish whimsy and daydreams. But now to have been thrust against a second handsome man, with a devious glint in his teasing, taunting eyes—well, Gillian's pretty head felt slightly giddy.

She wondered if she might not be actually experiencing any of this. Was it just a fantasy—a wonderful, crazy dream?

Only in romantic dreams could a young lady meet *two* such handsome men as she had met in one day!

Chapter Six

John Foster sat quietly in his cozy parlor, listening to the lively conversation and lighthearted laughter, thinking to himself how nice it was to have two such fine young people under his roof. It made him aware of the joy he and his dear Nancy could have shared through the years if they'd been blessed with children of their own.

Oh, he'd never dwelled on it too much, but tonight it was having a very definite impact on him. How pleasant it had been, after their evening meal, to gather in the parlor, light up his favorite pipe with the fine tobacco Stephen Lafferty had brought to him, and listen to the young man tell his tales of adventure from traveling all over the vast seas and lands.

What an exciting life this man had experienced for one so young! John realized that he'd lived a very simple, tame life in comparison.

John goodnaturedly teased the young man. "Now, you tell me, young man—what are we to call you? Steve, Stephen, or Captain Lucky?"

Steve Lafferty gave an infectious, deep laugh. "Well, sir— my men call me Captain Lucky. Those people who do not know me too well, or have not known me too long, call me Stephen. But my best friends call me Steve."

Nancy quickly responded by declaring, "Well, we'll call you

Steve, won't we, John?"

"For sure, my love," he said.

There was a pleased grin on Steve's handsome face. Suddenly his green eyes turned in Gillian's direction and there was a devious glint in them as he inquired of her, "And what will you call me, Gillian?"

Those piercing eyes made her feel flustered and she felt a sudden flush come to her cheeks. In a stammering voice, she mumbled, "I—I guess I shall call you Steve, too." She gave him an uneasy smile. Why did she suddenly feel so unsure of herself? Was it the heat of those magnificent eyes locking in with hers?

She prayed that the others in the room could not see the trembling of her body or hear the pounding against the bodice of her muslin frock.

"Good, that is what I'd like," he said. It was a great relief to Gillian when John directed an inquiry to Steve and he took his eyes off her. She was given some precious moments to regain her composure.

Being a man of experience where ladies were concerned, Steve sensed that Gillian was nervous in his presence. He figured that she'd possibly never yet been kissed or courted by a man. That made her all the more attractive to him. He realized that she had lived her whole life in this Arizona territory where the closest neighbor might live miles away.

Secretly, he thought to himself that if she'd lived in any of the port cities where his ship was constantly pulling in, or the city of Bristol which was his home, she would have surely known the ardor and admiration of many a dandy.

Such untouched loveliness as Gillian's was rare, and he damned well knew it. He cautioned his hot-blooded nature as best he could, but it wasn't easy. Steve Lafferty had never restrained himself from going after what he wanted, and he usually succeeded in getting it. But he was also clever enough to know that Gillian Browne was different from every other woman he had known.

After all, she was not the sort of maiden he might meet casually in one of the seaports where he docked to load a rich cargo, bound for another part of the country. After all, the Fosters were dear friends of his dead father. He could hardly come here and enjoy their generous hospitality and then take unfair advantage of Gillian.

But it was more than that, Steve had to confess to himself. She was like no other woman he'd ever met before. Her strange, magical charm had captivated him completely. He reminded himself that she was hardly more than a child, even though her supple figure was that of a most seductive woman! He could not resist turning his eyes to gaze admiringly over her lovely features. He saw a look in that sweet, innocent girl's eyes. The look was provocative, stimulating his wildest desires.

He suddenly realized that John Foster had been speaking to him and he'd not absorbed a word he'd said. He had to apologize and ask him to repeat.

John wasn't so old yet that he didn't realize it was Gillian who held Steve's attention. He tried to suppress an amused smile. He wondered if Nancy had made the same observation as he had.

Knowing his beloved Nancy and that eagle eye of hers, he should have known that nothing went on in her parlor that she was not aware of. In fact, she realized that the time was long overdue when she and Gillian had to have some talks about the things that go on between men and women. Gillian wasn't a child anymore!

It took the arrival of Steve Lafferty to wake her up to that fact. Sitting there tonight, she realized that she might be just a little nervous as long as he was sleeping under the same roof. Like John, she was not so old that her eyes could not admire a handsome, virile young man like Steve! He was enough to set any woman's heart to fluttering!

When it was time to go to their sleeping quarters, Nancy suspected that she might not sleep soundly this night. She wondered if she dared to speak to John about this—would he

49

find her apprehensions foolish?

She decided to say nothing but she would have been comforted to know that he was tossing and turning just as much as she was—and for the same reasons.

Another young man was unable to sleep that night, for many things troubled his sleep. Hawk tossed and turned, still intoxicated by the charm and beauty of Gillian Browne.

Solange had been aware of Hawk's preoccupation since he'd returned to their cabin. All during their evening meal, he had been quiet and thoughtful. She sat at the table eating her delicious food while Hawk merely picked at his. The lamplight reflected on his bronze face and she swelled with pride to think that she had borne this grand young man. A mother's pride flooded her being. It was her great compensation for being deprived of so many luxuries she could have had but for the cruel hand of fate.

She almost giggled once when she spoke softly to Hawk and he didn't even hear her. She did not embarrass him by calling attention to the fact that she was trying to talk to him.

When her kitchen was in order and the floor was swept free of any crumbs, she moved outside the door to sit on the stone step so she would not disturb Hawk in his quiet solitude.

A lovely starlit night it was, she thought to herself as she sat down on the step. Over in the woods, she could hear the sounds of the nightbirds. She swore she smelled the aroma of the pines. There was a time, when she was a gay romantic, that she would have looked upon this night as a lovers' night. Oh, to be that gay, spirited young lady she'd been in France so many years ago, she mused! Just once more before she died she'd like to enjoy that same exciting ecstasy!

A twinkle came to her eyes as she thought about the Solange Touraine who had had her share of suitors back in France. Her fatal mistake was becoming the mistress of the man who'd brought her to this country. Had she not chosen to accompany him here, and had she not been taken the captive of Cochise, she would have lived a luxurious life and not endured the hardships of the last twenty odd years.

Her slender fingers sought to release the thick coil at the back of her head. She stared into the blackness of the night surrounding her. But for the stars and the moon, the whole countryside was shrouded in darkness. Slowly her fingers ran through her long tresses in a leisurely stroking motion.

No woman had lived or experienced more of love than she had. She'd known it all. In France, she had been the flirtatious coquette, so stunningly beautiful she turned many a man's head. She'd been the mistress of a wealthy French nobleman. She'd been the wife, according to Indian custom, of the feared chief, Cochise, and she had borne his son. She'd learned that there were those who looked upon Cochise as a noble warrior and others who considered him an Apache devil. She had considered him a savage, a horrible man.

Then she'd lived for several years as the wife of Tim McGrath, the woodsman who'd rescued her when she escaped from Cochise. Tim was a good-hearted, kind man, and she'd tried desperately to be a grateful wife because of what he'd done for her and her baby son, Hawk. But Solange had never been in love with him. She admired and respected him, but he never thrilled her when they made love. Solange realized that there were all kinds of love a woman could share with a man. She had loved Tim in a very special way. There was a comfort and security in sharing her life with Tim, and she'd missed that after his death.

She thanked God that Hawk had grown into such a fine young man. Now, he was her comfort and serenity.

But there were times, like tonight, when Solange yearned for a man who could hold her in his strong arms and make love to her. A son could not fill this void. This was one of those rare nights when Solange felt lonely. She knew why, but she felt no shame.

So deep were her thoughts that she had not heard Hawk

move through the doorway until he sat down beside her. His muscled arms came to rest on her shoulders. What a tiny lady she was! She was about the size of the lovely Gillian Browne.

"A beautiful night, isn't it?" he remarked as his hand patted her shoulder.

"Isn't it! I was just sitting here letting its beauty consume me. Have you ever done that, Hawk?"

"Ah, yes, Mother. I've done that many times. Are we different from most people, Mother? Do others enjoy such simple pleasures as we do? I've often wondered."

"Oh, I'd like to think so, Hawk," she said, smiling her lovely smile. Hawk had never seen a more beautiful face than his mother's until he'd gazed on Gillian Browne.

After all her years in this country, there was still a French accent to his mother's speech and expressions. Occasionally, she reverted back to her native tongue, which he considered the most beautiful language. Hawk had never told her how proud he was of his French heritage and how tormenting it was to him to be half Apache. Never would he hurt her for something she had no control over, but never could he respect the Indian who'd repeatedly raped his lovely mother.

There was no one he respected and admired more than he did his mother. It pained him to think of the sacrifices she'd made because of him. Never did he forget the burden she had carried for him. To be saddled with the brat of an Indian at her young tender age must have been a horrible experience. She'd proved herself to be quite a woman. There was never a time when he'd not worn clean clothes and been fed. Always, he'd known the loving warmth of her arms around him to comfort him when he'd needed it. He owed her so much!

They sat there in their shared silence. Something about this night had a strange, sentimental effect on Solange Touraine and she knew not why.

"Oh, my son—my dear son, I hope I live to see you happy with the woman you will love. You have such a capacity to love. I think she will be a very lucky lady."

He had only to look at her face to know that she spoke from the depths of her heart. He, too, was speaking from the depth of his heart as he replied, "Oh, you'll live to see her, Mother. I have you to thank for that capacity for love you speak about. I'm very proud of the French blood that flows in my veins."

She reached for his hand and held it tightly with her dainty one. So soft her voice was as she told him, "I thank you, Hawk for feeling as you do. I tried to give you the best life I could. You were and you are the pride and joy of my life. You have made it all worthwhile."

Never had he admired her more and never had he realized so deeply the price this lovely lady had paid. "If only I can find a woman who measures up to you, Mother. That is the lady who will claim my heart."

Hawk knew that he'd already met that lady.

Chapter Seven

It would have made Hawk very proud if he'd known that Gillian Browne was comparing Steve Lafferty to him as Steve awkwardly mounted the fine horse so they could go for a ride over the countryside the morning after he'd arrived at the ranch. Gillian's mare had found her way home during the night, and was none the worse for her adventure. Gillian had to conceal a smile as she mounted and waited for Steve to tighten his horse's girth. Lafferty was no expert horseman! In no way could he compare to the striking figure of the bronzed Hawk. Hawk and his pinto seemed to be fused together as though they were one.

She sensed that the good-looking, cocky Irishman was not so self-assured and confident this morning as he'd appeared to be in the parlor last night. Impishly, Gillian spurred her little mare into a gallop as they left the grounds of the ranch, just to taunt Lafferty.

He knew better than anyone that he was no horseman any more than he was a man of the land. He could not imagine anything duller than living day after day and month after month on a ranch like the Fosters. The sea with its daily challenge was what thrilled Steve. The strange distant shores he had yet to see were what he anticipated. Life would mean nothing to him without the adventure of the sea and the time

55

spent on his ship.

No one considered himself luckier than Steve did. To do what he loved and make a good living at it was all a man could ask out of life, he considered.

But right now he was wishing he could sit better on this damned horse. He had to be making a comical sight to Gillian, who was now a good distance ahead of him. The little minx was showing him up as an oaf and he suddenly realized this.

When he noticed her pretty head turned around to look back at him and saw that she was laughing, he knew exactly what thoughts were going through that auburn head of hers. Oh, he'd make that little miss pay, he vowed to himself. One way or the other he'd even the score!

He spurred the horse to go faster so he might close the distance between them, but she continued to outdistance him. She, too, spurred her spirited horse to gallop faster.

Steve's shrewd mind took over as he watched her far ahead of him and he veered the horse to the right instead of following her lead. There was a thick grove of trees there and he reined the horse in that direction.

Something urged Gillian to glance back a few minutes later. To her great surprise there was no Lafferty trailing behind her. In fact, there was no sign of Lafferty at all so she swiftly pulled up and urged the mare to turn around. She looked in various directions, but there was nothing to see, except the deserted countryside.

She was vexed, and her blue eyes flashed brighter and her long lashes fluttered faster. Gillian was irritated, the way a mother would be with a straying child who'd got himself lost. She grumbled and fumed, leading her mare back over the trail they'd traveled over.

Now it was Lafferty's turn to laugh. He had dismounted, and he stood at the edge of the woods observing her puzzled face, her auburn tresses swaying to and fro as her head turned to the right and the left attempting to see him. A devious grin lit up his tanned face.

It was at this moment that Gillian chanced to glance over in his direction and saw him standing there, posed with his legs parted and his hands on his hips. Seeing him standing there with that crooked grin on his face, she found her heart suddenly beating faster. Was this a bit of Irish trickery? There was no doubt that he possessed a fair share of devilment. She'd found that out when she'd bounded into the house yesterday to slam against him—and his arms had lingered around her.

As she rode up to meet him, she was determined not to let him fluster her as he had last night. He had a way about him, this Steve Lafferty. She did not feel at ease around him as she had with Hawk. Lafferty had a roguish way about him, and devious eyes that danced over her from the top of her head to the end of her toes. He seemed to undress her, and she felt bared of everything, as if he knew her most intimate thoughts.

Tilting her auburn head slightly, she asked, "Why did you stop riding, Steve?"

He gave a deep throaty laugh as he confessed truthfully, "Ah, a horseman I am not. It is the waves of the ocean I ride, not a horse, Gillian." Had he been absolutely truthful, he would have added that he had suggested that they go for a ride only so he could have her all to himself, without Nancy's eyes on him.

"Well, I don't suppose that anyone can master everything. I doubt that I could stand to be tossed to and fro on your fine ship as it plows through the rough waters of the ocean. I fear I'd get deathly sick."

He reached up his hand to her as she started to dismount. "Oh, maybe, and maybe not. But it's a thing one gets over."

How very delicate her hand felt! Dear God, he became suddenly aware of her petite body pressed lightly against his chest. Their lips were so damned close that all he would have to do was bend his head slightly to capture them in a kiss.

Slowly, her body slid downward until her feet touched the ground and came to rest. A wee little minx she was, standing there facing him. Her head barely passed his shoulders. But for the lovely curves and mounds of her body, he could have taken her to be a child, with that angel face of hers. This lovely miss was certainly no child.

She stood there, facing him, a smile on her face. "Well, I will never know that experience, for I shall never take a voyage on any ship, Steve. That is not our way of traveling in this part of the country."

"Ah, Gillian—never say never. You are so young and you have a whole lifetime to live yet. You can't know where you'll go as the years pass. I never expected to come to Arizona territory, but here I am."

By now they were strolling toward the edge of the woods to enjoy the shade of the trees and move out of the dense heat of the Arizona sun. It was pleasant there in the covered bower of the tree branches. It seemed degrees cooler as they sank down there on the ground and let their horses graze nearby.

She thought about what Steve had just said to her. "Perhaps you are right. Perhaps I might leave here someday. I had never thought about that before. As you know, the last two years have been a time for me to get over the nightmare of the day my parents were killed by Apaches. Maybe someday, I'll be able to do that—get over it, I mean."

"Oh, that day will come. That is exactly why you should get away from this place where the Apache still lives. Here, you'll always be reminded of that terrible day."

She noticed the serious look on his face. Maybe she had figured him all wrong. He was certainly a self-assured, conceited young man but he was more than that, too. He was a compassionate, understanding man as well.

"I never thought about that until you said what you did, but it is true. I'll always be reminded of that day as long as I live here in the territory."

He gave her a warm smile. "Well, Gillian, you must know that I've lived a few years longer than you and, God knows, I've experienced a lot more, so I feel that I've given you something to think about." It seemed only a natural thing for Steve to circle her dainty shoulder with his arm. It seemed right and comforting to Gillian, too, because she did not flinch.

She stared up at him, listening intensely as he spoke, and the effect of her adoring gaze entranced Steve. With no will of his own, he was a man bewitched. Softly he murmured his impulsive desire, "I'm going to kiss you, Gillian."

Before she could voice a protest, Steve's heated lips had captured hers in a passionate kiss.

Gillian had never known the fury of a lover's kiss before. It was like nothing she'd ever experienced. Steve's kiss instantly ignited a wild, wonderful excitement, flaming her entire body. Hawk's kiss had been a gentle one, hardly a kiss at all, compared to this.

Without any awareness, her pulsing body was pressing against Steve's broad chest. The sweet fragrance of her nearness was enough to spark every fiber of his being with blazing desire. Never before had Steve denied himself the pleasure of a beautiful woman's lips and body. When he would have played the gallant and released her, she arched closer to him. The feel of that soft, supple body pressed against him, sending a blazing fever surging through his body. It rendered him helpless to fight the wild desires consuming him.

"Oh, God! God, Gillian! You can't know what you do to me!" he sighed as he bent to kiss her again. She eagerly returned his kisses, helpless to resist his overpowering force. They were already floating to the heights of a lofty passion that had already reached a point of no return.

She surrendered to the featherlike touch of his long, slender fingers fumbling at the front of her tunic. When his sensuous mouth left her lips to trail down the soft flesh of her throat, she gave a breathless gasp. When those lips covered her breast she moaned with ecstasy, for she'd never known this strange, wonderful sensation before.

Feeling her undulating body beneath him, the fire in him mounted to a new height. He cupped her breast with one hand as his other hand lowered the riding skirt she wore. For a few brief moments, Gillian was not aware that she was lying on the ground with this handsome Irishman, completely nude.

His hand trailed down over the firm roundness of her hips, pressing her closer to his firm male body. Her pliant, heated body was yielding to him. "Dear God, Gillian—you want me to make love to you just as much as I want to love you. Tell me—tell me, my darling that it is so?"

"Yes, Steve! Yes—I do!" she breathlessly whispered.

That was all Steve had to know as he burrowed himself between her velvet thighs. With one strong thrust, he forced his entry to fuse with her, knowing that he was going to pleasure her with all the love he could. He felt her gasp, but quickly she was moving in tempo with his body. He felt her fingers pressing into his neck as her hands encircled his head.

God, he wished this moment to last forever but he had no strength left to resist the explosion ready to erupt within him. Like the mighty waves his ship rode over, Steve surged, his passion bursting forth.

For the longest time, he held her close in his arms, saying nothing. Would she suddenly push away from him and be sorry she'd surrendered to him? After all, he'd taken from her what he could never give back—her sweet innocent virginity.

When she did suddenly stir to look up at him, he asked, "Please don't be angry, Gillian. I didn't plan this. It—it just happened. I swear it!"

"I don't blame you, Steve, any more than I do myself. You did not force me. I gave myself to you willingly. I allowed you to kiss me as I've never been kissed before. I allowed you to make love to me and you must surely know I've never given myself to any man before."

"I know, Gillian, and I am glad—glad I was the first to make love to you. I just don't want you to regret this. I've never met anyone like you before, Gillian."

He wore such a serious look! His emerald green eyes searched her face. She gave a soft little laugh. "Well, that's nice to hear, Steve. I've never met anyone like you, either."

Reluctantly, he suggested that they should be getting back to the ranch as much as he would have preferred to linger here with her. He sensed that the Fosters had a very protective feeling for this young girl they'd taken into their home.

His hands reached out to lift her from the ground where they'd been lying.

It was this sight that caught Hawk's eyes as he rode in the distance on his pinto. Who was this sandy-haired young man with Gillian? He had seen no suitors coming to the Fosters' ranch. Every muscle in his firm body tensed and overwhelming jealousy flooded him as his black eyes watched them from afar.

Gillian could belong to no other man. She belonged to him!

Chapter Eight

Solange hardly recognized the son whose angry face stared at her across the table as they ate their evening meal by lamplight. The look in his eyes was as wild and fierce as another man she recalled this evening. That was not pleasant for Solange. She never wished to see any of Cochise's traits in her son. But she did tonight.

When she sought to converse with him, he mumbled some feeble reply, so she did not prod him to talk to her. Sunk into deadly silence, she spoke not another word to him as she cleared away the dishes and washed them. As she did every night after their evening meal, she swept her floor before dimming the lamp to move into her small front room.

It was only then that she noticed that Hawk had banked the hearth with some fresh-cut logs for her to burn in the crudely constructed fireplace. Seeing that his mother's eyes were focused there, Hawk told her, "The nights might start having a chill to them. I plan to cut up more wood for you so you'll be well supplied while I'm gone."

"You're a good son, Hawk. How long do you suppose this scouting job will take?"

"I have no idea, Mother. But there's no reason why I can't come by from time to time to check in with you. And Troy has promised to make a weekly trip over this way while I'm gone."

"Oh, I'll be fine, Hawk. The garden did fine this year, and we have plenty of grain for the chickens, so they'll keep laying eggs for me." She gave a soft little laugh and pointed out that she still had an ample supply of meat in the smokehouse and fuel for her lamps. "Besides, you can't possibly know, my dear son, how many candles I've stocked up, and I've enough jars of jelly and jams to last me a year. Never fear for a minute that I shall not eat well."

What a magnificent lady she was, Hawk thought to himself as he stood observing her, bold and proud. Few women could have survived the ordeal she must have endured and not come out of it scarred for life.

Solange saw her son's face mellowing and she was happy. She did not like to see him angry.

She wondered what had caused his anger, but she had no intention of asking him. It was enough to know his black mood had passed now. Perhaps some bigoted rancher had called him a half-breed, which she knew riled him. She'd known for a long time that he detested the Indian blood in his veins. She knew that it was only because of his great love for her that he never discussed his feelings. It had to be a terrible burden to bear all alone.

A pleasant smile was on her face as she spoke to her son. "You will be a good scout, Hawk—the best the Southern Pacific Railroad has. You know this countryside with all the rivers and canyons. The desert and mesa are no strangers to you, Hawk!"

Hawk was confident that he could be a good scout. What his mother said was true; he knew this country. But he was not prepared for what she was about to say to him.

Solange spoke before she realized what she was saying. "The smoke encircling the sky as they bake their mescal is always a telltale sign of an Apache camp. God, I can still remember that smell!" There was a look of utter disgust on her face. She was caught up in her musings of the past and did not notice the startled look on her son's face.

The frown on his face was not one of disapproval, but for the pain she'd suffered. He had no words to express himself. When Solange suddenly glanced toward her son, she realized what she'd said and its effect on him. "Maybe, my son, knowing this will help you to be a better scout. I will hope so. Once you smell the mescal baking, you will know the Apaches are near. I'm—I'm glad you were spared that and so many other things."

"So am I, Mother, but I wish you'd not had to know of them."

"Ah, but out of the bad there was good. There was you, Hawk! For me, it was all worth it to have you. You must know that!" She smiled, a mist of tears creeping down her cheek.

"I can't see how I could have been worth that much suffering, Mother."

Solange gave a breezy little laugh. "That is a son who is very modest. A lot of women would share the same feelings I have, I'm certain."

He grinned. "Guess I've just not met that many women, living back here in the woods."

"I realize that, Hawk. But you've a lot of living to do. A young man as handsome as you are will know many women." It had not dawned on her before just how sheltered a life he'd lived for a young man of his age. Back in her native France when a young man had reached Hawk's age he'd have had many love affairs, especially if he was as good-looking as Hawk.

A more serious look came on Hawk's face as he told her in a solemn tone, "The opportunity to do so is not there for me, Mother. Let's be honest." His thoughts were about Gillian and their brief encounter but today he'd seen her in the company of the handsome sandy-haired man—the type of man the Fosters would approve of.

"I understand, Hawk, but it only takes one fleeting moment for a man or a woman to fall in love. I knew a wonderful love once with a man who stole my heart the moment our eyes met."

"Is it truly possible, Mother?" Hawk asked.

65

"It is very possible. One experiences many loves in a lifetime, Hawk. I loved Tim McGrath for the kindness he showed you and me and I tried to be a good wife to him. There was nothing about that love that compared to the one I'd known back in France. It was not that thrilling, exciting love I'd known with that young man, whose eyes could make me feel all weak inside. Do you understand what I am saying to you?"

"I think so."

"Well, if you don't know now, there will come a day when you will." Never had mother and son engaged in such frank talk as this. Perhaps it was long overdue, Solange decided. She was certain that the quiet, reserved Tim McGrath had never spoken to Hawk as a father would talk with a son. A good man he had been, but there was no romance in his soul.

"What happened to this man you loved so much, Mother?" Hawk asked her.

"He came to the shores of France and left swiftly without me knowing it, Hawk. It was one of those rare experiences that one remembers always. I always shall. I knew that magical moment would never come again and it never has."

Hawk's black eyes surveyed his mother's lovely features for a moment before he sought to remark, "Bet you were the prettiest lady in this place called France." He might be her son, but he could appraise her fine figure with admiration and the loveliness of her face. What a stunning-looking creature she must have been some twenty years ago!

There was still the hint of the coquette about her as she grinned at her son admitting, "Well, I never lacked for attention from the young Frenchmen wishing to squire me, Hawk dear. As a matter of fact, you are right! I was a French belle."

For an evening that had started out so tense and strained this one was ending up very pleasant. Hawk could not recall a time when he'd enjoyed talking with his mother as much as he had tonight. He'd never given any consideration before to the fact that his mother was so worldlywise, nor had he thought about the life she'd lived in France before she'd come to this country. He'd never thought about the life she might have led before becoming the captive of the Apaches. He saw her in a whole different light now. He also understood why she seemed so different from the ladies he'd encountered on the ranches here in the territory. She was in a class all her own.

Hawk's sleep was not a restless one as he'd expected it to be. His mother had eased many of his tormenting thoughts.

Solange knew that she had softened her son's torture—whatever it might have been. This was enough for her to be pleased. So her sleep was peaceful, too.

But she feared that there would come a time when she would not be able to soothe her son as she had tonight!

John Foster returned to his barn to find Gillian's mare and the horse Steve Lafferty was riding still missing from the stalls. He marched from the barn into the cottage. He was as nervous as any father would be whose daughter has been absent too long. This was a new and harrowing experience for John. Nothing like this had happened since Gillian had come to live with them at the age of fourteen. But then, no handsome young devil had appeared at their door as Steve had. He and Nancy had not had to deal with this before. God, he should have realized that suitors would be knocking at their door with such a pretty miss as Gillian living under their roof!

The first thing he said as he bolted through the door was, "Is it just me, Nancy, or have those two young people been gone one hell of a long time?"

She gave him a weak gust of laughter. "Guess you and me have been thinking the same thing, John. Got to admit that I've been nervous as hell. Can't even get my chores done for peering out the window to see if they're coming down the trail. Everything has been so simple and easy about taking care of Gillian up to now."

John gave her an understanding nod of his head. Maybe if they'd raised one up from a babe it would have been easier than it was now. He remained silent as his wife went to the stove to get him a cup of hot coffee.

Nancy slowly sank down in the chair across from her husband, a sober look on her face. "I've been a failure, John—as a mother, I mean," she said. "I should have had a talk long ago with Gillian. Guess I was never pressed to do it 'cause no young dudes were coming around. Now here comes that handsome son of Roger's and dear God Almighty, he's enough to melt any young girl's heart. I'll—I'll never forgive myself, John—I swear I won't if something goes wrong because I didn't warn her about some things."

John's weathered hand reached out to clasp hers. "Now, you just hold up a minute, lady! You're being too harsh on yourself. No one could have given more to Gillian than you have. Everything is going to be all right. You just believe me!"

That plain face of hers never looked more lovely than it did at this moment when he saw such love and concern in her eyes. "Damn it, John, I want to believe you! But I'm not going to breathe easy until I see those two riding up that road out there."

John reached over the width of the table to plant a kiss on her cheek. "Breathe easy then, sweetie. They're riding up the lane right now."

"Really, John?"

"That's right, Nancy. Go get yourself a cup of coffee and relax those highstrung nerves of yours. Mind me, now!"

She did as he requested, for she felt the heavy weight roll off her chest. Lord, she'd never realized just how draining the role of a mother could be! She made a hasty, impulsive decision as she was pouring her cup of coffee. She decided then and there that she was taking Gillian with her when she went to Tucson to visit her sister, Helen. That, she knew, John would understand.

When the two young people strolled into the cozy kitchen

they found the Fosters sitting there, enjoying a cup of coffee. There was no hint of the tensions the middle-aged couple had been enduring just a moment ago.

But Nancy Foster's all-knowing eyes saw something in Gillian's face that told her she surely must have a talk with her and very soon. Nancy knew what caused such a glowing radiance as the one she observed on Gillian's flushed face. She'd felt that same flush on her own face the day John first kissed her.

Sweet memories flooded her as she recalled that first romantic kiss! She'd wager that Gillian had been soundly kissed by that good-looking Steve Lafferty this afternoon.

Chapter Nine

The next morning as Nancy busily moved around her kitchen preparing breakfast, she voiced her idea to John about taking Gillian to Helen's with her.

"Think that would be a wonderful idea. If my memory serves me right, your sister's daughter and Gillian are about the same age."

"They are. So you feel you could manage very well here without either of us?" she teased him.

"Well, I guess I can struggle along for a few weeks," he said. But he could not hold the serious look on his face for long. He broke out in laughter.

Nancy marched over to where he was sitting in the straight-backed chair and tousled his thick mane of hair. "John Foster, you are a character. You will probably do just fine without me around to boss you!"

He looked up at her with tenderness gleaming in his eyes. "I'll miss that bossing, honey, but you deserve a little pleasure visiting with your sister. I think it will be good for Gillian. Not too much to entertain a pretty young girl out here on this ranch. I can see her now when you and Helen take her into all those shops. Won't she have herself a time?"

A broad grin came on Nancy's face as she nodded her head. "I'm going to tell her today, John."

71

"I think you should. I think it would give her something to look forward to."

By the time the two young people had joined them in the kitchen, Nancy's spirits were high with her plans for the day. She was secretly happy to hear from Steve Lafferty that he had to leave today. He ate with relish from the plate Nancy set before him. Her flaky biscuits were the best he'd ever tasted, and those fresh eggs and slabs of ham were absolutely delicious.

He grinned like a young boy. "Would I be ill-mannered if I ask for one more slice of ham? I'm enjoying all this good food of yours, Mrs. Foster. I must leave today and I don't know when I'll be tasting something this good again."

His announcement came as a complete surprise to everyone at the table. Nancy quickly obliged him by passing the platter of ham. "Help yourself, young man."

Nancy glanced over in Gillian's direction to see what her reaction was to his announcement. She noted the sudden flashing of her eyes and the fluttering of her eyelashes. She noticed how Gillian was now chewing her food more slowly. It was obvious to Nancy that he'd not told her before that he was leaving.

What better time for her to lift her spirits with a trip if she was disappointed or sad about Steve's leaving, Nancy thought to herself as they finished their morning meal.

Two hours later, the three of them stood at the gate, waving their goodbyes to Steve Lafferty, whose green eyes lingered on Gillian. As shrewd and cunning as he'd credited himself to be, he'd found no moment to get her alone for the rest of his time there at the cottage. He'd hoped to find one brief moment to have some privacy with her and steal one more kiss from those luscious lips, but he was denied that ecstasy.

Gillian, too, was disappointed that they were not given a moment for a final farewell. But Nancy and John were with them every minute. The cottage seemed very gloomy after he rode away.

Shortly after Steve left, John went to the barn to do some chores and Gillian followed Nancy to the kitchen to help her with the dishes.

"Nice young man—that Steve Lafferty," Nancy casually remarked to Gillian.

"Yes, he was," Gillian feebly replied as she went about the task of gathering up the dishes as Nancy took the kettle of boiling water from the stove.

"We have ourselves a busy week ahead of us, honey. I have a lot of sewing to do. Got to make you and me some frocks before we catch that stage to go to Helen's. I'm taking you with me to visit my sister."

Nancy did not have to be looking at her face to know that she'd caught the young girl's attention. "I'm—we're—we're going to your sister's?"

"That's right. We're going to Tucson, honey. We're going to have ourselves a good time." She gave out one of her hearty laughs. "We're going to leave old John here by himself for a while and us girls are going to the city and kick our heels up."

Gillian broke into a gale of lighthearted laughter and the two of them stood there drying dishes as they laughed. There could never be another lady like Mother Foster on the face of this earth, Gillian was certain about that. She was one of a kind— that rare breed of woman!

"Mr. Foster will probably be delighted to be rid of us two pestering females," Gillian declared, still giggling.

"Yeah, honey—but we never tell him that."

"We don't?"

"Oh, never, Gillian. I see right now that you and me gotta have a talk. Maybe it is long overdue. Guess this dumb lady has just not realized how grownup you've become since you came to us. We're going to do a lot of talking. We're going to enjoy some good times at Helen's. She's a real nice lady and you'll like her."

"Oh, I'm sure I will."

"She's my baby sister and she has the sweetest daughter,

Melissa, who's just about your age. The two of you will enjoy each other's company."

Gillian found herself all caught up in the excitement of the trip. Suddenly, the gloom about Steve's departure was fading. The next hour passed quickly as they put the kitchen in order and talked about the journey they would be taking.

Nancy sensed the excitement she'd ignited in Gillian and she knew she'd chosen the perfect time to announce her plans. She could not wait to tell John about Gillian's reaction.

She had to admit to herself that John had been right and she wondered why it hadn't occurred to her that a pretty young thing like Gillian could get awfully lonely. All of her friends were left behind when her parents decided to travel to Arizona territory. Nancy's neighbors did not have many occasions for social affairs. Weeks went by that Nancy didn't even see her closest friend and neighbor, Clara Shannon and her husband, Frank. Clara's girls were too young to be company for Gillian, anyway. Their twin sons, Elbert and Edward, were a few years older than Gillian, but neither of them had appeared to interest her when they had come to call.

It was easy for Nancy to see why they hadn't drawn any attention from Gillian, for they were both homely and lacking any personality which would appeal to a young girl. Nancy might be far past the age of a young romantic, but she could recall her feelings at sixteen.

She had been lucky, because John's folks and her parents were neighbors. She had been smitten with love for John for as long as she could remember. The miracle for Nancy was the startling shock that John finally took notice of her and came courting.

As she busied herself around the house, doing her chores, her head was whirling as she thought of articles she'd have to purchase at the mercantile store. She was going to get John to take her into town tomorrow, if he could possibly manage it. She knew she had a lot of sewing to get done for Gillian and herself. Maybe, if there was enough money to spare, she'd let

Gillian pick out one of those pretty little bonnets with the velvet streamers. She'd look like a doll with that pretty face of hers framed with a fancy bonnet. With that auburn hair and blue eyes, Nancy decided it would have to be a rich deep shade of blue.

Nancy found herself in a gayer mood now about visiting Helen and she knew it was the excitement of Gillian sharing the journey with her. Far more enjoyable to have her company than to be all alone.

When John came to the back door he heard the lively tune Nancy was singing even before he saw her. A broad smile lit up on his face. It was obvious she was in a happy mood and he was a happy man when he spied the delicious-looking cherry cobbler, his favorite fruit pie. No one baked a better one than his good wife. No neighbor he'd ever visited put tastier food on the table than Nancy. He considered her the best darn cook in the territory.

"Pretty song you're singing, Nancy. Glad to see you in such a gay mood," he said, strolling over to the counter to help himself to a dipper of water from the pail sitting there.

When she turned around, John saw the glowing radiance on her face which reminded him of the young girl he'd fallen in love with so many years ago. John knew that beauty was in the eyes of the beholder, for most men would never have considered his Nancy a beautiful, sensuous lady. He knew her for a passionate woman, and he saw a most intriguing person in that tall stout woman.

She came rushing toward him, mopping her forehead with the bottom of her apron to declare, "You were right, John Foster. As you usually are, I might add." They gave each other a warm, loving embrace. As they released each other, she asked him, "Could you spare the time to run me and Gillian into Rock Springs in the morning? I'll like to make us a couple of frocks to take to Helen's. I thought maybe I'd take the money we don't need—you know there in the jar—and get Gillian one of those fancy little bonnets."

75

That was Nancy with her kind, gentle heart! She hadn't had a new bonnet in years, John knew, but she wanted to get one for Gillian.

"I think we can manage that, and a bonnet for you too, my dear. After all, two such lovely ladies as you two both need a new bonnet to go travelin', I think. Besides, I've been driving myself silly wondering what to get you in a few weeks when we have our twenty-fourth anniversary."

Her face mellowed with love. "You did remember, John?"

"Of course I did. Have I ever forgotten that day, Nancy?"

"No, but neither of us had mentioned it this year so I didn't know. After all, when someone has been married this long I guess it is understandable that a husband might forget."

He gave her a playful pat on the rump and a wicked little wink of his eye as he assured her, "Not this man, Nancy. So it is settled. Tomorrow, we'll go to Rock Springs to get the things you need for your trip and especially those fancy bonnets."

John excused himself from Nancy's kitchen to clean up from his day of labor around his ranch. Dear God, he was not about to say anything to dampen her high spirits. It was obvious that those busy eyes of hers had not seen their neighbor, Hank Marcus, ride in late in the afternoon. If she had, he knew that was the first thing she would have asked him when he'd walked through that back door. He was hoping she hadn't, especially after Hank had informed him why he'd ridden over to tell him the news. A number of his horses had been taken by a band of renegade Apaches.

John had no intention of telling Nancy anything about this, for she would cancel all her plans to go Helen's. He did not intend to tell her that he had posted some guards at various spots around the ranch tonight in case the same band of renegades tried to take the mules he was about to sell to the Army.

Hank's news took John by surprise, for the countryside had been peaceful for quite a while. "I knew that other parts of the territory were having some raids, but this is the first incident

I've heard about around here in a while."

"Has been. When President Grant sent General Howard down here and he got this Tom Jeffords to meet with Cochise, the two of them made a pact. Jeffords respected Cochise, as he did Jeffords. Cochise held his men in control because Jeffords kept his word to the fierce chief. But there's talk now that Cochise is dead, although no one can be sure. The talk around Rock Springs is that Jeffords has not been able to meet with him for over four weeks."

"How come—if they were so friendly?" John had asked of his neighbor.

"Who can say? Them Indians are a strange breed. Talk has it that the last time they met, Cochise told Jeffords that they would never meet again in this life. Jeffords thinks he's dead. The red devil who is now starting all this hell is called Geronimo. He and his Apaches have crossed the border out of Mexico and plundered and raided in New Mexico, and now they've moved this way. It seems he hopes to line up Cochise's Apaches with his band."

"Then we could be in for some rough times around here, my friend. From the tales I've heard about Geronimo, he is a far more vicious brute than Cochise," John declared to his neighbor.

"Geronimo is a man crazed by revenge against all white men. White men killed his wife. At least, there were those like Jeffords who felt Cochise was a wise man they could trust to keep his word if he gave it. Geronimo is so changeable—real peculiar."

There was a moment of quiet thoughtfulness before John Foster spoke again. When he did, his tone was very somber and serious. "Caution your good wife, Lois, not to say anything to Nancy or Gillian, should the two of them see each other. If Nancy knows this she'll not go to her sister's and she deserves this trip."

Hank Marcus gave him a pat on the shoulder and an understanding grin. He made his own confession to John. "I've

77

not told Lois or the children that it was Apaches who raided our corrals, John. I figure what they don't know won't give them sleepless nights. Only me and my men know that it was Apaches. I understand what you're saying exactly. Course, that don't mean to say that I'm not taking a lot of extra precautions. But I'm damned well trying to do it so Lois won't suspect that I'm nervous as hell."

John laughed. "And I'll sure do the same. The only problem I'll have with that, Hank, is that Nancy is about the smartest person I know. To fool that woman is almost impossible."

Hank Marcus could not deny that. He found his wife Lois a far more attractive lady than Nancy Foster, but smart she was not! "Well, John, I gotta say I've got an ace in the hole there. But if I have riders out and you post guards around, then maybe we have a chance to ward these damned renegades away from our ranches."

They had given each other a warm handshake and it was their bond to help each other in their time of need. This was the way it was in Arizona Territory. When you lived in these isolated valleys and canyons, neighbors had to join forces when danger threatened.

Discreetly, John prepared his arsenal of rifles and pistols as Gillian and Nancy cleaned up the kitchen after their evening meal. He hard their lighthearted laughter and he knew he was right to spare them any concern over the possibility of danger lurking in their valley.

Tomorrow, they would go to Rock Springs but he would take two of his hired hands, his best shots. Oh, he'd have to conjure up some lie to satisfy Nancy, but he knew he could do that.

Until this new fury calmed down, he was happy that Gillian and Nancy would be many miles away!

Chapter Ten

John Foster could not boast that he'd fooled that clever wife of his very many times in all the years they'd been married. But today, he figured he'd done just that! He would have wagered with anyone that Nancy could not possibly have guessed the intense worry consuming him as they'd traveled into Rock Springs. The two hired hands had been warned not to give anything away to the ladies about the threats of a possible raid from the Apaches roaming their area after wreaking their havoc in New Mexico.

When he watched Nancy and Gillian roam through the store, choosing from the bolt of material and lace at their leisure, he was glad he had dared to chance the four-mile trip from his ranch.

He moved in and out of the mercantile store as the women shopped and enjoyed visiting with some of his old friends just outside the door of the store. It seemed that they had heard the same reports that he had heard from Hank and he only prayed that the clerk in the store didn't mention any of these rumors to Nancy.

The longer he waited for Nancy and Gillian to make their purchases, the more tense John Foster became. The longer they lingered, the more John began to fidget.

He moved back into the store to see the two of them trying

on bonnets. In long striding steps, he moved down the counters toward them. Taking off his wide-brimmed felt hat he sought to tease them. "Shall I try this one on, my dears?"

It was enough to make the two of them explode into a gale of laughter. He quickly persuaded the two of them to make their choice of the bonnets they'd tried on several times. When they did, he applauded their choice. It was sweet relief to John's ears when they announced that they were through with their purchases.

It was even more satisfying to Foster when they had made the journey back to their ranch without incident. It really sank in on John just how apprehensive and anxious he'd been when he started unloading the wagon. He felt as if a heavy burden had been lifted off his chest as he turned the reins over to his hired man, Cal. While they'd been in Rock Springs, John had sent Cal and Brock to the feed store to purchase an extra supply of grains and feed.

"Think you ended up spending more than me and Gillian, John," Nancy teased him as they walked up the path to their front door.

"Guess I figured I might as well, while we were there. That way I won't have to make the trip in while you are away, dear." That wasn't exactly the whole truth, but it seemed to be good enough to please Nancy because she dropped the subject. John did not wish to be away from his home and ranch for the next few weeks. He intended to be right here on this land he'd always loved to protect it, just as he would protect the woman he loved.

If Geronimo was roaming through New Mexico and Arizona looking to kill and plunder, then this white man was going to give him one hell of a fight.

After they entered the house and he had obliged the two ladies by getting their purchases laid on the bed, he excused himself to go back out to the barn. "Gotta talk to Cal and Brock. See you girls later. I'm sure that you two won't miss me for a minute," he playfully taunted them.

What he said was true, for they were busily surveying all the lovely materials, many yards of lace and ribbon. Gillian could already envision the loveliness of the frock they could make for her out of the deep blue sprigged muslin. How perfect it would be with the new bonnet! The ribbons on the bonnet were a perfect match to the ribbon they'd picked to trim the dress.

Exuberantly, her arms circled Nancy's broad waist as she declared, "You're so good to me, Mother Foster. No daughter could be loved any more than you've loved and cared for me. I—I just hope I can pay you back someday. I—I don't know what I would have done without you."

Gillian could not know how Nancy Foster was fighting back the tears because the girl's sweet words had affected her so deeply.

"Oh, now, honey—you pay me and John every day by giving so much to our lives. Don't you realize that? Shoot, you better quit talking so sweet to me or you'll see one hell of a mess when I start blubbering." She wore a broad smile on her face as she patted Gillian's small shoulder.

"Well, I sure don't want you to cry. Why, I feel like it's Christmas with all these pretty things. Poor Mr. Foster, he didn't get a thing."

"I beg your pardon—I got enough yarn to finish up the sweater vest and a cap for that big head of his," Nancy informed her. Gillian marveled at this woman whose tone could sound so unfeeling, reflecting nothing of the emotion and warmth in that robust body of hers.

It was true that there was nothing tiny or delicate about Nancy Foster—not the features of her face or figure. She gave no special time to herself for styling her hair or any interest in fancy clothes. Never had Gillian remembered seeing her wear any jewelry except the simple gold wedding band on her finger. Never had she seen her dab toilet water behind her ears or at her throat as her own mother, Amy, always did. No, Nancy Foster was a plain, practical woman, but she possessed a heart of gold and a sparkle in those eyes of hers as brilliant as any diamond.

To Gillian, she was a rare gem!

Each day Hawk took the wagon and his saw into the dense woods and worked from sunup to sundown cutting the timbers to load his wagon. Back at the cabin, he split and stacked the wood. Only when he had satisfied himself that he had supplied enough wood for his mother to cook her meals and keep her warm from the chill of the evenings did he quit the trips to the woods.

Only then did he give himself the pleasure of a leisurely ride one afternoon in hopes of seeing the beautiful Gillian riding her mare down in the valley. God, he yearned so to see her and be with her for one more glorious moment before he left the region. He realized after seeing her with that handsome man that he was allowing himself a very foolish fancy to think she could ever be his or that she would ever love him as he loved her. But how did one tell the heart to stop loving?

He recalled Solange's revelation to him a few short nights ago. Never had she spoken so frankly about such things and never had he felt so close to her as he had after their talk. If he was to believe what she told him, nothing was hopeless or impossible. He could hold on to that ray of hope that Gillian could be his, for he knew his love for her was strong and endless.

As he rode through the woods, he heard the echo of rifle fire coming from across the way where his pal lived. Hawk figured Troy must be roaming the woods hunting game for his evening meal. Hawk pulled up the reins on his horse and listened to the sounds around him.

Once again, he heard the blast of rifle fire. He could not resist a chuckle, for he guessed Troy was having trouble hitting his target. A sharpshooter Troy wasn't, and Hawk knew it!

Slowly, he cantered his horse away from the trail he had been following. There was only a short distance to go before his sharp eyes caught sight of Troy Beane stalking through the underbrush with his rifle posed and aimed.

A devious streak in Hawk urged him to yell to his friend, "Hey, Troy! What are you after?"

Troy Beane jerked around, letting his rifle sink to his side as he turned to see Hawk astride his horse with a grin on his face. He took his worn, wide-brimmed black felt hat with its leather band decorated with colorful feathers off his head and flung it angrily to the ground. "Hell, Hawk—you just cost me my supper. Had me a wild turkey spotted and I would have got him but for your damned loud mouth."

Hawk roared with laughter. "A turkey, eh? Sounds to me like that turkey was giving you a heck of a challenge, Troy. Heard a couple of shots you got off so I guess my loud mouth was the cause of that, too, eh, Troy?"

"Oh, shut your mouth or I'll have me a half-breed for supper." Troy was probably the only person who could get away with such a remark as that. But then there was a very good reason he was allowed to do that; he was a half-breed, too.

Giving a good-natured laugh, Hawk told his friend, "Come on, Troy, and we'll get that turkey for your table."

Without any argument, Troy did as Hawk suggested. He knew what an expert marksman Hawk was, never missing his target as Troy did constantly, so it came as no surprise that Troy did have a fine young turkey for his supper. That bird was going to provide some mighty fine eating, for the meat would be good and tender. Troy invited Hawk and Solange to join him for the evening. "It's been a while since we've visited, Hawk."

As the two went their separate ways, Hawk hoped he had not taken too much liberty before speaking with his mother first. But it would be nice to spend an evening with their neighbors before he took his leave from the region.

He shrugged any concern about his mother aside as he rode toward the valley below. Right now, another woman took over his thoughts, and that was Gillian Browne. Would his long ride yield him no sight of her? Perhaps it would.

It was a beautiful day with a sun so bright and a sky so blue, he could not believe that she would dare stay in the house. As he spurred his horse to that lofty pinnacle where he had so often sat atop his horse to look down on the valley below, he could see the glorious colors of the fields. A most beautiful cover of daisies, Indian paintbrush and black-eyed Susans in shades of yellow, white, red, and pink raised their heads toward the sun there in the pastureland of the Foster property.

There could be no countryside more beautiful than this, Hawk was convinced when he thought about the dense green forest he'd just ridden out of. As he sat there surveying the valley below, he watched the graceful swoop of the red-tailed hawk diving down to search for its prey. He wondered what had urged his mother to name him Hawk. He hoped that it was because she was reminded of this bold, proud bird.

His black eyes followed the hawk as he flew from his lofty perch in one of the piñon trees to travel swiftly downward. It was as his eyes were following the hawk that he caught sight of the auburn-haired Gillian with her straw bonnet resting on her back as she was bending down to pick the wildflowers in the pasture. So absorbed was he in her glorious beauty, he did not notice the movement a short distance away in the tall pasturegrass. But when his eagle eyes glanced to an angle some two hundred feet just north of where Gillian was, and he saw the jet-black long-haired men with kerchief-tied bands around their heads stalking the woman he loved, Hawk came alive with fear, for he knew they were Apache. The coarse long hair swinging around their shoulders and dark, fierce faces as they slowly approached their prey were enough to set off a rage in Hawk. He spurred his horse into action to cover the distance and he gave out his own wild scream to alert them to his approach. With his rifle gripped as his horse galloped in the direction Hawk had demanded, Hawk pulled the trigger. It was enough of a distraction to save Gillian from their evil intentions. His bullet had felled one of the renegades, and the other Apache ran as fast as his legs could carry him back to the spot where his horse was tethered.

Hawk realized, as he galloped closer to the spot where Gillian stood, frozen with fear, that she was in a state of shock. Hastily, he leaped from his horse to rush to her, encircling her in his strong arms. Perhaps, he, too, was in a state of shock as he murmured softly in her ears to assure her she was safe. He was there to protect her. Gillian was assured that she was safe as he told her, "You are all right. No one will ever hurt you while I'm around. I promise you that."

She knew not how long she lingered there in the warm, loving circle of Hawk's strong arms. When her blue eyes looked up at his face and she pleaded with him to see her safely home, Hawk could not refuse her, even if it did mean coming face-to-face with the Fosters.

"Please take me back to the house, Hawk. My legs feel like jelly. Dear God, I was scared to death!" she mumbled in a faltering voice.

"You had every right to be scared, Gillian. Those Apaches would have taken you their captive. Hold on to me, little one, and I will see you safely home." He turned her swiftly around so she would not have the chance to see the one he had killed. So far, it had not dawned upon her that his bullet had marked one of them for death.

After what had taken place Hawk cared not that the Fosters would recognize him as a half-breed and raise a skeptical eyebrow. He had a need to warn John Foster that there were Apaches lurking near his ranch. He also had the need to inform him in private that there was one dead Apache out there in his pastureland.

He supported Gillian as she mounted her mare. "Hold tight, little one, while I go for my horse," he cautioned her. She assured him she would be just fine. But she'd forgotten the beautiful wildflowers she'd picked for Nancy's table.

Together, they rode side by side at an unhurried pace toward the ranch house. Hawk's black eyes were on her all the way, and once she glanced in his direction to see him looking intensely at her. "I am all right, Hawk. Really I am." She gave him a warm, sweet smile, and Hawk swelled with so much love for her that he knew he could never love any other woman the way he loved Gillian.

If he could not have Gillian, then he wanted no other woman in his life!

Chapter Eleven

John Foster could have sworn he heard rifle fire as he was sauntering down the length of his barn. He rushed out into the corral, his concerned eyes surveying the countryside anxiously, but it was a peaceful, quiet countryside that he viewed.

He chided himself for giving way to a case of nerves, but as he was about to turn around and go back inside the barn he saw Gillian's glossy auburn hair with the rays of warm Arizona sunshine shining on it. She rode toward the house with a stranger at her side. Who was he and what was he doing with Gillian?

As they came closer and closer, John noticed that the man's manner seemed very familiar with Gillian and she was obviously welcoming his attention. He was certainly no stranger to her. But then, why did he not know him? By the time they were only a few yards from the corral, John had a better view of the young man's face. The thick black hair and tawny skin told Foster all he needed to know: The man had some Indian blood in him. Perhaps Gillian would not realize this, for she was seeing through her young girl's eyes a most striking young gent with a firm, muscled physique. His dark twill pants and faded cotton shirt were molded to his trim body. He wore no hat atop his dark head. John noticed the matching pearl-handled pistols resting low around his waist, as well as

...e was carrying.

...ere was a bold arrogance about the young man as he came closer. John knew instinctively that this man bowed to no one. Gillian called out a greeting. Hawk realized he was being scrutinized by this man Gillian had told was John Foster.

By now their horses were halted by the fence and Gillian introduced John to Hawk. "Did you hear the gunfire?" she inquired. "Hawk saved me. Two Apaches were out there in your pasture while I was picking flowers for Mother Foster. Scared me to death!"

John took off his hat and ran his fingers through his unruly hair as he directed his words to Hawk. "I'm beholden to you for coming to Gillian's aid. Hawk—isn't it?"

"Yes, sir—Joe Hawk," Hawk replied, and now he was the one searching the expression on John Foster's face.

John suggested that the three of them go to the house. "My Nancy is going to be most curious about all this, I think. I'd hoped to spare her and you, too, Gillian. I'd heard the rumor that we might expect some trouble like this. Obviously, the danger is right here in Maricopa County." John had caught himself in time so that he didn't call the threat what it really was: the Apaches.

John's all-knowing eyes did not miss a thing as the two of them dismounted from their horses. It was obvious that Joe Hawk was enamored of Gillian. He noted the special way his tanned hands assisted Gillian down from her horse and the way his black eyes adored her as they looked at her. John's concern mounted as the three of them walked toward the house.

He noticed something else as the three of them walked together: John was a tall man but this man, Hawk, towered over him. Little Gillian looked like a child walking by his side. Off his pinto, John could certainly appreciate the fine figure of a man he truly was. It was not surprising that a young girl would be impressed by such a magnificent-looking male!

Nancy was sharing her husband's impression of Joe Hawk as

she watched the trio walking toward the house. Concealing herself behind her ruffled curtains, she stood watching them walk up the pathway lined with hollyhocks. Why wasn't John bringing them to the front door instead of the back door, she wondered? Mercy, her kitchen wasn't in order to parade through it!

When John called out to her, Nancy moved out of her parlor and into the kitchen where the three of them were standing. Nancy was impressed by the formidable figure as John introduced her to Hawk. There were few men Nancy Foster had ever encountered that she had to look up to, for she was a tall lady. But this was one of the exceptions!

"Well, it's nice to meet you, Joe Hawk, and may I invite you to join us for some coffee and a piece of cake?" Nancy suggested.

Hawk accepted her offer. He instantly admired Nancy Foster and he sensed that she formed an opinion as swiftly as he did: She liked him!

"I'd enjoy that very much, Mrs. Foster," Hawk told her with a warm smile on his handsome face.

Nancy knew that either Hawk's father or his mother was Indian. Only the blending of an Indian with a fair-skinned individual could have produced such an offspring.

As they sat around the Fosters' kitchen table drinking coffee and eating Nancy's cake, Nancy observed that he was a well-mannered young man, whether he was a half-breed or not. John did not have to be told that his good wife was favorably impressed by the young man sitting at their table. He knew that she was a good judge of people and he respected her judgment, but his concern was for Gillian. Would she feel this warm and friendly should this young man be part Apache? Could she ever forget that it was a band of Apaches who had killed her parents? He rather doubted it!

John looked at her radiant face and he wanted nothing to take that glow away from her. She liked this young man and he knew it. As a man John knew the way another man would look at a woman he loved and he saw that expression in Hawk's black eyes. Ah, yes, there was great depth of passion in those smoldering black coal eyes of Joe Hawk!

He wondered if Nancy was sharing some similar thoughts as he was as he watched the young people. He wondered just what Nancy was feeling since she had learned about Apaches invading their property. Would she cancel her plans for the trip to Helen's? If she had changed her mind, there was nothing he could say that would change it. She was one stubborn cuss!

John heard Nancy asking Joe Hawk where he lived and various other questions. When he chanced to speak of his mother and called her by name, Nancy gave a sigh, declaring, "What a very pretty name— Solange! Don't know that I've ever heard it before."

"She came from France, ma'am. But I agree with you. I have always considered it a beautiful name. My mother is beautiful, too, as you'd see should you ever meet her."

"Well, you can't tell, Hawk—we might just meet one day."

"She would like that, I'm sure." Hawk realized that he should never have had any qualms about meeting these good-hearted people but he knew why he had been uneasy about it. Some of the white people living in this area were not so kind or considerate as the Fosters. Some could be very cruel and heartless as he'd found out as a young lad. It had left a very painful impact on Hawk.

It amazed Hawk that he was feeling so comfortable in the company of the Fosters, and because of this pleasant, relaxed atmosphere he lingered longer than he had expected to. Now that he knew he must leave, he ponderd how he could speak to Foster alone. He must do that before he left.

He graciously thanked Nancy Foster for her kind hospitality and his eyes glanced warmly over to Gillian. He did not wish to bid her good-bye but he knew he must. So instead of saying the words to her he'd have liked to express, he sought to say very casually, "I'm sorry we forgot your lovely wildflowers back there in the pasture."

She gave a soft little laugh. "Oh, Hawk, those flowers were the last thing on my mind when everything started happening. I can always gather more wildflowers."

A frown creased his dark, handsome face as he gently warned her, "Oh, I wouldn't do that, Gillian—not alone. Not for a while!"

"Hawk is right, dear. You must not go that far from the house for a while," John quickly agreed with the young man. As Hawk moved out of his chair, John offered, "I'll walk you out to the barn, Hawk."

Hawk was grateful, for John had provided the moment of privacy Hawk wanted to have with him.

It was only after they had left the house and were walking toward the corral that Hawk told John Foster about the dead Apache in his pasture. "I fear I did you no favor, sir. I regret that I had to kill him on your land. It may cause big trouble for you."

John gave him a comradely pat on his firm shoulder. "You had no choice, son. You did what had to be done. You saved our Gillian, and nothing else matters to me or Nancy. Whatever comes, we will try to give it a damned good fight. I've dealt with a lot of big trouble in my life."

"I've no doubt that you have, Mr. Foster, and I appreciate your kind words."

"Kind words? No, no, Hawk—the truth, young man! It was the Apache, wasn't it, Hawk? I'd heard that Geronimo had crossed the border out of Mexico with his renegades to gather up his forces to raid in New Mexico and Arizona Territory. Damned if I expected him to be so close as he obviously is." His next words stabbed into Hawk as sharply as the arrow would have pierced his broad chest. "Cochise is dead, they say. Geronimo has appointed himself the chief of the Chiracahuas. Obviously, that is what he's trying."

Hawk's face could have been granite, but John did not take notice of this as they continued to walk toward the corral. But

91

Foster's declaration kept ringing in Hawk's ears. Cochise was dead!

Hawk was a man in a trance when he left the Foster ranch, but he was pleased to know that the man who'd fathered him and caused his mother painful torment was dead. Never again could he hurt anyone. Never again would he lead a raid on wagon trains to kill innocent people as he had done to Gillian Browne's mother and father.

He rode toward his mother's cabin with a tremendous feeling of release in his soul and his spirit. Never again would he have to look upon the fierce face of the Indian chief, Cochise, as he had two years ago. He hated him with the same intensity as he loved his mother, Solange.

The warmth of the Fosters had also given Hawk great encouragement and a new hope that he'd never felt before—hope that he could be accepted by people like the Fosters. The brand of the half-breed was not to be a damnation to him all his life.

Never again would he feel that he was an inferior person because he was half Apache!

Chapter Twelve

A purple-hued twilight glowed radiantly over the country-side as Hawk rode out of the valley and back to his home in the mountains. He realized now that he'd been wrong to torment himself about how the Fosters would feel about him. No one could have been more gracious to him than they had been during his short visit to their home.

He was a young man filled with a new surge of confidence. The stigma of being Cochise's son did not have to forever damn him. There was an overwhelming feeling of pride within him, knowing that he'd saved Gillian. It was obvious that this deed had won him the favor of the Fosters. Now, he would feel free to pay a visit to Gillian when he wished. No more would he have to be content to watch her from that high mountain peak as he'd done so many times over the last two years.

The truth was he would have lingered longer had he not promised his friend Troy that he and his mother would have dinner with him tonight. As his pinto, Tache, galloped along the narrow trail lined with pines and he heard the calling of the piñon jays perched in the branches of the trees, he was a man returning home in the highest spirits.

As he was riding around the last bend in the trail before he reached his mother's cabin, he noticed one of the yellow-winged butterflies. Forever he would think of Gillian when he spotted one of them, for he'd spied one flitting over Gillian's head just before his keen eyes had spied the Apaches ready to pounce on her as she plucked her wildflowers. It sickened him to think what could have happened to her if he had not been nearby.

But he was there as he would always be when Gillian needed him. It was a promise he would keep!

As he tied Tache at the hitching post and walked up the pathway toward the cabin, there was a jaunty air about him that Solange noticed immediately. To see his mood so lighthearted and gay made her break into one of the little French songs she'd learned back in her native country so many years ago—a lifetime ago!

But she could not sing her song without her dainty feet insisting on keeping time to the melody. This was the sight greeting Hawk as he came through the door of the cabin. He said not a word but just stood watching her glide around the plank floor of their cabin. Forever, he supposed she would look youthful to him and it always amazed him, knowing the hardships she bore and the horrors of her young life.

He watched her small figure move and sway. Her silver-streaked hair hung loose around her shoulders, for her usual braids or coils did not restrain it.

She whirled around with a gay smile on her face to greet him. "Ah, it is a happy time when you can sing and dance—yes, my son?"

"Yes, Mother!" He grinned. It was as if she already sensed his feeling of happiness before he'd had a chance to announce his good news learned from John Foster that Cochise was dead. Never again would he have the chance to put an evil blight on either of their lives.

She reached out for Hawk's hand, insisting that he follow her as she danced around the room. "Someday, my son— someday you shall be wanting some pretty girl to dance with you and I shall teach you."

Hawk stumbled around the room awkwardly with her and

broke into a roar of laughter. "Mother, there is little I'd refuse you, but I am clumsy ox. You looked magnificent and I would look like an absolute fool!"

She flung herself into a chair and laughed. "Ah, my son—there are those rare times that I guess I pretend that I am that gay little French maiden back in my country and this was one of those times. You've just seen your mother make a fool of herself!"

"Never, Mother—never you." He sat down in the chair close by and suddenly his demeanor turned serious. "I've—I've something to tell you, Mother. I heard some news today that made me very happy and I think you will welcome it, too."

"What did you hear, my son?" she inquired, sitting up straight in the chair with an intense look on her face.

"Cochise is dead, they say."

"They say? Who says?"

"I was at the Fosters' ranch. John Foster told me this."

"Ah, yes—our little Gillian—yes?"

"Yes, the people Gillian lives with." He went on to tell her what else had happened and how he'd rescued her. "I also killed one of the Apaches."

"It sounds like you had no choice, my son, but to do what you did," she declared, her eyes searching his face to see if she saw any remorse of regret for his act. She saw none.

"Not if I wished to save Gillian," he told his mother.

"And Gillian—is she all right?" Solange noted the instant sparking in his black eyes at the mere mention of her name. She knew, as only a mother can know, that this young lady was very special to Hawk.

"She is fine. Oh, there were a few moments of fright when she heard the gunfire, but she is a spunky young lady. By the time I got her to the house she seemed to be over her fright."

Solange's next question was about the Fosters. A pleased smile came to her face when Hawk eagerly told her how welcoming they were. "You would like Nancy Foster, Mother. She's a very friendly lady. We sat in her kitchen and had coffee along with some little cakes she'd baked."

This did not surprise Solange about the people who'd taken Gillian into their home. She was sure that they would have to be good, kind-hearted people.

"So you have had a very interesting, exciting day, I would say, Hawk?"

"You could say that, Mother."

"Good, I am glad! I am so happy to know that Gillian is all right. I am so glad you happened along when you did, Hawk."

He was almost tempted to confess to her that he'd kept a vigil over Gillian Browne for the last two years. There were few secrets Hawk had kept from his mother, but this was the exception. Something stopped him from making his confession.

Perhaps it was because he suddenly noticed how his mother was scrutinizing him as he'd stood up from his chair to move across the room.

He wondered what thoughts were going through her head as her all-knowing eyes surveyed him so carefully. "Mother, you have a strange look on your face. What are you thinking?"

She spoke slowly, amazed that she'd never thought about it before. "*Mon Dieu*, Hawk—I'd not realized it before now, but now I know who it is you are the image of! I'm shocked that I'd not noticed it before this. You are the image of your great-grandfather! My father was a short, little man but his father was a giant of a man." You're like your great-grandfather Touraine!"

"You think so?" he quizzed her.

"I know so! There is no doubt in my mind at all." She smiled. The look on her face was enough to convince Hawk she spoke the truth. Hawk felt a pride in that heritage; he admired everything about his dear mother.

"I'd like to think that this was true, Mother. I truly would," he confessed to her.

"Believe me, my son. I would not say it if it wasn't true."

"I've always believed in you, Mother."

Such glowing warmth gleamed in her eyes as she stood there,

96

holding her towering son's hands in hers. "No mother could be prouder of a son than I am of you, Hawk. I know I always shall be."

"I thank you, Mother, for such high praise, and I shall always try to make you proud of me," he told her.

He suddenly took notice of the sweet and spicy aroma permeating the small cottage. He knew why when he saw the numerous bunches of gathered wildflowers. It was obvious how his mother had spent her afternoon and he knew that she intended to hang them in the little back room to dry. When they were cured and dried, she would enjoy the wonderful aromatic fragrance she enjoyed when she placed them in little jars and containers around the cabin.

He also noticed that there was no preparation for their evening meal as there usually was at this time of the early evening.

As she always could with Hawk, Solange noticed his dark eyes darting toward the stove and table and knew exactly what he was thinking. An amused smile came to her face as she laughed. "I've already accepted Troy's invitation for his fine turkey dinner tonight. He came by here on his way home after the two of you met in the woods. In fact, over there are two pies covered with a white cloth which we will contribute to the meal tonight. An apricot for Troy and a blackberry for you."

He could not resist laughing as he saw the teasing gleam in her eyes. "There's no other lady in the world like you, Mother. If there is, I don't know where."

"Oh, my son! I can't accept that and I do believe that you have a sugar-coated tongue," she teased him. "Now, quit trying to butter up an old lady like me and get yourself cleaned up so we can be on our way to Troy's."

As he had done all his life, Hawk obeyed his mother's bidding. She wore a pleased smile as she went to her bedroom and sat at her small dressing table to put her long hair in braids so she might make the two large coils at the back of her head. When she had them securely pinned, she went back to the room where all her wildflowers lay on the table to pluck a cluster to pin into her hair. Solange felt it was a festive occasion, so she intended to wear her prettiest frock. It was a deep purple color with dainty white flowers. The square neckline and cuffs were edged in ruffled lace.

Solange always felt very gay and lighthearted when she wore this dress, which was not too often. Tim had purchased this gown for her and it was what she'd worn when they'd married. The only jewelry she owned, except for the gold wedding band he'd placed on her finger when they married, was a pair of pearl earrings and a single strand of pearls. She treasured them, for she knew how many hours Tim had labored to earn the price those pearls had cost him. Often she had thought about that dear, gentle-hearted woodsman who'd taken her and her young son in and taken care of them. He'd honored her by asking her to marry him and she'd gratefully accepted his offer, for she had no one or nowhere to turn at that time in her life.

Never had she lied to him that she was in love with him, but there was a special love that grew through the years. In that secret part of her heart, she knew that he would never have been the type of man who would attract her if she had been back in France. Never had she envisioned her life to have been lived in the air of simplicity when she was a young French girl with romantic daydreams.

Yet, if she was able to ever go back to her native France to see her friends of yesteryear, she felt certain that most of them would not have attained the degree of happiness and contentment she had.

She looked now at the reflection in the mirror and saw a lovely lady. There were few lines in that satiny complexion, so fair and unblemished. With the flowers tucked in the sides of her hair, she could see the slight hints of the feisty coquette she'd once been. There was no denying that her figure was still trim and curved in the right places. While the gown she now wore would not have impressed her at one time in her life, she appreciated it very much now.

Tonight she would not be going to a fancy soiree with an amorous suitor, but she would be accompanying her fine son, Hawk. Solange intended to enjoy herself to the fullest, for it might be the last time this chance would come her way for a long, long time.

Once he left this mountain to hire out as a scout for the railroad, she instinctively knew that he would never be back at this cottage with her as he had been in the past. She was wise enough to know that it was inevitable. Oh, he was a dutiful son and he would return from time to time, but he would never be satisfied to remain here anymore.

Years had passed since she pondered what the future held for her. Now, once again, she was facing that frightening possibility. The last time she'd found herself in this dilemma was when she endured the days and nights in Cochise's camp, wondering how she might escape to freedom.

Because of her stubbornness and her determination to attain her freedom, she had achieved it. Now, she wondered if she was brave and courageous enough to manage alone, without Hawk there to comfort and console her when she needed him.

Mon Dieu, she could only pray that she could!

Chapter Thirteen

There was a festive air in the humble cabin of Hawk's friend, Troy, and the meal was scrumptious. It was truly a feast, with the roasted young turkey, cornbread dressing, fresh ears of corn, and Solange's fruit pies.

When the meal was finished, Troy picked up his fiddle and the others began to sing the tune he was playing. Solange looked at the happiness gleaming on her son's face and she, too, was happy. Never would he have imagined the heaviness in her heart that this would be the last time they might be sharing such a gay occasion for a long time.

There was a certain degree of tension hanging over the Fosters' house this evening. Gillian did not realize this, for she was excited about all the purchases they'd made. Innocently, she did not understand how serious the situation was, nor what it meant that Apaches had invaded the lands of John Foster. But Nancy Foster knew, and it was most disturbing to her. She mentioned none of her concerns when John returned from saying his farewells to Hawk, then went immediately to the barn. She watched as he and one of his hired hands rode out of the corral. He'd told her nothing about what he was doing.

But the minute he returned to the house, she cornered him and demanded to know. "John Foster—you—you tell me what is going on around here! I've got the right to know."

There was no doubt in John's mind that she was riled. He knew his Nancy and her firebrand temper very well after being married to her so many years. This was a part of her that he admired because it was a part of that spirit he would never have wanted to change. It was a trait that made her exciting and set her apart from other women he'd known.

A slow, easy grin came on his face as he sought to calm her. "You're right, my dear. I had an Apache to bury. Hawk shot him this afternoon and this is what he wanted to tell me, because he didn't think that Gillian realized that in her state of shock. Right there in our own pasture, Nancy."

For a moment, Nancy said nothing as her eyes locked with John's. When she did find her voice, she muttered, "I forgot to tell you, John, that this puts a different slant on whether I go to Helen's or not."

"I'd have expected you to feel this way, dear, but I've got a suggestion to make and I think you'll see that it is the right one. You go ahead on your sewing and preparations. Let me and the men do the worrying about any renegade Apaches stalking around this place. You know that a week or two could have them in another part of the territory. They're a band of nomads, as you well know. By the time you and Gillian are ready to leave they could be miles away from here. Now, wouldn't that be a shame for you to have given up your plans to see your sister?"

As he usually did, he spoke with a lot of good sense and Nancy could not argue. She shrugged her shoulders and a slow grin came to her face. "Well, guess I'll get busy on my sewing and let you get on with your business. And John, we got to lay the law down to Gillian, and she may not like it, but she can't go riding alone for a while."

"Already thought about that and I intended to do it in the morning." His hand gave her behind a gentle pat as she was turning to leave the room. Giving a good-natured laugh, he told her, "And if this absentminded man forgets to say anything, I know you will."

"That I will!" she declared firmly as she marched on out of the room.

The smile on his face quickly faded the minute she left the room and he ambled thoughtfully over to his chair in the parlor to enjoy a leisurely smoke. The incident this afternoon had left him deeply troubled. He had tried to hide this from Nancy and he felt he'd managed to do so quite successfully.

As he sat there in the parlor all alone and puffed on his pipe he did find himself relaxing. The night was a still one just outside the opened window. Only a light, gentle breeze seemed to be stirring the ruffles of the curtains, he noticed. His old collie had followed him and lay curled up by his feet to sleep the evening away. John's hand reached over the arm of the chair to give him a pat on the head. "You ate too much, too, eh, Champ? I know I did."

There in the peace and quiet of his home John Foster let his worries drift away. He could hear the voices of Gillian and Nancy echoing from the other room.

But all that serenity came to a sudden halt with the wild screaming out in the blackness of the night. John bolted out of his chair to dash to the front door. He saw one of his hired men running across the grounds toward the house. Out of breath and gasping breathlessly, he assured John, "Ain't no Indians, Mr. Foster—just a damned prowling bobcat over there by the woods."

"You sure it was a bobcat, Ed?"

"Sure was. Marshall spied him over there and he was thinking about riding out there to try to kill him but I told him you wouldn't want him to leave his post to do that. I was right, wasn't I?"

"You are absolutely right. I want Marshall right here and certainly not riding out at night into those woods. It might have been a bobcat he saw, but what if it was an Apache?"

"I know what you're saying, Mr. Foster, and that's what I told that young whippersnapper. That Marshall is sorta' a crazy kid."

103

John laughed. "Well, Ed—he's just not lived as long as you and me. He hasn't seen or done as much as we have. Guess we'll have to be a little patient with him, won't we?"

Ed Collins gave a laugh and agreed with his boss. He'd never known a man to equal John Foster. He remembered how he'd drifted into this territory without a coin in his pocket, and Foster had hired him, sensing he was down on his luck. Lord, he'd never forget that evening he arrived, just at twilight, so weary and hungry he could not have ridden any farther. Not only had John Foster hired him that evening but his good wife had invited him to share their evening meal, right at their table. Ed had been embarrassed about the way he'd gobbled up the good food Nancy Foster had prepared.

But that woman was a pure gem of a lady and she had that very special way about her that soothed any embarrassment he'd felt as she kept offering him the bowls of vegetables and platter of a juicy beef roast. He'd always sworn that it was the best meal he'd ever eaten and he lost count of the slices of her fresh baked bread he ate that night.

As far as Ed Collins was concerned, there were no people on the face of the earth as good as these two. He'd been here at the ranch long before they'd taken Gillian into their home. That young lady had become very dear to him, too, during the last two years. He would protect these people with his life if need be.

"Well, I'll be seein' you in the mornin', Mr. Foster," he told John as he backed off the porch to return to his post.

When John returned to the parlor, he heard the soft ring of laughter coming from the next room and he knew that neither of the women had known anything about the little happening of the bobcat. He was glad they were so engrossed in their silks and satins, lace and ribbons.

Once again, he settled down in his easy chair and lit up his pipe. He abruptly stopped to notice that old Champ had not moved a muscle. The collie must be getting deaf not to have heard the bobcat's scream.

Once again, John Foster settled cozily into his chair to enjoy a smoke. His nose savored the pungent aroma of the tobacco as he drew on the pipe. He could glance out the window to see the dark skies dotted with all the twinkling stars and a most beautiful halfmoon gleaming down on the land. As the clock chimed the hour of ten, John had just finished reading a rancher's journal. When the sudden screeching of an owl from a piñon tree just outside his window interrupted his peaceful tranquility, he jerked up in the chair, dropping the journal to the floor.

Dear God, his nerves were frayed! Now, there was no doubt in this rancher's mind that he was far more concerned about this thing than he wanted to admit to himself. It was going to be devilishly hard for him to hide this from Nancy. She knew him too well. Never would he be able to fool her! If she'd been sitting here in the parlor with him, as she usually did, and had seen him leap out of his chair as he'd done twice, she would have known instantly what was bothering him.

Ah, yes, Nancy Foster was too shrewd a woman for him to try to fool. He was like some jumpy old lady!

John found himself to be very weary. Locking the front door and dimming the lamps, he left the parlor to bid the two women good night and go to bed. It had been a long day.

When John came to say good night to Nancy and Gillian it dawned on Nancy just how late the hour was. She declared to Gillian, "Mercy, we did get carried away, didn't we?"

"I guess we did. I had no idea it was this late either," Gillian confessed as they started to gather up the piles of materials and trimmings covering the bed. When the task was accomplished, Nancy told her good night, leaving to go to her own bedroom. Seeing Gillian's enthusiasm about the pretty materials which would turn into lovely frocks for her to wear, Nancy could not possibly dampen her spirit even by hinting that the trip might not be made.

A feeling of sadness washed over Nancy as she walked into her bedroom and prepared to undress. They'd not been able to provide much in worldly goods fo the lovely young girl. God knows, such a beautiful girl should have fancy clothes and a few luxuries, but she'd never acted like she'd missed them during the last two years.

But Nancy recalled, as if it were yesterday, the day they rescued that poor bedraggled girl with her tear-stained face out of the smoldering ruins of that wagon train. As soiled as her dress was, it had been a nice one, and the little leather slippers were, too. There was a gold locket around her neck. It was obvious to Nancy that the Browne family were not any starving drifters. Things Gillian had told them during the first months led Nancy to believe that her father, Joseph, had been a good provider and that her mother enjoyed far more luxuries than Nancy had ever ever been used to here on the ranch.

Nancy had realized that she and Gillian's mother were two very different kinds of ladies. In appearance, she knew from Gillian's description of her mother, they were total opposites. Gillian's mother was a tiny woman with delicate, dainty features, while she was a big-framed, hefty woman. A rancher's wife in this land had to be a hardy, strong person. It wasn't a land for pampered, weak ladies.

With her nightgown on, Nancy slipped into the bed beside John, who was lying quietly there. While he remained silent, she sensed that he wasn't asleep. But she gave no hint of her suspicions.

There was one consolation for Nancy Foster as her head lay back on her pillow: she and Gillian's mother did share one thing and that was a love for the girl. That she knew for certain. It was a satisfying feeling for her to know that while they'd not been able to give Gillian much in the way of worldy goods, they'd given generously of their love. The young girl knew this and considered their home her own.

It was true that John had not been asleep when Nancy crawled in the bed, but the comfort of her warm body beside him was soothing and relaxing.

Gillian crawled in between the cool sheets and quickly

drifted off to sleep. But her sleep was not deep, and in the middle of the night, she found herself whirling back in time to the horrors of that early morning when the Apaches attacked their wagon. Never would she forget those wild banshee yells mingling with the screams of her mother. Echoing in her ears were the screams of the other travelers in the wagon train being killed by the wild savages attacking the wagon train.

In the struggle, as her father was stabbed and one of the braves was yanking the necklace from her mother's dainty throat, Gillian found herself falling behind the stacked baskets there in their wagon. When she fell she slammed her head against a huge cast iron pot. As blackness engulfed her, she was spared seeing her lovely mother stabbed to death like her father.

Miraculously, the baskets falling all around her had concealed her from the evil eyes of the Apaches and spared her life. When she'd next opened her eyes she was in the protective arms of the Fosters.

When she abruptly jerked up from her bed tonight, she suddenly realized that she was still in their protective arms and their home. But it took a few minutes to come back to reality from that horrible nightmare! Her body was drenched in dampness and her hands were still trembling.

At least, she was safe. No harm would come to her here!

Chapter Fourteen

There was a certain enchantment about this land that intoxicated a man, Steve Lafferty was beginning to realize. The land and a beautiful lady by the name of Gillian Browne were beguiling him in a strange mystic way he would never have believed possible just a few weeks ago.

Now that he was in this strange town called Tucson, and over a hundred miles separated them, he dreamed of her lovely face every night.

The peaceful Indians of this region had named the town of Tucson Stjudkhon. The old settlers of the region told Steve that it meant "at the foot of the mountain." Four mountain ranges did encircle the town there in the vast desert area. The rich Spanish heritage was reflected everywhere Steve looked. Most of the buildings were adobe with tiled roofs. The old courthouse standing near the plaza was an impressive structure in the Moorish style with its dome of tile.

Steve Lafferty had found the people of Tucson a most friendly lot. The man in charge of operations for the railroad company was a genial, jolly fellow. The evening Steve had arrived from Maricopa County, he had reported to the office of Howard Curtis. Curtis had insisted that Steve accompany him to his house for dinner before he took him to the hotel where he'd already arranged lodging for Lafferty.

Howard Curtis's family had given the good-looking Irishman a cordial welcome. He was certain that their home was one of the finest, most elegant houses in the town. Mrs. Curtis was a prim, neat little lady who possessed a most gracious air. It was obvious to Steve's knowing eyes that her gown was no simple frock like the ones worn by Nancy Foster or Gillian. Her jewelry was exquisite and expensive. Lafferty figured that Curtis was paid a fine fee for his services for the Southern Pacific Railroads.

If was only the tempting offer they'd made to him that had urged Steve to be away from his sea and his ship for such a long time. His fine ship could carry a huge load of cargo, including the supplies the railroad needed to connect the tracks to the existing rails, and go westward. That was the goal they sought to accomplish. Railroads had to go from the east coast to the west coast of this country.

When he was first approached to take on this job by the railroad officials, Steve was excited about being a part of this great enterprise, but he was not so sure he'd done the right thing for a man of his temperament. He had not counted on the number of weeks he would be away from his ship and the sea. Now, he must see it through, as he'd committed himself to doing the job.

There was one bright spot in all this, he consoled himself during that long stagecoach ride from Phoenix to Tucson: he'd met the beautiful Gillian.

He was truly not in the mood to accept Howard Curtis's offer to have dinner the first evening he'd arrived in Tucson. He would much rather have gone to the inn, enjoyed a bath to rid himself of the dust and grime of the long trail drive, and gone to bed. But he didn't have the heart to refuse Curtis.

No one could have asked for a more hospitable host. Curtis requested that his wife inform her cook to hold up dinner so Steve could enjoy the luxury of a bath. By the time he joined the Curtis family in their elegant parlor, he was feeling much less weary, but he realized that he was not the most impressive gent Howard's wife must have expected him to be. No doubt she'd heard all the tales about sea captains being a roguish lot and he'd be the first to admit that it was usually true. Tonight, though, he had no desire to play that role, so he did not respond to the attempts of Curtis's flirtatious older daughter, Virginia. He directed more of his attention to the younger, plainer daughter, Jeanette, who was curious about his ship and his life as a sea captain.

Much to Sue Curtis's chagrin, her prettier strawberry blond daughter did not seem to be attracting this handsome Irish sea captain at all. She was very disappointed, for he was a striking-looking man, but he was cold and aloof.

When she and Howard were finally alone in their bedroom, she voiced her displeasure about their guest. "I was expecting a more interesting young man, I must say."

"Oh, he is an interesting fellow, Sue dear. He was just weary from the long stagecoach ride from Phoenix. That was all. He just wasn't in the mood for a lot of idle chatter tonight. Maybe I should not have insisted that he come over for dinner tonight. We could have invited him to join us a few nights later."

Sue sat at her dressing table applying a layer of her special cream to her fair complexion which she feared was going to suffer from this fierce Arizona sun. Oh, Lord, she could not wait for Howard's assignment to be over so they could return to their palatial home back East, where all her friends were. She hated this miserable place with all her heart!

"Yes, Howard—I—I agree about that," she remarked. She noted, as she looked in the mirror, that Howard was not hearing her, for he was already asleep.

Across the carpeted hallway, in Virginia's room, the two Curtis daughters were having their own discussion. Jeanette had rushed through Virginia's door, her bright eyes flashing. "Did you ever see anything like him in your whole life, Virginia? Lord, what a handsome man! All I had to do was just look at him and I turned to jelly inside. Didn't you, Virginia?"

Virginia felt exactly the same way, but she dared not voice

this to Jeanette. Instead, she nonchalantly replied, "Oh, I guess he was all right. Awfully serious and quiet, I thought. I had hoped he'd be more talkative and amusing."

Wide-eyed and shocked by her sister's remark, Jeanette stammered, "You never cease to puzzle me, Virginia. I figured you would be as taken with him as I was. He's twice as handsome as any of those dandies coming here to court you."

What her younger sister said was absolutely true, but she was not about to agree with her. "Oh, go to bed, Jeanette, and dream about the sea captain you find so exciting. I've things I want to do," Virginia said, dismissing her from her room.

"Well, I might just do that, but I'll bet you might just be doing the same thing. The only thing galling you is that he didn't give you all the attention you're used to getting. That's what's bothering you!" Jeanette marched out of the room hearing the blast of her older sister's slipper as it was flung against the door.

As she angrily tossed the pins from her hair onto the dressing table, she decided right then and there that she was not going downstairs the next morning to join the family for breakfast. She'd remain in her room until her father and Steve Lafferty left the house. She cared not if it displeased her mother.

She had felt humiliated tonight that he almost completely ignored her. This wasn't the way young men usually responded to her. She'd not subject herself to that kind of treatment again in front of her family. She'd use her wiles on Steve Lafferty when she could do it away from her family, she thought to herself as she stared at her reflection in the mirror. She was beautiful and she knew it!

As she planned, Virginia made no appearance around the breakfast table the next morning, but Jeanette was there, eagerly questioning Steve Lafferty about his life at sea.

In that syrupy sweet southern accented voice of hers, Sue admonished her younger daughter, "Honey, please allow the captain to enjoy his breakfast. He'll never want to pay us a

112

visit again."

Steve saw the crestfallen look on Jeanette's face and gave a lighthearted laugh. "Oh, don't you think that for one minute, Mrs. Curtis!" Turning his green eyes toward Jeanette, he smiled. "Curiosity is a sign of intelligence, Jeanette, so I find your questions about the sea and my ship a pleasure to answer, or at least try to."

"Thank you, Captain Lafferty," she replied. But she asked no more questions during the meal.

By the time Lafferty rose from the table to go with Curtis to the inn where he would be quartered during his stay in Tucson, he did not feel too fond of the wife of Howard Curtis. He found her a manipulator who liked to domineer and bully the people around her. Well, he had news for her—she'd not work her wiles on him! If she thought for one minute she was going to do some matchmaking for her older daughter with him, then she was crazy. He had met overzealous mothers like her before and he'd sensed that this was what she had in mind last night.

He graciously said his farewells to her and Jeanette as he left the house with Howard to go to the Old Pueblo Inn. When Steve was settled in his bedroom and adjoining sitting room, Howard told him that he would be sending one of his men back to the inn with a buggy or a horse.

"Which would you like, Captain Lafferty?" Curtis asked.

Steve laughed. "I don't care for horses and I think they feel the same about me. I'll take the buggy, sir."

"A buggy it will be then."

Curtis advised Steve to enjoy himself and take in the sights of the countryside. But when he extended an invitation that Steve dine with them again that evening, Steve made the excuse that he had some papers to go over before he came to Curtis's office the next day.

"Well, we'll do it another time then, young man. Our door is always open to you." Curtis bade him farewell and left the room.

Lafferty had no intention of hurting Curtis's feelings, but

113

his wife could prove to be a problem, and so could his daughter Virginia.

How often could he turn down a dinner invitation when it was extended to him?

He was glad to be finally alone in the privacy of his own quarters. It did not take him long to unpack.

Perhaps, he would do as Howard suggested—a little sightseeing. Maybe he might find some little trinket to carry back to Gillian which would please her and make those blue eyes glow with excitement.

Dear God, she made all other women pale for him! He thought about the three fancy-dressed ladies he'd seen last night; they didn't hold a candle to his pretty Gillian in her simple tunic and full gathered skirt. The high-fashioned hairdos were not half as beautiful as her hair of deep copper flowing to and fro over her dainty shoulders.

Never had he seen such sensuous, inviting lips on a woman and now that he'd kissed them, he knew the honey-sweetness there. Just thinking of her now made him hunger to taste that sweet nectar. His strong arms yearned to encircle that tiny waist and press her close to him.

He was like a man who'd drunk a potent love potion. All he could think about was Gillian and how much he adored her.

Chapter Fifteen

By the time Steve Lafferty returned from his sightseeing jaunt around Tucson, he was ready to go to his suite, have a bath and his dinner served in his room. He was not interested in going to the main dining room this evening. So when he went through the lobby of the inn, he made his request to the desk clerk before he went to his rooms.

By the time he had bathed and shaved, one of the waiters was bringing the dinner he'd ordered along with a bottle of red wine. Ravenously, he devoured the thick beef steak and the tasty, well-seasoned fresh vegetables. By the time he finished the bottle of red wine, he was pleasantly sated and ready to go to the soft bed and enjoy a night of sleep.

He was certain that Curtis had spoken the truth when he'd told him that the Old Pueblo Inn had the best food in Tucson.

He must compliment the fine lady who ran this magnificent inn. She had an expertise as to what lodgers wanted in an inn. Lafferty had stayed in a goodly number of inns and lodging houses all over the world. His room was neat and clean and the food was superb!

When sleep overtook him, he dreamed of the girl whose lips were as red and sweet as the wine he'd drunk. He dreamed of the lilting sound of her gay laughter as she'd ridden with him over the Arizona countryside that last day he was at the

Fosters' ranch. Her hair had been like dancing flames of fire. He swore that no one had ever spoken his name so softly as she did with that special mellow drawl of hers. He was glad that she called him Steve instead of Stephen.

Had Gillian known the bewitching spell she'd cast on the handsome Steve Lafferty, she would have been elated. Never would she have imagined the impact she'd had on him by the time he left the ranch. She was not like the worldlywise ladies Lafferty usually spent his time with. So naive and innocent to the ways of the world, Gillian only knew what she felt in her own heart. She knew not how to use her beauty and her wiles to entrap a man—but she had done it nonetheless.

She realized that something wonderful and exciting had happened between her and Steve. She could not feel any shame for giving herself to him as she had. She could not believe that it was wrong, and she knew she was not a cheap, lowly lady because of what she'd shared with Steve.

But he had said goodbye without any promise of the future, a voice reminded her as she lay in her bed that first night after Lafferty had left. She tried to shrug that aside, but the voice continued to haunt her as she tried to fall asleep.

She tossed and turned, not wanting to face the truth the voice was telling her. Had he only had his pleasure with her and perhaps played her for a little silly fool?

Oh, surely a man could not love so tenderly as he had and then forget the special ecstasy they'd shared that day in the woods. Surely, he could not do that! She had to believe that he cared for her as she adored him. Had not his green eyes adored her as they'd looked so lovingly into hers?

He did love her, she told herself. He could not have held her and kissed her that way if he had not felt as she did, she soothed herself as that tormenting voice kept pestering her.

116

When she was able to convince herself that Steve Lafferty surely loved her, she was able to fall asleep. She needed to believe that he was as lonely as she was since he'd left the ranch to go to Tucson.

The proprietress of the Old Pueblo Inn was sorry she'd not been roaming the lobby as she usually did this morning, chatting with her guests. But she had some business to discuss with her lawyer and that took most of the afternoon. By the time she returned to the inn, her desk clerk informed her that Mr. Curtis had arrived with their new guest.

"I trust you took good care of him, Jason," she said.

"Sure did, ma'am," the clerk declared to Melba Jackson, who could be a very intimidating woman at times. She allowed no excuses for her orders to be carried out during her absence from the establishment. It was rare that she was gone from the inn more than a few hours at a time.

"So he is now in the suite—this Captain Lafferty?"

"Yes, ma'am. But no, he isn't there now. I just saw him walk through the lobby and leave in a buggy that Mr. Curtis sent for him to use during his stay here."

"Hmm, guess Curtis and the railroad people consider him rather important," Melba said, as she went behind the desk to check the ledger and pick up some papers she wanted to take to her private office to look over as soon as she had a light lunch.

In that flippant, perky way of hers, she gave the young clerk a wink of her eye as she quipped, "I'll leave it in your capable hands, Jason. I've got some things to do this afternoon."

This was the Melba Jackson Jason liked to be around. But there was another side that made him quake in his boots. He'd seen her that way a few times since he'd come to work at the inn. God forbid, he didn't want to ever be in that position again. Diligently, he worked at his job! Like most people in Tucson, he respected and admired the woman who'd taken this

117

old place with its overgrown grounds and made it into a magnificent inn with beautiful gardens. She'd become a prosperous businesswoman whom the gentlemen of the town admired and respected for her clever intelligence. Few ladies could have accomplished what Melba Jackson had managed to do in the town of Tucson or anywhere else.

As usual in the afternoon, the lobby did not have the milling crowd of the early morning or evening. A few couples sat in the large room just off the lobby where comfortable wicker furniture was arranged to make a pleasant atmosphere for reading or visiting with the other guests of the inn. Huge urns of ferns and blooming plants gave it a pleasant tranquility. The undraped windows allowed the viewer to gaze out over the courtyards and the rippling waters of the fountain streaming down into the pool. A flagstone path circled the area. Numerous blossoms of reds, pinks, and purples made a glorious sight for the guests to enjoy.

There were no gardens in the fine homes of the wealthy families in Tucson that surpassed the courtyard gardens of the Pueblo Inn.

It took Melba most of the afternoon at her desk to put her books in order for the week. By the time she wearily left her office to go back to the desk in the lobby, she saw that Jason was no longer there and her other desk clerk, Frances, had taken over for the evening.

"Hello, Frances—didn't realize it was this late. Worked longer than I'd planned," she greeted.

"Keep tellin' you, Miss Melba, that you work too hard," Frances gently scolded her boss. But after all, she'd been with Melba since the first day she'd opened the inn. Forever, she'd be beholden to her, for the salary she made at the inn supported her and her two children. Like Melba, she'd been married to a no-good man who'd got himself killed in a local saloon while he was playing poker.

"Never knew anything but hard work all my life. Wouldn't

know what it was to live the leisurely life." She gave the young woman a warm smile, but Frances thought her dark eyes looked tired. But she also knew that she'd go to her suite, take a refreshing bath, and dress in one of her fancy gowns to be the vivacious hostess as her evening guests started to fill the elegant dining room this evening.

In all the years, she could not recall an evening that Melba had not appeared to play her role as the hostess of her establishment.

"By the way, Frances—our new guest, Captain Lafferty—has he come back yet?"

Frances informed her that he had, just a few moments ago. "Stopped by the desk here just as Jason was leaving and I was taking over to give me his order for an early dinner. Said he wished it served in his room 'cause he intended to retire early."

"I see. Thank you, Frances." She turned to stroll slowly down the long, carpeted hallway to her private quarters. It seemed that she would not be satisfying her curiosity about this dashing Irishman Curtis had told her about when he'd engaged the lodgings for Lafferty here at the inn.

If she was to wager a bet, she would bet that he was one handsome rascal, just like her own Irish husband had been. No doubt he had a silken tongue that could sweet-talk a woman into anything he desired. Lord knows, that husband of hers could surely do it, and did for years, she remembered.

The chances were that this Lafferty would leave a few broken hearts around Tucson before he left to go back where he had come from.

But by the time she entered her suite, her musings about her past and Lafferty were put aside, for she had to take a bath and get dressed for the evening. She forgot her feeling of weariness and prepared to make herself the attractive, lively lady her patrons expected her to be. By the time her thick hair was attractively fashioned atop her head and deep green taffeta gown smoothly molded her fine figure, she was ready to put on her emerald teardrop earrings, which were her most prized piece of jewelry.

The reflection she saw in her mirror lifted her spirits. She had to admit that there was still an attractive lady there and that was enough to please a woman of her age.

Life had been good to her, she figured!

Part Two

Two Loves Have I

Tormented by feelings
exciting and new,
her mind is a whirlwind!
She's torn between two.
—Sheila Northcott

Chapter Sixteen

Howard Curtis knew he'd made the right decision in lodging Lafferty at the Old Pueblo Inn when Steve arrived at his office the next morning singing the praises of his suite and the fine food at the inn.

"Met Melba yet?" Curtis asked him.

"No, sir—I haven't."

"Well, it's quite a story around Tucson how she took that old spacious adobe house with its red tiled roof and converted it into an attractive inn about fifteen years ago. She was forced to make a living for herself after her gambler husband got himself killed and, by God, she sure as hell did that and a lot more."

"Sounds like she must be quite a woman!" Lafferty remarked, appreciating all the beauty he'd already seen around the grounds. Just outside his sitting room, he'd observed the huge saguaro cacti that stood over five feet tall, along with the small clustered pink blossomed cacti surrounding the small patio. The shade of the many trees and shrubs on the grounds was a cool refuge from the harsh Arizona sun.

"Her place is far nicer than the hotel downtown. When the miners come into town to let their hair down that can be a noisy street, I can tell you."

"Well, I've stayed in a lot of places like that. When you've hit all the ports in this world that I've hit, you know you can't always be as lucky as I am having the quarters I've got at the Old Pueblo Inn. I thank you, sir. I thank you very much."

Howard smiled. "Well, Southern Pacific wanted the best for you, and that is what I tried to do."

After they'd talked for a while, Curtis told him that he had to excuse himself to go have a talk with his man, Barstow, about the scout they were hiring. "Make yourself at home here in my office, Lafferty. I'll try to be back by lunchtime."

"I'll be fine, Mr. Curtis. You just go along, and if you aren't back by lunchtime, I'll assure you I won't starve." Steve laughed.

Curtis rose from his chair and got his hat off the peg on the wall. "See you later then, young man."

Steve watched him leave the room. He was interested in going over the many sheets of paper to see just how much of the rails and spikes had now been delivered here in Tucson from his ship moored back in San Diego. That would give him some idea about how long he would be expected to remain around here.

Completely engrossed in the sheet he was scrutinizing, he did not hear the arrival of a buggy just outside the building, nor did he hear the door slowly open.

Nothing could have pleased Virginia Curtis more than to find Lafferty alone in her father's office, for this was how she had planned that it would be. She found him the most devastatingly sensuous man she'd ever met. As he sat there now, with his shirtsleeves rolled up to his elbows and that unruly mass of sandy hair falling carelessly over his forehead, the sight of him titillated her!

Looking at those firm, muscled arms exposed with his sleeves rolled up, she could well imagine how it would feel for those powerful arms to hold her. The very thought made her tremble with excitement.

It had not been by chance that she had made this trip to her father's office, for she'd overheard her father tell her mother

124

before he had left the house that he was going to have to be out of his office most of the morning to discuss the hiring of this new scout, who was half Apache.

That was when she set into action her little scheme to pay a visit to his office in hopes that she might encounter Lafferty there alone. It had worked out exactly as she'd planned.

She'd even gone to the trouble of having their cook, Martha, prepare a basket of nice little finger sandwiches, a couple of her delicious meat pies wrapped in a flaky crust of dough baked a golden brown, and a carafe of steaming hot coffee. Martha had packed a basket of picnic foods and included two generous slices of her special applesauce cake, just baked when Virginia came into her kitchen.

The delectable aroma coming to Steve's nose was what made him rouse from his paperwork. His green eyes flashed bright with surprise at the sight of Virginia Curtis standing there smiling down at him. Tilting her head saucily to the side, she addressed him. "You look surprised to see me, Steve. But I often bring Father's lunch. He works so hard, you know. Today, I brought enough for the two of you."

"Well, that's very thoughtful of you, Virginia. But as you can see, your father isn't here."

"Oh, isn't he just out back? You mean he is gone somewhere?" She made a feeble attempt of pretending shock that he was away from his office. Lafferty almost felt embarrassed for her. She was so obvious!

He carefully laid the papers aside as he told her, "I'm afraid so, but then I can't say just when he will be coming back. It could be any minute or it could be hours. You see, Virginia, I've not learned your father's work routine. Having just arrived I have no knowledge about the workings of his job."

She took a seat and lifted the basket up on her father's desk. Sweetly she purred, "Well, at least you will have a good lunch, Steve."

"Oh, I hate to eat alone," he said. "You must join me."

"Well maybe just one of the little finger sandwiches."

She began to take out all the things Martha had prepared and Steve had to admit that his appetite was whetted as he saw the good foods she was placing in front of him.

"Christ, this is a feast." By the time he'd eaten one of the juicy little meatpies, he was ready to try another. It was no wonder that Howard Curtis had such a potbelly with a fine cook like Martha overseeing his kitchen. "My compliments to your cook, Virginia."

"Oh, she'll be thrilled when I tell her that. You must come to dinner again, Captain Lafferty," she said, as she half-heartedly nibbled at a sandwich. "Maybe you might come tonight?"

He hesitated for a moment, for he'd just taken a hefty bite of food. In a hesitating voice, he mumbled, "Oh, I—I regret that I can't make it tonight, Virginia."

She was not used to being refused, and she had to restrain the desire to ask him just why he couldn't come. Instead, she gave out a nervous little laugh. "For a stranger in town, you are terribly busy, it seems."

Lafferty had to suppress an amused grin as he watched her rise up from the chair. He sensed that she was in a huff and fuming, but she dared not let him know it.

"Well, there are times when business must come before pleasure, I guess!" Lafferty said as he helped himself to a cup of strong black coffee.

Virginia whirled around to face him as she stopped putting the leftover food in the basket. There was a flirting gleam in her eyes as she taunted him. "Why, you truly surprise me, Captain Lafferty. You seem so serious compared to all the tales I've heard about sea captains."

Steve looked up at her and his deep voice questioned, "Now just what is it you've heard about us seafaring fellows and I'll try to enlighten you."

"Well—just a lot of things," she stammered as his eyes pierced her. Virginia suddenly realized that this man was nothing like any of her suitors, past or present. He was older

126

and possessed a worldly sophistication she found difficult to contend with.

"You must have heard that we have a lady in every port and that we're a bunch of wild, reckless rascals. To tell you the truth, we are just that!" he admitted boldly. He noted the sudden fluttering of her eyelashes and that wide-eyed look on her face and knew that he had astounded her by his remarks.

But before she had a chance to say anything the door flew open and her father walked in. He was shocked to see Virginia alone in his office with Steve Lafferty.

For a moment he was at a loss for words and when they came they were directed at Virginia. "Well, missy—I did not know that you were planning on coming down here today. Your mother know you're here?"

There was no way she could lie to him about this, for he'd find out the truth as soon as he came home that evening. The truth was, Virginia did not want her mother to know about this. So she was left with confessing the truth that it was her idea. "I—I thought that it would be nice if I brought you and Captain Lafferty a nice lunch from Martha's kitchen. I had no idea you wouldn't be here, Father."

"Well, that was mighty sweet and thoughtful of you, and I'm sorry I missed sharing it with the two of you, dear." Howard didn't believe for one minute that she'd had any thought about him sharing that lunch. Virginia had an eye for the captain and she did not have his approval for being so bold with Lafferty. Tonight, he planned to speak to Sue about their daughter's unseemly conduct.

He dismissed her graciously. "Well, dear—we've work to do now. Tell your mother that I'll try not to be running too late—all right?"

Virginia picked up her basket and her reticule, for it was obvious to her that her father wished her to leave immediately.

Giving both of them a hasty farewell, she turned around to march toward the door. Her pretty face was flushed, for she was feeling foolish and embarrassed by the tone of voice her father had used. She knew he was displeased by her presence at his office, alone in the company of Steve Lafferty.

Dejectedly, she reined the buggy to go in the direction of home. Home was the last place she wanted to go right now. Besides, this place they called their home here in Arizona Territory was not what she considered her real home. Home was back East, where all her friends were. She had no friends here in this godforsaken place. The young ladies her age shared no common interests with her and she certainly didn't relate to them.

Steve Lafferty was the most exciting person she'd met since she'd been here and her little scheme to attract him had hardly gone the way she'd anticipated it.

The way her father had spoken to her just now, he probably looked upon her as a child.

Right now, she was so mortified that she didn't know how she'd ever face Steve again if he *did* come to the house for dinner!

Neither was she looking forward to the admonishment she'd be getting from her mother!

Chapter Seventeen

The grand reward of Howard Curtis's day was to return home and be greeted by the smiling face of his vivacious wife, Sue. He'd always blessed the day that he'd chanced to meet her as he walked down that cobblestone street in Boston many years ago.

As he guided his buggy up the long drive and saw the bright lights welcoming him, he found himself already anticipating the good meal he'd enjoy along with a fine bottle of wine from his cellar. After his hearty appetite was sated, he would relax in his favorite chair to read the paper and have his usual evening chat with Sue.

But he did not look forward tonight to discussing Virginia with his wife, for he knew that she was very prejudiced where her older daughter was concerned.

The moment he walked through the door he smelled the grand aroma coming from Martha's kitchen. He was determined that when they did return to Boston he would take Martha along.

He took a fleeting glance in the elegant parlor, looking so inviting and colorful with the fresh-picked flowers in crystal vases, but there was no sign of Sue so he knew she must still be upstairs. He moved on down the polished tile floor of the hallway toward the stairs.

When he opened the door of their bedroom, he saw his wife sitting at her dressing table, putting on her earrings. She looked so attractive in her gown of mauve with black braid trim! The jet black earrings dangling from her ears were a perfect match for that gown and for her fashionable hairdo.

He sought to tease her. "You look so beautiful. Don't tell me I forgot some special occasion, my dear!"

"No, Howard—you did not forget."

He immediately noted something in the tone of her voice that told him she was very displeased.

"You—you don't sound too cheerful tonight, my pet." He ambled across the room to stand behind her and place his hands on her shoulders.

"I am not happy, Howard! I find it very insulting the way your Captain Lafferty is snubbing your family. Just who in the devil does he think he is?"

Curtis stared down at his wife. "I—I find myself at a loss to know what you are talking about, my dear. Perhaps, you'd best tell me." He sank down in the blue velvet chair beside her dressing table.

"I will be glad to. I came home from shopping this afternoon to find poor Virginia in tears, Howard. She confessed to me that she had Martha fix a basket of food to take to you for lunch and there was enough for Captain Lafferty if he was to be there in the office with you. Well, you were gone so this—this Lafferty ate his fill. Being the gracious young lady I've taught her to be, she extended him an invitation to dinner this evening, and he refused. I think he must be a very rude man, Howard."

How was he to tell Sue that her daughter knew just exactly how to play her so that when he came home this evening with intentions of discussing her behavior, it would be futile? Virginia had outfoxed him.

He'd suspected from the first night Lafferty had arrived in Tucson and dined with them that Sue had set her mind to a little matchmaking between Virginia and Lafferty. Now she was disgruntled that he had not been taken by the charms of their daughter.

"Well, my dear, there is a remedy for all this. It is not demanded of us that we invite Lafferty for dinner again during his stay in Tucson. So let's leave it at that!" He got up to remove his coat and change into a clean shirt before going downstairs to dinner.

Sue sat at her dressing table, slightly confused. She was not prepared for this reaction from Howard. In a soft, meek voice she prodded him. "But dear—would that not make *us* seem rude, too?"

From his dressing room, Howard answered her. "Not at all, my dear. Lafferty will only be here a short time, so what does it matter? Remember, dear—he is a seafaring man and he stays nowhere too long. We wouldn't want Virginia to get involved with a man like that and have her heart broken, would we? When you think about it, Sue, you'll see what I'm saying makes good sense."

She continued to sit there, thinking about all the things her husband had just said.

As soon as the bright Arizona sun descended, the Old Pueblo Inn came ablaze. Candles burned in all the candelabras in the spacious dining room. Lamps glowed in the lobby and the sitting room, but Melba Jackson liked the effect of the flickering candlelight in the dining room. Each table had its small cut-crystal vase filled with flowers picked daily from her gardens.

Melba's voluptuous figure was draped in a soft pearl gray gown tonight and she wore sapphire and diamond earrings and brooch. She emerged from her quarters to circulate around the lobby. She always enjoyed her dinner at a late hour after all her patrons had left. After all these many years, she knew no other way of life. Perhaps it was not the conventional style of the people in Tucson, but how could she fault it when she enjoyed the luxuries she did? No lady in Tucson had as many expensive gowns or as exquisite a collection of jewels as Melba Jackson possessed.

The moment she walked into the lobby she noticed that it seemed to be a busy night for midweek. This was enough to delight her. She spotted some of her older guests gathered in the little sitting rooom off the lobby, enjoying themselves in conversation.

One glance in the dining room was enough to make her shout with joy. Every table was filled and occupied. This was amazing for a Wednesday night at the inn.

Some faces she recognized as her regulars and there were those who were just stopping over at her inn for a few nights as they were traveling west or going back east.

Suddenly, those scrutinizing dark eyes focused on a sole diner sitting at a table by himself. Instinctively, she knew that handsome gentleman had to be the elusive Captain Steve Lafferty whom she'd been so anxious to meet. Now it would seem that she was finally going to get that opportunity.

But for a minute she wanted to stand where she was, to just take in the whole image of this young man.

A handsome devil he most assuredly was! What amazed her was that he was dining alone. He might be a stranger in Tucson, but with his rugged good looks it didn't take long for some pretty young lady to be fawning over him. From what she'd heard about Curtis's feisty oldest daughter, she would have suspected that Lafferty would be having dinner at their house.

But then she'd also heard the rumors that Curtis's wife was a bit of a snob who felt herself too good for the people around here. That could explain that, Melba speculated as she began to move into the dining room to welcome the young Irishman to her inn.

She had a few people to greet along the way as she wove in and around a half dozen tables. A couple of the tables were occupied by regular patrons, so she stopped to chat a moment. But all the time she moved closer to Captain Lafferty's table, she noticed how he was just picking at the food on his plate.

He gazed over the dining room from time to time, aimlessly, his thoughts many miles away. It was not until she was standing beside his table that Steve became aware of the attractive middle-aged lady greeting him with a friendly smile. Steve knew immediately that she must be the owner of this inn, the one whom Curtis had spoken briefly about the day he'd arrived.

She was a fine figure of a lady in her pearl gray dress and brilliant sapphire earrings. He rose and invited her to join him.

"Ah, I'd like to for just a moment at least, Captain Lafferty," she said as Steve moved around the table to assist her into the chair opposite him. A well-mannered gent as well as a handsome one, Melba thought to herself.

"I'm sorry I wasn't at the inn when you arrived. I have to admit I've been anxious to meet you. We don't have an Irish sea captain stopping our way often." She gave a warm laugh.

"Well, it's my pleasure to meet you, Mrs. Jackson. Everything Howard Curtis said about you and your inn is certainly true. Never stayed in any nicer place than this," Steve told her.

"Well, I'm glad to hear that. We strive to give our patrons the best so they'll want to return again and again."

When Steve invited her to share a glass of wine from the bottle he'd ordered with his dinner, she agreed to have just one before she left him to go about her duties.

By the time she'd finished the wine and was preparing to leave, she sought to tease the young captain. "Now, tell me something, Captain, for you see I'm a most curious lady. Was your meal tasty tonight? I couldn't help noticing that you were not eating it with relish."

A very perceptive lady she was, Lafferty concluded. She was aware of everything that went on at her inn, he'd wager.

A sly grin etched his tanned face as he confessed, "I plead guilty. My thoughts were not on my food tonight."

Melba laughed and gave him a wink. "Bet she's a pretty little thing—this lady occupying your thoughts so intensely that you could not eat my good food."

She slowly started to move away from the table as Lafferty smiled. "She is! Goodnight, Mrs. Jackson. Nice to have met you."

"Nice meeting you, too, Captain Lafferty." She maneuvered around the tables, pausing to speak to the couples dining nearby. She was a warm, genial woman, Lafferty thought. A person felt like he'd known her for a long time. Howard Curtis had pegged her right—she was quite an admirable lady!

When he left the dining room, he did not go directly to his room. Instead, he took a leisurely stroll through the courtyard gardens. Now that the sun was down, a gentle breeze cooled the air. Other people staying at the inn seemed to have the same idea about taking a moonlight stroll around the gardens. He saw a couple sitting on one of the benches and he figured them to be newlyweds, for he'd seen them checking in late this afternoon. This was a most romantic setting and it made him ache with longing to have Gillian here with him.

Taking a puff on his cheroot, he ambled on down the path that would soon bring him to his own private patio.

He decided to sit out there a while to finish the last draw on his cheroot before going inside. Lafferty knew the reason for the discontent washing over him tonight. There would be no peace for him until he was with the two ladies he loved with all his heart—Gillian Browne and his ship, *Lady Luck*.

Chapter Eighteen

A gentle breeze rustled the branches of the tall, majestic palm trees outside his room. The back and forth motion of their branches reminded Lafferty of the surging movement of the ocean. To ride those waves again and feel the salt spray against his tanned face—that's when he'd feel alive again!

The day had been endless, just hanging around the railroad office, for there was not that much to occupy his time. Perhaps it was just his own black mood, but it seemed to him that Curtis was no longer the outgoing, friendly man he'd been the day before. The only thing Steve could figure out was that he'd taken offense about finding his daughter Virginia there with him alone. Damned if that was his doing! Curtis could fault his daughter for that. The truth was he wanted no part of Virginia Curtis. He'd learned a long time ago that her kind could get a man in a bloody mess of trouble.

But Lafferty knew that he was not just imagining it by the time the day was over and he went his separate way toward the Old Pueblo Inn. Curtis was distant and cool!

A deep purple haze was settling over the town that was surrounded by lofty mountain peaks in every direction. The streets were busy with people going toward home as he was returning to his own quarters.

He took no particular notice when his buggy passed the

powerfully built half-breed riding a pinto. Others stopped for a brief moment to stare as they viewed the coppery-skinned Hawk arrogantly riding down the street of their town. His shoulder-length black coarse hair and the high-crowned black hat with its wide brim caught their eye. But Hawk seemed not to notice them staring at him nor did he take any notice of the fellow he passed guiding his buggy down the same street.

Lafferty wore no hat atop his thick sandy mane of hair. He dressed for comfort in this place where the sun was so bright and hot. His faded blue shirt was unbuttoned at the neck and his sleeves were rolled up to give him the comfort he needed in this hot Arizona weather.

A bath and ridding himself of a day's growth of beard was bound to make him feel a lot better, he knew. It had seemed oppressively hot in Curtis's office by midafternoon.

By the time he arrived at the inn, dusk hung over the courtyard gardens and early diners were already arriving at the gates to go to the dining room. He decided not to go through the front entrance and through the lobby. Instead, he veered off the main path to the side of the inn and through the rhododendron bushes which would take him right up to his private patio.

As he had figured, he did feel much better by the time he'd shed his damp shirt and taken a refreshing bath. Removing the heavy beard which seemed to have so rapidly grown since the early morning hour and giving a light splash of lime tonic to his face gave a pleasant, clean effect. For a brief moment, he sauntered around his suite naked, helping himself to the silver case to get one of his cheroots and pouring himself a shot of Irish whiskey.

He sat there, leisurely relaxing, as he sipped the whiskey and puffed on his cigar. He let thoughts trail back to several days ago when he was there at the Fosters' ranch in the company of the sweet Gillian Browne. He adored this free-spirited miss who was so guileless and divinely naive. She was like no other woman he'd ever met, and he supposed that was what intrigued

136

him so.

When he'd emptied his glass of whiskey, he moved out of his small sitting room to go into his bedroom, took out a pair of pants, along with a clean white linen shirt, and flung them casually across the bed.

With lazy motions, he went through the routine of putting on his clothes and finally pulled on his black leather boots.

By the time he was dressed and the brush was put to his thick hair, he was ready to enjoy another glass of his Irish whiskey. A cool night breeze seemed now to be rustling through the tall palms just outside his room so he opened the door leading out onto his patio.

He decided to enjoy a moment or two there before going into the crowded dining room to have his evening meal. He couldn't say he exactly enjoyed dining alone. Usually he and his first mate, Driscol, shared the evening meal in his cabin when he was aboard his ship.

There in the darkness, his nose smelled a sweet fragrance he recognized as the one Melba Jackson wore the night before when she'd sat with him briefly in the dining room. Then he saw the matronly proprietress, ambling slowly toward his patio.

"Good evening, Captain Lafferty. You look very comfortable sitting there with a drink in your hand," she greeted him gaily.

She looked most elegant tonight in her basic black gown with pearls draping the neckline. Tonight her hair was styled in huge coils at the back of her head with a mother-of-pearl comb tucked at the top of the coils.

"I am pleasantly relaxed, Mrs. Jackson."

"Oh, Lord—please call me Melba. Everyone calls me that. Now, I'll be the first to say I appreciate your respect and I know that I'm old enough to be your mother, young man, but we're an easygoing, informal lot of people here in Tucson. I'll make a deal with you—all right? You call me Melba and I shall call you Steve."

Steve had already risen from his chair. He extended his hand

137

as he agreed to accept her request. "Now, I've also a suggestion to make to you, Melba. When your duties of the evening are through tonight, may I request the pleasure of your company to join me for dinner here in my suite?"

She rarely found herself at a loss for words, but his invitation took her by surprise. Then a slow warm smile creased her face as she declared with a tilt of her head, "Well, young fellow—you've got yourself a date! Been a long, long time since I've shared dinner with such a handsome dude as you so I'll look forward to seeing you in about two hours."

"I'll be here." He grinned. It had been an impulse idea to invite her and now he was glad he had. He knew he would find it far more pleasant to share dinner with Melba than to go to the Curtis's home and listen to the endless chatter of Curtis's wife and two daughters.

"I'll put in a special word to my cook. Any particular thing you'd like, Steve?"

"I'll rely on your choice, Melba."

"May I send up a bottle of champagne?"

He gave a deep husky laugh. "You certainly may." He watched her turn to move on down the stone path as she gave him a wave of her hand before she disappeared into the darkness of the courtyard gardens.

If he could not be with Gillian as he yearned to be, then he'd settle for the company of the interesting Melba.

The nights had seemed endless for Solange since Hawk left their mountain cabin to travel to Tucson. She'd managed to keep herself occupied during the daytime, but once twilight fell over the mountains, she found it very difficult to fix meals for just herself.

She suddenly realized that her whole life had revolved around her son. From the moment she'd given birth to him, he'd only been away from her a day or two at a time when he and Troy had camped in the woods to hunt.

Never had she felt so isolated back here in the woods until now. After a week, she was feeling an overwhelming desolation, and every noise she heard at night made her jump. Solange did not like being this way and tonight, she decided that it was an occasion to go to her cupboard to have some of her cherished brandy to quiet her frayed nerves.

Chiding herself was doing no good, she realized. How ashamed Hawk would be of her if he saw her this way! She would not be weak, she vowed!

The brandy did help, and an hour later, she was feeling more relaxed. In fact, she found herself pleasantly weary. Finishing the last sip of brandy, she moved to secure the locks of her door and go to her bedroom.

She vowed that she must accept being alone, now that Hawk was to be gone for weeks at a time. The truth was that Hawk might never live here again as he had in the past, she realized.

She did enjoy a peaceful night of sleep and when the bright rays of the rising sun came streaming through her window, she eagerly greeted the new day. Slipping into her wrapper, she went into her kitchen to prepare the fire and brew a pot of coffee. She did not relish the hearty breakfast which she was always fixing for her son so she settled for the little cinnamon spice cakes she'd baked the day before to munch with her coffee once it was done.

By the time her coffee was ready, Solange had changed from her gown and wrapper into her gathered brown skirt and ecru tunic with its drawstring neckline. Her long hair was neatly braided into one long, fat braid hanging down her back.

As she sat at her table thinking about the various things she might do today, a sharp rap interrupted her solitude. She went to her door, wondering who might be calling on her at this hour. Few people passed this way in the dense woods.

At the last minute before she released the lock of the wooden door, she was apprehensive; should she open the door? Cautiously, she finally opened it. There, to her great relief, stood Troy with a big grin on his face.

"Oh, Troy," she greeted him. "Come in!"

As he moved through the door, she happened to notice the little brown bundle he carried lovingly in his arms. It was a fat little butterball pup with a thick coat of brown hair.

"Who's your little friend, Troy?" She softly laughed.

"Well, he's a little stray and he's got a little sister. Guess someone just decided to desert them out there in the woods. Looks like a little bear, doesn't he?"

She could not resist reaching out to take the darling pup in her hands and nuzzle it against her cheek. She kissed the fuzzy little pup as its black eyes looked at her, seeming to welcome her warm loving touch.

"You are a little bear, young fellow. Poor baby, left in that old woods to be killed by some big critter out there," she murmured softly in the pup's ear. Troy wore a smug smile, for he knew his idea had been a good one.

He stood allowing her all the time she wished to snuggle the pup before he sought to speak. Once he was convinced that she was taken with the little creature he'd fetched out of the underbrush, he told her the pup was hers.

"Ah, little Bear, I think I love you. You are adorable!" Solange declared, glancing over at Troy with a happy smile on her lovely face.

"That's why I brought him to you, Solange. Thought he might be company for you since Hawk's gone. Hell, he's even got those same mean black eyes of Hawk's." Troy laughed lightheartedly. "Look at them!"

She held the pup out to scrutinize the two little jet-black eyes staring down at her. "You know, you are right, Troy. Well, Little Bear, I guess I must claim you then." She had to fight the mist trying to come to her eyes. She knew why the good-hearted Troy had brought the pup to her. He realized the deep, lonely void she had to be feeling now that Hawk was gone, and she loved him for being so understanding.

"I thank you, Troy, from the bottom of my heart. I don't think I've ever had a nicer gift given to me. Little Bear and I are going to enjoy many good times."

Solange Touraine was one of the bravest, strongest ladies Troy had ever known. This morning he saw her as he'd never seen her before, for she was overcome with emotion. He promised himself that he was going to make the effort to come over often to see how she was getting along, now that Hawk was gone.

It wasn't easy for a lady to be alone back here in these woods. There were all kinds of threats in this untamed area where no laws existed except the ones the settlers made for themselves.

"Glad you like the little fellow."

"Like him, Troy? I love him already." She allowed the pup the freedom of her cabin by placing him on the plank floor as she invited Troy to share coffee and spice cake with her.

"I figure that he might as well get acquainted in his new home. While he's doing that, we'll have a nice chat over our coffee, eh?"

Troy accepted her invitation and as they sipped their coffee and ate the spice cake, they noticed that Little Bear enjoyed himself on each and every crumb that happened to fall on the floor.

They both broke into a gale of laughter. By the time Troy made his departure, he knew this was a day that Solange was not going to be lonely. Little Bear was going to keep her well occupied.

When he left the cabin to mount his horse at the hitching post, he threw up his hand to wave goodbye. As Solange returned his wave with one of her own, he saw Little Bear there at her feet, happy and content.

He had already accepted Solange's cabin as his home!

Chapter Nineteen

Little Bear filled the lonely void in Solange's life. It was comforting to feel him curled at her feet or snuggled up on her lap during the long evenings. He was something to talk to during the days as she went about her chores or roamed through the woods when he followed her around like a little shadow.

Being a woman with so much love inside, Solange gave the little pup all her affection and he eagerly accepted it. He responded by giving her a lick on her cheek or hand to show her how much he loved her.

During the first week Little Bear was at the cabin, she found he had an insatiable curiosity and this intrigued and amused her. She would watch him and be entertained for an hour or so.

She'd cautioned him more than once about lunging at the bees as they stopped to take a share of the nectar from the flowers growing around her cabin. There came the day when he was to learn his lesson the hard way when one lit on his little black nose, giving him a stabbing sting. He went into a frenzy as he yelped and ran around frantically until she captured him up in her arms. She took him into the house to apply some of her soothing ointment to ease the pain of the sting.

"Ah, Little Bear—now, maybe you'll leave them alone, eh," she softly admonished him. "I tried to warn you, but you just

143

had to go and find out for yourself. Well, you did and it pained you, didn't it?"

He looked up at her with those black eyes of his as if he understood every word she'd spoken. Looking into his black eyes, she was reminded of Hawk. She prayed that he was not finding the new world he was now existing in too painful. After all, he'd never been away from these woods he'd grown up in with only her and Tim, along with a few friends. The outside world could be a very cruel place for Hawk, and she could think about all kinds of problems he might face.

As gentle a soul as Hawk was, there was a fierce side to his personality. She'd seen that side of him emerge only a few times in all his life.

This was something that could cause him a tremendous amount of trouble out there in the white man's world. That was the part of him he'd inherited from the savage warrior, Cochise. It was the part that filled her with distaste. But she could not fault Hawk for that.

Little Bear was a smart little pup, as Solange realized in the following days as they strolled through her yard. No longer did he try to catch the bees as they lit on the blossoms, but his curiosity was still there and it was obvious it was going to lead him into many a dilemma as the weeks went on. He pursued a toad frog who had fled under the stacked woodpile and got himself caught between two pieces of wood. In panic, he yelled out for Solange to come to his aid.

"Ah, little one—you are proving to be a handful, I think," she sighed as she managed to free him.

A week after Troy had brought the pup to her cabin, he came by to see how they were doing. It was obvious that they were doing fine. Solange told him about all the little incidents which had happened and Troy broke into laughter.

Satisfied that she was in good spirits, Troy left her a half of his catch of fish in the mountain stream before he departed to go home.

Solange and Little Bear had a grand feast that evening on

144

the crispy fried fish she prepared in her cast-iron skillet. It amazed her how much she and that tiny pup ate. The platter of potatoes and cornbread cakes was empty by the time they finished the meal. By the time she cleaned up her kitchen, she was ready to get into her nightgown, which was loose and comfortable.

She and Little Bear sank into the soft feather bed and a deep, heavy sleep engulfed both of them.

The strange, disrupting noises of the town and the streets did not induce sleep for Joe Hawk. He was more than ready to start out on his job of scouting when he would be riding the trails and the canyons instead of living in town. He could not relate to any of this. He could not fault this nice room in the hotel which his boss, Warner Barstow, had secured for him until they were ready to send him out.

His duties would not begin until the supplies of spikes and rails, along with other materials, arrived by wagon trains from the coast. Warner had told him the ship had arrived and the cargo was now on its way overland.

Hawk liked Mr. Barstow, who'd been very generous to him since the moment he'd arrived in Tucson. However, as he'd explored the town he'd realized what prejudice existed here for anyone with Apache blood. Like venom, various fellows he'd encountered had spit out the hatred they felt for a half-breed like himself. Each time it had happened, Hawk had flinched with pain and hurt. It made him yearn for the serene surroundings of his mother's warm, cozy cabin.

The only thing driving him to endure whatever he must to compete in this white man's world was thought of the place he could make for himself. Never could he do it if he remained in that secluded woods, as Troy had done and would do the rest of his life. Hawk wanted more and he was determined to get it. Whatever it cost him or whatever sacrifices he would have to make, he was prepared to do so.

There was another powerful force for Hawk to prove to himself that he was as good as any white man. If he dared to try to win the affections of Gillian, then he must prove himself to be worthy of such a lovely lady's love. That was all the incentive he needed to endure anything.

Each night, he lay on his bed dreaming about the beautiful Gillian and the sweet, glowing loveliness of her face. She was everything a man could ever hope for and he worshiped her as much now as the first moment he'd laid eyes on her. That perceptive instinct of his assured him that he held a part of her heart.

Most of Hawk's time was spent with Barstow when he was not sequestered in his hotel room, alone. When he did venture out in the town, he sought to visit the numerous little shops, purchasing trinkets which he knew would delight his mother. He'd bought her a huge woven basket to gather her flowers in and he'd found a pair of hammered silver earrings to match the link belt she wore with that swishing brown skirt. But the thing he'd bought which he thought would be so attractive in her thick, glossy hair was a magnificent comb with stones of turquoise encircled in silver.

These trips to the various shops were the most enjoyable times for Hawk, when he purchased things he knew would bring joy to those he loved so much back in Maricopa. The most expensive purchase he'd made was a very dainty necklace with one small gem, a sapphire. It had reminded him of the deep blue of Gillian's eyes. Hawk knew the day would come for him to give it to her and declare his love for her. That was going to be a grand and glorious day.

Until that day, he was willing to be a patient man and wait. But with all his strong will, Hawk could not keep his thoughts from straying back to Maricopa County—back to the two women he loved.

When Warner Barstow had told him to join him and the high official of the Southern Pacific Railroads, Howard Curtis, for lunch at the Old Pueblo, Hawk's chest swelled with pride.

Half-breed he might be, but he was going to be dining with a most eminent gentleman from back East. Few half-breeds could ever boast of that. This, he knew!

He went out that day to purchase himself a nice pair of pants, a coat, and shirt. That night he worked on his boots to give them a high shine. He would not wear his hat with the multicolored feathers, he decided.

When he left the hotel to go to the livery to get his pinto to ride to the Old Pueblo Inn he thought he'd never been more excited or nervous. But he felt a great exultation that he had now entered a new world he'd always dreamed about.

Hawk rode his pinto, his dark head held high with arrogant pride. His private thoughts were that he was going to make his mother feel proud of the son she'd sacrificed so much for. He'd be a man Gillian Browne could look up to and respect as she would any other young man she might fancy.

Hawk felt he was riding toward his destiny. He felt sure that this destiny would give him all the things his heart desired.

So strong was this feeling that his heart was pounding crazily and his palms were sweaty. He felt that he could be the proper young man to woo and win Gillian's heart.

He was very nervous about this lunch he was to share with two important railroad officials. He had been ill at ease from the moment he'd arrived in Tucson. All the crowds milling around were intimidating. Strange noises had made him flinch, for this town was not like the solitude of the canyons or the serenity of the woods.

When he reached the inn, he leaped down from his horse, slowly tying the reins. His dark eyes were taking in the grand-looking place he would soon be entering to join Curtis and Barstow. Barstow's presence was a comforting thought to Hawk as he ambled up to the iron gate leading into the grounds. Once inside he stood for a moment to view the magnificence surrounding him, for he'd never seen such a place as this. He was entranced!

Melba Jackson was there, on her way back to the inn with

her wicker basket filled with the fresh-cut flowers which would be placed in small individual vases this evening in her dining room. It was a nightly routine that those little vases held four little sprays of flowers.

She noticed the tall figure of Hawk standing there by the gate. She watched his black head turning slowly to survey her grounds. Something about the way he looked told her he was awestruck with admiration for the beautiful grounds. This always filled her with pride, for she had put a lot of labor and love into this place.

"Good day to you. Pretty sight, isn't it?" she addressed Hawk with a bright, cheery smile on her face.

Hawk jerked around on his booted heels to see a middle-aged lady standing beside the walkway. She wore a wide-brimmed straw hat with a bright scarlet band around the crown. As she moved toward him she pulled up the skirt of her frock. It was a bright floral material with as many colored flowers on the material as there were in the gardens here. The drawstring tunic blouse reminded Hawk of those his own mother wore. He was thinking as the lady approached him how he'd like to purchase a similar-looking skirt to take back home for Solange.

"Good day to you, too, ma'am. It is beautiful here," he said in a stammering drawl. "I—I can't say I ever saw anything more beautiful in my life unless it was those golden brown canyons near my home."

"Well, I take that as high praise, young man," Melba said. "May I introduce myself. I'm Melba Jackson, the proud owner of all you see. Now tell me your name?"

She looked up amused to see his black eyes sparking with disbelief. For a brief second, he could not find his voice. When he did, he muttered, "You, ma'am—you own this grand place?"

She gave a soft little laugh. "I certainly do. Now, young man, are you going to tell me your name?" There was a teasing little glint in her eyes as she looked up at him.

"Oh, I'm sorry. I am Joe Hawk, ma'am, and it is a pleasure to meet you, Mrs. Jackson."

She extended her hand. "And it's a pleasure to meet you, Joe Hawk. Shall I escort you to my inn, young man?"

A broad grin came to Hawk, for he felt honored indeed to be accompanying the owner of the inn. He walked beside her, trying to slow his long-paced steps to accommodate her gait.

But he was to find out that this was a feisty little lady and there was nothing slow about her movements as they walked up the pathway to the inn's entrance. As they walked, he told her who he was due to meet for lunch in her dining room.

"Ah, yes—nice man, Howard Curtis. My goodness, you make the second young gentleman I've been privileged to meet in the last week. I must thank him the next time I see him. Hopefully some duty won't call me away before he arrives here to meet you. The chances are he will be running a little late for the lunch."

By the time they walked through the front door of her inn, she noticed Hawk hesitating as though he were fearful of walking over the plush carpeting. The very sensitive, perceptive Melba Jackson realized that her young companion was out of his element and was a bit bedazzled by all he saw. She felt a particular warmth engulfing her for this fine-looking young man, knowing he felt ill at ease.

She handed her basket of flowers to one of her young workers as she and Hawk walked on into the lobby. She decided that she would keep Hawk company until Curtis arrived. She led him to the far end of the sitting room area where she knew she could view the doorway.

"Come sit down here with me, Hawk and we'll have time for a short chat. My goodness, I don't have a chance to talk wtih handsome men every day," she playfully teased him. She saw a hint of a smile come to his coppery face.

He welcomed her company and she knew it!

Chapter Twenty

Hawk felt as most people did after they'd talked with Melba Jackson: he felt as if he'd known her all his life. He thought to himself, if everyone was as nice as she, what a wonderful world this would be. The short period they'd talked before Curtis and Barstow appeared in the sitting room was enough to make Hawk relax and feel more sure of himself.

While she would never know it when she walked away to leave Hawk with the two gentlemen, she had enabled him to make a more favorable impression on Howard Curtis. Warner had already formed his opinion about the young half-breed. There was something different about Joe Hawk, setting him apart from half-breed Apache scouts he'd hired in the past. As yet, he couldn't pinpoint it, but he figured as the days went on and they worked together, he'd come to know Hawk better.

Already knowing Warner Barstow helped Hawk feel more at ease as they left the sitting room to go into the spacious dining room to have lunch. But by the time the lunch was almost over, Hawk realized he had nothing to be so tense about. Howard Curtis had been very cordial and friendly during the meal. He'd told him, "Warner says you're the best around these parts so that's good enough for me."

"Well, I appreciate Mr. Barstow saying that, sir, and I know one thing, I'll try to be," Hawk had replied.

As Warner had been impressed by that honest tone of Hawk's voice, so was Howard. Just looking at the formidable air of the man was impressive to Curtis. He saw little about this good-looking fellow that would remind him of any of the Apaches he'd seen. His manners were those of a white man.

Only once did Hawk feel his flesh crawl and that was when Curtis brought up the subject of Cochise and how they no longer had to fear his renegades. It was Geronimo and his horde coming, back across the border from Mexico, who had to be watched.

"I'm told that there will be no bargaining with Geronimo. He is a man of changeable moods and, of course, his wife being murdered at Janos has made him ready to take his revenge on any white man, woman or child."

Hawk was glad when the conversation suddenly went to another subject—the railroads, and the supplies arriving to begin the laying of the tracks.

By the time the three men parted company to go in their separate directions, Hawk was feeling very pleased with himself. He was now satisfied that he could make a place for himself in the white man's world even though all his life had been lived in the backwoods.

As he'd told Curtis, he was a good scout, for he knew all the remote canyons that the Apaches considered impregnable sanctuaries. "Maybe all the soldiers sent out from the fort can't find these places, but I know them, sir," Hawk had told him with an assured air that Curtis could not doubt for one minute.

When they left the inn, Howard directed his buggy toward his home. Warner had some work to finish back at his office, but he patted Hawk's muscled shoulder and assured him before he got into his own buggy, "You met with Howard Curtis's approval, young man. Now, you enjoy the next few days before we send you out on that trail. We want you wide-eyed and bushy-tailed."

"Yes, sir—I'll be ready anytime you say the word," Hawk

told him.

It was a day Hawk would remember forever, he thought as he rode his horse back into town. Not only had he seen the grand splendor of the Old Pueblo Inn but he'd met the grand lady, Melba Jackson. He could not wait to return home and tell all this to his mother. How proud she would be of him. He had shared lunch with two of the Southern Pacific's officials. He gave a deep, throaty chuckle, then threw his head back in laughter. "You're going to do fine, Joe Hawk!"

His spirits were so high he could have been drunk on some of Troy's whiskey. By the time he reached the street where his hotel was situated, Hawk had acquired a certain air of arrogance he'd never possessed before. He realized how small his world has been!

Hawk did not know quite how to explain it to himself as he entered the lobby of the hotel, but there was a certain swagger to his walk. He held his handsome head high with a pride he'd never felt before.

With this new assured attitude, the milling guests in the hotel did not disturb or bother him. He walked right by them and he even had a couple of friendly greeting nods from two gentlemen passing by. There was no disapproval on their faces.

By the time he reached his room, Hawk's thoughts were on Gillian. He could be the man she would be proud of. He closed the door and marched over to the mirror to look at his face. It was not an Apache face, dark and coarse as Cochise's had been. The reflection he saw there was the fine-chiseled features of his French ancestry and a golden, tawny skin hardly darker than the bronzed complexion of the young man he'd seen with Gillian that day back in Maricopa County.

He was not Apache! He hated the Apaches, and that hatred would make him the best damned scout this railroad could possibly hire. He took pride in his French heritage.

The rest of that afternoon and evening his thoughts seemed to drift back to Maricopa County to the two ladies who were the dearest to his heart. He thought about his mother and the girl who'd captured his heart some two years ago.

Knowing the way of the Apache thinking and action, he figured that the marauding Indians had moved on by now. With an Apache killed in Foster's pastureland, they would have to figure that the rancher was prepared and ready for them if they returned. The Apache liked the element of surprise when they raided or attacked.

Hawk had no way of knowing that the girl so possessing his thoughts that evening was now traveling toward the town of Tucson.

It had been a quiet, uneventful week around the Fosters' ranch and John was at the point of calling off the guards and night riders around his property. He knew that Nancy was feeling less apprehensive about leaving him alone while she made the trip to Tucson to see her sister. He was happy that she had continued to go forward with her plans.

Like beavers, Nancy and Gillian had worked day and night at the sewing, and he'd seen a couple of the frocks they'd stitched. Gillian's traveling ensemble of deep blue with its tight fitted jacket was a perfect match for the fancy little bonnet with the blue velvet ribbons tied under her chin.

Nancy's dark bottle green would be flattering to her. He noticed that his Nancy had not stitched her jacket to fit so snug. That lady of his could not be bound by restraining clothing, he mused.

The day he helped them board the Butterfield Overland Stage was not exactly the happiest day of his life. Never would he have allowed Nancy to know how lonely he was going to be with her away. That cottage was going to be ghostly quiet without her and Gillian.

He patted himself on the back that he'd been able to carry out such a deceptive act as he'd bid them farewell and the reddish-brown cloud of dust ascended from the rolling wheels of the stagecoach. It was only when the stage faded from sight that John turned away to mount his mare. Had he been a drinking man he would have been tempted to stop at the nearby tavern for a few shots of whiskey to ease the pain and loneliness of the empty house he would be returning to late that afternoon.

John reined his horse homeward. Instead of whiskey, he'd feast on all the good food Nancy had prepared for him to enjoy while she was away, and he'd enjoy the company of his old dog, Champ.

Once he was back in the cozy warmth of their cottage with all the things surrounding him that reflected the very essence of Nancy, he did not feel so lonely. By the time he'd eaten his evening meal and fed old Champ, he was ready to get comfortable in his favorite chair and fill up his pipe with tobacco as he always did after the evening meal.

It amazed him that the evening did not leave him as lonely as he expected, and he realized that it was this cottage that comforted him. As long as he was here, Nancy was with him in spirit, for everything about this little home of theirs was a part of her.

Sleep overtook him as swiftly as it did old Champ as he slept at the side of his bed.

Everything was peaceful around the Foster ranch as well as Maricopa County. The one Apache who had escaped Hawk's deadly aim of his rifle had rejoined his band of renegades to inform them about what had happened. They had moved on to raid the cattle of the ranchers in the next county.

By the time John Foster had retired for the night, the stagecoach carrying Nancy and Gillian toward Tucson had already made its first station stop on the hundred-and-eighteen-mile trip and was rolling toward the next one. It didn't matter to Gillian that the countryside was now shrouded in darkness; she was too excited to sleep. Never before had she traveled in a stagecoach and she was finding everything about this adventure exciting.

She knew that Mother Foster had made this jaunt before, so she was not so exhilarated as Gillian was. In fact, after they'd boarded the stage after the last station stop, Nancy had got herself cozy in the seat and folded her shawl against the side of the coach to lay her head against it. It wasn't long before she was asleep.

No other passengers had boarded the stagecoach at the station, so Gillian and Nancy had it all to themselves. Gillian had moved over to the other side of the coach and cautiously lifted Nancy's feet up to the seat to make her more comfortable. So sound was her sleep that she never knew she'd been repositioned. Gillian smiled with amusement.

She settled comfortably on the opposite side and removed her pretty new bonnet. When she first gazed out the window of the stage, she'd seen a beautiful starlit night, but a short time later she noticed that the sky was black, with no twinkling diamondlike brilliants.

As the coach traveled a straight southeast trail, the heavy cloud cover seemed still to be with them as they moved through the Picacho Mountains. She'd overheard one of the men up there on the perch of the stage mention something about the mountain pass being their next station.

She sat in the solitude of the dark coach, her thoughts divided between two handsome young men. There was Hawk with his simple, genuine honesty which endeared him to her, for she knew that he cared for her. How could she not know that he adored her when she saw those black eyes of his worshiping her everytime they looked her way?

She questioned why her restless heart could not settle for that. Perhaps she could have, if fate had not placed that good-looking, green-eyed Irishman, Steve Lafferty, in her life. He was a completely different man from Hawk. His air of arrogant and worldly sophistication was exciting to her. Something about the devilish gleam in his eyes when he looked at her made her weak all over. The infectious charm of that crooked

156

smile of his was enough to render her helpless when his strong arms urged her to move toward him.

Gillian could not deny that his masterful force could make her surrender willingly. He seemed to be able to bend her to his will effortlessly.

She could not deny that Steve Lafferty held power over her. That was why he frightened her. That Irish sea captain had the charm to bring out an abandoned wild desire to succumb to his will. Never had she felt that way before about a man.

There in the dark stagecoach, she could feel the heat of his green fire eyes on her!

Chapter Twenty-One

It was an endless night's drive for Burt Morton because his stagecoach's only passengers were women. He'd hoped to pick up a couple of husky men back at the last station and as a rule he would have. He knew that his pal, sitting next to him on the stage seat with his shotgun cradled in his arms, was feeling the same way. Like him, Moses Goss was an old-timer out here in Arizona Territory and this trail they were traveling over tonight was Apache land.

Both men knew that the Army could send in dozens of soldiers and troops, but they'd never clear out those damned Apaches infesting the mountains and canyons.

Maybe they'd separated the huge bands of roaming Apaches and cut down their numbers, but Moses and Burt knew what a small band of Indians could do to a stagecoach and the drivers.

They both recalled when three of their good friends at the stage station at Apache Pass were killed by Cochise, who wanted to settle a score with the Army who were holding some of his relatives hostage.

Neither of them sought to idly chat as they traveled down the dark, deserted dirt road. It was as if they were both listening for any sounds in the night.

The next station was some thirty miles east of Tucson, and it was only when they arrived there that Burt felt he could breathe easier. As good a rifleman as Moses was, he'd play hell keeping a band of four of those wild, crazy Apaches at bay while Burt guided the stage. That was why he'd have welcomed a couple of fellows for passengers on this particular strip between Maricopa and Red Rock.

There wasn't much he didn't talk to Moses about because they'd ridden side by side on a stage many a time. But tonight, he could have sworn he smelled Apaches nearby so he pushed his team of horses harder than he normally would have.

It wasn't easy to fool a man like Moses. He knew his friend far too well not to figure out why he was driving the team as hard as he was. But he said nothing to him.

As Gillian had been watching the night skies, so had Moses, and he'd seen the sudden invasion of clouds moving in to blot out all the sparkling stars that had been shining so brightly only moments ago.

He suspected they might be faced with one of those early-morning thunderstorms which hit the mountains around this time of year. Moses figured it was safer to be hit by a thunderstorm than by a band of Indians waiting for a stage to pass on that narrow mountain road.

But when the first rumblings of thunder resounded in the distance, both men jerked alive and exchanged glances.

"Guess you could say that me and you are both a little jumpy tonight," Moses said.

"Guess we are. I feel damned concerned for those two nice ladies in the back there. When one's as pretty as that young one and there's only one shooter around, I gotta' admit I get nervous as hell." They traveled on a few more miles before Burt openly confessed to his friend that some ten miles back he could have sworn he sensed Apache varmints nearby.

"Knew something was spooking you, Burt. Hell, you know better than to think you could pull the wool over my eyes," he said, spitting a spray of tobacco juice to the side of the coach.

In a few minutes the thunder which had been over in the distance was closer and Moses and Burt grabbed for their slickers at the back of the seat. By the time they slipped into them, the first drops of rain were beginning to fall. Heavier rains were pelting their faces by the time they saw the flickering light of the lamp hanging from the high post outside the Duncan Ranch which served as a stage station. It was a most welcoming sight.

It looked like a wee, twinkling star at that moment, but it grew brighter as the wheels of the stage rolled closer and closer. The blowing, gusting winds forced Gillian to close the flaps at the window. That and the rumbling thunder woke Nancy up and she sat up straight in the seat to declare, "God Almighty, it sounds like we've run into a good one. Raining cats and dogs, isn't it?"

"It certainly is and it all came up so suddenly. One minute I was looking out at the beautiful stars and all of a sudden they were gone," Gillian told her. The coach swayed back and forth from the force of the gusting winds and rain as Burt urged the team faster so they could get to the shelter of the station.

Gillian and Nancy felt the coach come to a halt and Moses and Burt leaped down to assist them down onto the muddy ground. Already, huge puddles of water were standing. They were going to be drenched before they reached the door. The rains swept across them as they trudged across the ground to the house.

Gillian knew without looking that her lovely new frock was wet and mud-splattered. Poor Nancy was drenched with only the shawl covering her shoulders. But for Moses's hand steadying her, she would have fallen when she stepped into a hole filled with water.

She muttered disgustedly, "God Almighty, this is what I call a gully washing rain!"

"You're right, ma'am." Moses gave a chuckle, holding her arm tighter, for she was no pint-size lady like the one Burt was leading into the house. But he liked her down-to-earth air. When he'd seen the two ladies board the stage, he figured her to be one of the local ranchers' wives. Her plain face was tanned by the hot Arizona sun so it was obvious she was not a woman content to spend her time inside the house doing needlepoint or embroidery.

"Well, I thank you for saving me from falling flat on my face back there, mister," she told Moses as they stepped up on the porch. It was good to be under the shelter of a roof with the rains not beating down on them. The station worker was there at the door to usher them inside the cozy warmth of the house.

"Come in, ladies," he said. "Ain't a fit night out there tonight even for a cur dog. There's some coffee brewing over there in the pot." Nancy had already flung her shawl off, for its dampness was penetrating into her frock.

Gillian hastened to get her pretty bonnet off so she could shake off any lingering moisture. She was so very proud of her new bonnet, for it was the loveliest thing she'd ever owned. Anxiously, she began to vigorously whip it off with her handkerchief. "Oh, Mother Foster, I hope my bonnet isn't ruined. I'm going to be sick if it is."

"Can't be helped, sugar. Damned if we just won't get you another in Tucson if it is," Nancy promised her, patting her dainty shoulder.

Wisps of her auburn hair were wet where the bonnet had not covered or protected it. The young station employee, Monty Harmon, couldn't take his eyes off the lovely blue-eyed angel who'd just walked into the station. He'd never seen anything as lovely as the girl standing there looking so unhappy about the rain-spotted bonnet she held in her small hand. In fact, he was so smitten by her beguiling charm that he completely ignored his old pals, Burt and Moses.

Moses removed his own hat to give it a flinging motion and noticed the direction Monty's eyes were focused. He gave Burt a nudge and grinned.

"Monty, how about getting these ladies some warm blankets to wrap around their shoulders while they have their coffee," Burt said, but Monty didn't hear a word said to him, for he was too bewitched by Gillian.

162

When repeating the request, Monty blushed with embarrassment, realizing what an oaf he must have made out of himself. Awkwardly, he moved out of the room, soon returning with two wool blankets. He handed one to Nancy and the other to Gillian. He knew there had to be a rosy flush on his face as he gave Gillian hers.

Burt figured that this was as good a time as any to tell them that their stay at this station was going to involve a lot more time than just changing teams of horses.

"Now, ladies, if you'd like, the both of you can rest a while. There's a guest room where you might like to refresh yourselves or lay down to sleep for a while. We're going to have to let this storm pass by before we make that final thirty miles to Tucson," Burt explained.

"Lordy, sounds good to me. Don't it, Gillian?"

"Very good. Monty will get you some clean towels 'cause I can see that you both have wet hair. Don't want to get you to Tucson feeling ill." Burt grinned. "How about fetching these nice ladies some towels, Monty, when you show them to the room?"

Gillian moved hastily to follow Monty, for she was eager to remove her new frock and hang it up to dry.

As soon as they were inside the room and the door was closed, that was exactly what she did. Nancy Foster did the same. Luckily, Nancy had not been wearing her new bonnet when she left the coach. She had tucked it under her shawl, for she'd been sleeping just before they'd arrived at the station.

Gillian, still devastated that her bonnet might be damaged, was blotting it with the towel Monty had given her.

"Hang it on that peg, sweetie, and I bet it will be fine when it dries," Nancy suggested to her.

Like an obedient child, she did as Nancy suggested, then sat on the side of the bed to remove her damp slippers. It seemed that there was nothing about her that wasn't wet or damp. Her stockings were wet, too.

Snuggled with the blanket around her shoulders, she

propped herself on the pillows on the bed. "Guess we're going to be here a while from the way it sounds out there," she declared, hearing the sharp blasts of thunder and seeing the reflection of flashing lightning on the drawn curtains at the two windows.

"That's what I'm thinking," Nancy agreed with her. "We might as well try to sleep until they wake us up." With the blanket wrapped around her, Nancy crawled on the other side of the bed and dimmed the lamp on the nightstand.

Both women felt warmed by the blankets draped around them, and the comfort of the soft bed was enough to induce sleep quickly.

Back in the other room, the three men sat around the cast-iron stove drinking coffee. After the ladies had left the room, Monty had brought out the bottle of brandy. He had finally relaxed with a few generous gulps of the brandy and coffee. By now, he was tolerating the playful teasing of his two pals about the fact that he was acting like a lovesick pup around the pretty lady.

"Hell, I don't deny it. Never saw anything as pretty as her anywhere in my whole life. God damn, I would like to just look at her lovely face all night long," Monty told Moses and Burt.

Moses laughed as he took a gulp from his cup. "Hell, Monty, you were wantin' to do a lot more than just look."

All of them roared with laughter. Monty admitted, "Well, wouldn't I be a stupid fool to try to deny that, Moses? Never been known to not appreciate a pretty gal. That's got to be the prettiest one in all of Arizona Territory."

Moses could not argue with him about that so he didn't try to. Neither did Burt.

For a moment, none of them said anything as they sat there enjoying the stimulating warmth of the brandy-laced coffee.

It was Moses who finally broke the brief silence. "I'll tell you something, fellows—if I'd met a lady like that when I was a young dude like you, Monty, I'd have moved heaven and hell to have won her. Now an old codger like me can only dream. In fact, that's what I'm going to do is hit that cot back there and sleep and dream."

"Well, Moses—by this time tomorrow she will be gone so I guess I'll just have to consider that she was something I dreamed about," Monty replied.

Burt set his cup on the counter and rose up out of his chair. "Figure it this way, Monty—you happened to meet a lovely goddess on a rainy, stormy night. If you're lucky, you might have that chance again."

"That's what I'm hoping, Burt. I'm coming to hope that I'm here at the station when she goes back to where she came from," Monty told his friend.

"From Maricopa County is where she's from. She'll be returning there, I feel sure of that."

"Then I'm going to be here every night!" Monty declared.

He was lovestruck, Burt and Moses realized as they made their way to the cots to get a little sleep. Neither of them could fault the young rascal, but they could envy his youth.

Age did take a toll on a fellow after he reached forty!

Chapter Twenty-Two

There was nothing but beautiful blue sky up above them as Nancy and Gillian boarded the stagecoach the next morning. There would be no dust as they traveled down the rutted dirt trail, for the rains had settled it and left a fresh smell in the air.

As Moses and Burt had been amused by the young station worker, Monty, the night before, Nancy sought to tease Gillian after they were inside the coach. "Think that young man took a shine to you, missy. Yes, sir, think you got yourself an admirer standing back there on the porch."

Gillian giggled. "Oh, you do, do you? Guess I should begin to have a few of them, wouldn't you say?"

"Sugar, I suspect you might have several if you weren't living out at that secluded ranch of ours. Don't give you much of a chance to meet young folks."

Gillian reached over to give an affectionate pat to Nancy's hand. "Oh, Mother Foster, I've had a wonderful two years at the ranch. The only loneliness I ever felt there was when I first arrived. That was because I'd lost my parents."

Nancy's face mellowed with love. "I'm glad you've been happy with us and so is John, I know."

Nancy urged Gillian to look to the left across the way, for she didn't want her to miss the picturesque Spencer Canyon. "Ain't it a beautiful sight?"

167

Gillian looked in the direction she was pointing. The canyon was glowing with its layered soil in varied shades of golds and rusts. With the bright sun shining down, there seemed to be little sparking brilliants splattered there in the sides of the canyon.

"Look, Mother Foster—a rider. See him?"

Nancy turned quickly back toward the canyon. "Where, child? I don't see where you're talking about. A rider, you say?"

"Yes, ma'am. There." She pointed toward the southeast. Nancy strained to see but she still could not spot the rider. Her first thought was that it could be an Indian spotting them so he could go back to report to his band of renegades. But no, they were too close to Tucson now.

She settled back in the seat dismissing that thought. "Guess my eyes are going bad on me, honey," she said.

It was a welcoming sight to Helen Clayton as she and her daughter, Melissa, saw the Butterfield Overland Stage turning the corner to come down the street to the station. It was several hours late and she had been concerned about her older sister. Nancy was more than a sister to her because she'd taken the place of their mother after her death.

When the stage came to a halt and Moses leaped down to help the two of them to the ground below, Gillian lingered back a moment to allow the laughing and crying reunion of the sisters to take its course.

Melissa Clayton stood as Gillian did, without saying anything. But the two of them exchanged friendly smiles.

Finally, Nancy broke the warm embrace with her sister and reached out to take Gillian's arm. "Come here, honey—want you to meet my sister, Helen Clayton, and that's her daughter, Melissa."

"So very nice to meet you, Mrs. Clayton and you, too, Melissa," Gillian said as Nancy urged her closer.

Helen was a small lady who barely topped her older sister's robust shoulders. She had a fairer complexion and lighter hair than Nancy's. Melissa Clayton must surely look like her father, Gillian immediately decided as she noticed her dark complexion and deep, chocolate brown hair. She also sensed that she was a very shy person. If she was to guess, she would imagine that they were about the same age.

As they gathered up their luggage and it was loaded into the buggy, Helen and Nancy sat in the front seat and she and Melissa sat in the back. Gillian had a chance to observe the fine deep green ensemble Melissa wore, with a matching velvet bonnet in the same shade of green. She had its ribbons tied attractively to the side of her pretty face. Gillian must remember to tie hers that way instead of under her chin. It was far more fashionable, she thought.

By the time they arrived at the Clayton home, Gillian was convinced that they lived in a far grander style than the Fosters. She was probably going to be a little embarrassed to compete with Melissa and her fancier wardrobe.

While Gillian was musing about this young lady, Melissa was having her own thoughts about this Gillian Browne they'd been hearing about for so long. From her aunt's letters about Gillian's background and the circumstances bringing her to the Fosters' ranch, she seemed to be some kind of heroine to Melissa. But now that she'd met her, she seemed so delicate and fragile. Unlike her aunt living out there in that godforsaken country on her ranch where the weather had tanned her face, Gillian possessed a flawless complexion. Melissa had never seen a more glowingly beautiful head of hair. She thought to herself that she certainly didn't want her suitor to set eyes on Gillian. When he came to court her, he might just be swept away by the sight of this auburn-haired beauty.

Just before they arrived, Gillian sought to engage Melissa in conversation by remarking, "I'm going on seventeen. Are you about my age, Melissa?"

"I'm eighteen. I just had my birthday last week. Daddy gave

169

me this," she told Gillian, lifting her dainty hand to display a lovely pearl ring. Gillian looked at the ring and told Melissa how lovely it was and that she was lucky to have such a thoughtful father.

Helen was not so occupied guiding her horse that she'd not overheard her daughter's remarks. She could not suppress a smirk. That pearl ring had been bought with the funds from the many loaves of raisin bread she'd baked and sold to the Old Pueblo Inn. He'd helped himself to the money in her cookie jar and taken it to buy the exquisite ring for their daughter. As it was and always had been with Kent Clayton, he took the full glory as his daughter had excitedly hugged his neck to thank him.

Helen couldn't play the role of shrew as she ached to do and tell her daughter that the ring was not the fruit of his labor, but of *hers*. The cost represented hours and days of baking all those many loaves she'd delivered to Melba Jackson. In fact, the last three days she'd labored many extra hours to get her baking done before Nancy arrived so she could enjoy visiting with her sister.

Oh, she could not fault her lovely daughter Melissa who looked exactly like her father with his dark good looks. Kent was a man who'd always been able to charm anyone around him. But he had a taste for the grandeur his earnings could never provide. Had it not been for her earnings as an expert baker to supplement their income, they would have had constant problems from creditors.

Helen was glad she'd only had one child because she'd realized after Melissa was born, and she and Kent had been married less than three years, that she really had two children: Melissa and Kent.

By the time they alit from the buggy and entered the two-story frame house, Gillian was sure she was right when she figured Mother Foster's life was harder and less luxurious than her sister's. The furnishings were much nicer and there were dainty starched doilies on the chairs and highly polished tables. Fancy silk pillows lined the matching settees in Helen's parlor and rested at the back of the overstuffed chairs.

What Gillian could not possibly know was that many of the pretty things Helen had in her home were gifts from a wealthy lady who appreciated Helen's kindness throughout the years because Helen baked her delicious pies and cakes. Weekly, she took a pie and a cake to Sabrina Fairchild.

Nancy ambled through her sister's parlor, surveying all the special touches Helen had put in her home. "Wish I had that talent you've always had, Helen. Your house is always so in order—so pretty. Just wasn't my talent, I guess."

Helen gave a soft little laugh, knowing exactly what Nancy was talking about. When they were young, Nancy was considered a tomboy.

"But had I lived on a ranch, I would have been utterly helpless, Nancy. I couldn't have done the things that you can handle with such ease."

Gillian smelled the delectable aroma of the spices from the baked foods lining a table in Helen's kitchen. Two huge wicker baskets were filled to the brim for tomorrow's delivery to the inn.

Nancy could not argue with her; Helen would not have made a rancher's wife. But neither could Nancy have put up with that prancing peacock, Kent Clayton. As far as she was concerned, the only worthwhile thing Helen had ever got from her marriage was a very lovely daughter. Kent was a wastrel and poor Helen had paid the price for it.

Nancy pointed out to her sister, "Well, you happened to have married a city man and I married the rancher. By the way—is Kent still with Golden's Mercantile Store?"

"Oh, yes. Mr. Brien died last year so Kent was made manager." Helen didn't add that she just prayed he managed the store better than he did his own finances.

While Helen and Nancy sat in the parlor having their leisurely chat, Melissa showed Gillian to her bedroom upstairs. Gillian found the upstairs as nice and neat as the downstairs. It was obvious that Helen Clayton took great pride in her home and spent time trying to make it as attractive as possible.

"You'll be right across the hall from me. Momma calls that room the Blue Room." She laughed. "Mine is the Pink Room because that's my favorite color. She's funny—likes to label everything."

Gillian was a little startled to find that now that the two of them were completely alone, Melissa was turning into a chatterbox.

"Does Aunt Nancy do that?"

"No, I can't say that she does, but I think it's rather nice." Melissa opened the door to the bedroom, and Gillian could see why it was called the Blue Room. There was a blue-and-white coverlet on the bed and matching little ruffled curtains at the double window made from the same material.

Everything looked spic and span. The small nightstand by the side of the bed had been painted white. A lamp and a blue vase of posies sat on it. There was a white wicker rocker with ruffled pillows made of the same blue material as the coverlet.

"How very pretty!" Gillian declared as she appraised the bedroom that had been decorated with such special care. Across the two double windows in wicker stands were a variety of green plants and one huge, magnificent fern flourishing where the bright light came through the windows. "Your mother obviously has a green thumb," Gillian remarked as she viewed the plants.

"Everything Mother does is always perfection. She's that type of person. Her home, her plants and her baking are a complete obsession," Melissa replied.

Gillian sensed a hint of a scornful air, and she wondered why. "I think it's wonderful to try to be as good as you can possibly be. I must say I admire her and I'm sure you must, too."

Melissa shrugged her shoulders as she mumbled, "I don't want that for myself. I mean I can't see anything so exciting about being a slave to a house. Guess I'm like my daddy. He

172

likes to enjoy life and laugh and be gay."

Gillian laid her shawl and her reticule down on the rocker as she turned to face Melissa. Her piercing blue eyes locked into Melissa's as she pointed out, "Oh, Melissa—I doubt that your mother considers herself to be a slave. She loves what she's doing, I'm sure. If that is the case then your aunt Nancy is a slave to her ranch, but it is only because she loves the ranch and the land."

"Mercy, you are a serious one, aren't you?" Melissa said cattily.

Gillian raised her fine-arched brow as she retorted, "Oh, I have a frivolous side, Melissa. But I am most serious when it comes to the people I love. You must know I lost my own mother and Mother Foster has been like a mother to me the last two years. You must appreciate the wonderful mother you have. How lucky you are, Melissa!"

The lovely Melissa was befuddled by this strange young lady's blunt remarks. For a moment, she stood there unable to find her tongue or utter a word.

The truth was she was now intimidated by the straight-forward honesty of Gillian Browne. In a stammering, faltering voice, she hastily excused herself. "I'll—I'll leave you to get settled in, Gillian." She turned swiftly to make her exit.

As she sought the refuge of her own room and gain the composure Gillian had blunted, Melissa felt like a stranger in her own home. Gillian Browne was not only beautiful, but she was also very clever. Those blue eyes of hers had seen right through her, Melissa realized.

She must play her cautiously!

Chapter Twenty-Three

The minute Gillian's head hit the soft pillow she fell into a deep sleep. It had been a long busy day and a most entertaining evening when the five of them gathered around the dining room, eating by candlelight. Such a happy, gay atmosphere abounded in the Claytons' dining room and Gillian had to confess that Kent Clayton was certainly an entertaining, charming man. She found him to be a lively, dapper middle-aged gentleman, and if she had to be truthful, she'd have to admit that he looked younger than his wife, Helen.

Somehow, she observed a certain forced politeness that seemed to exist between him and Mother Foster. If she was any judge of people, she concluded by the time the meal was over that Nancy Foster was none too fond of her brother-in-law. Neither did he find her company too pleasant.

He rose up from the table after the dessert was served and he'd finished his piece of cherry pie. "If you will excuse me, Nancy, I still take my evening stroll after I finish my meal. An old habit I can't seem to break, I guess." He gave them a gracious bow, moving around the chair. "I'll leave all you lovely ladies to enjoy yourself."

All Gillian had to watch was Melissa's admiring eyes following her father out of the room to know how much she adored him. For a moment there was silence engulfing the room. But when Kent went out the front door, Nancy was the one to break the silence by saying to her sister, "Mercy, I'd hate to think about trying to walk anywhere after such a feast, Helen. It was so good! Tell me, Helen—what does Kent do when it's raining at the dinner hour?"

Melissa answered before her mother had a chance to. "Nothing stops Daddy from his walk. He considers it good to walk after a meal."

"Now, my John would take exception to that. He marches straight to his easy chair and old Champ curls up there beside him. They both take themselves a nice nap." Nancy laughed.

Melissa remembered their last visit to her Aunt Nancy's how desolate and isolated it had been. "Well, I can see why Uncle John would not care about going for a walk. There would be nothing to see out there."

Before Nancy could reply to that, Gillian hastily declared, "Oh, there are all kinds of things to see and hear in the quiet of the night. Mother Foster's yard is filled with night-blooming flowers that always smell sweeter after dark. Over in the distance when the moon is full and bright you can see the tops of the mountains. Sometimes, you can hear the scream of a bobcat over in the nearby woods."

Helen could not restrain a smile as she gazed at her lovely daughter who was not impressed at all by these things. She turned back to look at Gillian Browne's expressive face as she spoke about the things which seemed to intrigue her. What a lovely, unspoiled young miss she was! How lucky for Nancy she was not the selfish, demanding girl Melissa had turned out to be. It used not to be so with her. It was only after her sixteenth birthday that Melissa had changed, and Helen was perplexed as to how to deal with her.

As Helen and Nancy cleared the table and washed the dishes, Melissa and Gillian were left in each other's company. "I feel very lazy not helping out in the kitchen," Gillian confessed to Melissa.

"Why, for heaven's sakes?" Melissa asked.

176

"Because I'm used to helping Mother Foster in the kitchen. Don't you help your mother, Melissa?"

"Not if I can get out of it! Besides, she is always shooing me out of the kitchen. She'd rather me and Daddy not get in her way. That is her little kingdom. So we do as she wishes. Daddy goes for his walks and I go out on the porch and swing if I don't have my beau coming over."

"Beau?"

"Yes, my beau. My goodness, don't tell me you don't have a beau who comes to court you. I have three young men calling on me at the present time. I must say it's Caywood I like the best, though," she boasted.

"I must confess I have no beaux who come to court me."

"Lordy, Gillian—I can't believe that. A girl with your face and figure would have a lot of fellows eager to come to call and bring flowers and candy if you lived here in Tucson. Lordy! Now, don't tell me you've never been kissed, or I shall surely faint!"

Gillian gave a soft laugh. "I'll spare you from fainting for I have known a man's kiss."

Melissa's dark eyes sparked with curious interest. "Tell me, did this man's kiss thrill you as my Caywood thrills me when he kisses me?"

"Now, how can I answer that, Melissa? I don't know how this Caywood kisses. But I can tell you that I liked being kissed by one particular man."

Melissa suddenly decided that perhaps Gillian wasn't as dull as she'd first suspected. Now, she was spurred to talk about all her various suitors and the amorous moments she'd experienced. Gillian proved to be a patient listener.

However, after an hour of this Gillian began to find Melissa dull and boring. She welcomed Nancy and Helen joining them. She welcomed even more the time when everyone sought to retire, for she was ready for the sweet comfort of the bed.

*   *   *

177

Helen had her own family's breakfast cooked and served by the time Nancy joined her in the kitchen. Kent had already left for the store. Nancy confessed to her sister that she could not remember sleeping so late for years.

When Melissa joined them in the pleasant, bright kitchen, Helen startled her daughter by asking her to take the delivery this morning to the inn. "Might be fun for Gillian and you to make the delivery. I'm sure that Gillian would like seeing the inn with the beautiful courtyard gardens. Melba would enjoy meeting Gillian, too. So I'm going to let you handle that for me, Melissa." Helen was not surprised by the stunned look on Melissa's face, but maybe it was about time she insisted her pampered daughter earn a little of the money spent on her. After all, this was what bought her all those fancy frocks and dainty slippers she wore.

Before she took Nancy for a stroll in her gardens to feed the birds their morning meal, she pointed out to Melissa the baskets to be delivered. Melissa sat, eating her breakfast, and gave her mother a halfhearted nod.

It was so very pleasant in the garden that the two sisters sat for over an hour just talking and enjoying this special time they had with each other. The birds flocked for the seed Helen had tossed on the ground in the shallow clay container.

When they returned to the house, Melissa was no longer in the kitchen. The baskets were gone, so Helen assumed that her daughter was on her way to the Old Pueblo Inn. It was not until another hour had passed that she chanced to glance out one of her windows which gave her a view of her front porch. There was no mistaking that lovely crown of auburn hair. That could only be Gillian she saw sitting there in the swing.

Helen rushed toward her front door. Bolting out the door, she went around the corner to approach Gillian. "Good morning, dear. I must apologize to you that you've had to entertain yourself. Nancy and I have been out in the gardens. You haven't had any breakfast yet. Oh my goodness!"

Gillian gave her a bright smile. "Oh, yes, ma'am. I helped

myself to those delicious biscuits and some of that good jam sitting on the kitchen table. That and two cups of coffee was enough to get me wide awake, Mrs. Clayton. I was just enjoying your swing."

"Glad you are, dear. By the way, did you see Melissa?" Helen already figured out what had happened.

"Yes, ma'am—she came into the kitchen while I was eating and said she'd see me later. Said she had an errand to run."

"I see," Helen mumbled. Melissa had not wanted Gillian to go with her. Rarely did she find herself as vexed with her daughter as she now was. What a little snob she had raised, and she had not realized it until just recently. Well, she was going to take some steps to correct that. Right now was a good time to start.

A week ago, Melissa had flung four of her dresses on the floor of her bedroom to announce to her mother that she didn't want them anymore. "Give them to the Brewster girl," she'd haughtily announced.

Helen had taken them and laundered them. There was nothing worn out on any of them. One was a pretty little calico frock with a frosty white collar and cuffs. Helen remembered the number of loaves she'd baked to purchase the fancy vivid blue dress with its scooped neckline edged with delicate white lace. How pretty and feminine she'd always thought Melissa had looked in the little frock with its puffed sleeves and the full, flowing skirt of a black material with a garden of little dainty white flowers splattered around.

Another garment Melissa had thrown to the floor was one she'd stitched with such care and for so many hours. It was a deep blue taffeta skirt with a bodice of blue and white stripes. A short bobbed jacket of the same blue taffeta completed the ensemble. Such loving care Helen had given to this garment!

All of these pretty things would be Gillian's if she wished to have them, and Helen felt she would certainly receive them gratefully. Melissa would not be receiving any new frocks from the fruits of her labor for many, many months. She could go to her father for her next new frock, Helen decided.

An hour later, Gillian was taking all the lovely dresses up the stairs, so excited and delighted that she was still trembling. She had believed Helen's story that Melissa had added a few extra pounds so she couldn't wear them anymore. Melissa's gained weight had proven to be her good fortune. How sad she must have felt to have to part with such lovely dresses!

When she'd first gone to live with the Fosters, Gillian hadn't missed the frilly dresses her mother had always dressed her in. It had only been lately she'd started to realize what a simple, meager wardrobe she possessed. If she was to be honest, it had all happened when Steve Lafferty came to the Foster ranch and she found herself wishing she had a pretty dress to wear. She recalled how she'd spent an unusually long time that evening before she'd joined the Fosters and Lafferty, fussing with her hair.

She'd worn the one and only frock that had any hint of being attractive and pretty. Compared to these four dresses, it was plain and ordinary.

It was only when she was in her bedroom hanging the dresses carefully to keep them free of wrinkles that she asked herself what Melissa might think about her mother giving them to her. She hoped she wouldn't be displeased

She sat there in her room, thinking about when she'd wear each of them. The deep blue with its jacket would be perfect when they went shopping. How grand she was going to look, she thought to herself.

Tonight, she might just wear the dress with the puffed sleeves edged with white lace. All those pretty little white flowers on the black material reminded her of the wildflowers growing back in the Fosters' pastureland. She was sure Mrs. Clayton would not mind her helping herself to one of the many white blossoms in her garden to wear in her hair. Tonight, she'd look as elegant as Melissa had last night when they gathered around the dining table.

She lost track of the time as she sat there in her lighthearted daydreaming state. She had no awareness of the heated argument going on just outside the carriage house at the back of the Claytons' house.

Helen had been looking out the window so she might see Melissa returning in the buggy. She wanted to spare Nancy from the scene which was going to take place, for she intended to let her daughter know in no uncertain terms that she considered her behavior to be despicable. She had no intention of tolerating it for the rest of Gillian's and Nancy's visit. She could do nothing about Kent's aloofness toward her sister, but Melissa was not going to snub this sweet girl.

She'd paced back and forth in the room under various pretenses so Nancy would not suspect just how vexed she was by Melissa's long delay in returning home. The trip there and back delivering the baskets of bakery items should not have taken more than an hour. The girl had been gone almost three hours. Now, where was she dallying so long?

Finally, she recognized the buggy coming up the street. Trying to make her voice sound calm and casual, she said, "Excuse me a moment, Nancy. I have to get something out back. I'll only be a minute."

"You just go about your chores, Helen. I understand that everything can't come to a halt just because I'm here." Nancy went back to her mending her skirt she'd torn the night of the storm when they'd rushed from the stage.

Pleased that Nancy was so absorbed in her sewing, Helen rushed out of the back of her house and down the pathway toward the carriage house.

Helen stood with her hands firmly placed on her hips. She yearned to slam the smirk off Melissa's face as she descended from the buggy.

"My money, Melissa—every last penny of it! If you spent any of it, you'll march right back and get my money back."

"Oh, don't worry, Mother—I didn't spend any of your precious money. Here." She handed Helen the funds Melba had given her. Had she not been anxious to meet Caywood as he went out of his office to go to lunch, she would have spent some of the money, rewarded herself with some little trinket. But she had waited in vain for over an hour and then she had begun to feel embarrassed as she sat there in the buggy. If someone had recognized her who knew her father, she would have had a lot of explaining to do.

As casually as she might shrug off her mother's reprimand, she didn't want her father to be displeased with her.

"You didn't even have the good manners to ask Gillian to go with you, did you, Melissa? I think you should feel very ashamed of yourself."

"Ashamed?" She laughed haughtily. "Why should I feel ashamed because I didn't wish her company? She's your guest, Mother—not mine!" Lifting her flounced skirt, she swayed around her mother to go up the path toward the house.

Helen's next words were sharp and cutting. "Perhaps it is better she didn't accompany you, Melissa. She probably would have been very bored with your company!"

Black fire flared in Melissa's eyes as she stared at her mother. She stood there frozen and stunned because never had she spoken to her like this.

Helen watched her turn sharply and march to the house. Oh, she loved Melissa dearly, but right now she did not like her very much!

Chapter Twenty-Four

Tucson was situated some one hundred miles southeast of the Fosters' ranch. Gillian swore that never was there a more beautiful sunset than right there on the ranch at twilight time. But here in Tucson on the desert plateau surrounded by mountains with their peaks reaching nine thousand feet, she was awestruck by the glorious splendor she viewed as she'd rushed out to pluck a white flower to wear in her hair.

She was a spectacular sight. The frock of black sprinkled with white flowers was far more alluring on her than it had been on Melissa, for Gillian's breasts filled the bodice, and the low scooped neckline gave a hint of cleavage. The full puffed sleeves enhanced her dainty feminine charm.

She was truly the vision of loveliness that had enchanted Steve Lafferty. She was the image of sweet innocence and smoldering passion, all wrapped up in one petite miss.

Caywood Barron saw this lovely vision dashing down the steps of the Claytons' house and into the garden and he stopped just to absorb the magnificence of her shapely figure and flowing auburn hair. He didn't have to be closer to know that the fine features of her face were beautiful. But who was she, he wondered?

He ambled around to the side of the house instead of going on up to the front door. As she bent over to pick a cluster of white flowers that had caught her eyes, Caywood stood, admiring her curvy body. No one appreciated a pretty young lady more than Caywood did. That was why Melissa Clayton had caught his eye when he first saw her.

When Gillian turned to go back to the house, she was startled to find a striking-looking young gentleman standing right behind her, giving her a warm, admiring smile. "Hello! I trust I didn't startle you."

She gave a soft sigh. "Well, I *was* a little startled. I didn't hear anyone approaching." Gillian's blue eyes were appraising his fine attire and his trim physique. His black mustache matched his neatly brushed black hair. His black eyes twinkled as they looked her over from head to toe.

"I think you were too absorbed in the pretty flower you were picking. No doubt to wear in your lovely hair, I'd wager? By the way, I'm Caywood Barron. I was just arriving at the Claytons' when I happened to see you."

Two people observed the scene taking place in the garden. Melissa happened to be looking out of her upstairs bedroom to see his carriage pull up. She was puzzled to see him going around the corner of the house instead of coming up the front steps. A few seconds later, she saw why he had been distracted. What she found disturbing was the expression on Caywood's face as he stood with Gillian in the garden. She knew that look and that smile. Caywood could be a charmer when he wanted to be. It was obvious he was trying to impress Gillian.

She seethed as she continued to watch them!

After three hours of baking in the late afternoon, with Nancy helping her, Helen had completed her next order for Melba Jackson and the loaves were already packed away.

The two of them working together had filled the cast-iron pot with beans to cook throughout the afternoon and seasoned it with some hefty chunks of ham. Nancy had brought a couple of jars of her pickle relish which she knew Helen loved. They'd laughed that Kent might not enjoy their dinner tonight but *they* would.

Once two pans of cornbread were ready to be removed from the oven, Helen and Nancy went upstairs to refresh themselves. Now, she'd returned to her kitchen after she'd put on a fresh, clean dress and recombed her hair and fashioned the thick coil at the back of her head. Thinking about what Nancy had said about Kent, she grinned. It was true that he would turn his nose up at the meal they'd prepared. It mattered not to her, for she and her sister would thoroughly enjoy it.

It was at this moment she chanced to glance out the window to see Caywood arriving. Melissa had said nothing about inviting him to dinner tonight. As if she wasn't agitated enough with that young lady, this really riled her.

For a moment, she thought Caywood was going to the back door, and she pondered why. Then she looked out the south kitchen window. The scene she viewed explained everything. She could not help being amused as she watched the two young people in her garden.

Maybe Melissa found Gillian dull, but it was obvious her beau Caywood found her bewitching. It could be a very interesting evening if Caywood did stay for dinner.

The little conceited upstart needed to be taken down a notch or two and Gillian might just be the one to do it!

From beginning to end, it had been a very interesting evening for Helen Clayton. She'd been privy to seeing Gillian and Caywood stroll together from the gardens to the house. She also did a little eavesdropping to see if Gillian remained in the parlor with him, but once she'd escorted the young man into Helen's parlor, she graciously excused herself to inform Melissa that he was here. Helen's esteem was heightened for the young lady. She was a well-mannered young girl, one whom Nancy could be proud to have taken into her home.

When she heard Gillian's soft footsteps ascending the stairway, Helen went into the parlor to ask Caywood to join them for dinner. While he waited for Melissa, she offered him a glass of sherry.

Melissa rushed through the parlor doors a few minutes later. It was Helen's observations that Melissa was unduly sweet to her before she took her leave from the young couple. Maybe she was just a little shaken and unsure of herself this evening, knowing that Caywood had already had a chance to meet and talk with Gillian.

By the time Helen's family and guests had gathered around the dining table and the meal had been served, she knew that Melissa was indeed very nervous.

If she'd pondered earlier that Kent and Melissa would have made some sarcastic comments about their dinner of beans and ham, she had nothing to worry about once Caywood raved about the tasty meal. "Oh, Mrs. Clayton—I got to tell you I've not tasted anything this good since I left Georgia."

Helen wore a real smug look on her face as her gaze turned quickly from Kent to Melissa. "I thank you very much, Caywood, and I'm glad you are enjoying it. It's one of Nancy's and my favorite meals."

"Include me, too," he declared. "What a lucky man you are, Mr. Clayton!"

Kent mumbled a response to the young man's praises of Helen's cooking. Privately, he thought to himself that her good cooking was about the only pleasure he got from her. She certainly gave him no pleasure in bed and she hadn't for many, many years.

Because she was consumed by jealousy by the time chocolate cake was being served, Melissa hoped to embarrass and upset Gillian, who was enjoying herself. Melissa could not bring herself to admit how fetching she looked in her castoff gown. In a syrupy sweet voice, she purred, "I'm so glad you are able to use my old dress, Gillian."

She sat there with a smug smile on her face, knowing that the lavender gown she'd picked out of her armoire was far more in fashion than the black frock with white flowers which was over a year old.

186

"How lucky for me that you could no longer get into it, Melissa!" Gillian said.

Caywood added sting to the sharp bite of Gillian's words when he commented, "Well, I sure don't ever remember seeing you wear that, Melissa. I guess on Gillian it must look different." Secretly, he was thinking that Melissa could never fill out a gown so alluringly or appealingly as Gillian Browne did.

As they finished the meal, Gillian sensed the tense atmosphere around the table. Kent Clayton sat tight-lipped and very quiet. Melissa had a pout on her pretty lips and Caywood was suddenly acting very ill at ease. Only Nancy and Helen seemed to be enjoying themselves as they chatted away like two magpies.

Gillian decided to excuse herself as soon as possible. This was a special time for Mother Foster to spend with her sister and she certainly did not wish to be the cause of any turmoil in the Clayton household. But when she tried to excuse herself Caywood protested, "You must join us, Gillian. I was going to take you and Melissa for a nice stroll down the street and over by the park. It's a lovely night."

She thanked him. It wasn't easy for her to lie, but she did. "I've—I've a terrible headache. I'd not be very good company." She made a hasty exit from the room, for she did not wish to look into Mother Foster's all-knowing eyes.

But she'd not been in her room ten minutes before Nancy Foster was there, asking her why she had left so swiftly.

"You've never had a headache for as long as I've known you, honey. What suddenly upset you downstairs? Now, I want you to tell me, Gillian. You were so lighthearted and enjoying yourself, and suddenly it all changed. Was it that spoiled brat, Melissa, and her smart remarks? Did she hurt your feelings?"

"I just felt I was causing a problem and I wanted to get away, Mother Foster. Nothing should cloud your visit with your sister. Melissa just doesn't like me and that is all right with me."

Nancy went to her and embraced her warmly. She was worth a dozen Melissas. Helen had herself one spoiled, rotten daughter and she'd known that from the minute they'd arrived. Poor Helen! Better never to have a child if she was like that ungrateful Melissa.

She broke her embrace to look into Gillian's bright blue eyes, so honest and true. "No, dear, she doesn't dislike you. The main thing riling Melissa tonight was all the attention her young man was giving you. She was pea green with jealousy, that was what she was!"

"But, Mother Foster, I'm not interested in Caywood. So she has nothing to worry about from me."

Nancy patted Gillian's shoulder. "Ah, honey, but Caywood was sure interested in you!"

"Then she should have been mad at him and not me!" Gillian said.

"That's right, she should have. Her anger with you was because your beauty is so striking that you could turn any young man's head."

"But Melissa is a beautiful young lady, Mother Foster," she pointed out.

"Gillian, few women have a beauty like yours, which is more than just a face and a figure. It is your heart and soul that make you so special!"

For a moment, Gillian was struck dumb by the high praise Mother Foster had paid her. When she did find her tongue, she mumbled, "I shall hope I can live up to all your expectations of me, Mother Foster. I would never want you to be disappointed in me."

"No, dear, I never want you to think you have to do anything for me. Remember, Gillian—what you do in this world you do for yourself. You'll never disappoint me, I'll assure you of that. I appreciate now why you made your swift exit tonight. I also realize now that you're even smarter than I'd given you credit for."

"Thank you, Mother Foster."

188

"Now, don't you worry about me having a nice visit with Helen. Melissa isn't going to mess that up for me, nor is she going to mess it up for you. I'll see you in the morning, dear." She gave Gillian a kiss before she left the room.

It was only after Nancy Foster had left and she sat there all alone on the side of her bed that it dawned on her that Caywood Barron's dark eyes reminded her of Steve Lafferty's green eyes when they'd danced over her. She had not thought about that until now.

Where was that handsome devil tonight, she wondered? Did he ever think about her as she did of him? Did she haunt his sleep as he did hers? She doubted it!

If she had known how close he was to her that night as she crawled into her bed, her sleep might not have been so sound.

Less than two miles separated them!

Chapter Twenty-Five

Two days later, when Helen once again sent her daughter to deliver her baked goods to the inn, she saw to it that Gillian went along. "Think it would be pleasant for you two to take a little jaunt around the town and Gillian could see some of the interesting sights of Tucson," Helen suggested. "You might even stop in at Brady's Tearoom."

Before they left, Nancy had cornered Gillian to tuck some money in the reticule she carried on her arm. "Now, just in case you see something you'd like to buy for yourself while you and Melissa are going around town."

"Thank you, Mother Foster." Gillian smiled and leaned over to give her a kiss before following Melissa out the door.

As they rolled along in the buggy, Gillian decided to ignore Melissa's cool air. She was going to enjoy herself in spite of the chilly treatment she was getting.

When they arrived at the inn and Gillian was taking in the beautiful panorama, she sought to linger to admire the grounds. Melissa made no effort to wait but continued on up the pathway with the two baskets.

"Come on, Gillian! These baskets are heavy and I want to be rid of them," Melissa snapped at her impatiently.

Gillian rushed on up the pathway, insisting that she could take one of them.

"Never mind now! We're almost at the entrance."

"I—I just never saw such a beautiful place as this," Gillian said.

Melissa had no time to comment as she spotted Melba Jackson in the lobby and rushed forward to catch up with her. "Mrs. Jackson!" she called out when she was about ten feet behind her and Melba turned to see Helen's daughter with her delivery again. She wondered if Helen might be ill since this was the second time the girl had brought the bread.

Melissa did have the good manners to introduce Gillian to Melba, and that eased Melba's concern about her friend. She was obviously at home enjoying herself with her older sister from Maricopa County.

"Come with me, young ladies, into my office, and I will get the money I owe your mother, Melissa." Melba turned her attention to Gillian as they walked across the lobby. "Gillian is a beautiful name and you are a very beautiful young lady, my dear."

"Why thank you, Mrs. Jackson. Your inn is so wonderful it's taken my breath away."

"Well, now it is my time to thank you, Gillian. You have my permission to come anytime to stroll or enjoy my gardens. When you can arrange it, please be my guest for lunch."

Gillian's bright blue eyes sparkled excitedly. How very nice this lady was to invite her to lunch! She could not wait to tell Mother Foster about this.

"Oh, Mrs. Jackson, I—I'd be honored to have lunch with you." Gillian smiled warmly.

"That invitation includes you, too, Melissa," Melba added as she handed her the money she owed Helen Clayton.

Melissa thanked her and told her that they must be on their way. She figured it would take her forever to get Gillian to the buggy, for she'd want to ogle the gardens.

The two girls took their leave and Melba watched them go, thinking that the little auburn-haired girl should have been Helen's daughter instead of the snobby Melissa.

Knowing both of the Claytons, Melba felt Melissa was like Kent and not Helen. Oh, she most assuredly was Kent Clayton's daughter!

Steve Lafferty chanced to be standing by the window and caught a fleeting glance of two female figures walking through the gardens toward the iron gate of the courtyards. He had to be hallucinating, logic told him, but damned if the lovely image he saw was the vision he'd been daydreaming about for the last long week or more. No one could have hair like that but Gillian Browne!

The next hour or two, he was like a man in a daze, going through the motions but not really concentrating on what he was doing. More than ever he vowed to get back to Maricopa County to claim the girl he'd left back there. He should have never left without declaring his love for her and now he knew it. Gillian Browne had made all women pale, as far as he was concerned.

No woman he'd seen or met since coming to Tucson held his interest. Howard and Sue Curtis's daughters, Jeanette and Virginia, had not ignited any interest, but it certainly wasn't because Sue Curtis hadn't tried. He'd seen right through her the second time he'd gone there for dinner. When the third invitation had been proffered, he'd politely told a little white lie to get out of it because he didn't wish to offend Howard.

It took him two days to convince himself that the auburn-haired girl he'd seen in the garden was not—could not have been Gillian. But his restless heart was inconsolable regardless of what his head was telling him.

He found it necessary to lie again to Howard Curtis about having a previous engagement so he wouldn't have to go to their house for dinner. The good-natured Curtis nodded his head as he remarked, "Oh, I understand how that is, young man."

Instead of dinner at the Curtis's, Steve sat alone in the

dining room of the inn. Melba Jackson had just locked her office door and was preparing to go to her private suite. It had been a long, tiring day and she couldn't wait to sit down in her comfortable chair and kick her slippers off to pad around the thick carpets in her bare feet.

Few patrons were left in the dining room as she sauntered by the archway and chanced to glance in. It was a thoughtful Lafferty she saw picking at the food on his plate. Now what had him so preoccupied, she wondered? A handsome gent like him certainly didn't spend his evenings alone.

He did not hear her approach until she stood at the side of the table. "Hope it isn't my food that's made you lose your appetite, Lafferty?" she said.

"Hardly that, Melba," he replied. "It's me, not the food."

She smiled. "Good! I'd hate to think that." She told him good night and went toward her suite.

Lafferty knew what he must do, but he couldn't do it until he had fulfilled the contract he'd made with the Southern Pacific Railroad. But for the fact that he'd met the beautiful Gillian, he would have wished he'd never taken it on. He'd been on land too long and he was feeling the strain of it! He needed those wide open spaces of the sea and to be at the helm of his ship. That was what made him feel alive. This existence would kill him.

He could fault no one but himself and the greed of the high price the railroad had agreed to pay him for his services. But he was stranded here until the last wagonload of supplies were removed from his ship and brought here.

Steve had not considered how many loaded wagons it would take before the hold of his ship was emptied of the railroad's supplies. By the time he was ready to leave this country, he'd be faced with hiring a whole new crew.

Tomorrow, Curtis should be able to give him some idea of how many wagons had arrived in Tucson from the California harbor where his *Lucky Lady* had docked.

*　　*　　*

Reluctantly, Helen Clayton had been convinced by Gillian that she could drive the buggy to make the deliveries to the Old Pueblo Inn. Nancy had laughed, assuring her sister there was nothing to fuss about where Gillian was concerned. "She can set a horse or drive that buggy just as well as you or Melissa."

Melissa had not come down from her room this morning and Helen was pressed to put out a double order for the inn's kitchens.

"You are sure you know the way and wouldn't get lost, dear?"

Gillian grinned. "Perfectly sure."

"Helen, she won't get lost. This is a girl who rides all over our countryside. Let her do it if she wants," Nancy encouraged her sister.

Thirty minutes later, Gillian left the Clayton house with two huge baskets filled to the brim with baked goods. Helen and Nancy watched her guide the buggy down the drive to the road running in front of the Clayton house.

"See, Helen—told you that girl could drive that buggy of yours," Nancy said, nudging her sister playfully.

"It was sweet of her to want to run the errand for me," Helen declared, knowing that her daughter was faking illness.

The two of them turned away from the window to go back into Helen's kitchen to make more of the loaves. Nancy suggested to her sister that they do a double baking schedule today and declare themselves a holiday tomorrow.

Any concerns about Gillian were forgotten as they labored at the counter.

Gillian took not one wrong turn on the road going to the inn and she found Melba Jackson immediately. Melba insisted that she could surely share a short visit to her dining room for some coffee and one of her own fresh baked tarts. Gillian could see no harm in that, so she accepted. The two spent a pleasant hour, chatting as though they were old friends.

By the time Gillian left the inn, it had become dark. It was only as Melba went back to her office that she noticed the ominous gloom shrouding the inn. She felt guilty now that she'd detained the young girl so long. Had she not insisted she join her for some refreshments, she would have been back at Helen's by now. As it was, she was going to get caught in the middle of a storm. A hard pelting rain was already assaulting the grounds outside the inn.

Gillian had barely walked out the front entrance and turned to follow the pathway down to the gate where her buggy was hitched to the post just outside the courtyards when the rain began to fall. She'd not even brought her shawl to fling over her head!

After Steve had taken his horse to the stables and started to walk to the inn's entrance, he, too, had felt the downpour of rain, so he sought the shortcut to his room by going to the side entrance.

This time the vision he saw rushing alone down the path could only be Gillian Browne. He turned swiftly to dash after her. This time he wasn't going to allow that vision to fade away.

When she had almost reached the gate, Gillian could feel the dampness penetrating her new gown. She was almost tempted to turn around and seek the shelter of the inn to wait out the storm, but what would Mrs. Clayton and Mother Foster think? She didn't want them to be worried about her. No, it would be better to try to make it back to the Clayton house, even if she arrived drenched.

That slight moment of hesitation on her part enabled Steve to catch up with her before she rushed through the iron gate. About the time his two strong arms reached out to grab her, a loud rumble of thunder erupted overhead. She felt herself being lifted upward in a pair of powerful arms. As the rain beat down on their faces, she realized that the face was Steve Lafferty's. Too fierce was the storm over them for her to question his actions as he rushed across the grounds with her.

It was not until they'd reached the comfort of his sitting room and he'd slowly lowered her to the floor with his arms still circling her waist that she breathlessly mumbled, "Steve? Dear God, it is you!"

For a fleeting second, he let his green eyes devour her damp lovely face. Then his hand went gently to her face to remove the stray wisps of hair. That devilish grin lit up his face as he said, "It is, my little Gilly."

Suddenly, his head bent down to take her half-parted lips in the kiss that he'd yearned for nightly since he'd left Maricopa County. His strong hands pressed her petite body closer to his. Her damp gown was molded to her body and he could feel each and every soft, rounded curve.

Like the bolts of lightning striking outside his room, Steve was struck with a fury of passion. It was a passion so fired and fierce and he was a man so hungry for the sweet nectar of her lips! He could not let her escape this time.

Gillian found herself caught up in overwhelming force she was helpless to escape!

Chapter Twenty-Six

The stormy violence outside the inn was no more fierce than the untamed, savage desire Steve was stirring in Gillian as his hands caressed and touched her. She had never known anything like this.

She felt the featherlike touch of his warm lips against her ear as he whispered tender words of love. "God, Gillian—I've dreamed of you every night since we were last together. I've missed you so much."

She gasped breathlessly. "I missed you, too, Steve!" She felt his fingers unfastening the front of her bodice.

"Let me love you, Gillian. Let me love you as I want to do. Tell me, darling, that you want that, too," he huskily pleaded with her.

"I—I've never felt this way about a man before. I guess I must love you," she softly moaned as his lips captured hers again in a long, lingering kiss.

"Let me convince you once and for all that no other man could love you as I can, little Gilly. Let me!" By now, his eager hands had gently removed her frock until it hung at her waistline. His head moved downward to kiss one breast. In unhurried, leisurely strokes, his tongue teased and tantalized the tip until he felt the sudden arch of her petite body against his. He knew she now flamed with passion and desire.

"Ah, yes, Gillian! You were meant to be mine! I knew it the first moment you rushed into my arms back there at the Fosters. You felt it, too. I saw it in your eyes."

Swiftly he sought to remove her clothing and his own. The heat of their two nude bodies touching ignited a rampaging fire he knew he could no longer control.

Steve felt her soft, velvet flesh pressing urgently against him, and his own passion mounted. He burrowed his nose in the sweet fragrance of her hair as he moved to place himself between the silken softness of her thighs. In a husky voice, he gasped, "Oh, God—God, Gilly!" He wished he could make time stand still!

"Oh, Steve!" she gasped as she clung to him. His strong arms drew her closer as though he never intended to release her.

For the longest time they lingered in that sweet aftermath of intimacy that only true lovers ever know. Steve loved the feeling of just holding her close to him, feeling her breasts heave as she breathed.

After a few minutes, he whispered in her ear, "Oh, Gilly—I thought I was dreaming when I saw you. Tell me how this all happened?" She told him why she was in Tucson. She suddenly realized how many hours had elapsed since she'd left the Clayton house. She broke from his warm embrace with a distraught look on her pretty face. "Oh Lord, Steve—Mother Foster will be worried silly about me. I was only to deliver her sister's baked goods to the inn and return to the house."

Without any concern for her nakedness, she leaped out of his bed and began to get dressed. For a moment, Steve continued to lie there and savor the sight of her satiny flesh so wonderfully displayed.

Slowly, he too rose up from the bed and began to get dressed. "I shall accompany you home, Gillian," he said. "I will tell Mrs. Foster that it was I, who insisted you stay with me until the storm had gone by."

She stopped buttoning the front of her bodice and there was

a startled look on her face as she stammered, "You're—you're not going to tell her I was here in . . ."

"You little monkey, I'm not going to tell her about anything that took place between you and me. That is nobody's business but yours and mine. That is too precious to me. I hope you feel the same." His green eyes searched her face for a response.

Gillian's blue eyes flamed bright with the love consuming her as she stood there, realizing that she'd given herself to this handsome man. Perhaps she should have been embarrassed or maybe she should have felt ashamed of herself, but she didn't. In a very honest, calm voice she replied to him, "I have never known such a moment before and I might never know it again, so for me it will always be precious and private, Steve."

He took her in his strong arms, assuring her, "Ah, yes, my darling, you will know that moment again and again. It will be with me!" No words she could have uttered would have made him happier than he was now, standing with her in his arms.

He would protect her, he promised himself. That was why he intended to see her to the Claytons, so she would not be blamed for her long absence.

When she was fully dressed, he made her sit in the chair for a moment while he rubbed her lovely hair with a towel to absorb some of the lingering dampness. "God, I've never seen a more beautiful shade of hair, Gilly. It looks like polished copper. Who did you inherit that from—your father or mother?"

She gave a soft little giggle. "Neither of them. I got this from my grandma." She fingered the long tresses hanging over her shoulder.

Now Steve knew that it *was* Gillian he'd seen a couple of days ago. He didn't even have to ask if it was so. The young girl with her must have been Mrs. Foster's niece.

Knowing how tempers can mount when someone is worrying about a person she loves, Steve figured he'd better get Gillian back to Mrs. Foster. Damned if he wanted to take her back! He'd have liked to keep her there at the inn with him.

Once he'd made the arrangements for a horse for himself and secured it behind the buggy Gillian had driven to the Old Pueblo Inn, the two of them departed.

Anyone seeing the two young people seated side by side on the buggy seat would have known that they were lovers. Melba Jackson happened to be privy to the sight and she had to admit that it stunned her to see Lafferty in the Clayton buggy beside the auburn-haired Gillian. Had she been at the inn all this time in the company of Lafferty? Over two hours had gone by since she and the young lady had parted company and she'd been concerned about her safe journey homeward. Now it would seem that she'd never headed for home.

Could that devious Irishman have enticed that sweet innocent girl? She'd feel like tossing him out of her very respectable inn, she swore, if she found out he had. Gillian was a sweet, innocent child.

As she reined the mare drawing her own buggy into action, she knew what she was going to do. She was going to get to the bottom of all this or her name wasn't Melba Jackson! What went on at this inn was very much her business, she figured! She'd not have that charming Irishman using Gillian!

Both of the sisters had paced the floor of the parlor for more than an hour and a half. Helen blamed herself for having allowed Gillian to leave the house in the first place.

Nancy had quickly chimed in, "No, you're not to blame. There was no hint of a storm brewing when she left here. She'd have been just fine going and coming if that hadn't happened." She assured her sister that Gillian had most likely pulled in to some shelter to wait it out. "I've known that gal for over two years now, and she's got a sound head on her shoulders."

The fierce storm and sharp bolts of lightning had urged Melissa out of her room and she sat there in her gown and robe, listening to all the fussing and fuming of the two older women. Darling little Gillian was in trouble. She intended to sit right there to see her get a tongue-lashing for being tardy in getting back home. Oh, she couldn't wait to witness that!

In her sweet, syrupy voice, Melissa said, "She must surely know how worried we all are about her."

Nancy glanced over to Melissa to give her a skeptical look. What a little hypocrite her niece was!

Just as she would have made a comment, Nancy observed the buggy turn the corner. "Well, I'll be damned!" she muttered, seeing the handsome Stephen Lafferty riding with her.

Helen rushed over to the window. "What is it, Nancy?"

"It's Gillian and she's fine. But Stephen Lafferty is with her and that's what surprises me."

"Stephen Lafferty? Now, who's he?"

Melissa had joined her aunt and mother at the window. What she saw made her livid with jealousy. A handsome man was there by Gillian's side and his face was so impassioned as he looked at her!

"Well, now we know why Gillian's been gone so long, don't we?" she cattily declared.

"My, what a good-looking man." Helen sighed. Once again, she inquired of her sister who he was, but Nancy shrugged it aside, saying she'd tell her about him later.

The ring of lighthearted laughter was heard as Gillian and Lafferty came into the parlor. Strange, mixed expressions greeted them.

"Mother Foster, I'm sorry I've been delayed so long but can you believe it—we met at the inn."

Steve found this was the moment he should take charge, which he did. "Mrs. Foster, it's nice to see you again. I must shoulder the blame for Gillian being so late, but I could not let her ride through that storm." He gave a husky laugh. "I was in a state of shock at the sight of her. I had no idea of seeing Gillian or you. It's a wonderful surprise."

Such charm as Lafferty's was hard for any woman of any age to resist. Helen was already impressed by the handsome young man and Melissa was completely entranced. Never had she seen such a magnificent specimen of masculinity. Those devastating green eyes could beguile anyone. She knew no man with such a set of broad shoulders and chest and such a trim waistline. She swore his tall, towering figure was a few inches over six feet.

He made Caywood look like a dwarf, she thought as she stood there admiring him. By the time Gillian had introduced Steve to Helen and her ogling daughter, Steve figured that Mrs. Foster had accepted his explanation. At least, that was his impression.

He graciously accepted Helen's offer of some coffee and took the opportunity to explain to Nancy Foster about his business here in Tucson. "They hope to have the Southern Pacific Railroad here by 1880. That is the plan, to have the tracks laid all the way to Tucson."

"Oh, wouldn't that be wonderful, Nancy?" Helen exclaimed.

"Sure would. Beat the heck out of a stage that runs every two weeks."

"Well, ladies—if you can just bear it a few more months, I think you will have that pleasure," Lafferty told them.

Trying to vie for his attention, Melissa purred softly, "Oh, how exciting it must be for you, Captain Lafferty, to be a part of something so important."

"I suppose so. However, I'm a selfish man, Miss Clayton, and it's meant time away from the thing I normally do. I'm a man of the sea. I'm not a man to linger long on land."

"Oh, really?" Melissa's eyelashes fluttered as she glanced over at Gillian. She gave a lighthearted giggle as she sought to tease him. "A fair lady in every port for you, Captain?"

His green eyes measured her cautiously. He knew the little game she was trying to play and the bait she was throwing his way. "Well, Miss Clayton—that is true until a man finds the one lady he can't walk away from." His eyes darted over to Gillian. There was no one in the room who could have doubted his affection when he looked at her.

"I must go now," he announced as he turned to Nancy Foster to ask if he might come again to see Gillian.

"Why, of course you can, Steve," Nancy told him.

"Thank you, ma'am." He took Gillian's hand. "Would you walk me to the door, Gillian?"

She rose to join him, feeling the sweet warmth of his hand holding hers. She knew that all their eyes were upon them as they left the room. She was feeling a little smug as they got to the front door.

Before he was to take his leave, she swayed closer to him without shame to inquire, "Could you walk away from me, Steve Lafferty?" A twinkle of mischief was in her blue eyes as they gazed up at him.

He planted a quick, hasty kiss on her forehead. "Never, my little Gilly! Never in a million years!"

She watched him walk away, believing that he'd spoken the truth!

Chapter Twenty-Seven

Those first few days in Tucson had left Hawk unnerved and confused. His half-breed nature could hardly accept that this so-called civilized place, Tuscon, was as civilized as his untamed woods back in the mountains. He'd walked down the streets to see the drunken patrons of the taverns pitched out into the streets by burly bartenders. Rough and rowdy miners flocked into the town, and it was obvious to Hawk that they were hellbent to get into a fight with anyone who dared to cross them.

So far, he'd managed to stay out of harm's way. Hawk had never met a man he was afraid of, but he was no fool; he knew the prejudice he would face as an Apache half-breed.

He'd made his first run as the railroad's scout and covered the first fifteen miles of the terrain to vouch that it was safe. Now he was free to do as he wished for a few days before he started to survey the countryside again. Only today, when he'd been in the office of Warner Barlow to check in with him, Warner had praised his scouting ability. "The workers are making good time laying the tracks thanks to you, Hawk. Haven't had one bit of trouble from any renegades. From what I hear, the same is not true over by the fort. Forage for the horses is becoming a hell of a problem. It seems the Apaches are setting fires all around there. The range grass is being burnt to a crisp."

A slow, easy grin broke on Hawk's bronzed face as he pointed out to Warner, "That's an old Apache trick, and they are usually very effective with it."

"Well, they sure as hell have been from what Sergeant Wallen told me yesterday. Southern Pacific is lucky to have you working with us. If we can keep going as we are, then we will make that deadline in 1880."

"I'm happy, sir, if I can contribute a little to making that happen. Knowing what that will mean to this territory is worth a lot to me." What Hawk would not say to Warner, or to anyone, was that it was a personal battle he'd won against the Apaches. That meant everything to him.

"Well, young man—you've earned yourself a few days' holiday. So go on now and enjoy yourself, take in the sights around Tucson. When you go back to Maricopa, you'll take back some wonderful memories. I know I will when I return to my home in the East. Don't miss a visit to San Xavier del Bac Mission. It was built years and years ago and the same old adobe walls are still standing."

Hawk bade him farewell and, since the day was still young, he took Barlow's suggestion. He traveled south out of the town down the dirt trail road. Nine miles to the south of Tucson, Barlow had told him.

Once he had covered the distance between the mission and the outskirts of Tucson, he saw ahead of him what had to be the mission, a stone-and-adobe structure rearing up above the old stone wall of the grounds. He tied Tache's reins to the long hitching post just outside the walls. As he was about to go inside the grounds, he noted the pinto's feisty, pacing moves. Hawk knew the horse was riled at being restrained at that hitching post. Tache had not been too contented with his new surroundings, for he and Hawk were not enjoying their usual daily rides.

"I won't be too long, Tache," he told his pinto. Since the time when Tim had first brought the pinto to the cabin as a gift for him on his fifteenth birthday, Hawk had talked to him as if he was a good friend.

It was Solange who'd given him the name of Tache. She'd never seen a spotted horse before, and when Tim led the horse up to the cabin she'd called him Tache, which meant "spots" in her native tongue. She'd found him a strange-looking beast but Hawk had adored him at first sight. The name Solange had given him had stuck.

Once Hawk entered the gates of the mission wall, he knew why Barlow had insisted that he visit this place. Perhaps Barlow was a more feeling, understanding man than he'd given him credit for. A great peace engulfed Hawk as he strolled leisurely amid the towering, regal palm trees and massive spreading branches of tropic greenery flourishing everywhere. Clusters of brilliantly colored cactus blooms were everywhere. He felt the same serenity he enjoyed back at home with his mother. He was glad he'd taken Warner's suggestion. This mission was truly a garden of paradise, Hawk thought as he ambled along the trail in the garden.

It was obviously a sanctuary for birds, Hawk noticed as he watched them gather to feed. He sat down on a bench to watch them, wishing he had a basket of bread crumbs, as Solange had when she fed the birds that flocked to their yard at home.

For the first time since Hawk had arrived in Tucson, he felt at ease.

San Xavier del Bac Mission seemed to possess a magical enchantment for all who entered its portals on this particular day. Never had Gillian lied to Nancy Foster from the moment she'd come to live with her over two years ago, but today she had. To keep a rendezvous with Steve, she'd deliberately lied to Nancy and Helen to get the use of the Claytons' buggy. By way of excuse, she'd offered to deliver Helen's goods to the inn.

She felt a qualm of guilt as she drove away from the house. She was discovering things about herself she'd never known before, thanks to Steve, who had unmasked her secrets.

With a sweet look of innocence and honesty, she'd also lied to Melba Jackson when she'd delivered the bakery items. Melba had hoped she and Gillian might have a chance to get better acquainted this afternoon, but she could tell that Gillian was anxious to leave the inn. If she were to bet, she'd have wagered that it was Lafferty she was rushing out to meet.

Melba slowly turned to walk back to her desk and sit down. Was this little enchantress as naive and innocent as she'd first thought? she wondered. God knows, those sapphire blue eys and sensuous lips were enough to tempt a worldlywise gent like Lafferty. All that lovely auburn hair flowing over her shoulders was enough to urge a man to bury his face in it, her perfectly proportioned figure was enough to tantalize any hot-blooded man.

A gambling woman she wasn't, but Melba would bet that Gillian was a woman fired with a consuming passion when she loved a man. She couldn't fault her for that, for she'd felt that way about her gambler husband. When she was about Gillian's age, Ace Jackson had appeared in her life and swept her off her feet. Sitting at her desk now, Melba could see every feature of Ace's face. She could recall those wonderful times with her husband, with his winning ways and his silver tongue. More than ever, she knew that age was a state of mind. Never did she want to grow old. Forever, she wanted to think young!

Gillian wasn't thinking about Melba Jackson as she left the inn to be on her way to her rendezvous with Steve. So intense were her feelings for the man she loved that, by now, there were no feelings of guilt about what she'd done. Only one thought consumed her: she would soon be with Steve.

Since the moment she'd surrendered to him, he was all she could think about. She'd thought about the heat of his lips on hers and the burning touch of his hands as they'd caressed her breasts. Dear God, she'd never imagined that a man's touch could give such ecstasy and pleasure!

As she drove the buggy toward the old mission, she began to

understand those particular intimate glances she'd noticed between her mother and father. But at thirteen, she'd had no idea of their meaning. Now she knew. Now she understood!

It was strange and puzzling to her that she had felt no shame about being nude with Steve's green eyes adoring her. She had actually enjoyed it, and it had given her a certain exaltation to know that she could beguile him so. She knew she had done just that.

She was so engrossed with thoughts of Steve that the nine miles passed hastily. When her buggy came to the entrance of the mission, Steve was there at the gate waiting for her. The grin on his face was enough to make her glad that she had lied to Nancy and Helen. This stolen interlude of pleasure with him was well worth the lie, she comforted herself.

As she reined the mare up to the hitching post, Steve swore he'd never seen a more beautiful sight. The blue gown she wore was a perfect match for her lovely eyes, and he decided then and there that the gem she should always wear was an exquisite sapphire. Not a diamond or a pearl for his Gilly; she must have the sapphire.

He rushed through the gate to assist her as she alit from the buggy. As he lifted her down from the buggy, his eager lips captured hers in a long, lingering kiss. "Oh, Gillian, I prayed you'd come. I had to see you before I left."

His statement stunned her. "You're leaving, Steve?"

"Only to go to San Diego, Gillian. I've a crew and a ship back there. I'm not a man of the land. I'm the captain of a clipper ship that has been in port far too long. The chances are my crew have become itchy and signed on to another ship, one that's ready to put to sea. Seamen are a strange lot, Gillian. They look forward to making port after they've been at sea for weeks, but after a couple of days and nights, they are ready to feel the salty spray on their face."

She felt his strong hand enclosing hers as they walked along the stone pathway. "Is this the way you feel, Steve? Are you ready to leave, too?"

"There is only one thing that makes me want to stay here, Gillian, and that is you. So I've decided that there is only one thing to do. I'll just have to take you with me." There was a devious twinkle in his green eyes as he looked down at her.

"Oh? I shall go with you?"

He laughed. "Oh, most assuredly, my darling. I would not think of leaving without you! Don't you know how much you mean to me?"

"I guess I don't, Steve. You tell me," she prodded him. "Tell me just how much I mean to you."

His eyes surveyed her very serious-looking face. He knew he should not lie to her, and he didn't.

"I'll not lie to you, Gillian. I've had my share of ladies and I felt no qualms of guilt. I could never feel that way about you. You tug at my heart as no other woman ever has. You are so different from any other woman I've known. The truth is, Gillian, you've completely confused me."

She could not suppress a lilting gale of laughter. "Well, Steve, if you think you've been confused, then I can assure you that I've been confused, too."

"Good! I'd like to think that you've suffered as much as I have." He laughed.

"Steve Lafferty, you are a wicked man! I know that for sure now," she said playfully.

"You're right, my little Gilly. I'm an evil, vicious man when I want something. Whatever it takes, I get what I want. There can be no doubt that I want you, Gillian. I have since the first moment I saw you and felt that exciting little body of yours next to mine. I knew that I wanted you near me for the rest of my life."

There was a seductive look in those blue eyes of hers and it had nothing to do with sweet innocence. "Are you asking me to be your wife, Steve Lafferty?"

His muscled arms enclosed her, pressing her closer to him. "Guess that is exactly what I'm saying, Gilly. Damned if it isn't! I want you more than anything I've ever wanted in my whole life." A smile came slowly to his face as he quizzed her. "Are you sure you're not a little witch who casts spells, eh Gilly? Tell me the truth?"

She snuggled closer to him, an impish grin on her lovely face and a wicked twinkle in her eye. "Now, do you think I'd tell you if I was?"

Chapter Twenty-Eight

Lafferty gazed down at Gillian's lovely face resting contentedly against his broad chest and it suddenly dawned on him what she'd done: That adorable little witch had gotten him to propose to her. Maybe that wily little minx was his conqueror instead of his conquest.

After all the experienced ladies he'd squired back in England and the port cities of France, he'd finally lost his heart to a little girl in Arizona Territory, a girl so tiny that his two huge hands could span her waist and whose head didn't come to the height of his shoulders. But, dear God, she had captured his heart completely!

He had surrendered to her bewitching beauty and the spell she'd cast on him.

Suddenly she broke away from him. "Oh, Steve, you said you were bringing a basket of food. Shouldn't we eat it? It's such a warm day and it isn't good for food to be out too long."

He laughed. "You insult me, Gillian! Here I am holding you in my arms and all you can think about is food. Shame on you!"

"Well, Steve—if you've gone to the trouble to get a basket of food from Melba's kitchen, then I think we should enjoy it," she told him, not wanting to confess to him that she was starved.

"Guess you make a good point there. Now, you just sit where

you are and I'll go get it." Before she could answer him, he had leaped up from the ground and darted through the greenery.

Soon he returned with a huge basket. There on the grounds of the mission they enjoyed a delicious picnic lunch from Melba's kitchen. Steve had forgotten nothing to make it a special occasion. He spread a colorful cloth on the ground, along with napkins. Melba's crispy golden-fried chicken and her delicious baked bread and her special fruit pies were included in the picnic basket.

As they ate, they agreed that Melba Jackson was a special breed of lady. "I feel like I've known her all my life. She's such a warm, friendly person," Gillian told him.

"Exactly my thoughts. Sounds like we think alike, my little Gilly."

"Why do you call me that? No one has ever called me that before."

His hand went up to lovingly pat her cheek. "That is why, my darling. It is my special name for you."

She stared at the handsome young man beside her. For all his power and strength there was a gentle, sentimental side to this formidable Irish sea captain.

He could not fathom her expression. She seemed to be measuring him for one brief second before she spoke. "You are a romantic, Captain Lafferty."

"Now how did you come to that conclusion, my pet?"

"I just know it. I feel it here." She gestured to her heart.

"No one has ever accused me of that, Gilly. Maybe that's why I knew you were the girl for me. You seem to understand me. Now I'm going to make a confession to you on these sacred mission grounds: I *am* a romantic. There, are you satisfied?"

She broke into a gale of laughter. "I knew it!"

So lighthearted and gay she was today! He wished he could linger in this interlude of paradise with her forever. He had misgivings about leaving Tucson tomorrow to travel to San Diego, but he had been away from his ship for many weeks and it was time he find out what was going on back there on the

California coast.

He'd discussed his concern with Curtis yesterday and Curtis had understood his feelings. "Can't fault you for that, young man. After all, you and your *Lady Luck* are going to be together long after this project is finished," he'd told him.

So Steve had decided to take the stage to San Diego, see how the railroad's cargo was being unloaded, and return to give Curtis a firsthand report.

Gillian took his news much better than he'd expected her to. It was refreshing not to have to deal with a sullen, pouting female. Oh, he saw her lovely eyes reflecting a moment of sadness, but Gillian was determined not to allow anything to mar this glorious day they were sharing together, especially if this was to be his last day with her for a while.

By the time he took the picnic basket to the buggy, she had a smile on her lovely face.

"You're the prettiest thing I ever laid eyes on, Gillian Browne. Do you know that?"

"No, and you can tell me that again and again, Steve Lafferty," she retorted.

"And so I shall—over and over again." He bent to kiss her rosebud lips. "Now give me your little hand."

She did as he requested and he fumbled in his pocket to take out the exquisite sapphire and diamond ring he'd purchased the day before. They were the finest Oriental sapphires and he was surprised to find them in Tucson. Slipping the ring on her finger he told her, "You're like a rare, beautiful jewel, Gillian. Every time I look in those blue eyes of yours I'm reminded of sapphires like this one."

She gasped with delight, for she'd never seen a ring so magnificent.

Never had she owned such a valuable piece of jewelry. She was so thrilled she could not utter a word. Finally, she stammered almost in a whisper, "Oh, Steve—I—I don't know what to say."

"Just say you love me with all your heart. That is my only

wish, darling."

She flung her arms around his neck and reached up to plant a kiss on his lips. "I do—and you know that! I always will!"

For all the days and nights he would be gone away from her, he wanted to take his fill of her sweetness. Praying that the high, flowering shrubs would provide them a private bower from those strolling down the pathway of the mission grounds, he loosened the front of her bodice as he laid her back on the grass. As his hands began to caress her, she was ignited with that flaming passion he always stirred the moment he touched her. He kissed her half-parted lips, taking his fill of the sweet nectar he found there. He let his hands and mouth tease and taunt her satiny flesh as she moaned from the sweet agony he was causing.

"Steve—oh, Steve!" She sighed, eager for him to fill her with his magnificent being. She did not have to make that request a second time; Steve eagerly obliged her.

Together they moved rhythmically until he could no longer stop the volcano ready to erupt within him. Gillian pressed him urgently against her so she could feel the full force of his power filling her.

Later, as they lay in that serene lovers' calm, he thought to himself how perfect she was for him. His darling Gillian was meant for him and him alone. Now, he knew why he'd fallen in love the first time he laid eyes on her.

While he would have sought to linger longer there on the grass, just to hold her in his arms, a sudden afternoon rain shower changed his plans. Hastily, they leaped up to gather their clothes and dress, but as they rushed to the buggy, the rains ceased and they both began to laugh about their hasty departure.

He teased her. "You sure you got everything back on? I don't want you arriving at the Claytons' in a state of undress."

"Steve Lafferty, you are a wicked man, do you know that? Of course I have everything back on."

"Just wanted to make sure. Don't want to get on bad terms

with Mrs. Foster. Got a feeling she could be a real hellcat if she was riled.

Gillian laughed, assuring him that she certainly could be.

"I figured that." He lifted Gillian up in the seat and moved around to the other side of the buggy.

Reluctantly, he directed the buggy toward town and the Claytons' home. More than ever he was going to find it hard to say goodbye to her.

Gillian was feeling the same way as she sat there on the seat. After this afternoon, she would be very lonely.

He had said he was taking her with him—but he had not said *when*.

Chapter Twenty-Nine

Gillian had never known such happiness. Tucson would always be a magical place for her, since this was where Steve Lafferty had asked her to be his wife. This eased the pain slightly of having to say goodbye to him when they arrived back at the Claytons' house.

Steve chanced to see her stealing glances every now and then at the ring on her finger and an amused grin broke on his face. Damn, he was glad he'd given it to her before he left for San Diego.

Once they arrived at the house and he stood with her by the gate to say their farewells, he inhaled the sweet fragrance of her as he tenderly kissed her cheek. He felt the flush on her face from their fierce lovemaking and as he drove away he was already anticipating their glorious reunion when he returned.

As she mounted the front steps she could still feel the overwhelming heat of Steve's warmth, even though he was already out of sight and his buggy had turned the corner.

She would have dashed through the front door, but a voice called out to her, "Well, Gillian—you look like you must have enjoyed yourself."

Gillian had not noticed Melissa in the swing on the side of the front porch when she and Steve were saying their goodbyes by the gate. Neither had she noticed her when she came up the steps.

"I've had a marvelous afternoon!" Gillian said. The radiant expression on her face was enough to tell Melissa that.

"Well, come sit down and tell me all about it. My afternoon has been a rather dull one. Caywood didn't come by as he promised. That cad! I'm about ready to tell him not to come around anymore," she told Gillian with a pout on her face.

"You surely don't mean that. I thought you adored him. Maybe there was a reason he couldn't come as he'd promised you," Gillian suggested as she sat down on the swing.

"Oh, I like him well enough, but he's sure not the handsome devil Steve Lafferty is. He sounds so exciting—an Irish sea captain and all! You truly amaze me, Gillian. You must tell me your secrets and how you used your wiles to attract such a sophisticated, good-looking man."

"Wiles, Melissa?"

"Oh, now come on, Gillian. Please don't play that dumb, innocent act with me. I know better. Maybe you haven't noticed all the grass stains on that new gown Momma gave you."

Gillian indignantly got up out of the swing. "Well, that isn't too hard to figure out, when you consider we had a picnic and sat on the grounds there at the mission."

Melissa gave a wicked little laugh. "I'm not talking about the *seat* of the gown. I'm talking about the back of the bodice, Gillian. I'd say you were lying back on the ground to get that."

Gillian's blue eyes sparkled with fire as she hissed at Melissa angrily, "And I'd say you've got an evil mind, Melissa Clayton. Don't judge me by yourself and what you'd have done."

She turned to march away as Melissa declared, "Well, I knew I was right about you. You've got a temper! There's a little of that hellcat in you for all that sweet angel face you wear around my mother and Aunt Nancy."

Gillian swung around to take a couple of steps back toward the swing. "There's a lot of hellcat in me, Melissa." She said quickly, "Remember, I'm a little old backwoods girl—a

222

country girl, you called me. I might just go wild and crazy and scratch that pretty little face up good if you rile me too much."

Without further ado, she turned and walked away, leaving a stunned, bewildered Melissa staring at her back. There was no smug look on Melissa's face now!

Gillian was relieved not to encounter Mother Foster or Helen as she made her way through the house and ascended the stairway to her room. But as much as she found Melissa a despicable, catty young lady, she had hit a sensitive nerve when she'd mentioned the grass stains on her frock. The innuendo that she and Steve were lovers was true, and Gillian could not deny that. A moment of guilt overtook her when she realized that she was indeed guilty of what Melissa had accused her of doing.

She decided to change quickly into another dress before Mother Foster might come into the room. She could not possibly wear the stained dress to the evening meal.

She changed into the pretty blue sprigged muslin which she and Nancy had made especially for this trip. She pulled all her thick, wavy hair back and tied the blue velvet ribbon around it, then dabbed on some of the lilac toilet water she'd purchased the day she and Melissa had gone shopping. She loved the sweet fragrance of the toilet water which reminded her of the lilac bushes outside her bedroom window back in Maricopa County.

The other item she'd purchased that day was a tooled leather pouch which she thought John Foster would enjoy for his smoking tobacco. Nancy had gently scolded her for not spending the money on herself, but Nancy could not argue with her when she'd said, "But, Mother Foster, he's been there all alone, doing all the work, while we've been here enjoying ourselves. I felt he needed a reward."

A broad, warm smile came to Nancy's plain face as she'd embraced the girl. "You're right, honey! Gillian, you have a good heart. Have I ever told you that, 'cause if I haven't then I'm telling you now."

Gillian thought back to this scene. She fingered the blue sprigged dress, wondering if Mother Foster would be ashamed of her if she knew how she'd given herself so wantonly to Steve Lafferty. God, she'd die before she'd shame the Fosters!

When she went downstairs to join the others for the evening meal, she was ready to face both Mother Foster and Melissa. She had dealt with the confused thoughts which had troubled her earlier, and had calmed any doubts plaguing her. She was no wanton woman. She sincerely loved Steve.

Nancy appraised her, thinking how very attractive she looked tonight as they gathered at the table. This trip had done wonders for Gillian. She'd needed an escape from that isolated ranch life. She swore that it was not just her imagination that there had been remarkable changes in Gillian. Was it a hint of a more sophisticated Gillian she saw there on her face? Whatever it was, Nancy had never seen her looking more breathtakingly lovely than she did tonight in the simple muslin frock they'd stitched back at the ranch.

Nancy Foster was not the only one admiring Gillian tonight. Kent Clayton compared her beauty to that of his own daughter, whom he had always considered a gorgeous-looking miss, but Melissa could never be the tantalizing temptress that Gillian was.

Damned if he didn't find himself stirred with desire for the little enchantress sitting across the table from him. Kent justified his lusty desires as he always had. Helen considered him a foul-minded man and he considered her a frigid woman who didn't appreciate his amorous attentions. She'd stifled him for years, so why shouldn't his eyes wander? He didn't feel his age and he knew for certain he didn't look it.

His ego was always heightened by younger ladies who gave him inviting, encouraging looks. Kent had the type of silken tongue ladies found charming, as he discovered when he sought to engage them in conversation as they shopped at the

ACCEPT YOUR FREE GIFT AND EXPERIENCE MORE OF THE PASSION AND ADVENTURE YOU LIKE IN A HISTORICAL ROMANCE

Zebra Romances are the finest novels of their kind and are written with the adult woman in mind. All of our books are written by authors who really know how to weave tales of romantic adventure in the historical settings you love.

Because our readers tell us these books sell out very fast in the stores, Zebra has made arrangements for you to receive at home the four newest titles published each month. You'll never miss a title and home delivery is so convenient. With your first shipment we'll even send you a FREE Zebra Historical Romance as our gift just for trying our home subscription service. No obligation.

BIG SAVINGS AND **FREE** HOME DELIVERY

Each month, the Zebra Home Subscription Service will send you the four newest titles as soon as they are published. (We ship these books to our subscribers even before we send them to the stores.) You may preview them *Free* for 10 days. If you like them as much as we think you will, you'll pay just $3.50 each and *save $1.80 each month* off the cover price. *AND you'll also get FREE HOME DELIVERY.* There is never a charge for shipping, handling or postage and there is no minimum you must buy. If you decide not to keep any shipment, simply return it within 10 days, no questions asked, and owe nothing.

mercantile store.

It had never bothered Kent that Helen wished to play the role of the ice maiden. He could not have cared less! There was and always had been some sweet feminine body to warm his bed. He'd never gone wanting.

Helen caught Kent ogling Gillian. She'd wondered how long it would be before he'd try to ply his charm on the pretty young thing. She was amazed he'd waited this long. Oh, she'd kept a watchful eye on him, for it was one time she wasn't going to allow him to have his way! From the minute Nancy and Gillian had arrived, Helen had determined that she'd not allow Kent to tarnish this sweet girl.

She'd put up with many things for some twenty years, but this time she'd not shut her eyes to the evil in this man she'd married. To play her falsely was one thing, but to have played his own daughter falsely—she could never forgive him for that. He'd convinced Melissa that he was some kind of paragon, and she was so naive she'd been an easy prey. Kent loved every minute of the hero worship he received from his daughter. That was when Helen found herself despising him the most.

Gillian happened to glance in Mr. Clayton's direction, and she noticed the strange look in his eyes. She felt a chill run down her spine. There was something about the way his dark eyes trailed from her face down her throat to the rounded mounds of her bosom. The expression on his face and the reflection in his eyes were enough to make her quickly turn away. The rest of the meal was not pleasant for Gillian, and she felt very ill at ease.

Helen happened not to be the only one to see Kent's face with the lusty look on it. It made Nancy fighting mad at her brother-in-law. She wondered why she hadn't thought about that possibility. It was no secret to Nancy that Kent Clayton had always been a womanizer. God knows, she'd tried to warn her younger sister when she was about to marry him.

She sat there at the table, recalling her exact words to the younger Helen, "He'll never give you contentment, Helen.

You'll never know a minute's peace. Kent Clayton couldn't be true to any woman." But her words had fallen on a deaf ear. Well, she couldn't save Helen from the likes of him, but she vowed she'd save Gillian.

Maybe it would be best for all concerned if she cut short her visit by a week. Thank God, she'd not mentioned to Helen just how long she'd intended to stay. She'd just said a few weeks, so one week short of what she'd intended would save any hurt feelings.

Besides, she was missing John and the ranch. She'd had a nice visit with her sister; they'd talked and enjoyed each other's company for over three weeks now. Helen had shown her the sights of Tucson and they'd managed a couple of shopping trips between the long hours they'd spent in Helen's kitchen preparing the baked goods she sold to the local inn. Perhaps Helen enjoyed it, and the money she received for all that labor, but Nancy found it drudgery and a most monotonous task. On the ranch, no two days were ever the same, and that was the life she preferred.

Tomorrow, she'd announce their departure, she decided.

When the evening was over and everyone retired to their own rooms, Nancy invited herself into Gillian's bedroom. When they were enclosed in the privacy of the room with the door closed, Nancy informed her of her plans. It took Gillian by surprise, but she tried not to show it.

"I think I should be getting back to John and the ranch. I've had a nice visit with Helen, but I feel I should be getting back. You understand, don't you, honey?"

"Oh, of course, Mother Foster," she agreed. What else could she do? But it meant that now she'd not be here in Tucson when Steve returned from his trip to San Diego. She'd just have to pray that he would come to her in Maricopa County.

She managed to mask how distraught she was until Nancy left the room. Only then did she fling herself on the bed and give way to tears.

Everything had changed for Gillian here in Tucson. She was not the same person anymore. An ecstasy had been hers she'd never imagined possible, and forever this place and the Old Pueblo Inn would hold a special place in her heart.

She wondered if she could possibly find any contentment or peace back at the ranch.

Chapter Thirty

Hawk figured if he got back to the hotel and sequestered himself in the privacy of his hotel room he would find the peace he sought. But the hotel room gave him no solace. He paced the floor like one of those cats that roamed the mountains near his mother's cabin. As he passed the mirror, he stopped to probe the image reflected there. His dark eyes took in the whole of him. His black hair was clustered around the nape of his neck, for he was wearing it a few inches shorter now. He turned to survey his broad chest and the taper of his trim waist. Moving back so he could survey his firm, muscled physique he measured his long, muscled legs.

To the emptiness of the room and himself, he muttered back at his own image in the mirror, "I'm not Apache. I don't look anything like him." He didn't have long coarse hair like Cochise, nor did he wear a band tied across his forehead. If they should be standing side by side now, Hawk would tower over his father. Never could he forget Cochise's fierce, dark face. He convinced himself that no one could possibly look at him and see on his own face the son of Cochise.

Perhaps he needed a breath of fresh air and some good food at the little place he'd found around the corner from the hotel. He didn't want to eat in the hotel dining room tonight. The little restaurant, El Cocina, served only the freshest vegetables seasoned with herbs, the way Solange prepared them back at the cabin.

Once he'd enjoyed a hearty meal, he might be able to get a good night's sleep. He needed a good night's sleep, to sweep from his mind what he'd done this afternoon to a man who didn't deserve it. Uncontrollable jealousy had ignited that fury in him, and he knew it now. But a strong man possessed a strong will, Hawk chided himself. He'd given way to raw, untamed instincts and he didn't like himself for it.

Had his old friend Troy been right when he swore that a pretty lady could cast a spell on a man? Troy swore it was true. He said that was why he preferred to be a bachelor and live alone. "That way I can do what I want when I want to. Besides, there ain't no woman going to put up with me and I'm sure not going to change," he'd firmly declared to Hawk.

As Hawk took the brush to his thick black hair, he pondered if this was what Gillian had done to him. Had she bewitched him with her breathtaking charms? He hadn't been the same since the moment he'd first encountered her. It had been different when he'd just observed her from the peak of the plateaus or seen her riding down in the canyons. But once he'd come close to her and they'd talked, sharing those precious, golden moments, Hawk was powerless to resist the beguiling effect she had on him.

He wondered now if that was why he'd seen that quizzical look on his mother's face once Gillian had entered his life. He'd never been able to mask his feelings from her. She could see right through him.

He put the brush down and turned to leave the room, making straight for the El Cocina. There was a brisk breeze flowing down into the valley from the mountains surrounding the town. He strolled along the street to enjoy it. The sounds of the town didn't bother him tonight.

The El Cocina's owners were warm, friendly people. As he entered the restaurant and took a table, the restauranteur greeted him. By the time he was eating the tasty food, Hawk felt relaxed. He'd wager that these people didn't see him as Apache. If they did, they didn't make him feel uncomfortable.

Hawk had not noticed the three bearded miners. Had he known that he was the topic of their conversation, he would not have been so relaxed.

The owners of the El Cocina, Matt and Lola Mathis, tried to make Hawk feel welcome in their establishment. Lola always gave him a generous portion, for she'd noticed how enthusiastically he'd eaten the first night he'd come into the restaurant.

Tonight, she didn't like some of their other patrons, and she told her husband so. "Those dudes back there are the rowdy sort, Matt. They are a foul-mouthed lot. Heard them talking about our young man over there. They are calling him a half-breed—an Apache."

Matt gave his wife an affectionate pat. "Well, dear—they are right about that. I would have to agree with them. I think he is."

"But, Matt, they weren't feeling like you are. They spit it out like it was filth."

A short time later when the miners paid their bill and sauntered by Hawk's table to leave, Lola Mathis was happy to see them go. Hawk did not even look up from his bread pudding.

The rest of the patrons in the place were regulars, so Lola could now relax. Hawk finished every bit of the pudding, then bid the Mathis couple good night and strolled out into the street. By now, there was no one on the streets. Everyone had gone home, Hawk noticed.

On the next street over were the taverns and the gaming halls, but Hawk had no intention of walking in that direction. As he turned the corner to go back to his hotel, he could hear the music from one of the nearby taverns blaring.

He started down the narrow side street which would take him back to his hotel. No lights burned in the small shops lining this street. Complete darkness consumed the area as

Hawk ambled along. He felt the need for the slow walk after all the food he'd eaten.

Hawk was totally unprepared for his attacker when he suddenly found himself pounced on. As clenched fists slammed at his face, he found himself rendered helpless by hands holding his two strong arms and hands behind his back.

He could not hold back a moan of pain as he felt the pounding blows to his gut and the sharp kick in his groin. He heard the sneering voice of a man spitting out at him, "Think you are as good as a white man, do you, half-breed? Well, when we're through with you, you'll know you're not! No goddamned Apache will ever be as good as the white man!"

He could not see for the blurring in his eyes. Somehow, he did manage to figure out that there were more than one—two, maybe, or three.

Hawk could not stand the punishment they were giving his strong body. In a fair fight he would have won over any of the three of them, but with their combined muscle and strength they had conquered him.

Giving a roar of boisterous laughter, the trio swaggered away, satisfied to have put the half-breed in his place, leaving the groaning Hawk in the darkness.

Another trio walked down the street, laughing in light-hearted camaraderie. Steve Lafferty's two comrades were curious about his fine ship and he'd been eager to oblige them by boasting that in twenty-four consecutive hours she could sail over three hundred and sixty miles. No vessel afloat could surpass that record.

One of the men gasped in disbelief. "Didn't know it was possible to go that fast."

"It is on my clipper ship." Steve laughed. "Want to sign on with me, guys? I will be needing some good men when I leave here."

A strange sound interrupted their conversation. They heard a soulful moan that sounded like a wounded animal.

"Did you hear what I heard?" Wayne asked.

"Sure did," Steve declared, starting to dash down the dark alley. The two others trailed behind Lafferty. They did not have to go too far before they came upon the limp, prostrate figure of a huge man lying helpless on the street.

"Holy Christ—someone really did a job on this poor bastard," Wayne declared, viewing Hawk's huge battered body.

Steve bent down and took the kerchief from his neck to wipe the man's blood-streaked face.

He called out to Hawk, "Can you hear me, fellow?"

The only response he got was a deep moan and a slight shake of Hawk's head. Steve assured him that they were there to help him and do him no harm. Somehow, Hawk sensed this.

At Steve's prodding, Hawk was able to give him a feeble reply that he lived at the hotel about a block away.

"Let's get him there so we can see just how bad he is hurt. We should send for Doctor Henry," Lafferty told his friends.

The three of them hoisted Hawk's limp body.

Once they arrived at the hotel, they ignored the staring people sauntering through the lobby. They wanted to get the injured man to the stairs and to his room.

Once they had Hawk on the bed, they worked in unison. One of them started removing his black leather boots while Steve got a basin of water and cloths to take over to the nightstand by the bed. Immediately, he began to apply the damp cloth to Hawk's bloodied, bruised face. Lafferty had doctored many of his crewmen when they were in port and ended up in fights in the local taverns. This poor man had endured one hell of a beating to his face, Steve realized.

It was a startling sight to Hawk when he opened his eyes to see that the man who was tending to his bruised face was Steve Lafferty—the man he'd seen with Gillian.

When he heard the other men discussing the possibility of calling in a doctor, he laboriously tried to lift himself up from the bed to assure them he needed no doctor.

"I'm pretty tough. I assure you I don't need a doctor. I'll be

233

all right. I'm most grateful for what you have done for me tonight."

"Lie down," Steve urged him, knowing that he was pushing himself to the limit. "You've nothing to prove to any of us."

Hawk had to admit he was as weak as a cat.

Steve and his companions stayed in the room with Hawk until they had satisfied themselves that he was all right. A good night's rest would put him back in shape except for a lot of soreness and aching muscles.

They all had a good laugh when Hawk was able to tell them that he, too, worked for the Southern Pacific Railroad as a scout.

"Well, I'll be a sonofabitch!" Wayne chuckled. "We were just taking care of our own and damned well didn't know it at the time."

One of the men pointed out to Lafferty that he wasn't going to get to bed as early as he'd intended so he could catch the early morning stagecoach to San Diego. Hawk insisted that they all take their leave. "I'm fine! I am going to feel terrible if you don't. You've done your good deed for me tonight and I owe all of you."

"Wasn't nothin'," Wayne assured him, moving out of his chair to stretch his legs.

Lafferty and the other railroad men got up out of their chairs. It was Lafferty who asked him, "If you are sure you're all right, then we shall take our leave so you can go to sleep. The rest is the tonic you need."

"I am sure, Lafferty," Hawk replied.

"Then we'll say good night, Hawk. Better luck than you've had tonight," Steve told him with one of his lighthearted Irish laughs.

"Let's hope so, Lafferty!" Hawk managed a little grin as the three of them marched out the door.

234

Part Three

The Restless Heart

Her heart's restless search
to fulfill her desires
chooses the one who
will share passion's fires
— Sheila Northcott

Chapter Thirty-One

Lafferty would not have felt so kindly toward the injured half-breed if he'd known that Hawk was as determined as he was to win the heart of Gillian Browne. All he knew was that he'd come across a man who had been unmercifully beaten.

Needless to say, he was still in need of sleep when he had to board the stagecoach for San Diego. Luckily for him, the coach was empty and he was the only passenger, so he could sprawl out on the seat and sleep.

Sleep was also a welcome luxury for Hawk. He took advantage of the time off he'd been given, caring not if he left his bed all day long. Its softness felt odd to Hawk's body and he pulled the quilts up over his shoulders and rolled over to drift off to sleep again.

When the noise from the street below his hotel window finally woke him up, it was late afternoon. Hawk was amazed to find that he could move much better than he'd expected. He sauntered over to the window to observe the parade of the street, then walked over to the washstand to pour some water into the basin and wash his face. He was ravenously hungry, but tonight he would not walk down any dark street here in Tucson. He'd eat right here, in the hotel dining room.

Something had happened last night to change Hawk's thinking about the white man. Three white men had helped him, out of the goodness of their hearts. How could he not have realized that he could enjoy a camaraderie with white men, as he did with Troy? Those three men had sat here in his room last night, enjoying a lighthearted conversation.

Maybe that was why he felt no qualms about walking alone into the spacious hotel dining room tonight. A new confidence in himself as a man in this white man's world had been born last night for Hawk. The three men had done more for him than they'd realized.

Solange would have been proud of her magnificent-looking son as he marched into the crowded dining room. With his head held high and proud, Hawk was ushered to one of the smaller tables, since he'd told the waiter he would be dining alone.

There were stares as his towering figure ambled by the tables, stares of glowing admiration from the ladies, both young and old. His impressive bronzed face with that jet-black hair and piercing black eyes were enough to draw attention. His height was enough to call attention from the gentlemen seated there in the dining room. Everything about him reflected his power and force.

By the time he was sitting at the table, he was feeling very pleased with himself. As he ate the good meal, a couple passed his table and the pretty young lady gave him a flirtatious smile.

He'd finished his meal and was enjoying one last cup of coffee when he observed a gentleman puffing on a long, narrow cheroot. Tomorrow he was going to purchase some of those cheroots, for he enjoyed the pungent aroma. But it was far more than just that, and Hawk knew it. He wanted to be like that very dignified gentleman. It was the same desire within Hawk to be like the Irishman, Steve Lafferty, so Gillian would be proud to accompany him in a buggy and be his lady.

An overwhelming feeling of loneliness washed over Helen this morning after Nancy and Gillian caught the early-morning stage to Maricopa County. It had been such a wonderful few weeks, reunited with her older sister, and Gillian was like a breath of fresh air. She wished that her Melissa possessed some of Gillian's fine traits. Gillian had been an inspiration for Helen, helping her to realize that all the luxuries she'd lavished on Melissa had not made her nicer or a better person. The future would be different, Helen secretly vowed.

She observed Kent and Melissa as they sat at the breakfast table. No one had to tell her that the two of them were glad Gillian and Nancy were gone. Helen said not a word as she went about her usual chores, but there was a smug smile on her face. There were going to be some changes made around this house, as of today, and she knew the two sitting at her table were not going to be pleased about them. She could already envision the cries of dismay and shock coming from Melissa when she was refused a new frock or slippers. Kent was going to start being a dutiful husband or he could find himself new lodgings, for she'd no longer continue to do his laundry and press his shirts.

No longer would those two be pampered as they had been in the past! They would do their fair share or they would do without. She'd made a decision while Nancy was here. Her marriage to Kent had not given her any pleasure for many years; she'd endured him for Melissa's sake.

The truth was she was alone now, even with the two of them here under her roof. If he were gone, she could survive. If he were gone, maybe she and Melissa could enjoy the pleasant mother-daughter relationship they'd had until Melissa was thirteen. Then it seemed Kent's influence began to make its mark on their daughter. Slowly but surely, as her admiration grew for Kent, it seemed to lessen for Helen. There was great pain to Helen as this happened, knowing how she'd labored to give her daughter so much.

Now that Nancy was gone, Helen would fill her days with her baking for the Old Pueblo Inn and make her deliveries herself. Only now those nice little fees she received from Melba Jackson were going to buy her some luxuries she'd yearned to have for so long.

Kent and Melissa sat at the kitchen table laughing and talking as though Helen were not even in the room, but it didn't disturb Helen—not this morning.

No longer did her heart hurt, for it was surprisingly cold!

The journey back to Maricopa County seemed to go faster than when Nancy and Gillian had traveled toward Tucson. Maybe it was because they were going home. The days were mild and the Arizona sun wasn't so hot. The nights had just a gentle chill.

As they rolled along the dusty trail, Nancy couldn't put her finger on it, but there was a change in Gillian. She seemed more grown up. Oh, they still talked and laughed in that easygoing way they'd always done, but Nancy felt there was a part of Gillian she was not sharing now.

Maybe she was having romantic feelings for young Lafferty. After all, they did see each other often, and he was enough to make any young lady fall in love with him. Maybe that was the secret mystery Gillian was masking and keeping to herself. Nancy supposed that was only natural when she recalled how she was when she'd first fallen in love with John. For the longest time, she could not confess to Helen that John had kissed her when they'd been out by the corral of her father's ranch.

What Nancy suspected was true. To Gillian, it seemed she'd entered a whole new world. She was not the girl who'd left the ranch and she would never be that girl again. Now she knew what it was to be loved by a man. The glowing embers of Steve Lafferty's lovemaking were with her still as she traveled back to the Foster ranch. Already, she ached for his strong arms to hold her and his sensuous lips to caress her. But these were thoughts she could not discuss with dear Mother Foster, or with anyone. These were too private and personal.

Did everyone feel this way, she wondered, when they were

in love? Was this the way Mother Foster had felt about John? She knew that her conception of love was different from Melissa Clayton's. While she'd claimed to be so in love with Caywood, Gillian had noticed in the tearoom that day in Tucson, Melissa's dark eyes were flirting with a couple of young men sitting at another table.

So consuming was her love for Steve Lafferty that no other man would draw her attention or her interest. Maybe there were different kinds of love for different people.

It was her private thoughts about Steve that made her drift into periods of sweet silence and brought a serene smile to her lovely face as she stared out the windows to gaze dreamily at the Arizona countryside.

She knew she'd be counting the days until Lafferty appeared at the Fosters' ranch. The days and the nights were not going to pass fast enough, she feared. She'd not find the contentment there as she had before he walked into her life.

When Gillian fell into her quiet mood, Nancy turned her own thoughts to John and what had been happening back at the ranch since she'd been gone. She just prayed those Apaches had hightailed it out of the county. Now that they were going back to the ranch, Nancy wondered if that young half-breed would be showing up. She'd make a point of asking John if he'd come around to see Gillian while they'd been away.

As much as she was beholden to him for rescuing Gillian that day in the pastureland, she'd have grave misgivings about Gillian becoming involved with him. Oh, he was a grand-looking fellow and a polite, well-mannered man, but the mere fact of his Apache blood was a barrier he could never break down. Nancy could never forget that it was a band of Apaches who had killed Gillian's parents.

But she also knew that passion and desire made many a young person forget things like that. Dear God, poor Helen was a prime example of that! All the gossip and rumors going around the countryside about the dapper Kent Clayton didn't stop her for a minute once she fell head over heels in love with

241

him. Neither did their parents' warnings do any good. Nancy's last-minute plea had also fallen on a deaf ear; no one could have saved Helen from making her mistake. No one had paid dearer, either, than Helen herself.

Like a bolt of lightning, it hit Nancy that John would not be expecting them to return for another week, so he'd not be in town to meet their stagecoach. But she wasn't going to fret about that. They'd hitch a ride out to the ranch.

Ah, it was going to be good to be back home again and see her dear John. She'd missed him!

Chapter Thirty-Two

Hawk welcomed the message for him to report to Warner Barstow's office two days after the beating had taken place. There were still a lot of aching muscles and stiffness in trying to move around, but Hawk was hoping the summons from Warner was to inform him to go out on another scouting job. He was ready to leave Tucson and ride those trails and canyons and breathe the fresh air of the countryside.

The city smothered him and he felt the need of the verdant dense forests and the majestic mountains with their winding narrow trails. Out there he could clear the cobwebs from his brain and think straighter, he told himself. Hawk knew now that big cities and towns were not for him and never would be!

He flinched with discomfort as he pulled up his pants and bent down to pull on his boots. Those bastards had really hit him with some mighty blows to cause this much pain for this long. He only wished he knew who they were and had gotten the chance to get a better view of their faces so he could have known who his enemy was. As it was, he could pass them in the street and he'd not know them if he was looking directly at them.

Once he was dressed and went to the livery to get his pinto, the discomforts were forgotten and he found moving around less painful. Once he sat in the saddle, he felt more like himself. He'd ride that soreness out!

By the time he arrived at Warner's office, Hawk was feeling much better.

"Trust you've had a nice stay in our city, young man?" the balding Barstow inquired.

"Yes, sir—had a real nice time taking in the sights around Tucson," Hawk told him.

"Well, it's time for me to put you back to work, son," Warner told him.

"I'm ready, sir."

"Well, we've had some rumors that Apaches were gathering some ten miles from where the tracks are now being laid. The trail between here and Phoenix seems to be our trouble point."

"You want me to leave today, sir?"

"Yes, I do, Hawk. Come on over here and I'll lay this map out for you to examine. I want you to scout around the territory for some twenty miles from this point here." Warner pointed to the spot that gave him concern.

Hawk looked over his shoulder and studied the area. He knew that the Apaches could pick such spots for a surprise attack on the railroad workers.

"I know the terrain, sir, and I'll check it out for you."

"I'll be looking forward to a report from you, Hawk."

"I'll be on my way then. I'll just hope the rumors you've heard are false. But if they aren't, then I'll try to find the Apaches and where they're camping."

"Good luck, Hawk. God go with you on your journey."

"Thank you, Mr. Barstow." Hawk turned to leave the office and be on his way.

Barstow watched the impressive, towering half-breed man walk out his door. He admired the young man very much. He wanted to help this young man make a future for himself, a future that would reach beyond this assignment. Joe Hawk had much to offer if only he was given the right opportunity.

He knew the plight of the half-breed men like Hawk. Life wasn't easy for most of them. But no one had to tell him that

Hawk was a very clever young man. One had only to talk to him to know that Hawk wasn't the most talkative person, but when he did talk his conversation was not of a frivolous nature. Joe Hawk was a very serious-minded young man. Warner wondered just who his mother was. He was sure she was a beautiful woman who had been taken captive by an Indian. Maybe someday, if he was around Hawk long enough, he'd find out about his background. He hoped so, for the young man had intrigued him since the first minute he'd met him.

As Hawk untied the reins of his horse and leaped up into the saddle, guiding the pinto into action, he questioned some things about Warner Barstow. He liked the man, and from the first minute they'd met, Hawk had felt the genuine warmth of Barstow. But never did he address him as Joe. It had always been Hawk. It was as if Warner knew that the name Joe was not his true name.

Hawk was the name Solange had given him at the time of his birth. He was the one who had changed it to Joe Hawk. Perhaps he had been wrong to do so. If it was good enough for his mother, then it should have been a good enough name for him.

It was only after he'd met Gillian that he began to think differently about his name and about so many things that had never concerned him before.

Now that he thought about it, everything in his life had changed from the minute he'd met her! Was it wrong for a woman to cast such a bewitching spell as she had on him? Was that beautiful girl with her hair of flaming fire a witch, possessing magical powers to render a man helpless? Sometimes, he felt that way. It was the only time that he could recall that he was not strong and determined. Gillian could make him weak with savage desire.

Never had he known such a wild, wonderful sensation could be experienced until he'd felt the sweet warmth from the nearness of her body.

By the time Hawk had gathered up his gear at the hotel and had it packed on the feisty little pinto's back, he was ready to make his departure from Tucson.

Hawk already knew where he would make his campsite, but between now and then, he had a good two or three hours riding.

As he left the outskirts of the city behind him, Hawk's spirits were already beginning to lift. He inhaled the refreshing air of the countryside. Lord, it seemed good to him to be riding his pinto across the land once again. It was good to see the tall green trees of the nearby forests.

Dotting the knee-high grassland, the heads of blossoming wildflowers popped up to greet him. When he spied lovely blue-violet flowers, he thought of Gillian and a pleasant smile came to his bronzed face as he rode along.

His heart cried out his love for her and he could not help wondering if he was dwelling in a foolish fancy to expect that she could love him as he loved her.

Solange had always told him that anything was possible if he wanted it badly enough!

But was that actually always true? Hawk had never questioned his mother's wisdom or her sage words, but he wasn't completely convinced she was right.

By the time he'd traveled for two hours, the sun was setting. Hawk reined his horse to a particular grove of trees which he knew would be the perfect spot to make his camp for the night. He knew there was a nice little spring a short distance away, and he remembered that crystal-clear water, so cold and refreshingly pure.

Hawk wasn't the only one who enjoyed those pleasant waters. He led Tache there to quench his thirst before unpacking the gear. Tache took his fill, giving a delighted whinney before Hawk led him away.

By the time he'd secured the horse to the trunk of one of the saplings near the spot where he would be placing his bedroll and making his campfire, all the marvelous noises of the woods and countryside could be heard.

Here in this wide-open country was where he belonged. No longer did he feel out of his element and his broad chest swelled as he inhaled the freshness of the verdant pine trees and the fragrance of the wildflowers. After the many hours of riding from Tucson, he felt no aches and pains from the brutal beating he'd suffered. What overwhelming hatred must have possessed those three miners as their fists slammed him with their mighty blows.

He was happy that his long ride through the countryside had yielded up no sign of any renegade Apaches. Perhaps they had all drifted to the south, Hawk decided.

As he reached the spot where he planned to make his campsite, he was already anticipating lying in his bedroll to gaze up at the starlit skies.

Nothing tasted finer to him than some game roasted over a campfire or the coffee brewed, black and strong. There was no reason for a man ever to go hungry in this countryside with all the fowl and wildlife in the woods and the fish flourishing in the streams and creeks.

Back in Tucson, as Helen Clayton guided her buggy homeward, she was feeling a state of elation she had not expected to know when she delivered her usual order to Melba.

It was Melba's usual routine to invite her into her office to pay her, but she was utterly stunned when she was offered a partnership in the inn if she would take over the full responsibility of the inn's kitchen.

It was an offer she couldn't turn down and the answer to many problems, mainly her trifling husband. Life was too short to endure him the rest of her life and she could never forgive him for what he'd done to their daughter.

Seeing him ogling Gillian had convinced her that she had to be rid of him. While her older sister had not said a word to her, she knew that was why she'd suddenly decided to return to the ranch. She could not fault her for that.

She'd left the inn, promising to give Melba her answer in a couple of days, but she already knew what that answer would be.

She could not wait to see the reaction in Melissa's eyes when she announced to her that she was to become a business lady like Melba Jackson!

But when she arrived, she would not find her daughter at home. Melissa was taking a buggy ride with Caywood. As they rode around the outskirts of town as twilight descended, Melissa sat beside her beau feeling very smug and satisfied about the little deed she'd done today after Helen had left.

Last night after dinner she'd gone to her room to write a vicious letter to Gillian Browne. Long before Gillian left Tucson, Melissa had determined to have her revenge on the backwoods girl who'd dared to stand up to her.

The visit of her aunt and Gillian had been unpleasant for Melissa from the day they'd arrived. That first evening, when Caywood had come by and openly admired the auburn-haired girl wearing her cast-off frock, she had seethed inwardly until she thought she'd explode at the dining table that night.

She resented being put in her place on a couple of occasions by Gillian. Melissa found her to be too sickeningly sweet for her liking.

When her dark, envious eyes watched that handsome Irish captain by Gillian's side being so attentive and enamored that he completely ignored her presence in the parlor that afternoon, a rage of jealousy was stirred.

What did this little backwoods girl have that she did not have, she'd wondered a dozen times, looking in her full-length mirror. Each time the answer came back to her that she was just as pretty as Gillian Browne.

Her resentment for Gillian mounted when she chanced to see her own father staring lustily at her across their dinner table. In that moment, she hated Gillian with all her heart. The look she'd seen in his eyes was not the same as the way he looked at her or her mother. She knew the look, for she'd seen it in that rascal Caywood's eyes.

That night she'd gone to her room, flung herself across her

bed, and cried until there were no tears left. She vowed that one way or the other she'd break Gillian's heart as Gillian had caused hers to ache and hurt.

What she'd done today should do just that, she figured. The letter she'd carefully written last night was sent off today. When Gillian got that letter and read her lies about the handsome captain, she'd be devastated, Melissa was sure.

To soothe her conscience, Melissa told herself that in part it was true, for she had seen the captain walking down the street with the strawberry-blond daughter of Howard Curtis. Virginia Curtis was acting awfully chummy and familiar.

Melissa had never met the young lady, for they moved in different circles, but she knew her on sight. No one could mistake that unusual shade of hair.

What Melissa could not know, having stood a short distance away to observe them passing by in the Curtis buggy, was that Steve Lafferty had accepted a ride to the stagecoach station with Virginia Curtis since Howard Curtis was unable to drive him.

Neither could she nor anyone else know that when Virginia tried to play the coquette, Steve found her outrageously obvious. With expert finesse, Lafferty let her know by the end of the ride that he was to be married as soon as he returned from San Diego.

It was a very quiet, stunned Virginia Curtis who stammered a fond farewell to Lafferty as he leaped out of the buggy at the stagecoach station. Gillian was the only woman Steve wanted, so he felt no need or desire to dally with the pretty Virginia.

But Melissa was not privy to all this. Her eyes saw only what she wanted to see. This was what her letter related to Gillian.

Caywood didn't know why Melissa was in such a pleasant and agreeable mood this evening. She'd not been so sweet and lovable with him for a long, long time.

He certainly planned to enjoy every precious moment while it lasted!

Chapter Thirty-Three

It was a strange sight to Kent Clayton to come home to a cold, dark house. When he entered the front door, his nose did not smell the delicious aromas of Helen's cooking. It was enough to startle him; this had never happened before. Helen was such a dependable person, always there to greet him with a good meal to fill his belly.

He wandered into the neat parlor. It seemed very lonely and desolate without the lamplight gleaming. The same was true when he roamed into her kitchen, and as he went into the hallway he wondered if he would find Melissa upstairs. As he mounted the second landing of the house, he saw the glimmer of light under the doorway of his daughter's bedroom.

He gave a light rap on her door and when the door opened, he could tell from the look on his daughter's face that she was as perplexed as he was by the absence of Helen.

"Daddy, Momma isn't home," she mumbled apprehensively, though she could not believe that Helen was not there. Tonight was so startlingly different that they were both a little stunned.

"I see she isn't. When did you get home, baby?"

"Well, Caywood took me out for a drive and I guess he brought me back about five-thirty."

"Five-thirty? Can't figure where Helen would be after that time," he drawled. The two of them went downstairs and lit the lamps in the parlor, as well as the kitchen.

As Helen reined her buggy into the drive, she smiled, for she knew she had surely set the atmosphere of confusion in her household tonight. She didn't care. It was no more than they deserved. Let the two of them hurt as they'd hurt her.

She was wearing the attractive bottle-green bonnet with the wide bow tied to the side of her face. She knew that the gentle breeze she felt caressing her cheek was making the pretty green-and-gold plumes flow gently. Already, she was anticipating wearing the pretty rich green frock she'd bought. There was also a reticule to match the bonnet and her new dress. Never had she been so extravagant and so completely selfish, buying only for herself.

She had surely put Minnie Collins into a state of shock as she'd made all her purchases at the dress shop. The two of them had enjoyed the hour they'd spent together and as Helen was preparing to leave, Minnie suggested that she close her shop a little early so that the two of them could go next door to Hattie's Cake Shop for a piece of cake and some coffee.

"Helen, come on. It's long overdue that you let that family of yours wait on you once in a while," Minnie pleaded with her old friend. Often Minnie had thought that it would have been better if Helen had been made a widow as she had been, early in life. Minnie'd opened her little dress shop and never sought to marry again. She'd never regretted the decision. She and Melba Jackson had both proved that a woman could be successful in business. A man didn't have a corner on the market.

Gathering up her packages, Helen agreed and Minnie hurriedly began to close her shop. When all the lights were dimmed and the sign was put on the door announcing that the shop was closed for the night, Minnie put her key into the lock and smiled. "Shall we go?"

"I'm ready if you are. Besides, I've just realized that my shopping has made me hungry." Helen gave a girlish giggle. She suddenly realized that she'd made herself a prisoner in her neat little house far too long. She would not do that ever again.

The two of them were like schoolgirls again, giggling and talking as they drank their coffee and ate the tasty apricot pie. Helen was enjoying herself so much that time was forgotten. She gave no thought that it was past the time she would have normally been setting her table for dinner.

By the time she turned her buggy toward home, there was not one cent left in her reticule. This did not disturb her either, because she would have another nice fee in a couple of days when she took her next order to the inn.

As she guided the mare into the drive and dismounted from the buggy, she thought about how, a short time ago, she would have been rushing into the house to announce her news to Kent and Melissa. But tonight she had no intention of saying anything to either one of them about it.

No, this was going to be her little secret for a while, she thought to herself. Gathering up her bundles, she moved through the darkness toward her front door. As she unhurriedly strolled down the pathway, she thought about her life and her marriage. A lifetime of devotion and love had not brought her any respect or love from her pretty daughter. Melissa's loyalty had gone to a man who'd done little more than sire her. So what was the secret to win a degree of respect, Helen wondered? It certainly wasn't enough to give unselfishly of oneself, for that's what she'd done for over eighteen years.

Lights blazed throughout the house as she let herself into the small hallway. Putting her packages down, she locked and secured the door for the night. She heard the slow mumbling sound of Kent and Melissa's voices coming from the parlor.

When they turned to see her standing in the doorway, Melissa's eyes went immediately to the packages. Her lovely face instantly brightened as she greeted Helen. "Momma, you're home!" She leaped up from the settee eagerly anticipating that the contents of those packages were for her.

"Yes, dear. I'm home and I'm tired, for I've had a long, busy afternoon, so I'm going right on up to my room."

Kent leaped up from the cozy overstuffed chair. "And what about our supper, Helen? We've not eaten yet." His handsome face was etched in a puzzled frown.

Helen shrugged her shoulders and began to move on toward the stairway. "Well, dear, Melissa can fix the two of you something. It's about time she started preparing herself to be a wife and know about cooking in a kitchen, wouldn't you say? I was cooking when I was much younger than she is now."

"Momma—what about you?" Melissa asked.

"What about me, honey?"

"You've not eaten yet either, have you?"

Slowly, Helen turned back around to face her perplexed young daughter. "As a matter of fact I have. I enjoyed a nice repast with my good friend Minnie. By the way, she asked about you, Melissa. So I'm not hungry. You two just don't worry about me. You just get your dad fed, Melissa, and yourself." Helen turned her back to her daughter, for she did not want to break out into laughter. She found it very gratifying to have put her husband in a state of confusion as he'd done to her all these many years.

"You—you mean I'm to cook our dinner, Momma? You're not going to prepare our meal?" Melissa stammered.

Helen turned and smiled. "I'm saying exactly that, my darling. You can do it, Melissa. Tonight, I'm turning my kitchen over to you and I'm sure your father will enjoy it very much."

"I—I don't know about that. I'm not the good cook that you are, Momma."

"Well, honey—you couldn't possibly be since you've not had the experience, but that is exactly why you should start practicing, isn't it?"

By the time Helen reached her bedroom, she was wondering why she'd not take this attitude with her family long ago. Why, Melissa was almost ready to shed tears, and the helpless look on her face was something Helen had not seen in a long, long time.

She turned up the wick of the lamp on her nightstand and

removed her pretty new bonnet. Her lovely new frock was laid out across the bed and also the new deep green reticule was taken out of the box. She admired all the fancy items she'd purchased. She'd wear them when she went to the inn day after tomorrow to deliver her order to Melba. Already, she'd made her decision to accept her offer.

All kinds of thoughts paraded through her mind. She wondered what Nancy would think when she wrote her that she was going to be a partner of the grand inn, the Old Pueblo. Helen considered it quite a feather in her hat since all she'd ever been was just a housewife and mother. She felt an overwhelming surge of pride that Melba had made her such an offer. She knew that such an opportunity would never come her way again so she could not possibly refuse it.

Once she was through admiring all the lovely things on her bed, she put them away and turned down her bed. With her nightgown and robe on, she sat down on the side of her bed to listen to the various noises from the kitchen below. Melissa was obviously in the process of attempting to cook supper. She was curious to know how it would turn out and what she would fix for Kent.

As she always did after she'd received her pay from Melba for the bakery goods sold to her, she made the entry in her little book. Realizing today what she was able to purchase for herself, she knew the amounts she'd spent on Melissa during the last year. Three orders a week yielded her a nice little sum of money. All that money had gone to keep her daughter dressed beautifully and a few attractive articles for her home.

As she was about to replace the little black book in her nightstand drawer, Kent stormed into the bedroom. He was in a fit of rage as he lashed out at her, "I'd like an explanation about all this tonight, Helen. If you were a drinking woman, I'd swear that you and Minnie had had too many glasses of sherry. I know better than that! In case you're interested, you've got a daughter down there in the kitchen in tears. She burned every damned thing she tried to cook and I'm going out to get myself a decent meal."

Helen sat there on the bed calmly without jumping up to rush to Melissa's rescue as she knew he expected her to do. In a low, cool voice, she replied, "Well, you just go on out, Kent. You do most nights anyway. And as for Melissa—she'll find a fresh-baked berry pie and a loaf of fresh-baked bread, so she won't starve."

"Damn you, Helen! Have you gone crazy?" Kent paced nervously, glaring angrily at her.

"Hardly that, Kent! I've just decided that things are going to go my way—not your and Melissa's way around here. It's as simple as that and if you don't like it, then you can get out! So can she! I'll not slave for you anymore." Her eyes locked with him and he saw the firm determination there that he'd never seen before. She meant exactly what she was saying.

For once, Kent's silken tongue was silent. This side of Helen Clayton he'd never seen or known before!

Chapter Thirty-Four

It did not surprise Helen that her husband had not come home all night. She had anticipated that he would go to his current lady friend to spend the night. No longer did it disturb her as it had over the years when she'd endured his philandering almost from the time they'd married.

But what had amazed her was the changed air about her daughter. Helen had not received such a friendly greeting from her daughter in a long, long time as she helped herself to a cup of coffee before taking her seat at the kitchen table.

A short time later, a sullen-faced Kent Clayton ambled through the back door and marched through the kitchen on his way upstairs to change his clothes before going to work. He said not a word to her or Melissa. Helen turned to glance in her daughter's direction. For the first time she saw the way Melissa was looking at him—with utter disgust and contempt!

Maybe now, Helen told herself, Melissa would quit worshipping this man who did not deserve it! Something had happened the night before when she'd left the two of them to fend on their own. God, she should have done it much sooner!

It was nice for Helen to hear her daughter offer to help her clean up the kitchen after she'd finished breakfast.

"Sure you can, honey." Helen accepted her offer. "It would help me get ahead with my baking."

In a meek, soft voice, Melissa remarked, "Guess I have never realized, Momma, just how much baking you do to buy all those nice things for me and this house."

Helen told her daughter, "When you love your home and your daughter, it's a labor of love, dear. At least, that's the way I felt."

It was at this moment that Kent walked into the kitchen. He felt the chill in the air as he passed his wife and his daughter, Melissa.

After Melissa had helped her mother in the kitchen, she excused herself to go up to her room. When she had closed her bedroom door, she flung herself across the bed and gave way to the flood of tears wanting to erupt since she'd seen her father come through the kitchen door. Dear God, she wondered, how many times had her mother put up with that after he'd been gone all night to some floozie's place? To think that she'd ever admired him and praised him, when it was her mother who'd deserved that loyalty!

But that was all over now. Last night, he'd revealed the true side of his character and her eyes had been opened with a rude awakening as to what a miserable fraud Kent Clayton was. She could do nothing about the wrongs she'd done to her mother, but she could certainly start making up for them, she vowed.

She lay there on her bed and allowed the tears of her pain to flow out. When there were no more tears to cry, Melissa slowly rose up from her bed to go wash her face and get dressed. By the time she'd dressed and brushed her long black hair, she realized she felt happier and more contented with herself than she had for a long time.

No longer was disillusionment clouding her thoughts. She could admit that she'd been a despicable little bitch to her mother and she regretted the letter she'd sent to Gillian. There was nothing she could do about the letter, she realized. Oh, she could write another letter, but the damage would be done once Gillian read the first one.

At least, she could make up to her hardworking mother for

the wrongs she'd done to her, and no longer did she worship her father. Kent Clayton was her hero no longer!

Over a hundred miles separated Nancy Foster from Helen, but that made no difference when you cared for someone as Nancy did for her younger sister. Her thoughts were of Helen as she tossed the grain to her flock of chickens. Maybe she didn't have the fancy little cottage Helen had in Tucson, but she had the love of a good, devoted man. She would not trade John for a dozen Kent Claytons.

Having promised her good husband some fried chicken for his supper, she looked over the flock to see which one she was going to choose for their supper tonight. Nothing pleased John so much as her fried chicken, her special cream gravy and flaky golden biscuits. This was what he was to have tonight.

She looked toward the mountains to see a haze gathered there. She found it hard to believe what their neighbor had told them the other day when he'd passed their way, since it was still so mild down here in the valley. He'd been up in the mountains hunting wild turkey, and snow had begun to fall before he came back down.

This had to be a strange part of the country, with flowers still blooming in the valley while only a short distance away there was snowfall in those mountains.

Up in those mountains where Nancy gazed, another woman roamed the grounds of her cabin, feeding the wild birds and her pet creatures of the woods. Solange's basket was filled with seeds and bread crumbs, along with the little balls of suet she placed for the birds' delight. She also filled all the containers with fresh water for the creatures of her woods to drink.

The aroma of the piñon wood burning in her stove permeated the air with its special scent. By the time she returned to her cabin she knew the water in her teakettle would

259

be steaming hot and ready for her to brew a cup of tea.

The repeated blows of an ax across the way told her that Troy was cutting firewood for the cold nights ahead. Hawk had provided her with an ample supply before he left.

At first, she'd worried about how Hawk would meet the challenge of his new world, but she'd come to terms with that, and she knew that she could live her own life without Hawk if she must. Those first weeks were the hard ones to adjust to, she realized now.

Besides, there was Little Bear now to lavish her attentions on, and he enjoyed every minute of all that love she had to give him. In turn, he gave so generously of his devotion to Solange. He was her constant shadow!

He'd followed each step she'd taken this morning on her jaunt around the ground and she felt sorry for the little pup, for he was breathing hard after keeping up with her. She picked him up to place him in her empty basket as she started toward her cabin.

Little Bear snuggled in the basket, grateful for the comfort of being carried back to the house. She looked down at the soft brown furry pup resting so cozily in her basket as she went toward her cabin and smiled. Nothing was more gratifying than love, whether it came from a small creature like Little Bear, a devoted son, or a man!

Now that she had made the full circle of her grounds and stood by the front step of her cabin, she was more than ready for tea. When she had rewarded herself with a couple of cups of her brewed tea, she prepared her iron kettle with water over the hot coals of her fireplace, for it was here that she would be slowly cooking the fine hen Troy had brought her yesterday. With her own herbs of tarragon, parsley, and chervil in the steaming water, she would cook the hen until it was tender. To that, she would add her egg noodles. She only wished that Hawk were here to share the fine feast she would have ready some six or seven hours from now.

As she set her cup in the dishpan and gathered together the

bowl and the ingredients she'd need to make noodles, her thoughts remained on Hawk and that world so strange to him. She hoped he was enjoying the challenge and proving to himself that he could live in that world. Solange did not want him to remain all the days of his life up here in the mountains and never know about the world outside his beloved woods. Hawk must not settle for that, she fervently prayed.

She began making her dough for the noodles to be dropped in the simmering juices of the chicken seasoned with the herbs she'd grown in her garden. She'd learned the recipe back in France, and she'd never tasted homemade noodles that excelled hers.

She happened to glance out her kitchen window as she was kneading the ball of dough to see that the snowflakes were falling faster and heavier now. It mattered not to her if it snowed. So she began to flatten the dough so she could cut the long strips. A smile came to her face as she noticed Little Bear curled up on the rug in front of the hearth, sleeping. She could not believe how he'd grown in such a short time. One day he would no longer be Little Bear, but Big Bear.

By the time she'd cut the last strip of dough, Solange broke into singing one of the old French songs she'd learned so long ago, back in her native land. Why should she not feel happy and contented, she thought to herself? She had a warm, comfortable cabin and good food cooking in her pot. Little Bear was there to keep her from being lonely and entertaining her with his antics. Just outside her back door, she had placed a bottle of wine to be chilled by the cold winds blowing through the tall, towering pines at the back of her cabin. She was anticipating a most pleasant evening.

But a sudden, sharp rap on her cabin door brought an abrupt halt to Solange's singing. She wiped the dough from her hands with the dishtowel as she moved to answer the door.

"Who is it?" she insisted on knowing before she released the locks.

"Troy, Solange!" His urgent voice called out to her that

something was wrong.

Without further hesitation, she unlocked her door to find Troy standing there with another man. It was obvious that the man leaning against Troy was injured. His fine-featured face grimaced with pain as his eyes met hers. She quickly urged Troy to bring him into her cabin.

"We were closer to your place than mine, Solange; that's why I brought him here. Stepped into a damned trap back there in the woods and really messed up one of his feet. Poor devil!" Troy told her as he gasped for breath to support the injured man. Solange saw the bloodstains on his pants and knew the damage one of those awful traps could do to a beast or a man. Her husband, Tim, had once fallen victim to one of them. She wasted no time getting together her ointments, clean cloths, and a teakettle of hot water.

In an authoritative voice which urged Troy to obey her without question, Solange ordered him, "Get his pants off, Troy."

The injured man's attention was distracted from his pain by the sight of the most beautiful woman his eyes had ever beheld. He'd watched her taking full charge from the minute they'd entered the cabin and it was easy to forget pain when a woman as beautiful as this one moved with such divine grace. His eyes had devoured the lovely soft curves of a small, petite body with her glossy thick braid of hair hanging down her back. What was such a glorious creature as this doing here in a desolate, isolated woods, obviously all alone?

The injured French Canadian found that hard to fathom. But then, how had *he* happened to drift this far away from his own home? Destiny, he supposed.

Aptly, she went about the task of cleansing his wound. It amazed Gaston Dion that she didn't flinch at the sight of it, for it was an ugly wound. He'd gritted his teeth not to give way to the feel of her gentle touch as she'd applied the ointment and wrapped his foot with the strips of cloth.

When she was finished, she rose up to take her teakettle

back to the wood stove. "It is late, Troy, and I've a delicious supper cooking, so you might as well stay."

"Don't have to tell me that, Solange. It smells good. By the way, think I better introduce you to this man you just doctored. This is Gaston Dion. He's a trapper."

She turned to see his grateful, admiring eyes staring at her. A friendly smile warmed her lovely face as she responded, "Welcome to my home, Monsieur Dion. I am Solange Touraine."

"*Merci*, Madame Touraine, for what you have done for me this night. You are a most kind, generous lady and I'll forever be grateful to you. Perhaps I can repay you some way in the future," Gaston declared. He found it impossible to take his eyes from her lovely face.

"Please—here in the woods we are very informal. I am Solange and you shall be Gaston, is that not so, Troy?" She gave a lighthearted, gay trill of laughter. She liked this man, Gaston. He had a kindly air about him and she saw a sincere honesty in his black eyes. There was something else which Solange had never expected to feel or experience again: she was instantly attracted to this handsome French Canadian.

He stroked his silvery beard as he looked in Troy's direction to say, "I'd say you should agree with the lady, Troy. I know I shall."

The three of them broke into laughter. Solange walked to her kitchen table and gathered up the strips of dough to place in her kettle in the hearth.

"Oh, Solange—I've not smelled food so good in a long, long time," Gaston said.

"And there is also a bottle of wine chilling just outside my door," she said.

A broad grin was on Troy's face as he told Solange, "Damned if it wouldn't be great if old Hawk was here tonight with us."

"Yes, I would like that, too, Troy."

An apprehensive look was on Gaston's face as he asked, "And who is Hawk?"

263

"That's Solange's son, Gaston," Troy enlightened him.

Gaston heaved a sigh of relief, for he had feared that they were speaking of her husband. "Ahhh, *oui!* It would be nice for your son to be here!"

Solange wore a sly smile as she measured the handsome stranger's face, for she noted the sudden changed expression on his face.

It delighted her that he felt this way!

Chapter Thirty-Five

Outside Solange's cabin, the snow fell heavily and the chill wind whistled through the tall trees. The creatures of the woods had sought refuge from the cold night air by scurrying to their nests and shelters. It was ghostly quiet outside the cabin, but inside, three people were thoroughly enjoying themselves.

Gaston Dion was enjoying himself so much that he'd forgotten the pain in his foot. He'd not enjoyed such a delicious meal in so long he could not remember when it was. To eat so much good food and enjoy the company of such an intriguing woman was more than he could have dreamed of experiencing this night. Crazy as it might seem, he was glad fate had placed him in the wrong spot and caused him to make a false move and step into a trap. Otherwise, he would not have met Solange Touraine!

He would have regretted that the rest of his life. In fact, he was already making his plans to try to woo and win this pretty lady. Ladies had always found him attractive and Gaston was very self-assured. As he'd drifted around the country, he'd never had trouble finding some lovely lady who was willing to give him the affection he wanted. Now, this lady was different. This was a woman he'd dreamed about finding but never expected to discover on the face of this earth.

She was a rare jewel, the hot-blooded French Canadian thought as he admired her lovely face and sensuous body. But there was more to Solange Touraine; Gaston had decided that almost from the moment Troy had brought him inside the cabin. She was a woman of strength and courage. This lady was no shrinking violet. She had taken charge and attended to his wound, and the ugly sight didn't give her a case of the vapors. He admired that!

He had no use for weak, spineless ladies like so many he'd met since coming to this part of the country. He saw much suffering and pain in her eyes and this whetted his curiosity.

No one had to tell Gaston that he was no longer the randy young rake he'd once been, but he was fired with a desire and passion that he'd not known for a long time. He wondered if Solange sensed the yearning beating so strong within his broad, husky body.

Solange sensed that Troy was suddenly getting nervous about what to do. The hour was growing late, but he was hesitating to return to his own home and leave her here alone with the injured Gaston.

She knew she must ease his troubled mind, for she had no fear of Gaston Dion. After all, she had dealt with the fierce Cochise! There was nothing about this French Canadian that stirred any apprehensions in her.

"Come, Troy—help me with these dishes and I'll let you go out on the porch to get the bottle of wine. I think there is enough for us to have one more glass." She turned to Gaston to say, "You see, I boss Troy as I would my son Hawk if he were here."

Gaston returned her smile with a warm one of his own, but he said not a word. It seemed to him that their eyes met with understanding, so no words were necessary. Solange was thinking the same thing as she turned to follow Troy.

Once they were in her small kitchen, she whispered softly to Troy, "It is all right, Troy. I will be fine. Gaston is a good man, I can tell. Besides, I have Little Bear here to protect me."

"Are you sure, Solange? If something happened, Hawk

would kill me! I know it and so do you."

"Hawk will not kill you, Troy, for he will have no reason to do so," she assured him. A more serious look came on her face as she added, "Troy, there is no man I shall ever have any fear of the rest of my life after all those months with Cochise."

A sober look etched Troy's face as he listened to her. He still found it overwhelming and amazing that such a delicate-looking lady could have endured all those months in an Apache camp as the squaw of Cochise and come out of it all as Solange had.

A compassionate look of admiration and understanding radiated on Troy's face as he looked at Solange. He'd never known anyone like her and he knew he'd probably never meet anyone like her for the rest of his life, up here on these mountains.

"Guess I just tend to forget, Solange. I just look at you and I see a tiny lady I must protect for my good friend, Hawk. I forget how very brave you are."

"I can't think of a nicer thing any young man could say to me, Troy, and I know Hawk will be very grateful to you for feeling this way," she told the young half-breed. "It—it makes me love you so much. It's a wonderful gift to have such a caring friend."

Troy went out on her small back porch to refill their glasses as Solange had requested and he returned to her front room, feeling free now to drink this last glass of wine and return to his own cabin. Solange could take care of herself. He had nothing to worry about, he realized.

When he took the last sip of his wine and turned to tell Gaston he would come by tomorrow, he knew his fears had been ridiculous. With great effort, Gaston sat up to extend his hand in a friendly gesture of farewell to Troy. "I owe you, my young friend. I thank you very much for what you did for me today. It will not be forgotten," Gaston told him.

A pleasant tranquility washed over Troy as he rode home. He could not recall an evening when he'd enjoyed himself more than he had tonight, and he wished Hawk had been there to share it, too. How nice that would have been!

By the time he'd secured his horse in the barn and walked the short distance to his cabin, the snow was falling more heavily. By morning the grounds were going to be covered with a few inches of snow. Before he went inside, he gathered up an armful of logs to bank up his fireplace.

He was pleasantly surprised to find that his little cabin felt warm as he walked inside. He placed the logs on the smoldering embers and quickly the logs began to spark with flames from the hot coals. A pleasant warmth consumed Troy as he started to undress. He was ready to get in his comfortable bed, for the hour was late. Usually, he would have been in bed an hour or two ago.

The late night hour did not bother Steve Lafferty as he sat in his familiar cozy cabin. To finally be back aboard his ship was sheer delight!

That endless stagecoach ride was enough to convince him that he was not meant to be on land. Just sitting in that coach, riding all those miles, was enough to drive him crazy with boredom. All the gold in the world would never persuade him to take on another assignment like this one with the Southern Pacific.

The truth was, he would have been tempted not even to return to Arizona Territory to collect his fee. He could always make arrangement for that. But what he could not arrange without returning to Maricopa County was claiming the woman he loved. He could not bear to think about pulling away from these shores without her aboard his ship with him.

Today, he had watched the last piece of cargo being unloaded from the hold of his ship. His obligation to the railroad had been fulfilled. He was free now! God, it was a good feeling!

After he and his first mate had shared supper, he'd taken a stroll around the deck and stood by the railing to gaze across the moonlit harbor. Lord, it was a beautiful sight! If only Gillian were standing there with him, his arm encircling her tiny waist, he would have been the happiest man in all the world!

When he finally turned away from the rail and went below to his cabin, the ache did not ease, for Gillian's lovely vision seemed to be there, too. He'd love to see that lovely nude body of hers lying on his oversized bed, her auburn hair fanned out on the pillow and her lips beckoning to be kissed.

He still could not figure out what the magic was about this tiny miss that so entranced him from the first moment they'd met. God knows, he'd never had any trouble getting a beautiful woman to come to his arms and surrender to his kisses, without making her any promises.

At first, he had not thought about asking Gillian to marry him; then suddenly he'd gone ahead and done it. That was something else he'd been asking himself: When had he suddenly decided to propose to her? Maybe the little minx had cleverly manipulated that, he thought as he recalled the afternoon they'd had a picnic on the mission grounds.

His sleep was sweet that night with dreams about his bewitching Gillian. The next morning, in his eagerness to get back toward Maricopa County, he wasted no time sending Driscol out along the wharves where the seamen gathered to talk and sit around on the crates during the day. "Find us a good crew, Harry," he said. "We're going to be sailing out of here before you know it. You know the kind of men I want."

"Sure do, Captain Lafferty." The first mate grinned, for that was the best news he could have heard. Like Lafferty, he was feeling stale and bored from being on shore too long.

Driscol turned and fairly dashed across the deck to be on his way and about the task of finding a crew for his captain. Lafferty had to smile, for he knew why Driscol was so exuberant. He was ready to leave this place and feel the swaying motion of the *Lucky Lady* as she plowed through the waters beyond that bay. Lafferty was feeling the same way.

He spent the morning going over every inch of his clipper ship to give it his special, careful inspection, while awaiting his first mate's return, hoping he'd lucked out and found some able, reliable men. A crew was not the easiest group to assemble. The seamen who sailed with Captain Lucky knew he was a stern but fair sea captain. But his orders were obeyed or a harsh, firm reprimand was doled out to the seaman shirking his duty.

Harry Driscol had found that out the first week he'd sailed on the *Lucky Lady*, but after that he'd come to respect the young captain. Harry had never had any urge to leave Lafferty to sail on another ship. He'd found that his loyalty to his captain had been aptly rewarded and his pay was good. It was a great satisfaction to Driscol that Lafferty had enough faith in him to leave the *Lucky Lady* in his care when he had to travel to Arizona Territory. Oh, he'd realized that the captain valued his ability of seaman after all the time he'd served aboard the ship as his first mate, but this ship was Steve Lafferty's pride and joy. To place it in the care of anyone else must have been a difficult task for him, Harry knew.

What a celebration they'd enjoyed the first night he'd arrived back from the territory! But Driscol noted a change in Lafferty that first night. He could not quite figure it out at first, but after a couple of days had passed and they'd talked more and gone ito town to eat in the evening, Harry understood.

Lafferty's green eyes did not roam the rooms to seek out the lovely ladies as they had in the past. In fact, when some very attractive damsels had sauntered by their table with an inviting gleam in their eyes, Steve had shrugged them aside. That was all Harry had to see to know what his captain was preoccupied about. It was a woman! Captain Lucky had found himself a lady who'd conquered his elusive heart.

Harry found that amusing, for he wondered if he'd ever see the day when Lafferty would fall for a woman, knowing how he'd bragged that he intended to remain a bachelor for a long, long time.

Some little lady had obviously changed all that. Some woman she must be, Harry mused. Knowing the type of woman Lafferty usually found most attractive, Harry was curious to meet this one.

Whoever she was, she'd surely cast a spell on Lafferty!

Chapter Thirty-Six

Steve plundered the big trunk in his cabin to check various items he'd collected in the ports where his clipper ship had docked during all his years of sailing the seas. He recalled many a memory as he plowed through the trunk. A sly grin came to his face as he remembered certain incidents. Always he had a little token to give to some fair lady who'd given him a night of pleasure.

He still had a couple of those lovely silk kimonos he'd picked up in the Orient. He gathered them up out of the trunk to place on the bed. He'd give those to Harry, he thought to himself. One of Harry's women might enjoy them.

On a separate pile, he placed the perfumed soap and oils along with the folded length of delicate lace he'd bought in France. He found a magnificent bolt of wool in a brilliant array of bright colors and some woolen knit shawls from his own native Ireland. There were several little teakwood chests inlaid with mother-of-pearl he'd obtained at a coastal harbor on the shores of Spain.

It was a strange interlude Steve spent during the late afternoon, for he was recalling the previous years of his life and his travels all over the world. God, he'd never have settled for less! He would have withered away on land! Nowhere was the air so fresh and clean nor the breeze so invigorating as it caressed your face, he would have sworn.

He had to convince Gillian that this was the life they must live together, for he could never leave her in port and sail away from that shore. No, she must accompany him!

Steve was convinced that he could persuade her, even if at first she refused his idea about how they should live. Her love for him would be enough to persuade her, he was sure.

Gathering up the items piled on the bed, he placed them in a black leather bag on the cabin floor. He was just locking the bag when he heard Harry calling. "You in there, Captain!"

"Yes, Harry. Come on in."

The door opened and the curly-haired, husky seaman rushed in. The broad grin on his ruddy face told Lafferty that he'd been successful in hiring some crewmen, but never had he expected six experienced seamen to be found in one day.

"All but one of them from the same ship, abandoned here when the gold fever took hold of the captain and his whole crew. These five are more than ready to get back to the sea where they belong. Think they'll be good men," Harry told him. "They're hungry, Captain—hungry for the open sea and the salty waters spraying their faces. You know how it is when a man of the sea stays on land too long. He grows stale!"

A sly smile came to Steve's tanned face and he gave a husky laugh. "For God's sakes Harry, I sure do know that. Let me ease your concern right now, for I assure you that I'll not take on another contract like this one. Believe me, I've regretted it! But it won't be long now before we leave these shores for the open sea."

"Glad to hear you say that, Captain," Harry said. "Sure am. Found time weighing heavy on my hands."

"Well, Harry—I'm going to leave the task of hiring the crew up to you while I return to Arizona and finish up the loose ends there. There's a rather fine fee to collect for all this time we've been away from the sea. I'm going to leave you the funds to lay on an ample supply of provisions, and I've already got an order for a cargo bound for England. How does that sound to

272

you, Harry?"

Harry gave a roar of delight. "Sounds like heaven to me! You can count on me, Captain. I'll have our old *Lucky Lady* shipshape and ready to sail when you arrive. I promise."

"I've no doubt of that, Harry. If I didn't I'd have never left my special lady in your hands."

"Appreciate that, Captain," Harry said. The captain's words confirmed what he felt was true, but it was gratifying to hear it from his mouth. Driscol was driven to live up to such faith, for never would he have wanted Lafferty to be disappointed in him.

Lafferty gave him a comradely pat on his muscled shoulders. "I couldn't have asked for a better first mate, Driscol," he declared. "We've shared a lot of time together and you get to know a man pretty well, I'd say."

Harry shook his head in agreement. "Yes, sir—I think you do. Time tells a lot of things."

Steve's spirits were high. He and Harry talking together was like the old times. It was a good feeling. "Let's go out, Harry, and get ourselves the biggest beefsteak we can find in San Diego. What do you say?"

Now this was more like the old Steve Lafferty! Harry Driscol responded eagerly. "That sounds damned good to me. I think I could handle a pretty big one. Been a while since I had one."

"Then what are we waiting for?" Steve moved toward the cabin door. He was going to enjoy an evening with his first mate and friend.

The two seamen left the *Lucky Lady* and jauntily walked down the long wharf toward the center of the city. Behind them, there was a golden setting sun reflecting against the waters of the bay where Lafferty's ship was docked. Other seafaring men were moving down the wharf, going into the city to have themselves a tasty meal and a carousing night now that their day's work was done. As warm as the afternoon had been, there was a slight chill in the air blowing across the bay now that the sun was setting.

273

By the time they left the wharf, the bright lights of the town were greeting them. Steve had found it an interesting place during the short time he'd spent there before going to Arizona. It was the oldest Spanish settlement in the state of California and the Spanish influence was still very prominent in the structure of the buildings.

New places and new people had always intrigued Steve. He supposed that was why he loved his life as a seaman, as his father had. Every strange port he'd visited was different from the last one.

He found the city of San Diego a most interesting place, more interesting than Tucson or Phoenix.

He and Harry passed a saloon where gay laughter and music were drifting out to the street. Right ahead, bright lights blazed from the establishment and a sign hung outside the double doors. The place was called the Blue Moon, and it was obviously a very popular gathering place. Driscol peered in the wide windows to see the many tables filled with customers.

"Think we might just find ourselves a big, thick steak in there, Harry?"

"Think so, Captain Lafferty!" Driscol grinned.

They entered and were guided to one of the tables draped in blue-and-white checked tablecloths. Each table was brightened by a burning candle in a small blue pottery holder. A waiter came to their table to greet them cordially. "Welcome, gentlemen, to the Blue Moon. We have a fine choice of entrees to offer you tonight. The Blue Moon always serves its special homemade bread, baked fresh daily, and there is a very tender roast, beef, or chicken or our choice beefsteak along with the catch of the day out in our bay if you prefer some good pan-fried fish. Then there is . . ." the waiter's voice trailed off as he noticed the two men exchanging grins.

Steve quickly explained that there was no need to go any further, for he'd already told them all they needed to hear. "That fine beefsteak is exactly what we came in here seeking. That and a bottle of your finest red wine would be nice, I think.

Sound good to you, Harry?"

"Sounds perfect to me, Captain."

"Very good, gentlemen. Let me know if there is anything you wish. I think you'll find our yeast rolls are the best you'll ever eat."

Harry had already spied a platter of magnificent rolls being served to the people at the next table. After the waiter left their table, Harry said, "Lord, I can't wait to bite into one of those rolls. You won't believe the size of them!"

A half hour later, the two husky seamen had eaten every roll on the platter. There was not one trace of the thick steak left, or the pile of roasted new potatoes. It had been a long time since either of them had enjoyed such a delectable meal as this one had been.

Now, it was just nice to sit there, pleasantly sated from all the good food, and sip the sweet red wine.

Neither of them sensed the approach of the very attractive lady swaying sensuously toward their table, but most of the people sitting close by recognized the proprietress of the Blue Moon, Alfreda Montera. Rarely did she come to the tables to greet her patrons. Most of her customers found her an arrogant woman, but that didn't keep them from coming to the Blue Moon to enjoy the finest food in San Diego.

It was the exotic fragrance she wore that made Steve Lafferty turn his head to look up at the voluptuous creature smiling down at him. "Good evening, gentlemen. I hope you've enjoyed your meal."

Harry Driscol was taken by surprise and utter delight by the sight of the alluring lady. He choked on the sip of red wine he'd just taken and allowed Steve to do the talking as he held the napkin to his mouth trying to smother his coughing.

An intriguing sight she made, standing there in her deep blue gown with its low scooped neckline revealing her magnificent cleavage. Her dark hair was pulled back into one large coil and at one side an aigrette of brilliant blue feathers with little seed pearls was pinned to it. Harry Driscol hadn't seen such a good-looking woman in a long time.

"We've had a most enjoyable evening," Lafferty said, gallantly rising from his chair.

"Please—be seated, Captain. I am Alfreda Montera."

Lafferty found himself unsure of how to address her, since he didn't know whether or not she was married, so he just gave her a charming smile as he spoke. "A pleasure to meet you, Alfreda Montera. I am Captain Lafferty and this is my first mate, Harry Driscol." Alfreda's eyes left Lafferty long enough to greet Harry. "Nice to meet you, Harry. I got the impression that you liked my rolls. I'm glad." She gave a soft lilting laugh.

"Oh, yes, ma'am. Thought I'd died and gone to heaven for sure," Harry exuberantly confessed. Steve and Alfreda both laughed.

"That is the nicest thing you possibly could have told me, Harry." Her sultry dark eyes went back to rest on the devilishly handsome captain. "I trust you will be here for a while, Captain Lafferty, and we shall see you again at the Blue Moon? We—we have many special dishes we offer if only one will request them."

The look in her sultry eyes was telling Steve much more than the menu, and he knew it. He'd met a lot of Alfredas all over the world. They were a dime a dozen and he had no intention of grabbing her bait. Besides, he'd seen the threatening shadow of a very angry man lurking at the door of the kitchen. He was a giant of a man, and Lafferty suspected he was her husband.

"That is good to know, Madame Montera," he told her politely. "For tonight, I guess all we need now is the bill for this grand meal we've had. Harry and I have an early morning call, so we'd best be on our way," he lied.

"Of course, Captain," she replied curtly. Turning sharply on her heel, she marched away to seek out the waiter so he could present the bill. She was no fool. She knew she'd been dismissed by Captain Lafferty.

There was no shadow of doubt in Harry Driscol's mind now

276

that Lafferty was in love with some pretty young thing he'd met in Arizona. Never would he have shrugged aside a pretty lady like Alfreda Montera, who was so openly inviting his attention. Captain Lucky had most assuredly changed!

As they left the Blue Moon, Harry deviously taunted Lafferty, "That was a lot of woman back there, Captain. A damned pretty one, if I'm any judge."

"You're right, Harry! But there are a lot of pretty women in this world, and Alfreda Montera is no lady. When you find a real lady, then you've found a rare jewel."

Harry had no comment to make, for he didn't have any need to: Now he *knew* what Steve Lafferty had found for himself back in Arizona Territory. He'd found himself a lady!

Harry was happy for him. It was high time Captain Lucky found himself a fine lady!

Chapter Thirty-Seven

It did not come as any surprise to Harry Driscol when Lafferty announced that he would be catching the stagecoach back to Arizona Territory. Driscol could see the anxiety written all over Steve's face as he spoke about his plans. But Driscol was a little puzzled that Steve had not sought to tell him about the lady who'd won his heart. But then, Lafferty was a very secretive person when the mood was on him. This had to be one of those times, Driscol figured.

They had little time to talk after that, because at dawn Lafferty was disembarking to make his way to the stage station in the center of the town. Driscol went his way to join the seamen aboard the ship.

Besides, Harry was ready for another cup of coffee down in the galley where the ship's cook, Corky, was preparing the crew's breakfast. Lafferty had not taken the time for one cup of coffee. It seemed he was most impatient to get on that stage.

Harry knew it would be a long time before he'd enjoy such a meal as he and Steve shared the other evening. Now he must content himself with Corky's cooking. He couldn't fault old Corky's vittles, though, for they were pretty fair eating to a drifting seaman like him.

*　　　*　　　*

After being back at the ranch for a few weeks, Gillian tried to resume the attitude and routine she'd had before going to Tucson. It wasn't easy and she only hoped she didn't give herself away around Mother Foster.

Back here, it seemed foolish to dress up in any of the lovely frocks Helen had given her and it certainly wasn't very practical. However, she often took them out and just laid them across the bed and fingered the soft material and lacy trim. After a while, she'd carefully hang them back up in the chest and close the door.

She realized something about herself during these times: To live on an isolated ranch would never satisfy her. She was curious to see the world outside this territory. A rancher's wife she could not be, she was thoroughly convinced.

Until now, she'd not asked either of the Fosters if she might take her mare out for a ride across the countryside. She knew they still remembered the incident that had taken place in the pastureland just before she and Mother Foster had left for Tucson, and they were still apprehensive. However, in all the weeks they'd been back, she'd not heard one word about roaming bands of renegades. Just to go out for a leisurely ride would be such a joy, and she decided this was the day to approach Mother Foster about it.

By the time she'd finished her morning chores, it was midday. After Mother Foster's hardy and filling breakfast, she needed no meal at noon. When she took the last egg out of her basket and put it with the others she'd just gathered, she was ready to go to the house.

The day was a glorious one for a trek over the valley, and for some unknown reason, she glanced toward the majestic mountains and thought about the friendly woman she'd once met there. There was no one Gillian could think of at the nearby ranches she'd like to visit, but it would be fun to ride up the mountain trail to that enchanting little cottage in the woods. She could recall the pleasant aromas permeating the cottage from Solange's dried flowers and herbs.

She still remembered that delicious herbed tea, and the gracious lady who had been so kind to her when she needed care. Gillian convinced herself, by the time she'd walked from the barn to the house, that it had been very thoughtless of her not to have made a visit long before now. Perhaps she was lonely, too, as Gillian was. After all, few people must pass that way. Those thick, dense woods swallowed up her cabin.

She said nothing to either of the Fosters when she entered the house and saw the two of them having their lunch at the kitchen table. They thought nothing about it, for Gillian rarely joined them for the midday meal. Such a glowing radiant smile was on her lovely face that neither of them perceived her discontent or loneliness.

"Does it strike you, Nancy, that Gillian is glowing with more beauty? Seems she just keeps blossoming prettier and prettier all the time."

"You're right, John," his wife agreed. "I've noticed. Can't put my finger on it, but I guess that trip to Tucson really brought out a sparkle in her."

Once Gillian was in her bedroom, she poured water in the basin and washed her face. After her morning chores it felt refreshing to scrub her face with the soapy cloth. When she had finished, she sat down at her small dressing table to take the brush to her thick hair, all tousled and blown by the breeze as she'd roamed around the barnyard and stables.

She braided her auburn tresses in two long braids and tied bright blue ribbon on each end, then tucked her blue tunic inside the waistband of her dark blue divided twill skirt.

She stood for a moment in deep thought. What nice little token did she have that she could give to Solange, if she was allowed to take her little mare out for a run? Some of the long strips of ribbon she'd purchased in Tucson, perhaps?

She rushed to the chest to choose four varied colors of ribbon. Yes, Solange would make use of them, for she, too, wore her hair in long braids. Then she thought about the snow that would soon come to those mountains. She had no need for

281

three woolen shawls, and Helen had given her a lovely knitted cape that Melissa didn't want anymore. She picked the pearl gray crocheted woolen shawl out of the drawer and smiled, satisfied with the gifts she would be taking to Hawk's mother.

She left her little bundle on the bed and sought out Mother Foster. She was glad she found her alone in the kitchen. A bright smile lit up Nancy's face when she saw Gillian coming to join her. "Well, don't you look as pretty as a newborn babe!"

Gillian gave a soft giggle. "From what I've heard they are always red, wrinkled, and ugly."

"Not always, Gillian Browne," Nancy corrected her. "Seen some sweet-faced little angels during my lifetime. Bet you were one when your momma first held you in her arms. I'd bet my egg money on that! Speaking of egg money, John's gone into the mercantile store this afternoon and I never thought to ask you if there was something you'd be needing. Lordy, I'm sorry Gillian."

Gillian quickly soothed her concern. "I don't need a thing, Mother Foster. Did he go by himself or take one of the men with him?"

"Oh, he went alone."

"I just wondered. I'm glad the Apache threat has died down. There haven't been any more raids around here, have there?"

"None that we've heard of, child. You're not still concerned about that, are you, Gillian?" Nancy inquired.

"Oh, mercy no! From what I've heard there was no trouble around here while we were in Tucson."

Nancy heaved a deep sigh. "Thank God for that!"

Gillian strolled around the kitchen before she approached the subject. "Is there anything else I can help you with this afternoon, Mother Foster?"

"Not a thing, honey. You just do what you want to do," Nancy told her.

"What I would like to do is go for a ride. It's been so long and I would enjoy it so much. I would not think about it if I thought I'd be in any danger."

Nancy had to admit that she could see nothing wrong with Gillian going for a ride. The poor girl must be terribly bored, confined to this house and barnyard after the hustle and bustle of Tucson. She did not have the heart to refuse her this freedom even though she did not know what John would have said if he'd been here. But he wasn't, so she'd have to assume the blame if something went wrong.

"If you don't wander too far, I can't see anything wrong with it, Gillian. I know you need an outing, dear. Go—have your ride, but be sure you get back before sunset or John will be stewing." She laughed.

"Oh, I will, Mother Foster," she promised, giving her an assuring embrace before rushing out of the room. Nancy watched her as she left the kitchen. What a shame her niece Melissa was not more like Gillian! More than once when she was at Helen's, she'd wanted to slap her niece's smug face. Nancy wondered when the change had come about in Melissa, for she used to be such a sweet young thing.

Nancy had found herself out of patience with her sister when she allowed such behavior from her daughter. Why did Helen accept it without a harsh reprimand to that prissy miss?

Maybe the good Lord knew what he was doing when he didn't bless her with any youngster of her own, for she would not have tolerated such insolence.

A wonderful carefree air washed over Gillian as she spurred her little mare into motion. She broke into a feisty, fast pace with her tail and her head high in the air as though she was as glad as Gillian was to be galloping across the valley.

The sun's brilliant rays shone down on them as they rode past the pastureland to enter the verdant, dense forest.

Gillian slowed the mare's pace as they wove through the thick woods, for it was such a pleasant setting. She enjoyed the pungent aroma of the pine and cedar trees flourished in the forest. As she rode along, she saw the thicket with tangled vines laden with wild berries. She was almost tempted to stop to gather some, but she continued on the trail toward Solange's cabin. After all, if she were to visit her for a while, she could not linger on the trail, or she'd never get back to the ranch before sunset.

She could tell the trail was growing steeper as she rode along the narrow lane, but it seemed to be taking much longer than it had when she and Hawk had traveled it some months ago. She knew she was taking the right path, for there had been no forks in the lane from the moment she'd entered it off the main trail. But she could not fight the wave of apprehension she was starting to feel when there was no sight of Solange's cabin. If she had chanced to look to the west she would have spotted the circling smoke rising up above the tall, towering pines, but her blue eyes kept looking straight ahead.

When she was about to convince herself she was surely lost, the sight of a familiar figure bending over to pick berries caught her eyes and she recognized Solange Touraine. What a welcome sight she was!

Solange had already heard the sound of hoofbeats on the trail. Her first thought was that it was Hawk coming home, but it was not his little spotted pinto she saw trotting toward her. All she had to see was all that long flaming hair to know it was Gillian Browne riding up the lane.

A delighted smile glowed on Solange's face as Gillian drew nearer. So often she had thought about this young lady and she'd hoped to see her again. Their encounter had been a brief one, but Solange was a person who was ruled by first impulses and instinct. She had liked Gillian Browne immediately. She knew that her son was beguiled by her youthful beauty. As his mother, she could have given him her wholehearted approval to court such a pretty girl. Oh, how honored she would feel to embrace Gillian as her daughter-in-law, but Solange had grave doubts that this could ever be.

She placed her basket on the ground, smoothed back the straying wisps of her silver-streaked hair, and gave her skirt a swift shake.

Gillian knew why she wanted to pay this visit. Such a

glowing warmth of welcome was reflected on Solange's face! Gillian swore she'd never seen a more beautiful lady, and she was very curious about her. She found herself wanting to know more about her and why she lived back here in this isolated woods. A woman as lovely as she was could have had a more luxurious life, it would seem to Gillian.

"Hello, Mrs. Touraine. You remember me? I'm Gillian— Gillian Browne."

Solange's eyes sparkled with delight as she threw up her arms in a welcoming gesture. "Ah, *ma petite*—how could I possibly forget you? Of course I remember you, Gillian Browne, and I've thought about you so often. I've—I've hoped that you would come back to see me and here you are. This is the nicest thing I could have had happen to me."

Gillian pulled up on the reins of her horse and leaned down. It seemed very natural to go into the woman's extended arms and accept her warm embrace.

When Solange released her and held her back to look at her, she survyed a more beautiful girl than she'd remembered. That instinctive sense of hers took over as Solange sighed. "You've changed from a pretty young maiden to a most enchanting young woman, *ma chérie.* Has that much time passed or can such miracles happen?" Her alert keen eyes danced over the girl's face.

"Has it really been so long?"

"It must have been, because spring came and went and the summer is over now. Now it is autumn. Time passes so very fast. Up here in the mountains winter comes much faster than it does down in the valley where you live. We've already seen our first flurries of snow. You'll have a bright sun and a mild day down there while I will be sitting close to my fireplace to stay warm up here. I am so glad you came before that happened."

"So am I," Gillian told her, understanding what Solange was talking about, for she would have felt more comfortable if she'd worn the twill jacket she'd left behind. She noticed that

Solange wore a very raggedy-looking knit shawl and she was glad she had brought the pretty pearl gray one.

"Come, Gillian—we shall go to my cabin."

Gillian turned to mount the mare and follow her. A few moments later, they approached the cabin. The smoke ascended from the chimney as Solange pointed out to her that it was already necessary for her to burn logs in her fireplace for warmth.

"Hawk cut me an ample supply to last while he was away," Solange said, as they entered the cabin.

"Hawk is a kind, thoughtful person and a very devoted son," Gillian declared as she followed the older woman through the door.

Naturally, Solange was pleased, as any mother would be, to hear her son praised. Something about Gillian had drawn her to the young girl from the minute Hawk had brought her to the cabin the day she'd been thrown from her horse on the mountain trail. What was it that drew two individuals together or could repulse them at a first meeting? Solange did not know the answer to that, but she knew it was true. She felt as if she had known Gillian all her life, yet she knew that this wasn't true.

As she invited Gillian to have a seat while she put her basket in the kitchen, she was glad that Gillian could not read her thoughts. If only Gillian could love Hawk! But a nagging thought persisted that this could not be.

After all, Hawk was half Apache. How could Gillian ever forget that, even if she loved him dearly? It was a stigma that could not be swept away by love, Solange feared.

While Solange placed her basket in the kitchen and checked her kettle to brew them a cup of tea, Gillian dwelled on her own private musings. Her heart was heavy about Stephen Lafferty and how he'd probably deserted her. Here she was, left with his baby and no father for the poor little thing. What shame this would bring to the Fosters who'd been so good to her!

She knew not where to turn except to Solange Touraine!

Chapter Thirty-Eight

Out of the corner of her eye, Solange caught Gillian's pensive look. The girl was troubled about something, she suddenly realized.

She must think of some way to make it easy for Gillian to confide in her.

"Would you like one of my spice cakes with your tea, Gillian?" she asked. "I think I'll have one. I worked up an appetite." She continued setting up the tray with their cups on it.

"Yes, Solange—I would love one!"

Solange opened the kitchen door so she could talk with Gillian while she fixed the tray. "I can't tell you how long I've been baking these little cakes. Hawk was a wee one when he first held one in his fist. He liked them so much that I had to bake them constantly."

"How—how old were you when you had Hawk?" Gillian asked.

Solange turned to look at her. "Not much older than you are now, Gillian. Funny, now that I can think back on it, after what I'd been through, the thought of having a baby did not disturb me for a minute."

"I can't say that I'd be that brave."

"Well, my dear little Gillian, you have not been captured by

287

Apaches and lived in those horrible camps. I thank God that you haven't."

"But for Hawk, I could have been, Solange," Gillian quickly pointed out to her. She reminded Hawk's mother of how he'd rescued her from three renegade Apaches.

"He told me about it, Gillian. I'm glad he was there when you needed him."

"I owe Hawk so much and I shall never forget it."

"I think Hawk knows that you are a good friend, Gillian."

"I hope so. I consider you and Hawk two of my dearest friends," Gillian confessed. "I—I feel just like I did the last time I was here in your cabin, Solange—there is such a warmth here. I can't explain it."

"I understand, dear—truly I do. I was brought to this cabin by the man who rescued me the day I fled from that Apache camp and Cochise. Later, he honored me by marrying me and helping me raise my infant son." She told Gillian about the woodsman she'd married and had grown to love. "It was not the exciting romance I'd known back in France, but it was a good love. There are many kinds of love in a lifetime, Gillian. When you have lived as long as I have, you will know what I'm talking about."

Gillian suddenly remembered the gifts she had brought for Solange. She excused herself to rush out to the hitching post where her mare was tethered. With the small bundle in her arms, she dashed back into the cabin just as Solange was bringing the tray of refreshments into the front room. After she'd set the tray on the small oak table, Gillian handed her the small bundle. "This is for you. Just a little something I thought you might like."

"Oh, dear—for me?" Solange was overcome with emotion; a mist of a tear welled in her eyes as she opened the bundle to find the soft pearl gray shawl and the strips of colorful ribbons. She did not cry easily, for life had made her hard in many ways. Nevertheless, it had still not destroyed the sentimental person she had always been.

"Ma petite—I—I know not what to say. I thank you for being so kind to me."

"I thought the shawl would come in handy up here in the mountains with winter coming on. I hear the snow gets quite deep during the winter months."

"Ah, it does, and you probably saw my ragged old brown shawl when you were here before. I was ready to give it up and now I can." She gaily laughed. "In fact, it will make a very cozy bed for my Little Bear. He will love snuggling in it."

"And the ribbons are for your hair. You have such lovely hair," Gillian told her.

"Now speaking about beautiful hair, I must tell you what Hawk calls your lovely tresses—flaming fire."

"Flaming fire! I like that. I've never had my hair called that before."

"I don't think he'd ever seen that brilliant auburn shade of hair until he met you. I'll never forget him remarking about it."

Gillian was enjoying herself so much that she did not realize that the last golden rays of the sunset were invading the thick grove of trees surrounding the cabin.

The merry laughter inside the cabin was ringing out as Gaston Dion walked up the pathway. He'd seen the strange horse tied at the hitching post.

Not knowing who it might be, he was hesitant about entering the cabin, but he'd shot a young turkey and he knew it would provide a tasty meal for Solange.

For a brief moment, he stood outside the door to listen to the voices inside. It was another lady paying a call on Solange, he realized as he heard Gillian's soft voice. He knocked on the door and waited for Solange to open it.

A warm, loving smile was on her face as she greeted him. "Ah, Gaston, *mon cher*—you have returned, and not empty-handed, I see. You have managed to provide us with a grand turkey."

"Well, I suppose I can't expect it for our supper tonight since the afternoon is gone, but perhaps tomorrow night—

oui?" He gave her a husky laugh as he emerged through the door, for it was obvious to Gaston that Solange did not see fit to conceal her feelings for him from her guest.

Solange Touraine was all woman, with not one ounce of fakery about her. He could not say that about any other woman he'd met, even though he'd traveled all over the world.

It still boggled his mind that he had found such a rare gem here in these mountains, completely secluded and isolated from the outside world. To think that he'd been here before and never happened upon her cabin!

He was determined that if he could manage to persuade her to be his wife and leave this little enchanted cottage, he'd take her back across the border with him to Canada. His fur trading business in Canada was a very lucrative enterprise which he and his partner, Aaron Bass, had formed some years ago. For three months out of each year, Gaston left Canada to check out the various regions south of Canada. He always posed as a trapper, living in the primitive conditions that such a role demanded, for it did not prove any hardship to him to live in the woods. He loved it and it was this love that had sparked his interest in the woods and the furry creatures dwelling there. Those furry little creatures had reaped him a handsome reward and an astronomical fortune.

Back in Canada, he lived in a palatial mansion with grounds patterned from the gardens of England's finest country estates. His appearance was nothing like the image he presented up here in these mountains in Arizona Territory. He was clean-shaven and his hair was not teasing his shoulders. His clothes were finely tailored and made from the finest imported wools. A faithful valet catered to his every need and demand.

Gaston rather enjoyed switching back and forth between the two roles he played. It kept his life from becoming boring and dull. This little three-month jaunt had finally given Gaston the answer to what he'd been searching for all his life. He'd found that answer here at Solange's cabin. Now, he wanted to give her the life she deserved. He could only pray that she'd accept his proposal.

Time was growing short now, and he would have to return to Canada soon. Never had he been so scared or apprehensive about something, for he knew if she refused him he would be crushed.

He was encouraged as she led him into her front room to introduce her to the lovely auburn-haired lady sitting there. "Gillian, I'd like you to meet my dear friend, Gaston Dion. Gaston, this is Gillian Browne."

Gallantly, Gaston extended his hand to Gillian. "Mademoiselle Browne, it is a pleasure to meet you. I am sorry if I interrupted the pleasant visit the two of you were enjoying."

"Not at all, Mr. Dion. The truth is I'd lost all track of time and I should have been riding back to the ranch an hour ago," Gillian told him. She'd seen that twilight was already upon the mountains when Solange opened the door to invite Gaston Dion in.

She hastily prepared to depart. "Please come back again, Gillian," Solange urged as Gillian dashed toward the hitching post to mount her little mare.

Gillian turned back to give her an assuring nod of her head. She heard Solange call after her once again, "And I thank you from the bottom of my heart for the lovely shawl and ribbons."

Gillian smiled as she waved goodbye, spurring the horse into action. Gillian knew she must push the mare into a fast pace to get back to the ranch quickly. Even so, she couldn't possibly arrive when she'd promised Mother Foster she would.

Time had just flown. She'd never met anyone like Solange. She could not blame Mother Foster if she was vexed at her, but she just hoped she wouldn't be too worried.

Her eyes anxiously searched for the clearing which would tell her she was ready to ride down into the valley below. It hadn't appeared. She could only pray that she'd not strayed from the trail now that there was no bright sunlight to guide her way. The dusky twilight was consuming the thick woods and she could already hear the night birds calling as they perched above her in the branches.

Now, there was not even the hint of any lingering light. The gathering twilight would soon turn to the dark of night.

It was then Gillian saw the break in the timbers all around her and the clearing up ahead. She gave a deep sigh of relief and spurred the little mare to go faster.

It was a welcoming sight to see the lights of the ranch house across the way. Like little fireflies on a dark spring night, the lamplight was flickering and welcoming her back to her home.

Her keen ears heard an eerie sound coming from behind her but she didn't stop to listen. She could not distinguish whether it was a roaming mountain cat or the whinnying of a horse. It really didn't matter, for either one could mean danger to her, so she kept riding as fast as she could, watching the lights from the house grow brighter and brighter.

Breathlessly, she arrived at the corral fence. The first sight she saw was a scowling-faced John Foster leading his horse out of the barn. He stopped, frozen in his tracks, as he spied her there by the fence. Without saying a word, he led the horse back through the barn door. She didn't have to be told that he was preparing to go out to search for her.

Dismounting from her own horse, she guided the little mare through the barn door to put her in the stall. She dreaded coming face-to-face with John. Rarely did John Foster display any anger, but she knew he was angry with her tonight. It pained her deeply to be out of favor with him.

When she was placing the mare in the stall, she stammered, "I'm—I'm terribly sorry. I have no excuse for not returning home as I promised, except that I visited too long and lost track of the time."

John's back was turned to her as she spoke, and this was the way he wished it. Never since she'd lived at their home had he been so riled at the young girl. He hardly knew how to handle himself right then.

"Get on in the house, Gillian, and I'll tend to your horse. There's a lady in there concerned about you—has been for well over an hour," he snapped harshly.

"Yes, sir, and I am truly sorry," she said in almost a whisper. She rushed out of the barn, fighting back the tears.

Nancy Foster had seen her ride up to the fence, but she remained in the house to try to gain her composure before facing Gillian. Obviously, the girl was all right and her worry and concern had not been necessary, but how was one to know? She found it hard to believe that Gillian could have been so thoughtless, knowing how she would be fretting when she didn't return before dark.

It was more than just a leisurely ride; Gillian had been gone for more than four hours. Usually she was gone an hour when she rode in the afternoon. No, Nancy was no fool! There was more to it than that. Was she meeting some young man on the sly?

She'd had such faith in that girl! Nancy knew she'd be shattered to discover that Gillian would lie to her. Oh, she prayed that wasn't so!

Gillian was feeling very ill at ease after the reception she'd received from John Foster. The two women faced each other with looks of uncertainty.

"I'm sorry, Mother Foster—sorry I didn't return when I said I would. I forgot about the time while I was paying a visit to Solange Touraine—Hawk's mother."

"This was where you went, Gillian? I'd not known you were going there. I thought you were going for a ride."

"I suddenly decided to ride up there, recalling how nice she'd been to me several weeks ago. I guess you could say it was an impulse, Mother Foster." She lied to Nancy for some unknown reason.

"I see, child. Well, I'm just glad to see you back safe and sound, for that trail up the mountain could be very dangerous for a young lady all alone. I would have thought you'd realize this."

"I guess I should have, Mother Foster, but I didn't. It was such a beautiful afternoon and I knew the way."

Nancy tried to act calm as she moved slowly over to her kitchen to attend to the supper they were yet to eat because of their concern about Gillian. Pretending an offhanded tone, Nancy inquired of Gillian, "Did Hawk escort you part of the way—through the woods?"

"No, Hawk is away, Mother Foster. He is still scouting for the railroad." Gillian began to take over her usual kitchen chores. "I'm sure Solange enjoyed my visit, too. She must get very lonely with her son away all this time. She's up there in that isolated cabin, all alone."

Nancy stirred the vegetables in her pots. "Oh, I'm sure she does, dear." She found it hard to be out of sorts with the pretty girl, and she did appear to be telling her the truth. Nancy wanted to believe her.

It did not take her long to mellow her feeling toward Gillian, but John wasn't so forgiving, so the meal was a little strained for all of them. Gillian was glad when supper was over and the kitchen was put in order so she could go to her own room to be alone with her thoughts.

As she sat at her dressing table to unbraid her hair and brush it, she found her thoughts not on the Fosters or Solange. She thought about Steve Lafferty, and she sat there enjoying an interlude of sweet daydreaming. She remembered the fairy tales her mother used to read to her when she was a small child, when the handsome knight came riding to the castle to rescue his lady love. She yearned so desperately tonight for Steve to come charging through the door and sweep her up in his strong, muscled arms, to carry her away from this house and Maricopa County!

She allowed herself to give way to wild, wonderful imagining. She could envision the two of them boarding his fine ship to sail the seas of the world. Together, they'd travel to all the exotic places she'd only wondered about but never seen.

Most of all, she'd know the ecstasy of his love!

Chapter Thirty-Nine

Solange Touraine did not have to daydream about the ecstasy of love and passion that night, for she experienced it as the rugged, sensuous Gaston Dion held her in his strong arms and loved her ardently. It had been over twenty years since she'd been carried to such lofty heights of flaming passion. Never had she expected to feel as she'd felt in Gaston's arms. After all, she was past forty. It was a glorious discovery to know she could still feel such pleasure.

Now that they were both quietly contented, sated from the overwhelming, divine fury they were swept up in, she lay there thinking about it all. Everything had happened so swiftly, and she felt certain that Gaston would admit he felt the same way.

She had to admit that she was in a lighthearted, gay mood after Gillian's visit, for that was a most pleasant surprise. A long time ago Solange had willed herself to make the most of her life and never give way to self-pity, but she did get very lonely at times. Having a visit with Gillian Browne was like the times back in France when she and a friend spent the afternoon on a shopping spree or a visit to a tea room.

Perhaps there was a frivolous, girlish air about her by the time Gillian had left her cabin and Gaston arrived. Later, the two of them had enjoyed a simple meal by candlelight. It was good to have Gaston at her table. There was no denying that she found him very attractive. To be able to speak her native language was marvelous to Solange, too. The more they were around each other, the more they seemed to share in their mutual likes and dislikes about life. She realized she was strongly attracted to this man.

After the meal was over and they lingered over one more glass of wine, Solange was thinking to herself that she'd not had such a wonderful day and evening in a long, long time. She had Gillian and Gaston to thank for that.

Finally, she moved out of her chair to clear away the table and gather up the dishes. Gaston moved around the table to help her. A sudden move of hers took him by surprise and he found himself pressed against her body and instinctively his arms enclosed her to bring her closer to him. Solange found herself being lifted upward until his warm lips could meet hers in a kiss. Once their lips met, such an explosion of heated passion erupted in both of them that they knew there was no stopping.

It was no surprise to Gaston, for he knew the minute he'd first laid eyes on her that this was a woman of passion. He was more than delighted to know that he had been right as he felt the supple curves of her body fit so perfectly to his and wish to linger there.

Solange felt lightheaded and giddy as the heat of his manly body pleaded for her surrender. She had no wish to deny herself this rare pleasure she'd not experienced for many years. Why should she? Perhaps it would never come her way again, but this night she would enjoy it to the fullest.

Abandoning herself to the savage hunger she'd known so many, many lonely nights, she gave no protest as Gaston lifted her up in his arms to carry her to the bedroom. His deep husky voice whispered sweet words of endearment to her in French. She felt no shame as she allowed Gaston to undress her or let his dark eyes savor the sight of her nude body. With Gaston, it seemed right and natural, as it had with her first lover, back

296

in France. *Mon Dieu,* it was a glorious feeling to recapture! She cared not what tomorrow would bring. Tonight was all that mattered.

His hands were magnificent and she did not have to be told that he had made love to many women, but that did not matter to Solange. His touch made her arch upward to absorb the overwhelming manliness towering over her.

"Oh, Solange—I—knew it would be this way with us from the very first. I sensed it," he gasped as his huge hands pressed her hips closer to him. "Oh, God—God!"

He heard her eager sighs of delight and it heightened his pleasure, but he did not wish this paradise to end too soon.

His lips caressed and tantalized the pulsing tips of each of her full breasts. He felt the frenzied undulating of her body beneath him and now he knew why he'd waited so long to claim some woman for his own. He'd waited all his life for Solange Touraine. He would have her now that he'd found her—come heaven or hell!

When he'd left no part of her unloved or untouched, he buried himself deep within her, forever claiming her as his own.

They lay there breathlessly in each other's arms. For a few moments, there was just a serene silence before Gaston murmured in her ear, "Solange, I love you—love you as I've never loved another woman. I want you to believe that."

"And I love you, Gaston, as I've not loved any man for many, many years."

His fingers gently touched her face and he removed the straying wisps away from her face as he tenderly teased her, "Then you must marry me so I won't have to live in sin with you."

"Oh, Gaston." She gave a light, little giggle. "Please, we are both too old to jest about this."

"I do not jest, lady! I cannot get down on my knees and propose to you, for the truth is I'm too damned weak, but I am most sincere when I say I want you for my wife so I can love and take care of you the rest of my life."

She rose up slightly to look down at his very serious face. "You are not just joking, are you, Gaston? You really mean it!"

"Oui, ma chérie—I truly mean it as I've never meant anything before. I love you, Solange."

Was it really possible, she wondered, that such a miracle could happen in her life after all the misery she'd endured? Was it possible such a good, fine man as Gaston wished to claim her as his wife? Surely this was not a dream, for she was too old for romantic girlish dreams.

There was a mist of tears in her eyes as she stammered in disbelief, "Are you sure, Gaston?"

"Just tell me yes, for I shall surely die if you say no. Tell me right now you will marry me," he said, pulling her down so he might kiss her lips. "Tell me!"

"Yes, Gaston—I will be happy to marry you. I just can't believe this is all happening."

"Believe it and nothing shall change it, Solange. Fate meant it to be and led me to your cabin so I could discover the woman I've been searching for all my life." He spoke with such sincerity she had to believe as he did.

It was a long night for Gaston and Solange. They propped themselves up on the pillows and Gaston told her all about his life as Solange had told him about herself and her past a few weeks ago after he'd first arrived at her cabin. She sat, listening, completely stunned by his revelations.

"So you are saying that we would be leaving here to go to your home in Canada, Gaston?" she asked.

"Ah, but we would forever keep this little enchanted cottage and come back from time to time. After all, there is so much sentiment to this place. This is where we first made love and you promised to be my wife. Always, we could spend time up here, just as long as you wished, *ma chérie.*"

"Oh, Gaston, you make me so happy."

"My precious Solange, I want to give you all the happiness you deserve. We can have a wonderful life, the best of two worlds. You will be my beautiful bride with all the gowns and jewels you desire once we return to my home. But never shall we forget this little place, and we shall come back here constantly to renew our vows of undying love. We shall roam the woods to pick the wildflowers and dress in our simple garb."

"Oh, Gaston, you make it sound so wonderful. But I still have Hawk to think about."

"If Hawk will accept me, then I shall accept him. In fact, as I've told you, Solange, I am a very wealthy man and I can open doors for Hawk if he'll allow it. But he must meet me halfway. I shall say one more thing. Hawk is a man now and the cord must be cut. His life will take one direction and yours another. When he finds some young lady he wishes to marry, are you to wither away and grow old all alone in this cabin?"

Gaston spoke with truth and wisdom she could not question. She sat there, thoughtfully absorbing his sage words. "You are right, Gaston."

"I'll bend over backwards to win your son's favor, Solange, but if he refuses, then I won't give you up. He and I will have a hell of a fight on that score. But I think I must point out something to you and that is when young men reach Hawk's age they're usually on their own. I sure was. When Hawk took this scouting job for the railroad, he left home. You were left here to take care of yourself as best you could. This isn't the easiest life for a woman like you, Solange. A lot of things can happen."

She'd thought about this on the many nights she'd spent at the cabin alone. What he said was true; she didn't want to live here the rest of her life all alone.

He cupped her face with his hands. "Solange, I know of no one who has given so unselfishly of herself as you have or who has endured so much as the beautiful young belle you were when you arrived here in this country. Some twenty odd years are enough. It is a time for you now to give a little to yourself. I will give you the rest of my life if you'll let me. Share the time we have left, *ma chérie,* and the two of us will share with your son if he'll let us."

She collapsed in his strong, comforting arms and gave way to a flood of tears she'd yearned to cry for a lifetime, it seemed. It was so very nice to have his arms to enclose her and a broad chest to lean on for comfort and security. He held her as she cried and cried with his lips gently touching her cheek.

For so long she had had to be brave and strong! It was a luxury to be feminine and weak. Solange indulged herself, snuggling in Gaston Dion's arms. She was willing to let him hold and protect her forever.

Gaston held her close until she fell asleep and only then did he slowly move to nestle down by her side so he, too, could sleep. It was nice just to lie there and hear the soft sounds of her deep sleeping. Gaston went to sleep a most happy man!

When the first rays of a new dawn came through the bedroom window, he opened his eyes feeling like a man starting a whole new life—and it was going to be a grand and glorious one. He slowly slipped out of the bed so he would not rouse the resting Solange. He pulled the curtains so the brief sunshine would not wake her.

This morning, he would prepare the coffee and have it ready for her. He was pleased that he was able to get himself dressed and slip out of the small bedroom without waking her.

Soon he had a good fire going in her cookstove and the coffee ready. He searched the cupboard to see what he could find to prepare a meal for them. Biscuits, he could not make, but he could cut some slices from the shank of cured ham he found in her pantry. He found the basket of fresh eggs Troy had brought to her and took six of them back to the kitchen.

As he placed the ham in the cast-iron skillet, he heard a noise outside the cabin. Sauntering across the cabin floor, he moved toward the front door. He was not given the opportunity to unlock the door; a mighty blow broke the lock as the wooden door slammed open and there in the threshold stood the bronzed, towering figure of a raging young man Gaston knew had to be Hawk.

His black eyes sparked with raging fire as he took two giant strides inside the cabin. Gaston knew that every fiber in this young man's body was tense with rage. But Gaston's towering height matched Hawk's and his broad, firm frame was even larger. The two indomitable individuals faced each other. Both seemed to sense that neither would give a quarter to the other and both were possessed of unwavering will.

"Where is my mother?" Hawk demanded.

"She sleeps." Gaston said, measuring the indignant young man standing in front of him.

Hawk's black eyes moved over him as he took a couple of steps closer. "And who are you and what are you doing here?"

Gaston went over to the stove to turn the sizzling ham over in the skillet. "I am a good friend of your mother's and my name is Gaston Dion. You are Hawk."

His casual manner threw Hawk off guard. "And how would you know that?" Hawk snapped back at him.

"Isn't too hard to figure out when you've heard a mother speak about a son she loves so dearly. Sit down and have some coffee. You've obviously ridden a long way to get here. Isn't as good as your mother's, but it will do." Gaston lifted the pot from the stove, ignoring the young man as he went about the task of pouring the coffee into two cups. "Here, see what you think." Gaston wasn't intimidated by this arrogant young pup!

Gaston lifted the skillet from the heat of the stove. "I'm going to hold up on the eggs until your mother gets up. I'm a fair cook of ham and eggs, but I'm not worth a damn on biscuits so I didn't try it. How's the coffee?"

A befuddled Hawk muttered, "It's all right." He was trying to figure out this stranger in his mother's kitchen. He'd been ready to slam his clenched fist into his face only moments ago, but something had stopped him. How did you do that to a man who offers you a cup of coffee?

Gaston sat down at the table and his eyes locked with Hawk's. "Let me enlighten you, young man. Your friend Troy

301

brought me here to your mother's when I stepped into a trap and injured myself. She nursed me back to health and we became friends. You are a very lucky young man to have such a mother and I was very lucky to have her tend to me when I needed help. It's as simple as that." He watched Hawk's face as he spoke.

Solange had been listening to the two of them and had opened the door just enough to observe them. She marveled at the expertise Gaston seemed to have in handling her firebrand son. She admired him tremendously.

Hawk sipped his coffee. "Troy brought you here, you say?"

"That's right."

"When was this?" the young man inquired of Gaston. The older man tried to keep an amused smile from coming to his face. After all, he had bartered and parried with men much smarter than this young man. Gaston knew he was curious about just how long he'd been hanging around the cabin.

"A few weeks ago, I guess. Don't exactly know, Hawk."

Hawk considered that an evasive reply. This formidable French Canadian was an impressive figure of a man that Hawk could not take lightly. Hawk knew he was not the slightest bit intimidating to Gaston, though his sharp features and fierce black eyes could give him a menacing look, he'd been told by Troy and others.

Solange considered that she'd delayed making her appearance long enough. She put on her robe over her nightgown and moved out of her bedroom to join the two men.

"My son, you have returned home," she said as she walked toward him with her arms extended. Gaston sat there to observe their reunion.

As the two of them embraced, Hawk told her, "Only for a few hours, Mother, and then I must be on my way. I'm still on my job. I merely took the long way so I could come by to see you."

"Well, that was very good of you, dear. Just to see you for a short time is wonderful to me after all these weeks." She looked over at Gaston and smiled warmly. "I see I have no need to introduce you to Gaston. Obviously the two of you have become acquainted over a cup of coffee."

"We have, Solange," Gaston told her. The breakfast could wait as far as he was concerned. He rose from the table and went over to the stove to put the skillet to the back. Marching over to take his woolen jacket and cap off the peg, he announced to the two of them, "I trust the two of you will excuse me because I've some traps to check."

He felt that if Hawk had only a brief time to spend with his mother, it was best he leave the two of them together. Solange knew immediately that this was his motive and she loved him all the more for it.

She made a hearty breakfast for Hawk, finishing up what Gaston had started to prepare for the two of them before Hawk's arrival. With the ham, she'd baked some biscuits and fried some eggs. Knowing Hawk loved the special gravy she made from the ham drippings, she prepared a bowl for him to enjoy with the biscuits. He ate ravenously as he always did. After he'd finished eating and they'd talked for a while, Hawk announced, "I must be on my way. This is actually railroad time I've spent here."

"Can you spend more time soon, Hawk?"

"I can't tell you, Mother. I don't know."

"You speak of many weeks then, or maybe months?"

"Possibly." He rose from the chair and gathered his jacket and hat. Solange followed him as he moved toward the front door and out to the hitching post where his pinto was tethered. She thought as she walked with him about Gaston's sage words—about how she'd be here all alone as Hawk went about his life. He was right!

Hawk bent down to kiss his mother's cheek and then he mounted the pinto to ride away. But he could not restrain his curiosity any longer. His black eyes searched her face as he asked, "What is this man to you, Mother? I think I have the right to know."

303

As she'd always done with Hawk, she gave him a straightforward, honest answer. "You certainly have a right, Hawk, and I'm most happy to tell you that I plan to marry Gaston. We love each other very much and I hope you will be happy for me that I've found such a fine man to care for me."

An expressionless look was on Hawk's face. His eyes gave her no clue to his true feelings.

"I always wish you happiness, Mother," he said, quickly reining the pinto into action and galloping away. He never turned to look back or wave to her as he usually did when he rode away.

As she slowly walked back into her cabin, she blessed the time that Gaston came into her life. For twenty years and more, she'd given her whole life to Hawk. Now it was time to take a little, before her life was over.

From this day forward, she would enjoy a few pleasures for herself!

Chapter Forty

Things had just not been the same here at the ranch since Gillian's visit to Solange's cabin. Gillian did not know how to please John Foster. Everything she did seemed to meet with his disapproval, and she also knew that his mood was causing trouble between him and Mother Foster.

Her afternoon with Solange had been so pleasant, and the time had passed so swiftly, that she never managed to bring up the problems plaguing her and the many questions she'd planned to ask Solange. Now she was embarrassed to speak of those things to Nancy Foster. After all, when they'd been returning home from Tucson she'd excitedly revealed to Mother Foster that Steve Lafferty had asked her to marry him. But then, after she'd been back at the ranch a few weeks there had been that letter from Melissa Clayton, relating to her that she'd seen Lafferty in the buggy with Virginia Curtis. She could imagine the supercilious grin on Melissa's face as she wrote that letter.

The same day she'd received her letter, Mother Foster had received one from her sister, Helen. She was so overjoyed by Helen's good news about her partnership in the inn that Gillian dared not say anything about the news Melissa had written about Lafferty. Besides, she did have her pride. Still, she yearned to throw herself into Nancy's arms and cry.

Instead, she'd waited until she went to her room to give way to the tears that flowed and flowed. Later, she consoled herself by telling herself over and over again that Melissa was a conniving little liar. It might not be true!

But when days and weeks passed and she received no word from Steve, nor had he arrived at the ranch, she did have to question if he'd played her false.

Today when their neighbor, Gregory Hill, stopped by the ranch on his way home from Tucson and she'd chanced to hear him telling John what was happening there, Gillian was numbed by his remarks about Steve Lafferty.

She'd heard him telling John, "Know that young man that paid you a visit back some months ago—believe you told me, John, that you and Nancy knew his father years ago. Isn't that right?"

"That's right, Gregory," John had replied.

"Saw him getting off the stagecoach coming in from San Diego. Had him one fancy lady in tow. She was some looker, I got to tell you."

"You sure it was Steve Lafferty, Gregory?"

"Know it was. Heard the driver address him as Captain Lafferty."

Gillian heard no more of their conversation as she staggered to her bedroom door. Flinging herself across the bed, she gave way to floods of tears. Steve did not love her, and he had himself a fancy lady who had returned to Tucson with him. All this sweet talk he'd whispered in her ear was for one purpose only, and that was to have his way with her.

She had to face the truth that she had his baby within her body—of that she was certain now—but she did not have his love. He had never had any intention of keeping those false promises he'd made her that day in the mission grounds before he was to leave for San Diego. God, what a foolish fancy she'd dwelled in!

But by the time she roused from her bed and wiped away the tears, she was angry! She'd show him. He would be the loser, and someday he might seek her out. She'd delight in flaunting the son or daughter that was his, but she'd have no part of him! If Solange would do what she did, then Gillian vowed that she, too, could have her baby and make a life for him or her.

She had nothing to be ashamed of, for her child would be a child of love as far as she was concerned. Solange could not say that about Cochise, yet, she loved Hawk dearly! Gillian still loved Lafferty. Her only torment was that he did not love her.

She could do nothing about that, but she could prove herself to be the woman she wanted to be. She could be the woman Solange Touraine was! That was enough to give her the courage and strength for whatever she might have to face in the future.

The next morning, it was not so painful to sit across the table from John Foster. Ironically, her new attitude had its effect on Foster.

She finished her breakfast in silence and left the table to do her usual morning chores. But Nancy Foster did not like discord in her house. She was tired of her husband's quiet, sullen air and she had no patience with it. She was a woman who spoke her mind and damned if she was going to let this thing fester any longer. Enough was enough!

When Gillian came back from gathering eggs in the barn, Nancy put down the basket of peas she'd been shelling. "You wnat to finish these, honey. I got something to do," she told Gillian.

"Sure, Mother Foster." Gillian watched her leave the kitchen to go out the back door, having no idea that she was so riled and disgusted with John's petty behavior.

Gillian finished shelling the peas and put them in the cast-iron pot to cook for their evening meal.

No one had to tell John Foster that his wife was not pleased with him. He knew this woman very well after all these years of being married to her. A look of her eyes could tell him immediately if she was irritated. Those occasions had been rare during the years they'd been married.

Had they had sons and daughters, John had realized the last few days, their lives would not have been as serene as they had been. The chances were they would have had many arguments. His gentle, forgiving Nancy would have been at odds with him numerous times, he realized.

He went to his usual place of solitude when he and she had experienced one of their little tiffs—on one of the bales of hay there in the barn.

Nancy knew exactly where she would find him when she marched across the barnyard. There was no woman who looked more fierce than Nancy Foster when her temper was ready to explode. "Well, John Foster—are you going to tell me what the burr under your saddle is all about? I'm riled—I don't have to tell you that, I guess!"

"I know that, Nancy," he told her, taking his unlit pipe out of his mouth. "I know how fond you are of that little girl. I just don't believe she told us the truth and I feel we both deserve that from her."

"Dear God, John! Maybe she didn't, but don't you sit there on your rump and tell me that you never lied to your own parents. Did that make you a bad son and did your parents treat you with the coldness that you have been giving to Gillian ever since she went to Solange Touraine's cabin without telling us?"

"Everything you say is true, Nancy. I won't argue with you about that," her husband confessed to her.

"There's—there's more to it, John, and you and I both know it. Lord, maybe it was God's will and wisdom that we didn't have any children." There was no mercy in her tone as she glared at him and he knew that she meant every word. The words pained him deeply. When his eyes searched her face, Nancy saw the hurt there. "Oh, don't—don't say that, Nancy. I don't like you to ever think that."

"Can't help it when you're acting the way you're acting, John."

"Well, sit down here for a minute, Nancy," he urged her. He had not planned to mention to his wife that one of their

308

neighboring ranchers had seen Hawk ride down from the mountain the morning after Gillian had been up at his mother's cabin. John recalled that Gillian had told her and Nancy that Hawk was away on a scouting job. Obviously this had not been the truth, John concluded.

When Nancy took a seat beside him on the bale of hay, he told her about this. "If he is scouting for the railroad, then how could he be back here in the mountains? Now Jeb knows Hawk when he sees him, Nancy."

John went on to explain to Nancy that he figured Hawk must have been visiting his mother. He could tell that his words made a stunning impact on Nancy.

It was rare that Nancy was struck numb, but it took her a few moments before she could speak. "Why—why, John would she fib to us about him being there?"

"Because she would not want us to know it. Maybe our little Gillian is attracted to Hawk. He is one handsome devil, I'll admit. But he's half Apache and there's no denying that. Maybe she might feel guilty about being attracted to a half-breed. After all, it was a band of Apaches who killed her parents. But I don't have to tell you when two young people are attracted to each other many things are forgotten."

Nancy chided herself privately for having doubted her devoted husband. She had been too harsh on him. "Well, I have no doubts that Hawk found Gillian very intriguing. His dark eyes adored her all the time he sat here in our kitchen that afternoon."

She reached out to take her husband's weathered hand as she told him, "Oh, John—I have nothing against Hawk. He seemed like a fine young man, but I question if Gillian could ever erase from her mind that he was part Apache."

Just the warm feel of her touch on his hand was all John needed to tell him that she was no longer angry with him. That meant everything to him!

"Well, Hawk is a man who could turn a young girl's head easily and her heart would rule her instead of her head. It would be later that the heartache would set in, and I don't want

309

that to happen to Gillian. I love that little girl as though she was the daughter we didn't have."

Nancy saw the mist in her husband's eyes, and her arms went around his neck. "Oh, John, please forgive me! You would have made a wonderful father! The best!"

That was his darling Nancy. She could be so blunt, with that honesty of hers, but she could so quickly sweep the hurt away with a generous outpouring of her love.

When the two of them emerged from the barn there were no more misunderstandings between them. They strolled across the barnyard holding hands like young lovers.

It was a wonderful sight to Gillian as she looked out the kitchen window. To think that she had caused problems for these dear, good people who'd been so kind to her had weighed heavily on her mind lately. Now that heavy burden had been lifted from her shoulders.

Surely, this was what love really was, Gillian told herself as she stood there, watching them walk side by side. This is what she would hope to have with the man she loved.

She watched them strolling along with their hands clasped together. She saw Nancy give one of her gusts of laughter and John's face brighten with one of his slow, easy smiles. Gillian knew this was the kind of love that was endless and forever.

She'd thought she'd found this with Steve, but the last few weeks had changed many things about her romantic fantasy. She could not allow herself to daydream about that fantasy any longer. She was faced with the stark reality that she was pregnant! She was also faced with the responsibility of that baby she carried within her, whether the father acknowledged it or not!

It no longer mattered that she loved him as she'd never love another man as long as she lived. It was obvious that he did not love her.

Gillian vowed now that she'd not be played for a fool again as long as she lived. She'd do whatever she must for herself and her baby!

Chapter Forty-One

A big broad grin creased Troy's face when he opened his cabin door and saw his good friend Hawk standing there. "Damn, Hawk—this is an unexpected pleasure. Had no idea you were anywhere around these parts. Figured you to be many miles away. Come on in."

Hawk crossed the threshold in silence but Troy took no notice of that, for there were many times when Hawk fell into a quiet mood.

"Seen your mother yet? She'll be tickled to death to see you, Hawk." Troy turned to stir up the logs in his fireplace.

"I've seen my mother. Also seen the stranger who seems to be making himself very much at home in our cabin. I've you to thank, Troy, for taking him there so I've been given to understand," Hawk's deep voice declared.

Slowly, Troy placed the wooden bellows down on the hearth. He didn't have to turn around and look at Hawk's face to know the violent indignation churning within his old friend. Nor did he have to be warned about the ferocious, dangerous person Hawk could be at times. He'd never expected Hawk to be threatening to him, but right now, he wasn't too sure.

Troy replied in a cool calm voice. "I did take Gaston to your mother's cabin, Hawk, because he was badly injured. I suspect if you'd come across the man as I did, out there in the woods, you would have done the same thing."

"And after the man was doctored and tended to by my mother, you left this stranger there when I was not home to protect her, Troy?" His black eyes sparked with fire. Troy was prepared for those mighty fists to strike out, and Troy was no fool: he knew he was no match for the husky Hawk.

All he could do was tell Hawk the truth and what he chose to believe was up to him, Troy considered. "It was your mother's idea that I come on home and let the man rest there overnight, Hawk. I—I've never questioned Solange's wisdom so I did as she suggested."

Had Hawk not been so enraged at what he'd found back at the cabin, he would have known there was complete honesty and truth to Troy's words. But it was not only Troy he was angry with. He was angry with his mother, too. Never had he thought about her marrying again. He'd never imagined anyone sharing that cabin with her except himself. Her declaration that she was going to marry this stranger had given him a stunning blow. When he rode away from the cabin and into the woods, he cared not if he ever returned there again.

"Did you know that since all this happened the man has not left there? He's remained."

"I knew he had stayed for a few days because I made a daily trip by there. When it was obvious to me that Gaston could move around on that foot and he assured me he was fine, I didn't go over after that. Solange seemed to be in fine spirits and handling everything as she usually does—just fine. Tell me, Hawk, what is it that has you so out of sorts?"

A frown came to Hawk's face as he moved a couple of steps closer to Troy. Troy figured this was it and clenched his teeth to receive the blow he knew he was about to receive. But the blow did not come. "She's planning on marrying this—this man she's known a few short weeks while I was away," Hawk said.

"And you put the blame on me for that, Hawk? Well, I won't accept that. Yes, I took Gaston there, for your cabin was closer than mine and the man was in need of help immediately. But Solange's decision to marry him cannot be put on my back." He turned to his stove to pick up the coffeepot. Somehow, the fear that Hawk was going to strike him no longer troubled him. "Want a cup of coffee, Hawk?"

But when Troy turned around he saw that Hawk had already turned on his heel to move toward the door. "No, Troy—I must be on my way. I've lingered here in Maricopa County too long as it is. Still got some country to scout out for the railroad."

He said no more as he moved out the door. There was no farewell, no promise to see Troy when he returned. Troy watched his friend ride away on the pinto and he wondered what was really tormenting Hawk's soul.

As he sat there sipping the coffee, he had to confess he was a bit baffled by the news Hawk had told him about Solange's plans to marry Gaston Dion. He'd never known her to be a foolhardy, impulsive woman. To have announced it to Hawk as she did meant she'd most certainly made up her mind to do it. It didn't seem like such a bad idea to Troy if the two middle-aged people had come to care for each other during the last few weeks.

How could Hawk possibly resent his mother for finally having a little happiness after she'd devoted all of her life to him?

By the time Hawk would have taken the fork in the road which would carry him back in the direction of the territory he was assigned to scout, a savage impulse took over and he gave way to it.

He rode to that particular spot which had been his lookout point on the mountain, the spot where his view of the valley was perfect for sighting of the comings and goings of anyone down there at the Foster ranch. How often he'd sat there and watched the beautiful vision of Gillian Browne walking around

313

the grounds or across the barnyard carrying her bucket of feed.

No one knew about the vigil he'd kept on that peak for over a year, long before he'd chanced to meet her in the woods after the fall from her horse. Once again he wanted to relive this pleasant secret time of his life. He needed the serenity of that spot, and if he was lucky, and his eyes might savor the sight of the beautiful Gillian, then maybe all this turbulence would subside. Maybe the foggy confusion of his thoughts would be lifted.

It mattered not to him that night had quickly come on the countryside, for he'd slept out in the woods many nights. As long as he had the woods to roam in search of his supper and a campfire to cook it over, his belly would be filled. Another twenty-four hours would make no difference on his job, he convinced himself.

When his pinto was secured in the grove of trees and Hawk had taken down some of his gear to place it in the spot which would be his campsite, he looked down at the valley. But there was nothing to see except the smoke circling skyward from the chimney of the Fosters' house.

He took out his rifle and laid it down on the blanket he'd spread on the ground. He'd shoot rabbit or a squirrel for his supper. Now that he thought about it, it had been a long time since he'd gone hunting in the woods or stayed out there a couple of nights to hunt wild game for his mother's table.

His dark face flashed when he glanced back down in the direction of the valley to see two figures moving across the barnyard. He quickly recognized John and Nancy Foster, so he returned to setting up his gear.

Before the sun went down, Hawk set out on foot into the thicker section of the woods to hunt. Since these woods were flourishing with many creatures and he was an expert marksman, he had himself two fine young rabbits for roasting over his campfire in less than an hour's time. Before the sun had finally set, he had them skewered and placed over his fire.

By now, he could see the bright lights of the lamps glowing

through the windows of the Fosters' house down below. He could picture the three of them gathered around the table in Nancy Foster's spic-and-span kitchen, enjoying a fine meal. How lovely Gillian's face must look, he thought to himself! He'd never seen her by lamplight or candlelight. But she could not possibly be any lovelier than she was with the bright sunshine gleaming on her fair, flawless skin.

The roasted rabbits were tender and juicy and he enjoyed the fine feast they provided. There were sweet wild berries, too, so he was sated by the time he finished.

The fire was now a glowing mound of smoldering coals, so he got up to add some additional branches to the fire. The heat warmed him and he realized the coldness in his heart had suddenly faded. Hawk was glad he'd decided to stay here alone on this mountain tonight. It had soothed the rage churning within him.

There in the quiet of the darkness surrounding him, he realized that he was wrong to be so angry with Troy. Everything Troy had said was the truth and he, too, would have carried the injured man to his mother to tend to. Knowing what a strong-willed, determined lady she was, he didn't even doubt Troy when he said that it was her idea that he go on home because the hour was late.

Dear God, he of all people should know that Solange Touraine was capable of taking care of herself!

All rage was gone for Troy and his mother. These two people had given him their devoted loyalty for years. How could he possibly have doubted either of them?

Hawk crawled inside his bedroll to get himself a good night's sleep so he'd be ready to travel back to Tucson at dawn's first light. His dreams were of Gillian Browne and the cabin he would build with his own strong hands. That Irishman could not build her a cabin, but *he* could. It would be a fine cabin because he would put all his love and devotion into making it so.

Gillian would look at it and fling her arms around his neck

with delight when she saw it for the first time. He would hunt and fish so they would never want for food. He dreamed of Gillian picking the beautiful wildflowers she loved and he dreamed of his mother teaching Gillian about herbs and teaching her how to dry and preserve them.

The dream went on and on until he dreamed of Gillian with a baby in her arms. But the baby did not have coarse thick black hair like his. The small infant had a mop of sandy-colored hair, unlike his or Gillian's.

He dreamed that he questioned Gillian about this and she looked up at him with those big blue eyes of hers, honestly confessing to him, "This is Lafferty's baby, Hawk."

This was enough to jar Hawk awake out of his sleep. He sat up in his bedroll to stare out at the blackness of the night surrounding him. His campfire had died down to embers now. He sat there for a long time before lying back down to try to go to sleep again.

In the valley below, Gillian stared out of her bedroom into the same darkness. She wondered what the reddish-golden glow was that she observed up on the mountain peak.

At first, she was startled by it, thinking that it might be a roaming band of Apaches. She thought about waking up the Fosters, but she hesitated, sure that they were both sound asleep by now. Instead, she just sat there in the darkness of her bedroom and looked up at the mountain.

When she noticed that the glow began to dim, she relaxed, and she also recalled hearing John Foster talk about the ranchers who went up in the mountains to camp out for a few nights to do some hunting.

Wild game flourished in those mountains all year long. She recalled how John Foster always went there to get himself a turkey for the holiday feasts. This was enough to ease the apprehension and fear when she first spied the flaming glow up there on the mountain.

Wearily, she lay back down, letting her head rest on the soft pillow. Sleep came quickly!

Chapter Forty-Two

Gillian was not the only one in the Foster household who spied the glowing fires on the mountain peak. Nancy's first thought was that a band of renegade Apaches were camped up there, plotting an attack on their ranch, so sleep did not come to her for many long hours. She was tempted to wake up her husband, but probably it was one of the ranchers up there, hunting. So she just lay there in her bed and watched, listening for any sounds that might alert her to danger.

Eventually, she drifted off to sleep from sheer exhaustion, but when the new day was dawning she was not ready to meet it, for she felt weary. John noticed the tired look on her face as she was preparing his breakfast. "You look tired, Nancy."

"Got to confess I am, John. I didn't sleep too well last night. Saw a strange sight up there in the mountains late last night that disturbed me. There was a campfire burning in the late-night hours. Couldn't sleep, thinking it might be some of those damned Apaches hellbent on doing us harm. Watched it until it died down and then I guess I finally went off to sleep."

"Sorry, honey. I don't think we've got that to worry about from all the news I've heard lately. That Geronimo is a different breed from old Cochise. He lingers not too long in one spot as the old chief did. They say he is a man of indecision and that is why no one can deal with him as they could with the

317

old Chiracahua. There's talk around town that he and his band are holed up in a remote area of the territory in those steeple-sided canyons where they know they are safe."

"Oh, I hope you're right, John." Nancy sighed.

"Sure I am, dear. Sooner or later even Geronimo must know he can't win this battle with the army. He's too far outnumbered and he can't fight those kind of odds. Cochise had come to realize it before he died. That's why he finally agreed to that treaty. Cochise was a man you could reason with, but Geronimo is crazy in the head."

John gave her an assuring kiss on the cheek as he prepared to go out to the barn while she finished up cooking their breakfast. Nancy felt better now that her husband had assured her that she had nothing to fear.

By the time he returned, she had his breakfast ready to serve and the two of them sat down at the kitchen table. Nancy was more like her old self, he was glad to see. "Me and Bill are going into town to get some supplies we're needing," he told her. "Is there anything I can bring back for you, honey?"

"As a matter of fact there is, John. I need some yarn. I've a lot of knitting to get done with the holidays coming on. I'll write you down a list of the colors I want. Got a little vest I've started for Gillian in the prettiest shade of blue, like the wildflowers out there in our pasture in the springtime."

John laughed. "She seems to be a sleepyhead this morning. Maybe she was up late last night like you."

"Maybe she was," Nancy remarked. She started removing the dishes from the table as her husband grabbed his old felt hat to leave the kitchen.

When she had finishied writing her list, she went to see if Gillian was still sleeping. It was unusual for her to stay in her bedroom so late in the morning.

When she cracked the door slightly, she saw the girl sitting there in her cotton gown. "Gillian, honey—are you all right?"

"Wasn't feeling too good this morning, Mother Foster. I didn't rest too well last night. I feel like I'm coming down

318

with something."

"Now we can't have that, sugar." Nancy marched over to the bed to place her hand on Gillian's forehead. "Don't seem to have a fever."

"I—I don't feel like I have a fever!" Gillian's blue eyes looked up into the woman's kind face smiling down at her. "I—I'm sure I'll be all right, Mother Foster. Really!"

"I'm sure you will be, too. By the way, John's going into town. You need anything?"

"Can't think of a thing. Are you going with him?"

"No, just he and Bill going in."

For some reason Gillian could not explain, she was glad that Mother Foster was going to stay at home. Now that the sun was up and the darkness was gone, she still remembered that strange sight there on the mountain peak late last night.

Nancy Foster sensed that Gillian was relieved to hear that she was going to be there at the house with her, and she wondered if Gillian, too, had sighted the campfire on the mountain.

With the light of a new day shining down on his coppery face, Hawk roused from his bedroll. He felt refreshed and ready to travel. He felt no need to eat after the hearty feast he'd enjoyed the night before, but he did feel the need for some strong, black coffee. He took the time to brew that as he packed up his gear.

Glancing down in the valley, he saw that no one was stirring around the ranch, but by the time his pot of coffee was ready he saw Foster's wagon move down the drive. There on the seat with Foster was one of his hired hands.

Once he had his fill, he tossed the remainder of the coffee on the ground. He was ready to ride for Tucson.

Leaping astride Tache, he spurred the pinto into motion and moved down the winding mountain trail which took him into the canyon below. From there, he'd take the southern route back to Tucson.

But as he came to the base of the mountain, he caught a fleeting glimpse of Gillian dashing from the barnyard to the small grove of trees where there was a crystal clear spring, its bubbling waters cascading over boulders. He yanked on the reins to watch her scamper through the meadow with her hands holding up the folds of her full, gathered skirt. Her long hair was flowing back, free and loose as she moved swiftly.

She reminded him of a wood nymph, too beautiful and enchanting to be real, Hawk thought as he sat there astride his horse admiring her.

When he knew he should have spurred Tache to move on toward his destination, he had to give way to the impulse to veer off the trail and guide Tache toward the grove of trees.

He could not deny himself a few precious moments with her. It had not been something he'd expected to have, but now that the opportunity had come his way, he had to take advantage of it.

His dark eyes could see her long before she realized that he was approaching. He watched her curvy figure bending over to fill her pails with the cool spring water.

Slowly, he cantered the pinto toward her. She did not turn to see him until he was within a few feet of her. She gave a gasp and then a soft little gale of laughter. "Oh, Lord, Hawk—you gave me a scare for a minute until I saw it was you!"

"Sorry, little one. I should have called out to you. Forgive me!" His dark eyes sparked warmly as they gazed down on her. She looked up at him with a sweet, lovely smile on her face. Setting her bucket down, she sat back on the grassy knoll.

"I didn't know you were back, Hawk."

"I just made a fast stop as I was close by, doing my scouting. I'm heading back toward Tucson now."

"I see. I know your mother was delighted to have you come by for a visit," she remarked as he leaped down from the horse.

"Oh, yes—she was pleased." Sinking down on the ground beside her, he cupped his hands to enjoy a cool drink of the spring water. "Nothing tastes so grand as spring water."

"Nothing so grand to wash your hair with, either," she declared gaily.

A teasing grin was on his bronzed face as he remarked, "Is that what makes that hair of yours so full of fire and flames?"

"I can't tell you that, Hawk. But I love to wash my hair with the spring water and I have ever since I came across this spring."

His long fingers reached out tenderly to touch one of the curling tresses hanging over her shoulder. "Beautiful hair, Gillian. I've never seen any woman with hair so beautiful."

Gillian remembered what Solange had told her about what Hawk called her hair, but she made no mention of that. Instead, she thanked him for his compliment.

His firm, muscled body was so close to her! She noticed how intense his dark eyes were, piercing her. She suddenly felt ill at ease, for she sensed that Hawk was going to kiss her and she knew not how she would react to his demanding lips claiming hers.

Suddenly, she felt the heat of his arm at her back. There was no more time left for thinking about anything, because Hawk's other powerful hand was on her shoulder, drawing her close to his broad chest, and his lips were upon hers, demanding that she respond to him. It was a lingering, tender kiss, unlike the fury of ecstasy Steve could ignite within her.

When he released her, his eyes searched her face for a moment before he sought to speak. "Remember, Gillian— always remember that if you ever need me, I will be there. I wanted you to know that before I leave here. Nothing would ever stop me from coming to you if you want me, little one."

Wide-eyed and breathless, she watched him rise up from the ground and saunter over to release the reins from the trunk of the tree where he'd tied Tache. With a swift leap to straddle Tache, he gave her a broad smile as he bade her farewell.

"Goodbye, Hawk," she murmured softly as she watched him gallop away.

321

She was left there with the quiet solitude of the trees and the bubbling spring. Over in the distance, she could hear the soulful call of a turtle dove, and she thought about Hawk's last words to her. Dear God, why couldn't she have given her heart and her love to a man like Hawk? He was so good and kind. With Hawk, she knew that all she'd have to do was ask and he would give her anything he could.

But if he knew that she carried Stephen Lafferty's child he might feel differently, she thought as she sat there quietly. All kinds of mixed emotions washed over her as she thought about the two men who'd become a part of her life.

Love was not exactly as her girlish daydreams had envisioned it to be! She feared she had allowed herself to be a silly romantic fool where the dashing Irish sea captain had been concerned. It would seem that he'd marched into her life and taken his moment of pleasure. As quickly, he'd disappeared!

How deceptive love could be, Gillian realized!

Chapter Forty-Three

Steve Lafferty felt like a man freed of bondage as he prepared to board the stagecoach. Back in Maricopa County he'd have his final meeting with Howard Curtis, shake hands on a job completed, and collect his handsome fee. And he'd see his beautiful Gillian and claim her for his own.

When he leaped up into the coach, he was not prepared for the sight of the woman sitting there in her flashy scarlet gown and her scarlet bonnet with dancing little black feathers.

He recognized her immediately. "Well, Señora Montera—I must say this is a surprise!"

"A pleasant one, I hope," she cooed, her flirting black eyes ogling him.

Steve moved on into the coach, taking the seat across from her without making a comment until he was seated.

"Where is your destination, señora?"

"Same as yours, I believe, Captain Lafferty. I'm going to Tucson. I hear that Tucson is going to be a booming place soon, with the Southern Pacific completed. I think it could take another fine restaurant. I plan to give the Old Pueblo Inn a run for the money that's going to be flowing there."

Lafferty laughed. "I don't think you're going to get a grand welcome from Melba Jackson, so I'd suggest that you not seek lodging at the inn."

"This Melba Jackson—is she the owner of the inn?"

"That's right! Best you stay at the hotel when you get to Tucson," Lafferty told her.

Tilting her head, she quizzed Steve, "And where do you stay, Lafferty?"

"I stay at the Old Pueblo, but my stay is going to be brief this time, señora."

The stage began to roll out of San Diego and Steve settled back in his seat, taking out the silver case to enjoy one of his cheroots. "It won't offend you if I smoke, will it, señora?"

"Not at all. But may I request that you quit calling me señora, Lafferty! It's a long ride we're going to be sharing. No point in being so formal, do you think?"

"All right, Alfreda! I'll go along with that." He knew exactly what this feisty woman had on her mind, but she was due to be sadly disappointed.

At the first station stop, a young couple boarded the stage for the ride into Tucson, so she did not have the privacy of the coach with Steve Lafferty.

The trip to Tucson from San Diego was miserably hot, and the countryside was experiencing a drought. Waves of dust invaded the coach.

The station stops did not provide the grandest accommodations, and the food was terrible. Alfreda's mood became waspish and Lafferty's Irish wit could no longer bring a smile to her face by the time they were nearing Tucson.

Privately, she was wishing she'd not set out on this venture. But what she had not told Lafferty was she and her husband had had a fierce fight, so she'd taken all the funds she could gather and decided to strike out on her own.

This was nothing new to Alfreda. Two years with Ramón Montera in San Diego were enough, and the job of helping him run the Blue Moon had lost its excitement. It was the same when she'd left a husband and his tavern back in San Francisco a few years earlier to wander southward down to San Diego. She always managed to leave with her reticule filled with

324

plenty of money.

So it was this time. Ramón would find himself short of funds when he discovered that she'd slipped out of the city to catch the stage for Tucson. But she also knew that there was nothing he could do once she was gone.

Steve's good-natured soul could not completely dismiss her when the stage did arrive in Tucson. Gallantly, he offered to see her to the hotel. She accepted his offer, anticipating the sheer joy of a comfortable room and the luxury of a bath.

He bade her farewell in the lobby of the Granada Hotel. "I wish you much success, Alfreda. I won't be around to see it happen, but I have a feeling you'll get what you want."

There was not one hint of the vivacious lady she had appeared to be earlier. Alfreda was weary and she had suddenly realized during this long trip that she was not getting any younger. In fact, the years were catching up with her. There was a weak, sly grin on her face as she told him quite honestly, "What I want right now, Lafferty, is a good, comfortable bed and a warm bath. Maybe our paths will cross again, but in case they don't, I wish you the best."

He gave her one last smile before he turned back in the buggy, on his way to his own lodgings at the Pueblo Inn.

Alfreda turned to follow the young man carrying her bags toward the stairway. By the time she'd climbed the stairway and walked down the carpeted hallways she had already come to the conclusion that her rooms were certainly not going to be so grand.

Once she was inside the room, Alfreda sank down on the bed to survey her new surroundings. They were drab and dull and it was enough to depress her. But she reminded herself that she'd been stuck in worse places than this more than once in her life.

She vowed that she wouldn't be here long. No, she'd change all this for something better, she promised herself as she started opening her bags. Right now, she had a bath to take and she'd get a good night's sleep. Then she could face tomorrow with a clear head.

Alfreda Montera had always made her opportunities happen and she had no doubt that she'd do it again right here in Tucson.

Hawk had ridden long and hard all day after he'd said goodbye to Gillian. He did not stop to make his camp as early as he might have, feeling that he should give the railroad some extra time since he'd given himself extra time to stop by his mother's cabin. There was no way for his boss, Barstow, to know this, but Hawk knew it.

He was bone-weary tired by the time he'd finally stopped and fixed himself a meal. He fell asleep as soon as he lay down on his bedroll.

When the first rays of the rising sun came through the trees to wake him up, Hawk came alive and prepared to put in another full day of searching the canyons and cliffs of the countryside.

He went over several miles by midday without seeing any bands of Apaches riding up on the high plateaus or canyons. Nor did he see any circling smoke from their campfires, so he was feeling encouraged that he would be giving a good report to Warner Barstow.

By late afternoon, he was satisfied that he'd put in a full day. In fact, the countryside was so quiet and peaceful, Hawk felt as if he were the only one around for miles and miles. He was sure that the railroad men would have no trouble laying their tracks.

One more night he would be camping out and sleeping under the starlit sky. Tomorrow night he would be back in Tucson.

He turned in early, but not because he was sleepy. Gillian dominated his thoughts, so he lay on his bedroll and thought about her as he gazed up at all the twinkling stars. They reminded him of the bright twinkle in her deep blue eyes. He yearned to be riding back in the direction where he'd just

326

come from instead of Tucson.

Then sleep did overtake him, he dreamed sweet dreams about the pretty girl with her hair of flaming fire, but an early-morning storm interrupted his dreams as it moved in over the mountains and swept down into the valley.

As quickly as he could, he gathered up his gear and mounted up on Tache to make it to the shelter of a cave he knew about that was only a short distance away. By now torrents of rain were falling and his shirt and pants were already wet. He spurred Tache into a fast gallop.

Once he arrived at the cozy enclosure and led Tache inside the cavern, he decided he might as well wait out the storm and brew himself a steaming pot of coffee. Once he'd started a fire, he roamed back farther in the cavern. A strange object caught his attention on the floor of the cave. It was a beaded and featherlike fan, and he picked it up to examine it more carefully. A short distance away, his dark eyes now came upon a dust-covered pouch. His curious nature urged him to go back a few more feet, and there he discovered an old two-piece peyote staff, along with a gourd rattle.

Holding these things brought a chill over Hawk, and he flung them back on the floor of the cave. Apaches had been here and he wanted no part of them. In a frenzy, he tried to rub the dirt and dust of them from his hands.

God, let the rains stop, he silently muttered as he turned on his heel to check his coffeepot. To drink a cup of coffee and be on his way was the only thing he wanted right now.

He poured the steaming brew into his tin cup and looked at the entrance of the cave to see the heavy downpour of rain falling from the sky. He realized there was no point in drinking the coffee hastily, for he had time to spare. He sipped the hot brew cautiously and slowly.

It was the strange whinny Tache gave that made him turn quickly around to look over his shoulder. When he did, he viewed a strange sight. Hawk wasn't sure he was seeing a man or an apparition back there in the cave. A band held his long black hair away from his wrinkled, weathered face. It was an expressionless face he saw, except for a pair of piercing black eyes. Hawk saw that his tunic and baggy pants were ragged and torn.

"Who are you?" Hawk's deep voice demanded.

"I am Loco of the Mimbres," the old Indian muttered in a cracking, faltering voice. "Who are you?"

"I am called Hawk."

"Ah, yes—Hawk—a fitting name for one so strong as you. Well, Hawk, could old Loco beg of you a cup of whatever you are drinking?"

Hawk could hardly refuse such a request from a man who looked so helpless.

"You been camping in here? You must have been far back there. I didn't know you were back there," Hawk told him as he handed him a cup of coffee.

"A while. And you—what are you doing here in this place, Hawk?"

"A refuge from the storm, until I can travel on to Tucson. I happened to remember this cave when the storm struck." Hawk noticed that the Indian studied his face most carefully.

"I sought refuge here, too, from Geronimo. I did not wish to ride by his side. He is a fool and he can't win, so he is only getting more people killed. I wanted no part of his crazy, hopeless plans so I came here to hide out."

"You knew Cochise?"

"I knew him and he was a far smarter man than Geronimo will ever be. He faced the truth, and if only he'd have lived many lives could have been saved. This was a favorite spot of his. Did you know this? He came here to smoke his pipe of peyote and think about what he should do for his people."

"No, I did not know this," Hawk told him. But as he listened to the old Indian, he found it interesting that he had been drawn here a few years ago. Was it that old devil Cochise who'd drawn him here?

"That is interesting, for this is a secret place—very secluded and concealed by underbrush. It isn't a place one just happens upon. In fact, one could ride right past it and not know about the opening of this cave."

Hawk offered the man some food from his saddlebag and Loco eagerly accepted. He noticed that the rains had subsided, and he decided to leave all the supplies of food he had left for Loco. He looked as if he could use them and he would be back in Tucson before nightfall so he had no use for them.

"You can have these, Loco. I'm going to be hitting the trail soon. The rains are over it seems."

"You are a good man, Hawk. I could follow you if you were the leader," Loco told him as he watched the formidable young half-breed gather up his gear.

"I thank you, Loco, and I would be honored to have you follow me. But I am not a leader."

"You remind me of another man I knew, an old, dear friend," Loco told him.

"Well, Loco—I hope he was a good man. And I wish you the best wherever you roam. I must leave you now, but I'm glad we met."

"So am I, Hawk. It was an honor to meet you and talk to you, for it was like talking to my old friend, Cochise. He was a good man. At least, as good as any man is in a lifetime. He would have been proud of a son like you."

A slow smile came to Hawk's tawny face. "I am the son of Cochise, Loco." He hastily reined Tache around to ride out of the cave. Never before had he confessed that to anyone.

Somehow, it seemed right to admit this to the old Indian, a member of the Mimbres tribe.

Part Four

Love Conquers All

Hell's savage fury
to tear them apart,
succumbs to the joining
of two lovers' hearts.
— Sheila Northcott

Chapter Forty-Four

Captain Steve Lafferty seemed to be the topic of conversation in a couple of offices in Tucson. Howard Curtis had gone to Warner Barstow's office to inform him that Lafferty had now delivered all the cargo. Barstow's crews could now go forward without delay.

Barstow was delighted to get that news and assured Curtis that he had to wait only for the report from his scout. "Joe Hawk should be returning any day now, I figure."

"So you are saying that if he brings back a good report your men are ready to go?"

"That's right, Howard. My crews are ready to start laying those tracks. I figure if everything goes as smoothly as I hope, then the Southern Pacific will reach all the way to Tucson. I think we can sit back and say we've done a hell of a job, Howard. We have the hardworking crews, along with Captain Lafferty and my good scout, Hawk, to thank for their services."

Howard Curtis heartily agreed with Warner. But there was an urgency gnawing at Curtis that Barstow didn't realize. He had no inkling about Howard's eagerness to get back to his home in the East. Barstow's family and the Curtis family had formed no close bond of friendship or spent much time together during Curtis's sojourn here in the territory.

Each week that kept Howard here had made his life more miserable, having to deal with his ill-tempered wife, Sue, and a whining, complaining daughter who were both homesick for their life back East. He knew he would have no peace until he got home. They considered this godforsaken country out here in the Southwest and the ways of the people very primitive and crude.

"What do you think it will take to get the rest of the tracks down, Warner?"

"Well, are you speaking of my end of the job or yours, Howard?"

"Mine!" It mattered not to Howard how long it took Warner, for he lived here anyway.

"I'd say that your part of it is over if Hawk gives me a good report. The rest of it is in my hands. But you and your family might like to stay for the grand celebration of the first run. That should be some kind of party."

Curtis gave him a mumbled reply, not committing himself one way or the other. The truth was he was eager to be on his way back East so Sue would give him some peace. Life had not been too pleasant around his house. Back there, she'd have the social life she loved, and it would be a better atmosphere for his daughter as well.

Now, he found himself anxiously awaiting the arrival of this scout, Hawk, as much as Warner was. Hawk's report could be his ticket to leave here and return to Boston.

Never had business been better, and Melba Jackson knew she'd made the right decision to bring her friend Helen into the inn as a partner. The load she'd taken off Melba's shoulders had been tremendous. The last few weeks had convinced the middle-aged lady that she was trying to do too much and it was wearing her down.

She also knew that Helen was pleased with the way her life was going. Her daughter Melissa was a changed person now that her husband's influence was no longer there. Helen and Melissa were close, the way they used to be. As for Kent Clayton, he suddenly left Tucson and no one seemed to know where he'd gone. When his creditors started to hound Helen to pay the debts he'd left behind, she flatly refused. "He's no longer my husband so I am not responsible for them. You'll have to talk to Kent about that," she'd strongly declared. Without further discussion she had turned her back on them to go about her own business.

As the two women shared a late lunch, Melba commented to Helen that Captain Lafferty had returned to the inn late the night before.

"I like that young man," Helen told Melba.

"Yes, so do I. He was a man in high spirits this morning. Said he was going shopping for his bride-to-be."

"He—he was meaning Gillian, I hope?" Helen inquired anxiously.

"Of course it is Gillian. Knew that a long time ago. First time I saw those two together," Melba remarked.

Helen gave a sigh of delight and confessed how fond she'd become of Gillian during the time she and Nancy had been visiting her.

"Those two were meant for one another, Helen. Knew that Irishman had lost his heart to that pretty little thing the way he was acting. A handsome dude like him don't sit and eat by himself unless he's head-over-heels in love. Too many gals around to snatch him up in a hurry."

They both laughed and nodded in agreement. But now their lunch break was over, and both moved out of their chairs to go their separate ways. The rest of the afternoon, Helen found herself thinking about the news Melba had told her. Would Nancy be pleased about Gillian marrying Captain Lafferty, she wondered? There was no denying how sad her sister would be when Gillian was gone from the ranch. The last two years had been so wonderful for Nancy, having the girl living there with them. There would surely be a deep void for a while.

335

When she left the inn and guided her buggy in the direction of home, she could not wait to tell Melissa the news about Captain Lafferty and Gillian.

But when she arrived, Melissa was not there. She found a note saying that she and Caywood had gone to a picnic. It seemed that Melissa was spending most of her time with Caywood lately; her other suitors no longer came around as they used to.

It wasn't that Helen disliked Caywood, but she knew he had a roving eye, just like Kent, and that did bother her. God knows, she didn't want Melissa making the same mistakes she'd made.

Since there was no rush for the evening meal, Helen took a leisurely stroll in her yard. A magnificent sunset lit up the western sky and she thought an artist could paint a masterpiece if he captured all this beauty. Vivid shades of purple faded to mauve and rose as the sun sank behind the mountains. She sat down on the wooden bench in her garden to enjoy the sight and the quiet peace that washed over her.

Finally, she could say that she was a happy, contented woman, and the feeling was grand. It seemed to Helen that it had taken her a whole lifetime to realize this state of bliss.

She took no notice of the time until a slight chill came to the air, since the sun was down and night was approaching. As she finally forced herself to go indoors, she thought the feel of the air was like autumn approaching.

Maybe she'd ask Melba for some time off around the holiday season so she could spend a couple of weeks with Nancy. Maybe that would fill the emptiness of Gillian being gone from the ranch when the holidays came this year.

It was late afternoon when Hawk made it to the outskirts of Tucson. On the chance that he would still find Warner working late at his office, he decided to go there first.

By the time he arrived at Barstow's office, darkness had

settled in. He was glad to see the lamp burning inside the office when he halted by the hitching post. By the time he dismounted and raced up to the office door, he could see Warner working at his desk as he'd passed the front window.

When he knocked on the door, Warner yelled at him to enter. Barstow turned to see that it was Hawk, and a broad grin broke on his face. "Good to see you back, young man. Been thinking about you a lot all day. Damned if I haven't! Come on, sit down. We've got lots to talk about!"

"Glad to be back, sir," Hawk replied as he walked over to take the seat by the cluttered desk.

"Can't help feeling a little concerned about you when you're out there scouting that wild country."

"It was as peaceful as it could be, I'm happy to report to you. Saw not one sign of any kind of threat that would endanger the job or your men, Mr. Barstow."

"That right, Hawk?"

"That's right. Geronimo might have appointed himself the leader, but there are just not that many to follow him—not here in Arizona, at least. Think the rumor that he hightailed it back across the border into Mexico might just be the truth. With more and more soldiers coming into the territory, he's got to know how outnumbered he'd be to try to fight against those odds."

"Damn, you'd think so. God, this is the news I've been wanting to hear. All the supplies have arrived from the coast so it would seem that the old Southern Pacific can go forward," Warner said. There was nothing to delay the crews and the wagons from moving out in the morning, he told Hawk.

As he leaned back in his chair, Warner happened to look up at the clock on the wall and realized he was going to be facing one irate wife when he walked through the door of his house.

"Young man, I'd say that we've both put in a good day for Southern Pacific." Warner walked around the corner of his desk with an envelope for Hawk. Handing it to him, he gave him a comradely pat on his shoulder as he praised him for the

337

job he'd done. "Have yourself a fine meal on Southern Pacific, Hawk. You'll find a little bit of a bonus for the good job you've done for me."

Hawk took the envelope and shook his hand. "Thanks, Mr. Barstow. I—I appreciate your kindness to me when I first came here to Tucson, and I'd like to think you'd consider me for the next scouting job when it comes along."

Warner laughed. "Oh, I expect this is just the beginning for us, Hawk. I've a couple of ideas I want to talk to you about after you've had a visit back home. I figure you've earned a few weeks back there in your mountains and a little time with that nice mother of yours."

Hawk was taken a little by surprise that he was now free to leave Tucson, but he was also thrilled to know he could get back to the mountains. This town held no magic for him.

Warner grabbed his hat from the peg and dimmed the lamp, and he and Hawk left the office. The older man turned and struck a bargain with Hawk. "Tell you what, Hawk—you take yourself a month off and I'll be expecting to see you back here in four weeks. I've a job to offer you I think you'll find to your liking."

A broad grin came to Hawk's bronzed face and he exuberantly agreed. "You can count on that, sir. I'll be back in a month."

Warner gave a nod of his head and told him that he'd be expecting him. Warner called out as Hawk was mounting up on Tache, "Good luck to you, young man!"

All the way home Warner thought about the young man he'd just left. Hawk was an exceptional man and he'd taken a liking to him from the first day they'd met several weeks ago. No one had to tell Barstow what an obstacle it was to be a half-breed in Arizona Territory. He'd lived here all his life and he understood the prejudice that existed. He could hardly fault it, for many had suffered from the hands of the savage Apaches, but there were those like Hawk who had not been guilty of

338

those atrocities. Yet, they were made to pay the price.

If he could help that fine young man, he was determined to do it. He'd already seen what Hawk's trust in him had done for the young man.

Warner had felt sorry for him at first, for he realized that he'd lived all his life in the mountains and this strange place must have been a little unsettling to him. He'd heard about the beating Hawk had suffered from the drunk miners, but Hawk had not been the one to mention the incident.

Warner knew that Hawk had not been prepared for the contempt a lot of the citizens of Tucson felt for half-Apaches. How could he know, since he lived in those remote mountains? But Warner had a vision that there would come a day when Tucson and Arizona would come to know and respect this man, Hawk. He would get great satisfaction in knowing he might have played a small role in making it all come about. He had the faith that Hawk would not disappoint him.

He was in such high spirits when he arrived at his cottage that he did not worry about being met at the door by an angry wife.

It was not until he arrived at the hotel and the privacy of his room that Hawk took out the contents of the envelope Mr. Barstow had handed to him. At first, he wasn't sure that he'd counted right.

He sank down in the chair and carefully laid out the contents on the nightstand. He had not been wrong the first time, but it was so much more than he'd expected.

In his whole lifetime, Hawk had never held so much money in the palm of his hand. His black eyes gleamed as he thought about what he could do with so much money.

He was rich! At least he felt that way at that moment. Why, he could give Gillian Browne anything her heart desired, he told himself!

For the longest time he just sat there, staring at the magnificent fortune. He was also convinced that he could one day become as wealthy a man as the cocky Irishman who'd intruded into Gillian's life.

Well, let him try, Hawk thought. But now he was determined to fight for the love of Gillian Browne.

In the end, it was Gillian who would pick the man she loved!

Chapter Forty-Five

It was hard for Gillian to wear a bright, cheerful smile around John or Nancy when she was feeling such anxiety. She felt helpless, not knowing what to do should Steve desert her, as it seemed he had certainly done.

Another week had gone by without any letter from him or any sight of him riding to the gate.

Finally, Gillian was given the opportunity she'd wanted for the last two weeks, a chance to go seek the counsel and advice of Solange Touraine.

Gillian was still asleep when Nancy rushed into her bedroom and shook her to wake up. "Honey, wake up! Are you awake, Gillian, enough to hear me?"

"Think I am, Mother Foster," Gillian stammered sleepily.

"Well, listen—the Hills boy is over here. He's concerned about his parents. They're both down in bed sick—so sick they can't raise their heads off the pillow. Poor kid—he's scared silly. So me and John are going over there. I'm going to cook them up some soup and tend to them all day and John's going to tend to the stock."

She quickly informed Gillian that John would be back by nightfall, but she might stay over. "Now, you don't worry that you'd be here after dark by yourself, honey."

"I'll be just fine, Mother Foster. You just go tend to your

341

friends," Gillian assured her. The minute Nancy went out the door Gillian wasted no time getting out of bed. She was dressed and had her bed made by the time their wagon was rolling down the drive. She saw the Hills's young son following behind the wagon on his horse. He couldn't have been more than ten or twelve.

She helped herself to some coffee as she went around the kitchen to put it in order. Instead of sitting down at the kitchen table she bustled around, taking a moment for a fast quick sip. When she was satisfied that everything was in order and all the dishes were washed and dried, she went through the rest of the house to see what might need to be done before she sought to carry out her own plans for the day.

In her haste to be on her way, she almost forgot to attend to her morning chores out in the barnyard. She rushed out to throw some grain to the chickens and gather up the eggs.

She found herself mumbling as she rushed back toward the house, "Now, have I done everything?" Satisfied that she had, she rushed back to her room to gather up the dark blue twill jacket hanging on the back of her bedroom door. There was a chill to the morning air. She also took the black wide-brimmed felt hat she often wore when she went riding at this time of the year.

Lately she'd been wearing her loose-fitted tunic outside the waistband of her divided riding skirt to seek more comfort, since her waist had expanded an extra inch. She wore a corded deep blue braided sash around her waist to conceal her gained weight from the Fosters. But she was overly sensitive about this, for she realized that to them she probably looked the same as she had weeks before.

This time when she rode the mountain trail there was no hesitation or apprehension about the lane she rode along. She knew the way! The ride did not seem to take as long as it had a few weeks ago.

But by the time she reached the lofty peak of the mountain, she was glad for the warmth of the jacket she'd worn. There in the little grove of trees was the welcoming sight of the little cabin. A trail of gray-blue smoke circled upward toward the sky, and as she pulled up on the reins of her mare, she was welcomed by the barking of Little Bear. He came running down the pathway to the hitching post.

At the same moment, the cabin door swung open and Solange called out to Little Bear, "Shame on you, Little Bear. That is our friend, Gillian." The furry brown pup seemed to know exactly what she said to him, for he immediately quit barking and began to wag his tail.

Gillian leaped from her horse and laughed. "You've got yourself a guard dog there, Solange."

"Oh, he likes to impress me that he is fierce, but I know better," she replied. Extending her hands warmly to greet Gillian, she smiled. "It is good to see you again so soon, *ma petite.*"

Gillian walked beside her up the pathway, but suddenly her attention turned to her hand down by her side that Little Bear was affectionately licking. She nudged Solange without saying a word and Solange saw what she was directing her attention to. "Ah, he has decided that he likes you, I think!"

As they entered the door of the cottage, Gillian was instantly entranced by the beauty and aroma of the little wreaths of Solange's mixture of herbs and dried flowers.

When Gillian remarked about them Solange told her that she must take a couple of them when she departed. "I enjoy making them to give to my friends. They are especially nice during the holiday season."

"I envy you the talent you have to make such beautiful things, Solange."

"That's sweet of you, but I'd bet you could do the very same thing."

"Well, you inspire me to try, Solange," Gillian told her.

She invited Gillian to have a seat while she prepared a pot of tea, and as she puttered around in her kitchen, she told Gillian, "You must have sensed that I was in need of some company

343

and a nice visit from you with Gaston away. I have truly missed him since he left."

"It is probably that I was in need of your company," Gillian confessed. Solange turned around to see the troubled look on the pretty girl's face. But she turned back to the task she was doing so Gillian would not know that she'd caught her pensive mood.

All the time she fixed the tray, Solange revealed to Gillian her exciting news about her plan to be married. "Oh, Gillian— I am like a young girl, excited about being in love again. You see, I never expected to love again like this. But this just proves we can be delightfully surprised about what life has in store for us."

"Oh, Solange—I'm so very happy for you. Gaston seemed like an awfully nice man and it was obvious that he adores you!"

"Oh, Gillian—that is what is so wonderful about it. I have no shadow of doubt that Gaston loves me and I love him with all my heart and soul. I—I fear my announcement to Hawk was a shock, but he will come to accept it in time."

As they sat sipping their tea, she told Gillian of their plans to live in Canada, but a part of the time would be spent back here in this cabin which was so dear to her. She gave a soft little laugh. "Would you believe me if I told you that Gaston is not what he appears to be at all? He is a very successful businessman in the fur-trading business. He only poses as a trapper to check out the woods. This was what he was doing here in these woods when he chanced to step into that trap that injured his foot."

Gillian had listened to her intently as she told her about Gaston. "Fate meant for the two of you to meet, Solange. It must have been that," Gillian remarked.

"I feel that is so, Gillian. Just as I feel that fate brought the two of us together. Life holds many mysteries that we don't understand. It is only later that we understand them. May I be frank with you, Gillian, and I can't explain it yet? But from the moment we first met, I felt a strange closeness to you and I felt that by the time you left and Hawk was taking you back home, you felt it, too. Is it not so?"

"Yes, it is so, Solange. I can't explain it, either." Gillian's face was solemn and serious as she looked at Solange. Solange's hand came out to take her hand in hers. Her soft voice was mellow with compassion as she spoke. "Well, we shall not try to understand it, *ma petite*. We both know it is there. If I'd been blessed with a daughter, Gillian, I would have wanted her to be just like you. So for one precious moment let me have my fantasy and talk to me as you would have her if she was sitting here. Tell me what is troubling you, for I know something is weighing heavily on that pretty head of yours. Maybe I can help you."

Solange was an easy person to talk to, for she was so warm and understanding. Without being embarrassed or ashamed, she told her about Steve Lafferty and how she'd fallen madly in love with him.

"Oh, Solange, now that I look back on it, I was so naive and allowed him such liberties. I must have taken leave of my senses. I had always considered myself a sensible person."

A smile was on Solange's face as she softly laughed. "Ah, Gillian, when your heart goes crazy the head has no control at all. I remember when I was that vivacious little coquette in France and I thought I was so very smart, but I was just as naive as you. It takes living life to become wise, and by that time we've experienced many mistakes and a multitude of pains from those mistakes. But this is life!"

Gillian dejectedly sighed. "Oh, I've suffered that pain, believe me! I'll grant you that my pride has taken a beating that I don't exactly like. However, that I can accept and dismiss. What I am troubled about now is not just about me and that I allowed myself to be played for a fool. What I am troubled about is a baby who will not have a father. I know that I am carrying Lafferty's child."

"Oh, you poor child! Oh, Gillian—now I know why you are

so troubled. Are you sure, *ma petite?*"

Gillian nodded her head and told Solange she suspected it when she'd come to visit her the last time, but she never got around to talking to her about it then.

"I remember that visit and I sensed that something was tormenting you then. Well, now that I do know, I can only say to you, Gillian, that you do not have anything to feel shame about and it is not the end of the world, not when I will be standing by your side. No, my Gillian, the babe you have within you is a child of love and I would not forsake you. You will have my and Gaston's help if you need it. You can count on that!"

Overcome with emotion, Gillian could not suppress the flood of tears demanding release, and she gave way. With tears streaming down her lovely face, she could only manage to stammer, "Oh, Solange—Solange! Now I know why I needed to talk to you."

Solange stretched out her arms and enfolded Gillian in them to hold her while she sobbed, tears also moistening her own cheek. She felt the young girl's body tremble and she was glad she was there for her to cling to. Many times she would have given anything to have had someone to hold on to for the comfort she knew she was giving to Gillian Browne right now. She recalled all those moments of fear she'd experienced in her young life and she knew that particular hell. If she could ease that for Gillian, she would certainly do it.

"I'm glad it was me, Gillian," she told her as she brushed her auburn hair away from her tear-stained face. "Everything will work out for you, I promise you, Gillian."

A special bond was formed between the two of them that would never be broken, and both of them knew it.

Chapter Forty-Six

Neither of the ladies sitting in Solange's cozy cabin had any inkling that an intruder had been standing in the doorway, listening intensely to the last few minutes of their conversation.

Hawk had never knocked on the cabin door before entering so he didn't do so this afternoon. He'd barely turned the knob and only slightly opened the door when he recognized his mother's voice making her declaration about the loves of her life, and he saw, in that same instant, the back of the auburn-haired Gillian. That was enough to make him stand frozen in the spot.

He could see Gillian's dainty shoulders and her thick coppery hair cascading down her back. He had never loved her more.

It didn't even matter to Hawk that he'd just heard her say that she could be carrying another man's child. The sight of her was enough to assure Hawk that his love was so strong that he didn't care.

He knew who that man was and he remembered what Warner had told him about Lafferty. He had already left Tucson so it was obvious he wasn't rushing back to Maricopa County. If he had done that, he would have already been here.

He could not remain silent any longer. In a low, deep voice

he let his presence be known. "My mother's sentiments are also mine, Gillian. We would never let anything happen to you, if we could help it."

Gillian, as well as Solange, turned to see the towering Hawk standing by the door. His black eyes were radiant with the love he was feeling for the two women as he walked slowly toward them.

In a stammering voice, Gillian asked, "You heard what I just told your mother?"

He smiled warmly at her. "I heard, little one, but surely you don't think this changes my feelings for you, do you?"

"I—I don't know."

"You are the same Gillian I've always known. Nothing could ever change that."

Solange looked up at his handsome face and she loved what she saw there—a kind, loving man with a capacity for deep understanding and compassion.

The words he spoke filled her with pride and she knew now what she'd suspected all along about Hawk's deep affection for the young girl. But she knew that Gillian's heart belonged to another and he would never possess her love. Now, Hawk must know it, too, she told herself.

"I appreciate that, Hawk. Your—your friendship means so very much to me. You and your mother seem always to rescue me in my hours of need. I don't know what I'd do without you."

"My cabin can always be your place of refuge, can't it, Hawk?" Solange remarked, smiling at Hawk. He sensed she was very pleased and proud of him and the attitude he'd displayed after hearing their conversation. She knew that he had heard her own remarks to Gillian

"Of course. This cabin seems to hold a certain power that way. I guess I shall always feel that way about it. There is a peace I find here that I find nowhere else," Hawk declared as his dark eyes left Gillian to gaze in his mother's direction.

She knew exactly what her son was trying to tell her in his

simple, straightforward way, and she appreciated very much that he felt that way.

"I have to admit it seems to cast a spell over me every time I come here. Once again, I've stayed far too long, Solange, and if I don't leave right now I'm going to be in trouble," Gillian declared as she rose up out of the comfortable chair by the hearth.

"Well, we don't want that, nor do we want you getting home after dark, since you are all by yourself," Solange said, going across the room to get one of the wreaths she'd promised to Gillian.

"I will see that she gets into her valley safely, Mother," Hawk offered.

"Oh, you don't have to do that, Hawk. You've just arrived home," Gillian said.

"But I wish to see you home, Gillian."

"Very well. Shall we be going?" She turned to take her leave, thanking Solange for another wonderful afternoon, and her lovely gift of the wreath.

"My pleasure, *ma petite*," she told Gillian as she reached over to give her a kiss on the cheek. "Supper will be waiting for you, my son, when you return."

Hawk followed Gillian out the door. Solange watched the two of them go toward the hitching post to mount their horses. Hawk could have made a most handsome companion for the lovely auburn-haired Gillian and she could not deny that she wished it could be her son that Gillian had lost her heart to instead of Steve Lafferty.

She watched them ride down the trail as long as her eyes could see them: What a striking pair they made!

Hawk glanced her way many times as they rode along the mountain trail. To him, she looked just as sweet and innocent as she had at fourteen. He felt just as protective of her as he had back then.

When they came to that spot in the trail where they would be descending into the valley below, it was Hawk's idea that they stop for a moment to linger there before they parted company.

He leaped down from Tache and secured him to a nearby sapling before he rushed over to help Gillian down from her mare. So fragile she seemed as he lifted her to the ground! For a moment, he remembered her telling his mother that she was carrying a child and he thought to himself that she was only a mere child herself. But he had only to remember those sweet stolen kisses to know that she was all woman—a very sensuous, passionate one!

Gillian was no longer innocent or naive to the ways of love, for Steve Lafferty had taught her well. She sensed instantly how Hawk was feeling as he helped her down from her horse. She saw the black fire of his eyes as they danced over her face and she felt the heat of his hands as they clasped her waist. She had to admit that she could give herself to Hawk if the devilish ghost of Steve Lafferty did not haunt her constantly.

Hawk said not a word as he led her to a cozy spot back away from the trail and urged her to sit down on a huge boulder. "There, isn't that perfect?" he asked as she sat down and leaned back against the boulders.

"Absolutely perfect, Hawk." She laughed. It was good to be with Hawk: she always felt so safe and secure when he was by her side. Somehow, she'd always sensed that Hawk would protect her from anything that threatened her. Maybe it was because he'd rescued her twice when she was in danger.

He sank down on the ground beside her. "It's wonderful up here in these mountains. I think you feel the same as I do about it, don't you, Gillian?"

"I find beauty in the mountains as well as the valley below. They're —they're like two different worlds." What she didn't say was that she yearned to see more of the world than just the mountains and valleys of Arizona Territory.

Suddenly, she felt the force of his hands on her shoulders. A serious look was on his face as he began to speak. "I can't let you leave me today without saying to you what I've yearned to

350

say for a long, long time, Gillian. It has nothing to do with what I heard you and my mother discussing when I arrived at the cabin. Long ago, I felt as I do now. I am asking you to be my wife. Marry me and you have no worries to face all alone."

Her hands cupped the handsome bronzed face bent so close to hers. "Oh, dear Hawk! I am so very fond of you and there are many kinds of love, but it would be so unfair of me not to love you as a wife should. I carry another man's child. I—I couldn't do that to you."

He gave a husky laugh and kissed her on the cheek. "Oh, little one—I know that you don't love me as I love you. But I love you so much that it would be enough for both of us."

"But there is also another man's child to consider, Hawk." Her blue eyes searched his face.

"That little innocent baby will be a part of you, won't it? So how could I not love it, too, Gillian?"

Tears came to her eyes as she slumped against his broad chest and sobbed until she could cry no more. Hawk tenderly held her close to him, allowing her to give way to the hurt that had been bottled up so long.

As if she were a small child resting in the arms of a doting father, Hawk soothed her and brushed the straying locks away from her tear-stained face. In a soft, consoling voice, he murmured in her ear, "As Mother told you and I tell you now, Gillian, our cabin is always open to you and so is my heart, with all the love I have to give. You don't have to give me an answer right now, but you will know that all you have to do is come to me or send for me. All right, Gillian?"

"I'll know, Hawk," she stammered. She sought not to move out of the circle of his powerful arms.

Hawk would have allowed her to remain there forever but for the fact that twilight was gathering over the mountains and down in the valley and he wanted no disfavor from the Fosters because she would be returning too late to the ranch.

"Come, Gillian—I must get you going toward the ranch so the Fosters won't be angry with us."

351

She suddenly came alive and gasped, "Oh, good Lord, Hawk—I'd completely forgotten about the time." She leaped up off the ground and made a dash for her horse as Hawk watched her with a big grin on his face. "Am I not going to get even a farewell from you?" he asked.

"Oh, Hawk—I—I'm sorry, but I just don't want them to be angry at me." After she had mounted the mare, she told him, "I'll—I'll think about what we talked about, but I don't want you to be gallant just because you feel sorry for me and the mess I've got myself in. I love you for feeling the way you do. I always shall!"

His black eyes gleamed warmly as he assured her, "Pity has nothing to do with it nor does it have anything to do with me being gallant, little one. Love is what it's all about!"

"Goodbye, Hawk, until we meet next time." She smiled as her fingers went to her lips in a gesture of throwing him a farewell kiss. Immediately she spurred the little mare into swift motion to make for the ranch, praying all the way that John or Nancy had not returned yet from the Hills.

Her wish was granted for the house was deserted when she entered after securing her horse in the barn. Hastily, she rushed to her room to remove her jacket before returning to the kitchen to tie an apron around her waist. Putting some kindling into the stove, she got a fire started and filled the pot with water and began to make a hearty stew for the evening meal. Never had she peeled vegetables so fast. Flinging the whole onions and quartered potatoes into the pot, she added the seasonings. By the time she'd cleaned the carrots and cut up the remains of a beef roast of the night before, she was breathless from moving so fast.

She slumped into one of the oak chairs at the kitchen table to gather her thoughts; she had to make the stew with the same perfection that Nancy always seemed to achieve when she fixed it for them.

She leaped up to get a jar of tomato sauce out of the cupboard and added it to the bubbling stew. Once that was done, Gillian sat down wearily willing to let the mixture simmer until the Fosters arrived. She was exhausted for it had been a long, long afternoon. But it had been a wonderful afternoon, and she was glad she'd gone up to the mountains to see Solange.

Luck was with her, for she'd gotten home before the Fosters returned. They'd have no need to know that she'd been gone from the ranch at all.

Being with Solange and Hawk had given her the courage she needed to face whatever the future held for her.

Before she'd allow her child to be born without a father, she decided, she would marry Hawk!

Chapter Forty-Seven

Gillian had drowsed off to sleep for a moment, and when she lifted her head she realized how dark the kitchen was. She moved from the chair to light the lamps in the kitchen and the front room and looked at the clock on the parlor wall. Would John not be returning to the ranch tonight? Perhaps the Hills had become worse and he was forced to stay there.

She was wondering if she should get a lantern and go to the barn to do the evening chores that John usually handled. By the time she got back into the kitchen, she smelled the delightful aroma from the cast-iron pot where her stew was steaming. She was pleased with herself.

She was about to light the lantern and go to the barn when she heard a commotion outside the house. To her delight, she saw that it was John, and Mother Foster was with him. Nancy Foster looked weary as she ambled through her kitchen door, but she gave Gillian a warm smile as she greeted her. "Lordy, something sure smells good!"

"Stew, Mother Foster, but it won't be as good as yours." Gillian smiled.

"I wouldn't swear to that! Smells dang good to me. I'm as hungry as a wolf," John declared, placing his hat on the peg on the wall. Gillian began to set the table while he went out to do his chores. "You can bet I'm going to get them done fast tonight." He chuckled as he left.

Gillian insisted that Nancy refresh herself and relax while she set the table. "By the time you do that, I'll have the cornbread ready to take out of the oven, Mother Foster."

Gillian could not find one thing to fault about her stew, for it was just as good as Nancy's. John complimented her again and again. He told Nancy she had taught her well.

"You're a whale of a cook, Gillian!"

Gillian smiled and thanked him. "I did have a good teacher," she said.

Nancy did not linger long after her hearty meal but sought the comfort of her bed, leaving Gillian to clean up the kitchen while John went into the parlor to sit in his favorite chair and enjoy smoking his pipe as he read the journal.

Once Gillian was in the privacy of her bedroom she began to undress and put on the batiste gown; she realized that the time was growing short for her to conceal from the Fosters or anyone else that she was pregnant. No longer did she have that wasplike waist, for it had thickened, and there was no denying that her breasts were much fuller.

In her soft batiste gown, she felt so comfortable as she sat down at the dressing table to stroke her hair with the brush. She looked at her reflection in the mirror and never had she glowed with more radiance. She'd heard that women always glowed when they were pregnant. Well, she certainly glowed!

But when she went to bed, Gillian slept better than she had in many weeks. Now she did not feel so alone and helpless. It was a good feeling to know that she would not have to be branded as a shameless hussy who'd got herself pregnant by some man and brought a child into the world without a father to give that child a name.

She was relieved to know that she would not shame the Fosters, for if she did accept Hawk's offer to marry her, they would never have to know of all these weeks of torment she'd endured alone. They'd just assume that the child was Hawk's.

A heavy burden had been lifted off her shoulders and she

was grateful, but that did not ease her aching heart. She loved Steve dearly and she always would. How could he have played her so falsely? He seemed so sincere and she'd believed him so completely when he'd vowed his love for her.

She was glad now that she'd replied to Melissa's letter as she had and let her know that she didn't care whether she ever laid eyes on Steve Lafferty again as long as she lived. It was not her way to lie, but lie she had. She'd told Melissa that she'd met another man who was occupying her time since she'd returned to Maricopa County. Gillian had gone so far as to write Melissa that she might just marry him. It had been a devious impulse on Gillian's part, but the letter from Melissa had had a devastating impact on her. Once her own letter was sent, Gillian had completely dismissed it from her mind. She had no way of knowing the changes that had taken place in the haughty, selfish Melissa she'd met and known when she'd been a visitor in the Clayton home.

That Melissa no longer existed. Once she'd seen her father for what he really was and realized that it was her mother who'd been slaving for her for years, Melissa's attitudes and ways made a drastic change. She'd regretted her contemptuous letter to Gillian but there was nothing she could do about it once it was on its way to Maricopa County.

But all this Gillian could not know.

For a week Steve Lafferty had waited impatiently in Tucson for a stage that would take him to Maricopa County. He had reached the point that he was not going to wait any longer, even if he had to buy his own buggy and a horse to get him where he wanted to go.

This was his intention this autumn afternoon as he left the Old Pueblo Inn. A week here in Tucson had been more than enough time for him to finish all the loose ends of his business with Curtis, and he'd acquired a magnificent ring to present to his bride-to-be.

But something happened to change Lafferty's plans that afternoon. He'd stopped by a tobacco shop in hopes of finding some of his favorite cheroots, and on the way out he'd met the pretty Melissa.

"Well, Melissa—isn't it?" he asked her as they nearly collided with each other.

"Yes, Captain Lafferty—it is Melissa—Melissa Clayton. I'd heard that you were back in Tucson."

"But not for long, I can tell you."

"And where do you go from here, Captain?"

"I go to Maricopa County, Melissa, to claim my bride."

"Gillian?" Melissa asked.

"Of course, Gillian—who else?"

Melissa felt a little sick inside. "Can we go somewhere to talk, Captain Lafferty?"

"I—I guess so. Does it have to do with Gillian? Something tells me that it does." Steve raised a skeptical brow as he looked down at Melissa. She saw the sudden sober expression his face had taken on.

"Yes, it is about Gillian you might say," she reluctantly admitted. Seeing the intensity on his face, she wished that she'd not said anything. How did she know what his reaction would be when she told him about her letter to Gillian and Gillian's letter back to her?

"She's—she all right, isn't she?"

"As far as I know she is fine. I—I had a letter just the other day from her." She noticed immediately that he breathed a sigh of relief to hear that news.

He urged her toward his buggy and helped her up in the seat. "We'll take a little ride and have this talk you wanted to have." He didn't know this young lady too well, having met her only briefly while Melissa was visiting, but somehow she seemed to have changed. She seemed more subdued and less flippant and haughty.

Steve reined the bay into action and moved away from the busy main street of Tucson toward the edge of town. Spotting a cluster of shade trees, he pulled up. "How about this, Melissa? I think this will give us the privacy for a talk."

"This is fine, Captain Lafferty." She thought to herself that it was not so far out of town that she'd have to walk a long way to get home should he be so angry about what she was going to tell him.

"All right, Melissa. I'm waiting."

Playing with her hands in her lap, she began to speak. "I have to go back to the time when Gillian and Aunt Nancy were here. I—I've changed a lot since then and you'll just have to take my word for that, nor will I bore you as to why I've changed. Anyway, when Gillian was here I—I wasn't very nice to her. It disgusted my mother and she was very displeased with me. Then my beau, Caywood, couldn't take his eyes off Gillian when he came to the house. This made me furious, as well as jealous. I wanted to get even with her because I blamed her for everything."

She stopped for a moment, gave a deep sigh, and let her eyes dart up to Lafferty's face. He urged her to continue.

"Well, after she left, I happened to see you riding in a buggy with that Curtis girl. I thought the two of you acted very friendly with each other, so I wrote this to Gillian out of spite. Now, I don't blame you for hating me for this, but I am truly sorry."

"God, Melissa! It was a bloody innocent ride, I can tell you. She merely was taking her father's place, who couldn't take me to the stage station when I left for San Diego. Oh, well, it isn't all that devastating, I guess. I may just be facing an angry little minx when I get to Maricopa County."

Melissa remarked, "I am afraid it could be more than that, Captain. As I told you, I had a letter from Gillian a day or two ago, and she talked like she'd met someone she'd become very fond of in the last several weeks. She said she just might marry him."

"She *what?* She said what?" he roared, grabbing Melissa by the shoulders roughly. "You aren't lying again, are you? You damned well better not be, Melissa Clayton!"

She had never seen a man look so fierce or menacing. She shook her head to indicate that she was not lying. At the moment she could not find her voice.

Gaining some control of his fury, Steve released his hold on her shoulders. When he did, Melissa began to fumble in her reticule. "I—I think maybe I still have her letter. Just a minute and maybe you can read it for yourself." A second later she was pulling the two-page letter from her reticule and handing it to Steve.

Obviously she had not been lying, he had to admit as he read Gillian's words for himself. Slowly, he folded the letter and handed it back to Melissa. "I'll take you home, Melissa."

All the way to the Claytons' house, Steve sat like a man in a trance, saying nothing. When he came to an abrupt stop in front of the gate, he got out of the buggy and went around to help Melissa down. He simply said goodbye and turned to get back in the buggy. Swiftly, the buggy rolled down the street and out of sight.

Lafferty made straight for Jeffer's Livery where he exchanged the buggy for the best saddle horse they had in their stables. He and the horse did battle with one another all the way back to the inn, but Lafferty figured that by the time they reached Maricopa County he would master the horse or the horse would master him. At least he could travel to Maricopa County faster on a horse than he could in a buggy.

Gillian Browne would marry no one else but him, he swore!

Chapter Forty-Eight

It was a wonderful reunion Solange shared with her son, and during those first two days Hawk was at the cabin, he got acquainted with Little Bear. The young dog took a liking to him immediately and started following him everywhere he went as he did with Solange.

It had been thoughtful of Troy to bring the pup to his mother. She told him how he'd kept her from getting so lonely while he was away.

"I guess, Mother—I guess I never gave that any thought— that you would be up here in the woods, completely alone except for Troy's visits," Hawk had confessed.

He sought to make up for his thoughtlessness by doing the things with her that she enjoyed, taking long walks in the woods or picking the exotic flowers. He put off his visit to Troy so he and his mother could have these special private moments together before Gaston returned to the cabin. She did not know exactly when he would be coming back from Canada.

"But the cabin will always be ours. Gaston has promised me that, and you can always come here, even when I cannot be here." She told him about the plans Gaston was making for them. "You can come to Canada, too, Hawk. Gaston has said that he would help you in any way he could. He is a good man, Hawk. Please—for me, Hawk—give him a chance."

"For you, I will, Mother. But I will not come to Canada. This is where I belong and this is where I will stay." He gave her a warm smile and that was enough to console Solange so she pressed for no more from him.

On his third day at the cabin, Hawk announced that he was going hunting. "The holidays are coming. I'll find us a fine, fat turkey for our table, Mother."

"Ah, Hawk—that sounds wonderful. And while you are out there, look for the perfect piñon tree to set over there in the corner for the holiday season."

"I shall, Mother."

He felt he could not postpone his visit to Troy, for the days were going by all too swiftly. Once Gaston returned to the cabin, Hawk knew he might decide to leave if the notion came upon him. He knew he had no control once that black mood came down on him as it possibly would.

"You wish me to bring you some branches of the cedars and pines for your wreaths?"

"Ah, yes, Hawk. I've already started stringing red berries. Did you see the huge basket of pine cones I've been gathering?"

"No, Mother, but I was sure you had." He laughed. Forever, his fondest memories would be of his mother's special efforts to make their humble cabin festive during the holiday season. As long as she'd been away from France, she still observed the traditions she was brought up with when she was a young girl.

Now that he was a grown man all these things meant much more to him. He was given a special heritage by this remarkable French lady that most of the half-breeds, like Troy, had not known. He had her to thank for that.

He took his tall crowned black felt hat from the peg and bid her goodbye. "Wish me good luck," he called back to her as he started out the door.

"Ah, I know you will have good luck, Hawk." She smiled.

He was gone and she turned back to attend to her chores. As she did, her thoughts were on Gillian. Hawk had said little after he'd returned back from escorting her part of the way home, and she had not pressed him. If Hawk had anything to tell her, he would have.

It suddenly dawned on her that there was no sign of Little Bear in the cabin. "Oh, *Mon Dieu*—he's followed Hawk!" she moaned. Now she could only hope that Hawk would be aware that the young scamp was trotting devotedly behind him through the woods. That little pup meant so much to her! She found she could not get her mind off him, praying that he would not get lost in the dense woods that Hawk knew so well.

Her heart was so heavy with worry over Little Bear that she could not eat, but she did manage to drink a cup of herbed tea. She harshly admonished herself that she was fretting for nothing and that he would be just fine. Demanding that she quit wasting the day, she got busy cutting little squares of muslin and poured a portion of dried flower petals into the center of each square. Gillian's colorful ribbons were used to tie a dainty bow. What a delightful scent came from her little sachets! She must give some of them to Gillian the next time she came to visit, Solange thought as she took them to place in the drawers of a chest in her bedroom.

Gaston stood outside the door of the cabin, but he could not open the door, nor could he knock, for his arms were filled with packages. He used his booted foot to slam against the wooden door. Solange rushed to the door.

Opening the door, she was greeted by the smiling face of Gaston standing there looking quite helpless, so burdened with packages. "Gaston! Ah, *mon cher*—you are back!"

"I am back, *ma* Solange." He hastily moved through the door to place the load he was carrying on a nearby chair. But he did not take the time to take her into his arms as she would have expected him to do. Instead, he hurried back out the door to grab up a jute bag there on the ground. Solange stood, watching him. Amusement sparked in his dark eyes as he came back into the house, for he saw the perplexed look on her lovely face. As he reached down into the sack to bring out a very bedraggled, wet pup, he laughed. "Found this little *gitan* down in the creek having a devil of a time trying to get back to the bank."

"Oh, Little Bear!" She sighed with overwhelming relief at the sight of him even though he was a pathetic mess. He trembled with chill from the mountain stream Gaston had rescued him from. She quickly got a towel and wrapped him in it as she rubbed his dark brown fur to dry it. Then she took the old woolen afghan from her chair and placed him in the center of it, tucking the folds around him. He snuggled cozily by the warm hearth, looking up at Solange as if to tell her he was glad to be back in the warm cabin.

"Now, *chérie*—now I shall collect my kiss," Gaston declared. He put his strong arms around Solange's waist and drew her to him. As he bent down to kiss her, he vowed, "Next time I leave this cabin, we shall leave together, for I have no intentions of ever being without you again, Solange. I was so lonely!"

"Oh, Gaston! Gaston, I love you so much. Neither of us shall ever have to be lonely again," she softly murmured as she felt his warm sensuous mouth meet hers.

Unhurriedly he allowed his lips to capture hers in a kiss as he held her there in his arms. Loving Solange was like savoring a vintage wine; he loved to have it last and linger. When they embraced, time stood still. Nothing mattered except that he held the woman he loved in his arms.

The kiss would have lasted even longer had there not been a rapping on the front door. Reluctantly, he released her as they exchanged smiles.

Smoothing back her hair and straightening her tunic, she went toward the door. It was Hawk, and the rapping had been done with his heavy boot. His arms were as filled as Gaston's had been a short time ago.

Solange gave an amused laugh as she saw him standing there with two jute sacks filled with vegetables and a turkey he'd shot.

"Troy insisted that I bring these to you after I took him one of the turkeys I shot," he told her.

"Did you tell him that you and Little Bear had become very good friends?"

She moved back to allow her son to put down his heavy load. "Gaston has returned and he, too, came bearing a load," she told him.

Hawk made no reply. He glanced around the openness of the two rooms but he saw no Gaston Dion. When he had laid the sacks on the floor of her kitchen, he picked up the turkey to go out the back door of the cabin. "I'll clean this big fellow for you, Mother."

"All right, dear. Oh, by the way, Little Bear tried to follow you and got himself lost. Gaston happened upon him in the creek, so he must have been trotting after you. Right now, he is very content to be snuggled up in a towel over here by the fireplace."

Hawk gave a gust of laughter which gladdened her heart. She wasn't too sure how he'd take the news that Gaston was at the cabin.

"Well, Little Bear has many lessons to learn, I think. I remember the first time I fell in that cold mountain stream."

"And I, too, remember that day, Hawk," Solange recalled. "You looked a lot like Little Bear."

They exchanged smiles as he started out the door with the turkey in his hand. She turned to see Gaston standing behind her. He thought she had the loveliest smile in the world. He'd listened to the two of them recalling a past memory they'd shared. There was a very tight bond between these two and he must always be mindful of that, he cautioned himself.

"Your son is a fine hunter," he remarked to Solange.

"A very fine hunter. He has us a fine turkey for a grand dinner I shall fix tomorrow. He also took one to Troy. Troy, in turn, sent us a nice assortment of his fall garden vegetables. That is the way it is with people up here in these mountains, Gaston."

"A shame it isn't like that in other places. Guess that is why we must never forsake this place but come back from time to time to keep in touch with this special cabin you've lived in so many years, eh, *ma chérie?*" His dark eyes were warm with love for her and she noticed that he had slipped into her bedroom to use the brush to his thick mane of gray-streaked hair when he'd found out it was Hawk entering the door.

"Yes, Gaston—that is why we must return from time to time." She moved closer to him, taking his hands in hers.

"I've given you my word on that, Solange. Now I've something else to give you—a token of my love for you." He reached inside the pocket of the leather vest he wore and handed her a tiny velvet pouch. When she opened it, she stared down and gasped at a magnificent diamond ring. Such sparking fire came from the stone there in the circle of gold! She'd never owned such an exquisite piece of jewelry.

"Oh, Gaston—what can I say to you? I'm overcome—I'm completely speechless!" Gaston went about the task of taking the ring to slip it on her finger. It was a perfect fit. "There, *ma* Solange—an exquisite gem for a lady who is a rare jewel!"

"You look at a lady who is so happy you came my way, Gaston Dion. I bless the day Troy brought you to my cabin." She reached up to receive his kiss.

When he finally released her, his eyes sparkled brightly as he told her, "You know, Solange—I should have brought that trap along with me that night or gone back to get it. We could have claimed it as our good-luck charm and always kept it in our home."

Hawk had happened to open the door on this very intimate scene, so he silently backed down the step into the yard. There he lingered with the turkey for several minutes before he attempted to enter the cabin for the second time.

This time, he found them sitting in the front room. His mother was putting on a long, flowing cape of imported French wool. The hood was edged in a luxurious sable fur. Hawk watched as his mother tried on the rich brown cape and thought she looked like a queen with the fur framing her face. This huge rugged man must surely care very much for her.

"That will keep you warm when we travel north, *ma chérie*. Arizona Territory never gets such cold weather as we shall be going to."

"You look awfully pretty, Mother," Hawk declared, letting his presence be known.

"Ah, Hawk—she does, doesn't she! In fact, we men declare you the most beautiful woman in the world, is that not true, Hawk?" Gaston gave one of his deep, friendly laughs. Hawk was finding it hard to find anything to fault the man with, so he returned Gaston's smile with his own.

"Come, Hawk—join us over here," Gaston invited. "I've brought you back a gift from Canada and I hope you'll like it." He pulled out one of the packages and handed Hawk a wooden chest of highly polished wood. Hawk took the chest and fumbled with the brass hook securing the lid. When he opened the lid of the fine mahogany case, he saw matched pistols with grips of ebony. There were scroll engravings of eagles and wolf head hammers.

Hawk could not utter a word for a moment as he appraised the fine pair of pistols. He let his finger run up and down the barrel. Never had he had a gift like this or owned such a fine weapon.

"You like them, Hawk?" Gaston knew the answer as he watched Hawk admiring the fine weapons.

"I—I don't know what to say. I can say I thank you, but that doesn't seem like enough to say," Hawk stammered, looking up at Gaston and then to his mother.

"That's enough for me," Gaston assured him. "If they are something you will enjoy and treasure then I am very happy with my selection of the right gift for you."

"I can't imagine anything I'd have liked better than these pistols, Gaston." Gaston was feeling happy about all the gifts he'd purchased to bring joy to the lady he loved and her son. This was his desire.

Solange patted Gaston's huge hand. "You are so generous, Gaston. I love you so very much."

He pulled her over to plant a kiss on her cheek, for he had no intention of restraining himself just because Hawk was there. It was not his way. He was a very demonstrative man and a very affectionate one. "And I love you, too, Solange."

Hawk could not help flinching, for he had not been used to Tim displaying his ardent feelings toward his mother when he was alive. Tim was a very restrained fellow where his feelings were concerned. There had been a stern, austere air about him most of the time as Hawk recalled.

So Hawk acted as though he'd not heard a word spoken between them. Instead, he allowed himself to be completely engrossed with the magnificent matched pair of pistols.

He'd never expected to possess such a prized pair of weapons as these were! As he sat there, he thought to himself that he'd bet Captain Steve Lafferty did not own something as fine as this.

But in the next moment, he thought of Gillian. To possess her would be more exciting and satisfying than owning these fine pistols, he had to admit.

Chapter Forty-Nine

A thick blue haze hovered over the high mountain peaks. The sun was rising and the smoky fog seemed to be creeping throughout the forest surrounding Solange's cabin.

It was all a little awesome to Troy's cousin who sat beside him in the wagon as she viewed this strange country they were traveling over. It was so different from the place she'd lived before being left at Troy's doorstep a few days ago! A friend of her family had brought her here after her mother died; Troy was the only relative she knew of, so she had nowhere else to go.

It was hardly a responsibility that Troy could refuse, for he had loved Shawna's mother, Violet. She'd cared for him when he was a young lad so he was glad to do the same for Violet's daughter. Like Troy, Shawna was a half-breed, but her coppery skin was much paler than Troy's and the mingling bloodlines of her father and Violet had produced a most beautiful young girl.

Troy had not known Shawna's father, but he must have been a handsome white man, and his Aunt Violet was a lovely Indian woman. Like his Aunt Violet, Shawna had glossy, thick straight hair that hung halfway down her back. But her eyes were a strange mixture of green and brown with flecks of gold in them and they were fringed with thick, long lashes. Troy was a small man but he stood a few inches taller than Shawna. He figured at the most she might reach five feet.

Her unexpected arrival at his cabin had prompted him to make this trip to the village to get supplies he badly needed for a young lady to live in his cabin. He thought it might be smart to stop by Solange's place to get her sage advice about particular articles.

"You'll like Solange, Shawna. She is a fine lady. I've known her for a long time."

"Oh, I'm sure I will like her if you do. I usually like most people, Troy." She smiled at him and he was reminded of his Aunt Violet when he gazed upon her lovely face. He'd already found her to be an outgoing, friendly person and quite a talker. Troy had to admit that this was taking a little getting used to. Being a bachelor all these years, he was used to the quiet and peace of his cabin, spending many hours all alone. It seemed he would be taking a lot of strolls in the woods if he wanted to find the quiet peace he enjoyed so much.

Leaping down from the wagon, he marched around to help his cousin down. Together they walked up the pathway. Solange had seen them coming and was already opening the door.

"Morning, Solange," Troy greeted her.

"A good morning to you, too."

Troy introduced Shawna. Shawna was not prepared to see such a lovely lady standing there. As the two of them exchanged greetings, Shawna told her, "Troy has talked about you constantly and I can see why."

"Well, welcome to my home, Shawna. My feeling for Troy is mutual, for we are very close, dear friends, aren't we, Troy?"

"We are, for sure."

Solange served them some of her fresh-brewed tea as Troy told her about Shawna's parents both dying and how she'd arrived at his cabin a few days ago.

By the time they'd spent almost an hour visiting with Solange, she realized the dilemma Troy felt himself to be in with a delightful little chatterbox like Shawna under his roof

370

day and night. She could appreciate that he was feeling a little flustered.

"We're going into the village, Solange. Is—is there something I could get for you while we're there?" Troy asked her.

Solange rose up to take his cup and quickly declared, "As a matter of fact there is a great favor you could do for me. I broke the blade of a kitchen knife yesterday, but come in the kitchen so I can show it to you. Would you excuse us a minute, Shawna?"

"Oh, of course," Shawna replied as her black eyes were busy surveying the quaint loveliness of Solange's cabin.

Once they were out of earshot in Solange's kitchen, she asked Troy what was really bothering him. He whispered that he was at a loss as to the things he should buy now that Shawna was to be living with him. Solange patted him on the shoulder and told him she would make a list with only the first three items being for her own needs. The rest was for him to get for his cabin.

"Oh, thank you, Solange." He felt much better as he went back into the front room to join his cousin.

As soon as Solange prepared the list, Troy and Shawna left the cabin to be on their way to the village. Troy had promised to drop off her things on their way home.

As she was preparing to close the door, she turned to see her sleepy-eyed son standing behind her. He'd caught a fleeting glance of Troy and the lovely copper-skinned girl with him.

"Who was that with Troy?"

"Troy's cousin, Shawna." She told him of the circumstances that had led to the cousin coming to live with him.

Hawk gave a roar of laughter. "Troy's got this girl living with him? Can't imagine old Troy with a woman in that house!"

"Well, dear, whether he likes it or not, he has her, and she seems like a sweet little thing and very pretty, too."

She turned her attention to the kitchen to prepare breakfast for her son and Gaston. The two of them made a fine pair, for

Gaston was a hearty eater, just like her son. By the time she had cooked enough to pile the two plates high with food, she saw Gaston ambling into her kitchen. He praised the delicious aroma that he swore had woken him up. He paused to give Solange a kiss before taking a seat at the table where Hawk was already sitting.

When she had placed the plates in front of Gaston and Hawk, she helped herself to a cup of tea and sat down with them. When Gaston had finished everything on his plate, he gave a pleased sigh. "That mother of yours is one fine cook, Hawk! It's no wonder you are such a strong fellow."

Hawk gave a nod of his head, for his mouth was full of food. When he could finally talk, he heartily agreed with Gaston. "I never knew just how good she was, either, until I had to eat at some of the places in Tucson."

"Pretty terrible?"

"Oh, I found a couple of places where the food was good, but still not as good as Mother's."

"Flattery from two such handsome men is enough to urge this lady to bake a special pie for supper, I think," Solange said gaily. "Now I know why you came home. You got hungry."

The three of them laughed. It made Solange happy to see that Gaston and Hawk were getting along so well together. She felt that Gaston would be able to win her son over if he was only given the chance.

The two men went out into the woods after they finally pushed themselves away from the table. Solange heard Gaston telling Hawk, "Might as well get the feel of those pistols and see if you'll like them, son. Besides, it will give you and me a chance to talk a little. I'd like to tell you about my fur-trading business."

When Solange finished the household chores, she went back into her kitchen to bake two berry pies so she could give one to Troy when he stopped by. It surprised her when Hawk returned to the cabin without Gaston a short time later.

"He wanted to do some more checking on the little furry

372

creatures he's interested in," Hawk informed her.

"I see. Gaston is a very serious man where his fur business is concerned." She saw Hawk's eyes appraising her fresh-baked pies and quickly informed him that one was for Troy and his cousin. "You'll have to wait until supper like the rest of us."

Hawk laughed as he strolled out of the room. She was rather glad that Hawk had returned so that he might have a chance to meet Troy's pretty cousin.

A short time later Troy was standing at her door with the articles he'd purchased for her, but Shawna had remained in the wagon. Solange gave Troy the money for the things he'd bought for her. "Wait just a moment, Troy. I've something to give Shawna and I want Hawk to meet her." Calling out to Hawk to tell him that Troy was there, she picked up the pie to go out to the wagon.

Hawk and Troy trailed behind her. As they came nearer to the wagon, Shawna's black eyes flashed bright as she saw the handsome, firm-muscled young man walking with her cousin. This had to be Hawk, whom Troy always spoke about as his best friend.

"For you, Shawna," Solange told her as she gave her the pie. "And I want you to meet my son, Hawk."

Her skin looked like copper satin in the bright sunshine. Her hair and eyes were just as jet black as Hawk's, Solange observed as she looked at the two of them as Hawk greeted her.

"I'm happy to meet you, Hawk," she said.

Hawk was damned if he could see how the two of them could be cousins. Troy with his ugly face certainly did not resemble this pretty miss. Troy spoke up. "Hawk, Shawna is Aunt Violet's daughter. Remember me telling you about her, and that I stayed with her when I was a boy?"

"I remember that, Troy."

"Well, folks, I have chores waiting for me. I'll enjoy that pie tonight, Solange. Thanks." He leaped up to the seat and called back to Hawk to come over when he could.

Hawk gave him a nod of his head, knowing that Troy was

going to have a need to absent himself from the cabin to enjoy some solitude in the woods. It was probably the reason he'd never got married; he enjoyed being alone a lot of the time.

Shawna waved goodbye as the wagon moved away from the hitching post. Solange stole a glance at her son as he strolled silently beside her back toward the cabin. She had the impression that Hawk just might have been entranced by Troy's pretty cousin.

"Pretty, isn't she?" Solange finally commented.

Occupied with his thoughts, Hawk mumbled, "Oh, yes, she is pretty. Doesn't look like old Troy though."

Solange laughed. "No, she doesn't."

After indulging themselves with Solange's good food, along with the berry pie, the three of them sat in the front room. While the two men did most of the talking, Little Bear curled up like a ball in Solange's lap, enjoying her hand stroking him.

She noted Hawk's keen interest as Gaston told him of his humble beginning and how he had accomplished a prosperous business in Canada through hard work and faith in himself.

"I was a really poor boy, Hawk, and I had no one to do it for me so I had to do it myself. Worked my butt off, I can tell you, but I finally reaped a rich harvest." As a father would talk to his son, Gaston spoke to Hawk. "A man can do anything he wants to if he wants it bad enough. It just depends on how much he's willing to give of himself. I was willing 'cause I wanted to be a rich man. I'd been poor all my life."

Oh, how she wished Hawk could have had a father like Gaston, she privately mused as she sat there watching the two of them together.

She found herself loving Gaston more and more all the time. God had surely sent him to her, she felt.

Chapter Fifty

Now that everyone in the cabin had retired for the night and Solange and Gaston were in the privacy of her bedroom, Gaston held her in his arms close to his broad chest. "He is a fine young man, Solange. One of these days Hawk is going to come to terms with the things that have tormented him. He likes the white man in him, but he does not wish to accept the part that is Apache. When he comes to a time in his life when that sore quits festering and paining him, then he will live a full, happy life."

"Oh, Gaston, I hope I can help him realize that."

"You already have, *chérie,* and now we will both help him. I'm going to try to make up to Hawk for the absence of a father's influence in his life. I don't speak ill of this Tim you were married to, but I don't think he gave much time to Hawk when he was a lad."

"Oh, Gaston—I find myself falling more and more in love with you every day." She sighed softly with a mist of tears gathering in her eyes. Why could they have not met many years ago?

"The feeling is mutual, my precious one!" His lips sought hers and his husky body moved to mold to hers. His deep bass voice whispered in her ear, "I am hungry, *ma petite,* but not for food. I'm hungry for your sweet, sweet love."

She softly laughed as she willingly gave him all the love filling her heart and soul.

Shawna's sleep was a restless one, for she was still feeling the effects of meeting the devastatingly handsome Hawk. Never had she seen such a man. He was everything she'd ever daydreamed about, the perfect romantic figure of her girlish fantasies. To think that she had come face-to-face with such an individual was more than she'd ever expected. To think that this was Troy's friend amazed her. The two of them just didn't seem like a pair who would be pals as they obviously were.

Her thoughtful mood had prompted Troy to question if she was feeling all right as they ate their evening meal. She quickly assured him that she was feeling just fine. "Guess the trip to the village and meeting your friends made for a full day for me, Troy," she lied.

But Troy was not as dumb as she might have thought him to be. He knew that neither the trip to the village nor the day had been that taxing on a vivacious girl like Shawna. He had sensed her quiet mood after they'd said goodbye to Solange and Hawk. No, Shawna was not that tired. She was lovestruck over Hawk, he figured, recalling how he'd seen those black eyes sparking so bright when the two of them were walking up the path toward the wagon.

How could he warn her, he wondered, that Hawk's heart belonged to a beautiful white girl living down in the valley? God, he'd heard Hawk speak about this Gillian Browne and that was enough to tell Troy that he idolized her.

He'd never said a word to Hawk when he'd spoken about Gillian, even though he'd been tempted to, just as he was tempted now to caution Shawna about losing her heart. Lord, how he'd wanted to warn Hawk that Gillian Browne was not going to love a half-breed whose kin had killed her parents! But he knew Hawk would only resent it and become sullen, so he had just listened and allowed Hawk to talk about her.

376

He didn't plan to be so reserved with his cousin. She was young and innocent. After all, she was his responsibility now that his Aunt Violet was dead.

"My friends liked you, Shawna. I think you liked them, too," Troy remarked, searching her pretty face as he spoke.

"I certainly did."

"Well, they're good people. There's no lady with a kinder heart than Solange Touraine and Hawk's one fine man. He's been scouting for the railroad. Just got back home a few days ago."

She nibbled her food as he talked. Troy just kept on talking about Solange and Hawk and the way neighbors became very close up here in these mountains. "You may find life a little dull, since you're so young, Shawna."

"Maybe I won't, Troy." She stopped eating to look up to smile at him.

"Well, no young people around. Maybe that's how I turned out to be a bachelor. Now, Hawk has his eyes on a pretty white girl down in the valley, but I think he's dreaming. That girl isn't going to pair herself up with him. You couldn't tell Hawk that though." Troy laughed.

"A white girl? Hawk likes her very much?"

"Oh, yeah. He says she has hair like flaming fire and eyes like the blue wildflowers that bloom down in the valley pastureland. Oh, he's smitten with her. I've never seen her, so I can't say what she's like. But she has been up to Solange's cabin on a couple of occasions, I've heard."

Shawna got up out of her chair without saying a word. She quickly started gathering the plates off the table and busied herself around the kitchen.

Troy knew he had probably given her a jolt when he'd mentioned that Hawk had his eye on a girl named Gillian Browne, but he felt it was necessary.

He left her alone in the kitchen to think about what he'd just told her. Hawk might be his friend, but he did not want his little cousin losing her heart to a man who loved another woman.

When Shawna had finished her chores, she came to the room where Troy was sitting to tell him good night. "I'm ready for bed, Troy, so I just thought I'd tell you good night," she said as she untied the apron from her tiny waist and folded it.

"Night, Shawna, and sleep well," Troy mumbled, for he was already half asleep. He felt a little guilty about what he'd done. It was obvious that what he'd said had made her very unhappy. Maybe he should have kept his mouth shut! He was the first to admit that he didn't know the ways of women. They were a very complex, puzzling people.

Shawna was not a young lady to give up without a fight, and now that she'd met Hawk she was determined to do anything it might take to attract him. So what if he thought he was in love with this Gillian Browne? Men had been known to change their minds, she told herself as she slipped into her nightgown. Maybe she'd just show this white girl that she had more to offer Hawk than she did. She could give him all her love and there were no barriers to mar the love she felt in her heart.

They were two of a kind; they were both half-breeds. That was something to bind them together, something he and this Gillian Browne would never have!

She sat on the edge of her bed and unbraided the long single braid of her thick hair and shook it vigorously to let it flow free and loose around her shoulders.

Once she dimmed the lamp on the small table by the bed, she crawled into bed, but she was not ready for sleep. She was ready to allow her wild imagination to flow. She envisioned the image of Hawk and she could almost feel the heat of his powerful presence hovering over her. The strength and the power of his strong, muscled arms would be holding her close, pressed to his chest, and his black head would be bending lower and lower so that their lips might meet in a kiss.

Shawna shuddered at the thought of what that sensuous mouth could ignite if it captured her lips in a kiss. No man had ever possessed her yet, but she had known the thrill of a man's kisses. She'd found out at a very early age that men found her attractive. Back where she'd lived, she seemed to have blossomed much earlier than a lot of the girls her same age.

Her mother, Violet, was always keeping her eagle eyes out protectively. Because of this, Shawna had realized she must be attractive. Her friends at the age of fourteen were still flat-chested with no curve to their youthful figures like Shawna. It naturally set her apart from the others that were her age.

It was long after midnight when she finally drifted off to sleep.

While Shawna lay in her bed dwelling in her fantasy about the handsome Hawk, Gillian lay in her bed at the Fosters' ranch house facing the stark reality that she must abandon herself to what fate had dealt her because she'd dared to love a man with her whole heart and soul. How could she deny any longer that he had deserted her? How could she continue to wait, week after week, in hopes that he was going to come to Maricopa County as he'd promised? Dear God, how many weeks had passed now? She'd lost count. But she did know that a whole season had passed into another one and that she was forced to make a decision about Hawk's proposal.

Tonight, she lay in her bed with her head whirling crazily. Should she go to Hawk and accept his offer of marriage?

A voice deep within her cried out against this plan and she was torn with the torment of it. Could something have happened to Steve that prevented him from getting back to her as he'd promised? Logic told her she was merely grasping at straws. There had not even been a letter from him since they'd said good-bye.

Gillian knew she must forget any foolish fancy she'd been harboring about Steve Lafferty!

By the time exhaustion and weariness was finally making her surrender to sleep, Gillian had made her decision. Tomorrow she would go to Hawk and accept his offer of marriage. She could not think selfishly only of herself and her desires. There was an innocent baby to consider.

Girlish romantic dreams had to be put aside now and she had to think of the child she carried. It wasn't as if she wasn't fond of Hawk, and she'd strive to be a good wife to him. He deserved that from her. But she knew that nothing would ever make her forget those magical moments she'd spent with Steve Lafferty!

She comforted herself with the thought that she could think of them once in a while and recall the exciting ecstasy. No one would ever know that she was thinking about him and the rapture they'd shared.

She wondered how many other women had faced this decision. How many women ended up marrying a man they were truly not in love with? She'd never figured that she would be one of them.

To love a man so completely as she had Lafferty could be a painful experience, she realized! She could almost hate him for it!

It was absolutely hopeless for Troy to expect Hawk to have an understanding ear when he tried to complain about his cousin. Watching him devour the slice of bread with great relish, he figured Hawk was stopping by the cabin more often than he had in the past.

He was a fine one to talk when he was having another thick slice just as Hawk was doing. Both were so engrossed in their eating that they did not see Shawna moving through the room, her arms piled high with bedding that she was taking out for a good airing. She wore an amused smile on her face as she observed the two of them eating like a couple of hungry wolves.

If what her mother had always said was true about the way to a man's heart being through his stomach, then she was going to give this Gillian Browne a run for her money. She wanted to find the way to Hawk's heart more than anything in the world!

When Hawk left Troy's cabin that afternoon, he rode Tache home at a slow, unhurried pace. There were some thoughts he was trying to sort out in his head. Never had he been interested in any woman other than Gillian, but he would be lying to himself if he tried to deny that Troy's half-breed cousin didn't attract his attention. He found her to be a fascinating little creature. But it was Gillian he loved, he kept reminding himself. He'd asked her to be his wife and this had been what he'd wanted for a long, long time. But there was another problem, too: Before too long he was going to leave for Tucson to meet with Warner Barstow.

If Gillian did not give him an answer very soon, then he would not be able to save her from the shame she spoke about to him. He would be many miles away, and he had no inkling when he would be returning to Maricopa County once he left this time.

Should she accept his proposal of marriage, he would take her to Tucson with him. As his wife, she'd be his responsibility. And he'd want her with him.

Tomorrow, he decided, he must ride to the ranch and explain this to her, for the days were passing swiftly. They had no time to dally if there was to be a wedding.

Although Hawk could not know it, the same thoughts occupying his mind that afternoon were also prodding at Gillian. All day, she knew that she was not imagining that Mother Foster was scrutinizing her expanding figure. She had to go to Hawk the next day and tell him that she would marry him if he was still willing to make her his bride.

The next day, she left the house to go for a ride. At least that was all she told Nancy Foster. She dared not say that she was riding up into the mountains.

She wore her divided skirt with the faded blue tunic unhampered by the sash because her mirror revealed that the sash emphasized the roundness of her belly, growing larger every day.

As she was leaving the area of the barn, John Foster was coming out of the barn. She waved at him before galloping away.

Wild like the wind, she rode the little mare across the pastureland, her auburn hair flying back from her face. It was not until she came to the spot where she and Lafferty had lingered for some stolen moments when he was here visiting, that she pulled back on the reins. She recalled that glorious afternoon when they'd sat on the grass in that small grove of trees.

Like someone in a trance, she dismounted from her horse and walked to the exact spot where they'd sat. Steve had plucked a little cornflower, blue like her eyes, and tucked it behind her ear. No flowers were blooming there now, but she sat down to reflect on that moment of splendor.

She was so deep in thought about that wonderful afternoon that she did not hear Hawk approaching the grove, nor did she sense that he had dismounted and walked softly up behind her.

He said not a word for a moment or two. He just stood there looking down at her and watched her nimble fingers playing with a blade of the green grass. Her flaming hair fell around her shoulders but he could not see the loveliness of her face for her back was turned.

Compassion flooded him as he thought about what a heavy load those dainty shoulders had carried the last several weeks. What a bastard that Lafferty had to be to have deserted her!

He had to convince her today that she must marry him!

Chapter Fifty-One

Finally he let his presence be known by calling her name softly. She turned, a startled look on her face.

"Hawk! I am glad to see you."

"Are you, little one? Well, I am glad to see you. In fact, that was where I was heading when I chanced to see you here. This is even nicer." He sat down beside her. His black eyes moved carefully over her face before he asked, "Are you feeling all right, Gillian?"

"Oh, yes, Hawk. I'm just fine—really!"

He took her small hand in his and his fine-featured face took on a sober look before he began to speak. "Gillian, we must talk today. I can't give you more time to make up your mind. I promised Warner Barstow I'd return to Tucson in four weeks. He offered me an opportunity that I can't miss. You must understand this."

"Oh, I do understand, Hawk. Truly, I do." She was about to add that she was on her way to seek him out today to give him her answer, but before she could say it, Hawk was telling her, "We must get married, Gillian, if this is what you want. Once I leave I don't know when I'll be returning. I don't want you to face this alone."

She grinned and put her fingers over his lips. "Now, if I may speak, Hawk, there will be no reason for you to say anything else. I was coming today to tell you that I accept your offer of marriage—whenever you say."

A boyish grin came on his bronzed face. "You're going to marry me?"

"If you still want me to." She giggled.

"I still want you, Gillian. I've always wanted you, since long before we ever met. I've loved you for longer than you can know." His arms went around her and he gave her a tender kiss on her lips, for he had no intention of forcing her to respond to his fierce passion. When she could come to him willingly, then he would be the happiest man in the world. Otherwise, he could settle for less.

He did not allow his lips to capture hers too long, for he was only human. As he released her, she reached up to place her hands on his cheeks and sigh, "Oh, Hawk! Hawk! I—I don't know what to say. You are so good to me."

"Oh, I'm not so good. I can be a mean son-of-a-gun, as you will see when a little time goes by. Ask my mother." He laughed lightheartedly.

"I shall," she retorted. Suddenly, she found herself realizing that life was not so desolate after all. She and Hawk could have a good life together and she would try to make up to him for what he'd done for her. He certainly deserved that much.

"Can we be married at the end of the week? A simple little ceremony is what I'd like, and I figure that's what you'd want, too. As soon as we're married I'd like to be on our way to Tucson."

Gillian looked up at him. "I suggest that we have a wedding early in the day and we shall leave Maricopa County right after the wedding. Our honeymoon shall be our trip to Tucson. Think about it, Hawk! We'll sleep out under a starlit sky and have our meals by a cozy campfire and listen to the night birds sing. What could be more romantic than that?" The look on her face and her exuberant air were enough to convince Hawk that she would find this exciting.

"You truly mean it, don't you, little one?"

"If I didn't mean it, I would not have said it." She grinned.

"Then it will be that way. Oh, Gillian—you've made me a very happy man!"

"And you've made me a very happy woman, Hawk. I shall tell the Fosters as soon as I get back to the house. I won't have time for a wedding gown, I'm afraid, with this short notice."

"Oh, Gillian—I feel a deep regret that I'll have no chance to get you a ring. I'm sure Mother will let us use the gold band Tim gave her when they married. But when we get to Tucson, you will have your own ring, I assure you!"

Gillian assured him that this did not matter to her. He hesitated for a moment to mention something else that was on his mind: She must be prepared for a trip on horseback. Even with a pack horse there was only so much they could take along with all the gear they needed for the hundred-mile trip.

"Gillian, you know that we're going to have to travel light. I'll buy you anything you need once we get to Tucson—all right?"

She laughed. "Oh, Hawk—I don't have that many possessions. Don't fret about that at all."

When they sought to leave the grove and go their separate ways, it seemed to each of them that in that short interlude under the trees they'd made all their plans for their future. Both rode away feeling as if a heavy burden was now lifted.

Gillian returned to the ranch feeling happier than she'd felt in a long time. At least she knew where she was going and the uncertainty and apprehensions no longer were there to torment her.

Hawk rode back up to the mountains with the news that he knew would delight his mother. Solange had always adored Gillian, and nothing would make her happier than the news he would be telling her tonight.

At the end of this week, Gillian would be his bride! He still found it hard to believe. This had been his dream for so long!

Lafferty had lost and he'd won after all, Hawk proudly told himself.

*　　　*　　　*

Steve Lafferty had completed his plan to travel to Maricopa County on horseback. He had to leave the majority of his luggage in Melba Jackson's care there at the inn. The one thing he was taking with him was the wedding band he'd purchased for his bride-to-be. There was damned well going to be a wedding, and nothing was going to stop it!

The strong, long-legged roan Steve had swapped for the buggy was recommended by the owner of the stables. "He'll get you there faster than any other horse I've got in my stalls right now. Them long legs of his will cover a lot of ground, I'll swear to that. Rode him myself a day ago," the man had assured Steve.

Steve had to take his word for that since he was no expert on horses. He already accepted the fact that his trip was going to be an experience he wouldn't forget for a long time. He didn't have a way with horses as he did with his ship and the sea.

He was going to challenge that big roan, for he felt the urgency to get to Maricopa County as quick as he could. The thought of Gillian giving way to some foolish impulse to marry another man was more than he dared to chance.

For the first two hours out of Tucson, he and the horse got along fine as the big roan made a fast and furious gallop along the dirt road. Steve was feeling a little cocky by this time. Maybe with more practice, he could get to be as fine a rider as Gillian was, he told himself.

He found himself relaxing as he swayed in the saddle as he and the roan moved across the countryside. Since it was late afternoon by the time he'd left the inn, it was already approaching nightfall. When he saw the outskirts of a town just ahead, he realized that he'd best see if there might be a place to get a meal, for he'd not taken the time to bring provisions with him.

A small sign by the side of the road informed him that the small hamlet was called Rillito. He questioned if he'd find a place to eat once he guided the horse down the one street lined with stores and shops. Most appeared to be already closed for the evening.

A tavern seemed to be still alive with patrons, but a drink was not what he was wanting. Besides, he had his own flask of good Irish whiskey. But a couple of doors down, he spotted light coming from the front of a small cubicle of a place. He was pleased to see that it was a restaurant of sorts with a half dozen tables occupied by a few customers.

He guided the roan to the hitching post and dismounted. Once he had entered and noticed the unswept floors, he figured the food would probably not be too tasty. By the time he'd ordered and eaten the so-called dinner special, he knew he'd been right. But at least it was something to fill his need until he could do better. Up the way there was a place, Red Rock, that had a nice wayside inn and lodging house. That's where he'd enjoy breakfast the next morning.

When he was preparing to go toward the front door, he heard a distant rumbling. By the time he was out the door, he saw an intense flash of lightning in the mountain area ahead of him.

He had not noticed the little wizened-face gent sitting on the floor and leaning against the wooden post. Steve gave him a nod as he prepared to untie the reins of his horse.

"Got us a good one comin' in from them mountains over there. Did you see that lightning?" he asked Steve.

"Yes, I saw it," Steve answered the old fellow.

Giving a spit of the tobacco juice, the old man inquired, "You ain't a'ridin' in that direction, are you?"

Steve laughed. "Afraid I am."

"Horses don't like lightning and thunder. They get spooked. Do real crazy things when they do. But then I guess you know that."

Steve lied and told the old fellow he knew that as he leaped up to mount the horse. He gave the old man a wave of his hand as he spurred the roan to move out.

But he'd not gone a couple of miles from the town when he saw that the storm was right ahead of him, just as the old man had said. The thunder was more fierce and the lightning was much sharper. The roan was becoming more fractious and unruly. Steve was finding him a handful to control. He was stubbornly determined to get out of the clearing and into the shelter of the woods just ahead so the lightning would not be obvious to the nervous animal.

It was a taxing battle for Lafferty for the next few minutes, but he managed to get the roan to the edge of the woods. But with a suddenness that took even Lafferty by surprise, the woods seemed to light up as a bolt of lightning struck close by. The earth shook under them from the deafening thunder. A maddening frenzy broke in the horse and he reared up not once but twice. Steve felt himself tumbling to the ground below. While he was slightly stunned, he saw the roan wildly galloping in and out of the trees of the woods.

He sat on the ground, brushing his tousled hair away from his eyes. With that damned horse had gone his prized silver flask filled with Irish whiskey, a change of clothes, and his shaving articles. The one thing he'd not packed in the saddlebag was the ring for Gillian.

He was grateful for that, at least!

Chapter Fifty-Two

Now Lafferty knew what the old fellow meant when he spoke of a horse getting spooked. But when he was about to get up from the ground and brush himself off, he felt the first drops of rain hit his face. In another second they began to fall faster and heavier and Lafferty knew there was a downpour in the offing. He sought one of the thicker branched trees to find shelter.

His keen green eyes spotted a fair-sized boulder with some thick underbrush, and he figured that it might be a good place to huddle down in. He crawled through the brush and snuggled as close to the boulder as he could.

The ledge of the boulder extended above him, providing a cover for his head, but it was hardly enough to cover his broad shoulders. He felt the pelting drops hitting his shirt. The underbrush's thickness seemed to protect the legs of his pants. He leaned back against the boulder, for there was nothing else he could do but sit and wait for the storm to pass.

Perhaps the pattern of the raindrops on the leaves and the support of the firm bolder against his back helped Steve give way to the weary feeling. Sleep overtook him.

The rains continued until the early morning hours. Just about the time the sun was rising in the western sky, a stooped figure moved through the woods, a jute sack flung over his back. He'd left Rillito an hour earlier to get back to his cabin in the woods. It had not exactly been his plan to stay the night in town, but the storm had made the decision for him. He'd traveled to Rillita to get a few supplies. He wasn't even good company for his dog, Pal, when he ran out of chewing tobacco.

Whistling a little tune as he moved over the carpeted grass of the woods, old Arlo Murphy made his way toward his cabin. His rheumy eyes caught sight of a strange sight sticking out from the underbrush as he walked down the narrow path. He saw that it was a fine leather boot and he wondered who it belonged to.

His hands parted the bushes to see what was behind them and he recognized the gent immediately as the one he'd spoken to back at the cafe. But Arlo saw no sight of the red roan he'd ridden away on.

He gave a jerk of the young man's leg. "Hey, young fellow! Wake up!"

Steve came alive with a startled look. "Wha—what?" His green eyes stared up at the figure hovering over him and he recognized the old fellow. "Oh, it's you! Sorry, give me a minute to get awake." Steve sat up to bring himself alert.

"You all right, young man?"

"I'm fine. Just still half asleep, I guess."

Slowly Steve crawled out of the bower to stand up. Brushing his sandy-colored hair away from his forehead, he gave a lazy stretch of his tall body and moved his long, muscled legs to give some life to them. A slow, easy grin came to his face as he told the old man, "Well, old man, my horse did get spooked last night—threw me and ran away like banshees were after him."

"Yep, told you so! So you're stranded—right?"

"Right!"

"Then I'd say you better come with me and we'll have ourselves some breakfast. Then you can decide what you're going to do."

"Guess you're right, old man. I can't think of anything better right now than having breakfast."

Old Murphy motioned him to join him along the path through the woods to his cabin. "Think it's about time we introduce ourselves if we're going to share a meal. Murphy is the name, son—Arlo Murphy!"

Lafferty grinned as he shook the old man's hand. "Nice to meet you, Murphy. I'm Steve Lafferty."

The old man's bushy eyebrow rose as he gave Steve a measured look. "Lafferty, is it? Well, I'll be damned—a good Irish name if I ever heard one. Am I right?"

"You are, Murphy, and damned proud of it. Would I be right if I figure you to be a little bit Irish, too?"

The old man chuckled. "You'd be figuring right, son."

Suddenly, they seemed to be leaving the woods behind them to enter a small area that was cleared of trees. In the middle of the clearing was a crudely constructed cabin.

"There she is, son. That's my little place—my home. Well, me and Pal's house. That's my old dog that's just about as old as I am."

Steve did not have to ask him if he'd built the cabin himself.

They had not gone but a few more paces before the massive black short-haired dog came running out of the cabin to greet his master. But the dog suddenly broke from Murphy to growl at Lafferty until Murphy soothed him, assuring Pal that Lafferty was all right. "Simmer down, Pal. He's a good Irishman like the two of us."

Lafferty and Murphy both laughed and the big dog seemed to understand and accept Lafferty after that.

But an hour later, when Steve sat at the small table to eat the eggs, slices of ham, and the flaky biscuits the old man had prepared, he had to confess that it was the best fare he'd enjoyed for a long time.

"Good, ain't it, son?" The old man grinned slyly as he watched Steve devouring the food.

While both of them enjoyed one more cup of coffee, Murphy admitted to Lafferty that he had no solution as to how to get him back on the trail. "My old mule died on me last week. That's why I had to walk into Rillito yesterday. Haven't been able to find me another one so far."

"Well, I might just have to start walking, too," Steve told him.

"You're about eleven miles from Red Rock, young man, and if you can walk it then you could find you a horse there. I've no doubt about that. That's about the best advice I can give you. I know a dude who has some horses, but that's almost ten miles and he might strike a bargain with you and he might not. So I say it's best you head for Red Rock."

"I'd say you're right, Murphy." Steve agreed with the man sitting across the table from him.

The old man gave him the directions to move to get out of the dense forest and back on the trail. When Steve tried to put a few coins on his kitchen table, Murphy shook his bushy head to declare, "If one Irishman can't help another in their time of need, then we're a poor lot."

While Steve took the time to wash his face and use Murphy's comb to plow through his unruly hair, the old man busily fixed him a pack to take with him. He cut some slices of the ham shank and bread and filled an extra canteen with water.

Lafferty would have given many coins for his razor, but in his hurry to be heading for Red Rock, he did not take the time to use Murphy's.

The two of them said their farewells and Murphy stood watching as Lafferty's towering figure moved farther and farther away, until he disappeared into the woods. He knew he would never see the young man again but it was nice to have had this brief encounter.

Lafferty's firm, muscled legs were feeling taut and tight by the time he'd walked for over four hours. He had no idea of how far he had to walk before he would be seeing the outskirts of Red Rock. He was certainly grateful for the canteen of water and the pack of food that old Murphy had packed for him. He seemed to be the only person in the deserted countryside. Not one wagon or rider had passed his way.

Onward, he walked down the trail toward Red Rock. Just as twilight was falling over the countryside, a flat-bedded wagon came rolling down the dirt road.

Lafferty welcomed the farmer's offer to give him a ride into Red Rock. It was a grand feeling to sit down on the seat of the wagon and rest his tired legs.

The ride into the town of Red Rock was a pleasant retreat for Lafferty after all the miles he'd walked. When he parted company with the farmer, he made for the lodging house where he knew he could find good accommodations. The owners of the inn directed him to the livery where he could acquire himself a horse.

Three hours after he'd arrived in Red Rock, Lafferty had purchased himself a new mount to replace the red roan and all the articles in the saddlebags the erratic horse had run off with.

By the time he walked into the dining room of the lodging house, he was feeling invigorated. He was clean-shaven and he'd purchased himself a new shirt.

A good meal was all he wanted and a good night's sleep before he hit the trail the next morning to be on his way toward Maricopa County.

Once he had returned to the comfortable room of the inn and tugged at his fine leather boots to remove them, he thought to himself that he surely must love that little auburn-haired lady. He was going through a lot of torment just to get back to her on time. As he sat there on the edge of the bed, all he could do was shake his head in disbelief. Never had he bowed to any woman in his life as he found himself doing to Gillian Browne. It had to be love! It had to be a love that he'd never known before! He had to also admit to himself that he never expected any woman to bewitch him as she'd managed to do. As crazy as it might seem, he honestly believed that she was not aware of her enchanting charms and how they affected a man.

Gillian's announcement to Nancy Foster had taken her by utter surprise and she was unable to speak for a minute or two. But she saw the look on Gillian's face as she spoke and she knew instinctively that she intended to marry Hawk and not Steve Lafferty.

"We can't get a wedding gown ready that soon for you, honey. Would you settle for wearing mine when I married John?" Nancy asked her.

"Oh, Mother Foster, I'd be very honored to wear your wedding gown," Gillian had replied.

"Well, it was early spring when I married John and it is late autumn now," Nancy told her.

"That does not matter to me."

"Well, it would please me very much, darling, for you to be married in my gown. We've got to get busy taking a lot of tucks in it."

"Oh, Mother Foster, we can get that done in a couple of days," Gillian assured her, patting her hand.

"Oh, I have no doubt about that, honey. What I have my doubts about is if you should be marrying Hawk."

For a moment Gillian could not reply. When she sought to speak to the dear lady who'd been so good to her for the last few years, her voice was soft and mellow. Those blue eyes of hers looked at Nancy Foster with such sincerity and honesty that Nancy could not argue with her. "Romantic dreams are wonderful but there comes a time in life that we must put them aside to face the truth. Hawk loves me and I know I can count on his love. What more can a woman ask of a man? I admit to you that I lost my heart to Steve Lafferty, but that was foolish fancy on my part."

Nancy knew exactly what she was trying to tell her, for she remembered Helen's infatuation with Kent Clayton. It had given her nothing but misery for years.

"Honey, it's your life and you've got to live it the way it seems right for you," Nancy told her.

"I thank you, Mother Foster. Hawk and I will be happy, for I will work to make it that way."

"Then it will be, Gillian!" Nancy declared. Maybe this marriage was right after all, she thought.

Chapter Fifty-Three

The rest of the day Nancy found herself baffled as she went about the chores when her thoughts drifted back to Gillian and her plan to marry Hawk. She had to admit that she'd not been as smart as she credited herself with being, for she thought Gillian so in love with Steve Lafferty that no other man could have won her away from him.

It had to be that the poor child was devastated by the fact that he'd not come to the ranch as he'd promised. Now that she thought about it, she'd not heard her mention his name for the last four or five weeks. She should have suspected that Gillian was becoming disenchanted with the handsome Irishman. She suddenly decided that it might be best that she go out to the barn so she could tell John before the three of them gathered around the table for the evening meal.

At least the shock of it would have a time to settle down. The unexpected news was going to be as mighty a blow to him as it had been to her.

She found her husband up in the hayloft pitching down some hay. She called up to him to come down so she could talk to him.

"Just a little more, honey, so you just sit yourself down on that stool and let me finish up here. My old legs aren't what they used to be so I don't want to crawl up and down those extra steps," he called down to her as he continued his task in the loft.

Nancy did as her husband suggested, and he did not make her wait too long before he climbed down the steps to join her. "Now, what's so urgent that it brought you out here to the barn?" He wiped his face with the kerchief he'd tied around his neck.

"Well, I just thought it would be better for me to tell you alone without Gillian around, John. She—she's going to marry Hawk and I got to tell you, it floored me. Here all the time I was just sure it was going to be Steve Lafferty."

For a minute, John just stared down at his wife, sitting there on the small oak stool, and made no reply.

"You heard what I said, didn't you, John?"

"I heard. Well, it would seem she's changed her mind for whatever her reasons. Guess we just got to go along with it, eh, Nancy? If she's determined to marry Hawk, then I guess that's the way it will be."

Nancy rose up from the stool, telling her husband she'd let him get back to work. She'd go on back to the house and finish up her housecleaning.

"See you in a little while, Nancy," he told her as she went toward the barn door. John knew that his wife had to be feeling a degree of sadness about Gillian marrying Hawk and leaving them. He had to confess that he was going to miss having that little girl around the place, but it was bound to happen sooner or later. Somehow, the news had not surprised him as it had Nancy.

With the holiday season coming in a couple of months, it would be lonely for the two of them. He wondered if Nancy had already thought about this. He'd wager that she had.

She had thought about that, about the void once Hawk took Gillian away as his bride. But she managed to hide her heavy heart.

The girl had to have a beautiful gown to be married in, Nancy thought, but there was the possibility that her lovely gown could be yellowed with age even though she'd packed it in a box very carefully.

Rushing into her bedroom, she yanked out a box that she'd not opened for years. Did she dare to hope that her own lovely wedding dress was still nice enough for Gillian to wear? There was time to get it hemmed up to fit her petite figure and tucked in at the waistline. She said a silent prayer as she lifted the lid.

The white satin material was not the snow-white color it had been the day Nancy wore it, but the lace inset yoke and stand-up collar were still in fine shape. The puffed sleeves had ruffled flounces. Venise appliqués covered the bodice. She pulled it out and gave the long, full, gathered skirt a couple of shakes. "Oh, glory be! That girl's going to have herself a beautiful wedding gown." She laughed. Some airing out on her clothesline and a bleaching from the hot sun would do wonders, she knew.

She rushed out of the house to get it out on the line. John did not know what she was so happy about when he heard her singing as she came back into the house.

An hour later Gillian came into the kitchen and Nancy took her to the back door to point out the dress she was airing. "It was my wedding gown and I'm getting it ready to be yours, too, honey," she told Gillian.

Gillian flung her arms around Nancy Foster. "Oh, how sweet and dear you are to me, Mother Foster. It's the most beautiful thing I've ever seen."

"Well, we've got ourselves a hemming job to do, and I'll get you to try it on so I can pin in the waistline and the hem." Nancy gave out a lighthearted laugh.

But this brought forth a wave of apprehension in Gillian. Mother Foster would surely take notice of her much fuller figure.

A short time later, Nancy was anxiously urging her into her bedroom where her little sewing basket was. Gillian followed behind her wondering what she could do to get Mother Foster to leave the room. She sat down on the edge of the bed to

397

remove her shoes. She unfastened her skirt and let it slip to the floor. Now it was time to get out of her tunic.

"Oh, Mother Foster—I forgot to add some extra water to that pot of beans," she lied.

"You go ahead and get your clothes off and I'll go tend to them."

Gillian heaved a deep sigh of relief and hastily used the time to rid herself of the tunic and slip into the lovely white satin gown.

By the time Nancy returned to the room, Gillian was standing there in her old wedding gown. Nancy laughed as she saw the gown with the skirt flowing there on the floor. "Knew we'd have a few inches to take off that skirt."

She busied herself pinning up the hemline. It was the waist that surprised her. She concluded that she must have been smaller than she'd realized when she'd first married John. About an inch on either side was all she'd have to take in. She told Gillian that she could take it off now, she had all the pinning done. While Nancy's back was turned to her, Gillian got back into her loose-fitting tunic. By the time Nancy turned around, Gillian was fastening her skirt, grateful that the fitting of the gown had gone so smoothly.

"It's an angel you're going to look like, Gillian honey," Nancy declared as she placed her sewing basket on her bed. "Going to start working on that hem tonight after supper."

Gillian had been pleased that the Fosters had accepted her news so calmly, for she had not been sure that they would.

After the evening meal, Nancy and John settled down in the parlor. Nancy started the tedious task of hemming the gown and John did as he usually did every evening after supper. He smoked his pipe and read the journal.

Gillian figured that it was not too soon to begin thinking about the things she should pack to take to Tucson with her after she and Hawk were married. She remembered what he'd told her about traveling light, so she realized that she could not take all the lovely clothing Helen Clayton had given her. She chose her cotton blouses and twill divided skirts to take with her.

They would be riding horseback so she couldn't wear the pretty sprigged muslin with the fancy little blue bonnet as she had when she and Nancy had caught the stagecoach.

She suddenly realized just how little she was going to be able to take with her when she started making the small pile on her bed. But then Hawk had promised her he would buy her what she needed once they got to Tucson. As for jewelry and keepsakes, those were easily placed in her one reticule. The savage torching of their wagon train by the Apaches had destroyed everything she'd cherished and saved for keepsakes up to the age of fourteen.

So she had little to carry away with her when she left Maricopa County. Just to think about this made her angry. Those devil Apaches had robbed her of everything. She sat there, thinking about it.

A small voice whispered in her ear that the man she was going to marry in a few days' time was part Apache, but she argued back to that voice that Hawk, with his gentle ways and tender heart, was not like those savages!

In the same calm subdued way the Fosters had received the news from Gillian, Solange responded when Hawk announced that he and Gillian were going to be married.

He had expected a little more exuberance from Solange, knowing how fond she was of Gillian. "Are you not pleased, Mother?" he inquired of her.

"Oh, Hawk—my dear son, I love Gillian already, so you must know that you have my approval. I want nothing more than you and Gillian to be happy. It just comes as a little bit of a shock, shall we say?" She gave him a warm, loving smile that was enough to satisfy Hawk. Solange was glad, for she dared not speak from the heart this night.

She listened as her son told her of their plans for a very

simple wedding so that they might depart for Tucson immediately afterward.

"Well, just as long as both of you are sure that this is what you want, Hawk. It all seems to be happening very hastily. You two are giving me or the Fosters no time for preparation."

"It's the way Gillian and I want it, Mother."

"Then this is the way it shall be, my son."

After Hawk left her, Solange wasted no time in starting to make her future daughter-in-law a special little nosegay. She chose from her collection of dried flowers the shades of white, blue, and pink, and the streamers of ribbon holding the cluster together were the same shade. They were from the collection of ribbons that Gillian had brought to her a short time ago.

The day Gillian had come to visit her and brought her the lovely gray shawl and array of ribbons, she'd never imagined that she would have been making this nosegay for Gillian to hold in her dainty hand when she married her son, Hawk!

Solange had grave thoughts. This could be a mistake for both of them!

Chapter Fifty-Four

When Hawk spied the beautiful nosegay, he knew his mother had worked tediously last night to make this for Gillian.

But she was not in the cabin, nor was Gaston, so he figured that the two of them had gone for one of their early-morning walks.

He helped himself to a couple of cups of coffee and decided to pay a visit to Troy. It was probably going to be his last chance to say goodbye to his old friend.

He grabbed a couple of the still-warm biscuits to munch on and rode down the trail toward Troy's cabin. A boyish grin broke on his face as he envisioned the expression on old Troy's face when he told him that he was going to marry Gillian Browne in three days.

As Tache trotted down the narrow mountain trail, Hawk finished the last biscuit. A cool breeze whistled through the verdant pines and he saw the busy scampering squirrels going up and down the trees, already preparing for the winter months that could be harsh up on these mountaintops.

None of that harshness was there now though. It was a glorious day!

He would never have heard the soft voice calling out his name if he'd been riding down the trail at his usual pace, but he and Tache were leisurely moving along. He halted when he heard his name called out again. At the third calling, he spotted the tiny figure of Shawna sprawled in the shallow ravine by the edge of the trail.

"I fell, Hawk. Think I messed up an ankle 'cause I can't stand up on it," she yelled up at him.

"Be right down to get you, Shawna." He leaped off Tache and scrambled down the incline.

"Lord, I'm glad you came along when you did. There's no telling how long I would have sat here. Tried crawling up a couple of times and ended up falling down again," she told him as he reached the spot where she was sitting.

There were a couple of smudges of dirt on her lovely dark face and her tousled hair gave her the air of an impish child who'd managed to get herself in a mess of trouble. He thought she looked adorable as she stared up at him with those big black eyes. "Tell me, Shawna—how did you manage to fall down here in the first place? There's plenty of bank on the side of the road."

Her black eyes flashed with fire and there was a tone of irritation in her voice as she snapped at him, "Very simple! I walked down the bank to get myself some of the wild ferns growing here to take back to the house, but I happened to lose my footing. I fell, damn it!"

Hawk could not suppress a roar of laughter, not because she had fallen but because of her spitfire temper. Troy had a little hellcat on his hands when she got herself riled, as she was right now with him.

He noticed her empty basket because she'd never ended up getting her ferns so he yanked out his knife. "A girl can't go home without the ferns she's paid so dearly for." He lifted enough out of the ground to fill her basket.

"Now, Shawna—shall we get you up off the ground and get you home?" His hands reached out to her as she laboriously moved to put all her weight on her uninjured leg.

"Sit back down on the ground, Shawna," he ordered her.

Bending down, he lifted her up in his arms and when she was securely cradled there, he reached over so her free hand could take the handle of the basket filled with ferns.

She smiled up at him, grateful for his thoughtfulness. All the pain in her ankle was gone as he held her in his strong arms. Her dark eyes stared at his handsome face and she knew that she loved him.

Holding her as he was, to walk up the incline and get her atop Tache, Hawk could not deny that the soft feel of her young body pressed against him was having an effect. The adoration in her eyes was obvious to Hawk. He'd not seen that yet in Gillian's eyes.

By the time he mounted Tache, and Shawna's hands were clasped around his waist as she sat behind him on the horse, Hawk was faced with a mixture of feelings he'd never expected to deal with. He'd never desired any woman in his life but Gillian Browne, but he could not deny that Troy's cousin was stimulating him in a strange way he could not explain.

He was glad that it was only a short distance to Troy's cabin. This was insane, he told himself. He could not be attracted to another woman now that he was to marry Gillian in three days!

By the time they got to the cabin and he'd lifted her off Tache to carry her into the house, Hawk was perplexed by his feelings. He only began to relax when he'd deposited her on the cot in Troy's front room.

"Think I hear Troy out in the back chopping some wood. You just sit there, Shawna, while I go out there," Hawk requested. She would have never imagined the turmoil she'd created in that masterful man she adored so much. He drifted in a state of strange confusion.

She had only to look at her ankle to know that it was already swelling, so she removed her sandals as she sat there. Shortly Troy and Hawk came through the back door.

Troy took charge of the situation the minute he looked at her ankle. "It's a pretty good sprain, I'd say, wouldn't you, Hawk?"

"Sure would," Hawk agreed as his friend went into the kitchen to get a pan of the cool water he'd brought up from the spring a short time ago. He wrapped the cloths dampened with cool water around Shawna's ankle and foot, hoping to stop the swelling. "Now you just stretch out there on the cot, Shawna, 'cause that's where you're going to be spending your time this evening," Troy informed her.

She gave him no fuss, for she knew that she could not put any weight on her injured ankle. She'd tried that before Hawk happened along.

"I thank you again, Hawk, for coming to my rescue," she told Hawk with a soft smile.

"I'm glad I did, Shawna." His eyes met hers. Something urged him not to linger any longer. "Guess I better get going now, Troy."

"I'll walk out to the gate with you, Hawk. You'll be all right, won't you, Shawna?"

"I'll be fine, Troy. Goodbye, Hawk."

When they were out by the gate, Hawk told Troy about his plans to marry Gillian. For a moment Troy could not speak, for it had all come about in such a hurry.

"Solange is pleased, I'm sure," Troy asked Hawk.

"I think she is. She loves Gillian, too."

"Then you certainly have my blessing, too. When is the wedding to be?"

When Hawk told him in three days, Troy was really stunned. But Hawk quickly enlightened him that it had to be quickly since he had to go back to Tucson.

"Well, we'll be seeing you next at the church, I guess, Hawk. I'm assuming that's where you and Gillian will be married, isn't it?"

"Yes—but not the one in town. We're going to be married at the one on Canyon Road."

Hawk mounted his pinto, urging him into a gallop. Giving one final wave back at Troy he headed for home.

By the time he was at the hitching post and leaping down

from Tache, the brief interlude of bewitchment Shawna had caused had faded. It was Gillian who was completely occupying his thoughts as he walked up the pathway, eagerly greeted by Little Bear giving a friendly bark and a fast wagging of his tail.

"Well, hello—little fellow! Happy to see me?" Hawk bent down to give him a friendly pat on his head.

Together, they went toward the front door. Solange turned to greet her son. "Hawk, you are home! You just missed Reverend McGrann. He stopped by to tell you that he would be delighted to marry you and Gillian on Saturday, but the ceremony will have to be performed before noon because he has to be in Guadalupe by two. Is that all right?"

"That is perfect. That way Gillian and I can leave early in the afternoon."

"Then you should ride to the Fosters' ranch the first thing in the morning so you can tell Gillian and the Fosters. Take the nosegay I've made for your bride. I want you to take something else to her, Hawk. A bride should wear a beautiful strand of pearls around her neck and pearls on her ears. That will be my wedding gift to her."

Hawk began to protest. "But, Mother, Tim gave you those."

"I know, Hawk, and I enjoyed them all these years. But Gaston will give me a new strand of pearls and earrings. My gift will make your bride happy."

"If this is what you want, Mother."

"This is what I want, my son. Tonight, I will give you my gold band for you to place on your bride's finger until you can purchase one for her in Tucson."

Hawk had always adored his mother for her kind and generous heart, but never more than he did this evening. "Gillian will be thrilled by your gift and I thank you, too, for the ring, since I do not have one to give her. But she shall have a most magnificent ring, I promise you."

Solange looked affectionately at her son as she assured him, "I've no doubt about that at all, Hawk."

He sauntered into the kitchen where she moved about to put

her fresh vegetables into the pot. "What about you and Gaston, Mother? Will the two of you be leaving shortly after Gillian and I leave for Tucson?"

"Oh, yes—we shall, Hawk. Gaston has to get back to Canada very soon, but we will be here for a few days after the two of you leave. I don't have to tell you that this cabin is yours anytime you wish to come here, do I?"

"No, Mother—I know that."

She turned around to look upon the face of her son, so handsome and dear to her. She thought about all the years of the past, her joys and her heartaches. Her voice was mellow and cracked with the emotions she was feeling when she spoke. "Well, my son—it would seem that we are to go our separate ways into a new life, is it not so? It was bound to happen and one is never really prepared when it does come about. But I want you to know that I wish you a wonderful new life. I know you will have it. I shall, too. Gaston is a wonderful man and he loves me as I always wanted a man to love me, Hawk."

Hawk said nothing as he walked over to embrace his mother. "Oh, Mother—Mother! I love you! Life is going to be good to both of us. I know it."

Neither of them saw the bulky figure of Gaston standing at the front door. Gaston did not wish them to know that he was standing there, overhearing their most intimate, precious moments. But the emotion of the scene, and hearing Solange's endearing words about him, was enough to make his broad chest swell with overwhelming elation.

Dear God, how he loved that woman!

Chapter Fifty-Five

As far as Troy was concerned, that settled it once and for all. His little cousin must not set her heart on Hawk romantically because by this weekend he was going to be a married man. But how could he ease the pain for Shawna when he told her that? And he must tell her, he knew.

He'd seen her eyes following Hawk as he left the cabin. She adored his big, handsome friend. It was easy for Troy to understand how any young maiden could idolize such a handsome man as Hawk was. He hadn't been blessed with good looks and that was probably why he was a bachelor. Women had never found him that attractive.

As he'd walked back to his front door, he decided that he'd just tell Shawn the truth. It was the simple, uncomplicated way. This was Troy's way and always had been.

When he entered the cabin, he told Shawna, "Now I'll be the cook tonight, cousin, and you'll stay there and rest that swollen ankle."

She giggled. "I guess I'll have to let you have your way, Troy. I can't argue with you about that."

Troy went into the kitchen to prepare one of his very simple meals that would not measure up to the good meals Shawna had been preparing since she'd arrived at his cabin. His Aunt Violet had taught her well, Troy had to admit.

As he puttered around his small kitchen, his thoughts were about the marriage that was to take place this Saturday. He wished the best for Hawk and his new bride, but he questioned if it was right for Hawk. It seemed to Troy that Hawk would be a much happier man if he married someone of his own kind— someone like his pretty cousin. No one could want a more beautiful young wife than Shawna would be. While he'd had to begrudgingly give up his private times here at the cabin, he had to confess that she'd made the cabin more attractive with her special little touches and cleaning. This was the first meal he'd cooked since she'd arrived. He suddenly felt awkward trying to fix a meal.

When supper was ready, he fixed a plate for Shawna and filled one for himself so he could sit in the front room with her to share their meal.

"It's—it's very tasty, Troy," she told him after she'd taken a couple of bites. But Troy knew she was just being gracious because by now he was used to her good cooking. This was not as good as hers were.

"Well, I thank you, Shawna, but I must confess to you that I'm spoiled already with your cooking."

She laughed. "Well, I guess that means I've got to get well in a hurry."

Troy joined her in laughter. "Lord, I sure hope so."

When the two of them finished, Troy got up from his chair to go into the kitchen to wash the dirty dishes. Shawna urged him to bring that shirt of his that needed mending. "Lord, it is boring to just sit here and do nothing." She sighed.

So Troy went to the bedroom to get her sewing kit and his old faded blue shirt that he'd ripped the other day on a branch in the woods.

"There you are, Shawna. Seems you know how to do everything—good cook and fine seamstress. You'll make some man a fine wife someday."

A bright, radiant smile came on her face as her black eyes dashed upward. "You think so, Troy? I think so, too. I could be a very good wife." She wanted to add that she thought she'd be the perfect wife for his friend Hawk, but she decided to keep that opinion to herself.

"Well, you'll meet a nice fellow one of these days and I'll lose my cook and housekeeper," he teased as he went on into the kitchen.

By the time he had finished the dishes, Shawna had finished mending his shirt. By the time he joined her in the front room, he'd decided that he'd delay telling her about Hawk's marriage until the morning. Best let her get a good night's sleep because he felt the news was going to depress her.

It was decided that she had better just sleep there on the cot in the front room.

Shawna decided not to dim the lamp for a while; she could manage to handle that, since the table was beside the cot. But what she'd not thought about before Troy said good night and left the room was that she had no nightgown.

There was no way for her to get it, so she managed to slip out of her full, gathered skirt and tunic blouse. She'd just have to sleep in her undergarments.

She lay back on the cot and pulled the sheet up over her after dimming the lamp. She thought about the wonderful feel of Hawk's strong arms when he'd carried her up from the gully. She also remembered the feel of his firm, muscled body as her arms clasped him as she rode behind him atop Tache. The swaying motion of the pinto as they rode along and Hawk's nearness had sparked wild, wonderful sensations within her.

Had he felt the same way, she wondered, as her body pressed against his back? She hoped so!

She hoped he would be coming over again very soon. Somehow, she sensed that he had to be feeling something akin to her feelings.

It didn't matter to her that Troy had told her that Hawk was attracted to a girl down in the valley. She knew that men found her attractive and she could lure him away from that girl if she wanted to, she felt sure. At least, she was willing to use any wiles she had to. To win Hawk's heart completely consumed her tonight.

Just before sleep took over, Shawna vowed she was going to win Hawk's love.

It had taken Nancy Foster two nights of fine stitching to shorten her old wedding gown and take the tucks at the waistline. Now it was pressed and hung on the wooden peg in Gillian's bedroom. The task of pressing it had been Gillian's and it seemed an endless chore. But it looked so beautiful when the job was finished.

In the solitude of her bedroom, Gillian sat on her bed and an overwhelming wave of sadness swept over her. She was going to miss the Fosters when she left to go with Hawk to Tucson. This had been her home for over two years now. But there was more to it than that, and Gillian could not deny it. She could not stop herself thinking about Steve Lafferty.

There on the chest was the lovely nosegay Solange had made for her to hold when she and Hawk were married, and she knew the love that had gone into its making. Hawk had brought the nosegay and the pearls that were a special wedding gift from his mother this morning. How very sweet and generous everyone was being to her. Why couldn't she be overwhelmed with joy about this wedding that was to take place in just a few days?

That little tormenting voice that had plagued her quite often lately was doing the same thing tonight.

She sat there in her soft batiste gown, musing and gently stroking her stomach. Should she hate Lafferty? "But for you, little one, I might just wait forever for him to return to me, but this I cannot do. I've got you to think about," she moaned softly to the emptiness of the small bedroom.

She got up from the bed and strolled to the window, staring into the blackness of the night outside. Where was Steve tonight and who was he with? Was that fancy lady that the rancher Hill had spoken about keeping him company and pleasuring him?

She turned away from the window and glanced at the small pile of possessions she would be taking with her. It seemed like precious little. Hawk could ease his mind that she would be taking too much, she thought to herself as she finally ambled over to dim the lamp and crawl into her bed.

Only three more nights would she be sleeping in this bed, she realized before she drifted off to sleep.

When Steve Lafferty had left Red Rock, he planned to put in a long day on the trail to make up for the delay. At least he'd enjoyed a good night's sleep and a fine meal at the inn.

The weather cooperated as he traveled northwestward toward Casa Grande. That was well over halfway to his destination. With any luck at all, he'd have to spend only one more night on the trail before he'd arrive in Maricopa County and the Fosters' ranch.

The little filly he'd obtained in Red Rock seemed to be just as swift as the roan had been. She and Steve seemed to get along much better, for she was not as fractious or unruly as the big roan had been. He seemed to be able to control her.

The sun was not yet sinking in the western sky when he rode into Casa Grande. He was not ready to quit traveling when there was that much daylight left, so he pushed on, even though he did not know how far he was from the next town along the trail.

After today's ride, he was finding himself less repulsed by horses. The truth was, he might just get to enjoy riding in time if he could acquire as fine a little mare as this one. An hour later, he saw a sign by the side of the road telling him that he was now entering the southern border of Maricopa County. But he also remembered from traveling this way months ago that he still had several miles to cover before he reached the Fosters' ranch.

But when darkness began to shroud the countryside, he

knew he must stop for the night at the next place he came upon. That small village happened to be Ocotillo which was not as large as Red Rock, nor did it have any choice as to where he could seek lodging. There was only one rundown hotel and Steve did not like the looks or the smell of the place when he ambled through the front door of the establishment.

He didn't like the way three ugly hooligans sitting over at a table playing cards leered at him when he walked up to the desk to ask for a room. He had no trouble getting himself a room, and the young man at the desk told him there was a place across the street where he could eat. Steve thanked him and wasted no time going upstairs to his room. He had expected no special services here as he took the key he was given and opened the door to the dark room. As soon as he spied the kerosene lamp, he closed the door behind him and locked it.

The odor in the room was oppressive, so he opened the window and looked down at the street. He was glad he'd had the good sense to bring his pistols with him. He couldn't explain it to himself, but his first mate would have called it that Irish instinct of his. There was a smell of danger to this place.

He didn't like the looks of the blokes he'd seen in the lobby. Something about them reminded him of a time when he and Driscol had gone into a tavern in London. He'd had the same feeling then, and sure enough, when he and Driscol left the place they were jumped by four fellows who just didn't like *their* looks.

He washed the trail's dust from his face, and it felt good to shave off the day's growth of beard. Something urged him to not carry the expensive ring he was taking to his bride when he went across the street to get something to eat. Yet he hesitated to leave it in the room.

In the end, he decided that over his dead body would any bastard take that from him. He took out the matched pair of pistols and strapped them around his waist.

As he ambled through the lobby it was obvious that the card game had been disbanded. He saw no signs of the three who had been sitting there, but this made him all the more cautious as he went out the front door and across the street. While the hour was still early, there didn't seem to be any citizens of the small village around.

When Steve entered the small cantina, he picked a table facing the front door. A man with a soiled apron tied around his middle came to the table to ask what he'd like. Steve asked what they served.

The hawk-faced man told him, "Well, the special of the day was beef stew, but we may be out now."

Beef stew made in this place did not appeal to Steve anyway. "How about some eggs and ham then? Could you fix me a plate of that?"

"Guess we could. You're a stranger around here, aren't you?"

"Just riding through. That's right," Steve replied. "Got some coffee? I'll have a cup of coffee."

The tall, lanky fellow turned to get the coffee. Maybe it was because he was tired, Steve decided, but the coffee tasted fairly good. By the time he'd finished a second cup he was served a platter of ham slices and three eggs. As hungry as he was, Lafferty eagerly began to eat and he knew it had to be better than the stew would have been.

By the time he left the place he was feeling much better. At least he'd satisfied the ache in his stomach and he had thoroughly enjoyed the three cups of coffee he'd drunk. He was thinking as he left that if only he still had his silver flask with the fine Irish whiskey how great it would be to have a couple of generous belts of that when he got back to the room.

Except for the lights of the hotel, the rest of the street seemed to be deserted, and there was a ghostly quiet as he leisurely sauntered across the dirt street to go back to the hotel.

The three men lurking at the corner of the hotel watched Lafferty walking across the street. When he was stepping up on the plank flooring in front of the hotel, the three sought to

413

make their move.

Lafferty felt himself grabbed from all sides. In a fleeting moment, he'd let his guard down. But the three men didn't know that this Irishman was no dandy to be taken lightly. As a seaman he'd been in many a tavern brawl and a number of those times in a strange port, he and his first mate had been outnumbered. Lafferty knew many ways to defend himself. His hands and strong arms might have been restrained, but his forceful, powerful legs were free, so he used them. One of the men found himself falling to the ground and, in doing so, his hands released one of Steve's arms.

That mighty arm swung backward with a savage fury that the victim had never known and the thrust of that powerful hand making an impact against the man's throat rendered him utterly helpless. He fell to the ground, drowning in an abyss of blackness.

To see his two buddies lying there and to know that he was the only one left to do battle with this man was making Clint Blake want to hightail it out while he still had his head on. This guy was as mean as one of those mountain cats he'd encountered a few weeks ago.

But he did not get the chance to make his getaway, for Lafferty's fierce fists found his face. Two brutal blows to Clint's face were enough to urge him to join his two comrades on the ground.

A smirk was on Steve's face as he surveyed the three. He'd known they were up to no good when he'd spied them in the lobby. He swore that he could see this evil in a man's eyes and he had seen it in the three of them as they'd watched him so intently. There were those who would call this a lot of Irish blarney, but he knew it was the truth.

He turned his back on the three men and walked into the hotel. They would give him no more trouble tonight. Tomorrow he would be on his way to Gillian.

God willing, this time tomorrow night he would be with the woman he loved!

Chapter Fifty-Six

It was not until he was inside his room that Steve noticed the angry reddish spots on the knuckles of his right hand, the result of the savage force of his clenched fist when he'd struck the two men a few minutes ago. The ache in his hand was nothing compared to what they should be feeling, he concluded.

But when he got undressed and before he dimmed the lamp, he placed the oak chair against the door, just in case. If the three men were to try something foolish like bursting through the door, he'd have some extra warning.

He placed his pistols under the pillow and lay down on the bed. For a few moments, he stared up at the dark ceiling, for he wasn't quite ready to go to sleep; he was still tense. Once he began to relax, sleep came swiftly. But sometime in the middle of the night he woke up with a sudden jerk. He sat up in bed to listen and his keen ears heard the sound of footsteps just outside his door. His hand reached under the pillow to grab one of the pistols as he turned to move slowly up out of the bed. As he stood at the door to listen, he could hear the sound of the footsteps going away from his door and down the hallway.

It was obviously just another lodger going to his own door, Lafferty figured, so he sleepily stumbled back to seek the comfort of his bed. The next few hours before dawn were peaceful and nothing interrupted his sleep.

When the sun came shining through the small window of the room, Steve woke up, wide-eyed and alert, ready to get dressed so he could ride out of this place. In fact, he wasn't going to tarry long enough to have breakfast.

The minute he was dressed and his gear was in his arms he left the room and went downstairs. Depositing his key with the desk clerk, he marched out the door to go to the livery.

An old, bearded gent seemed to be in charge this morning instead of the young fellow who had been there last evening.

"Good morning. Ready to get my little mare and be on my way," Lafferty told him. He informed him that he'd already paid for her keep overnight.

The old fellow scratched his head and wore a frown on his face as he shook his head. "Don't exactly know what you're a'talkin' about, young fellow."

"My mare, damn it! Left my mare here last night while I spent the night at the hotel next door," Steve barked angrily.

"Well, you just look for yourself, and if you see a mare in any of these stalls, then I'll eat your hat," he told Steve with a shrug of his shoulders.

Without any hesitation, Steve Lafferty did just that, and the old man had been right. But when he demanded an explanation, the old man told him, "I came on this morning, young fellow, and you see all that's here is that wagon and that old brown nag back there in the stall. Can't help you, I'm afraid."

"What about the man who was working here before you took over?"

"Oh, you mean Ned? Well, I could direct you to where he lives, but you would not catch him there. He was leaving here to go to Florence Junction to visit his lady."

No one had to tell Steve who'd taken his mare. Those three bastards had done it and he had not figured on this, he had to admit. He was cussing himself that he had not finished them off instead of just leaving them unconscious on the ground. He

416

should have killed them!

"Tell me, fellow—would that nag get me a few miles, you suppose?"

"Couldn't guarantee nothing, son," the old man honestly answered. He told him that he'd make him a good deal on the nag and wagon. "They got to go together."

Steve asked him what he had to have for wagon and nag. The old man named a ridiculous price, but at least he could be rolling on down the trail and out of this miserable place.

Steve told him that it was a deal and the old man proceeded to hitch the horse to the flat-bedded wagon. A few minute later, Lafferty was once again on his way, heading for his destination northward.

He wondered, as the wagon wheels rolled over the dirt road, just how many more obstacles he would have to overcome before he got to his ladylove. That little auburn-haired imp better not have got herself married before he got there to stop her. He'd bloody well kidnap her if that was the case.

Traveling in this old wagon was not as fast as riding the little filly. In fact, he had begun to take a liking to her. He'd never figured to feel fondly about a horse.

Friday mornings Troy usually hit the mountain stream not too far from his cabin to catch a line of fish. He was usually lucky enough to catch enough for two good evening meals, but he figured that he'd better not go this morning since Shawna was so helpless with her ankle injured.

After they ate breakfast, she teased him that he better not fail to make a good catch today. "But I didn't figure I better go with you the way you are," he remarked.

"I'll be fine, Troy. Now you go on like you would if I wasn't here. I'll not have you changing your plans," she told him. Her black eyes sparkled as she teased him, "I'm not completely helpless." She rose up from the cot and held onto the back of one of the wooden chairs to show him how she could support herself.

Troy grinned. "Guess you're right. I will go catch us some fish for supper, if you are sure."

"I'm sure!" she assured him.

As he gathered his fishing gear, Troy decided that just before he left the cabin, he would tell her about Hawk, for tomorrow was the day of the wedding. He could delay it no longer. Maybe this was the best time to tell her, so if she had tears to shed, she could have the privacy to do it without him around.

When he had his gear and his pole placed out on his small front porch, he went back into the front room where she sat on the cot propped up against some pillows, stroking her long black hair with the brush before she put it into two braids.

"Sure you'll be all right for a couple of hours or so?" He stood in the doorway, his old wide-brimmed straw hat atop his head.

"I'll swear, Troy—I'm going to throw this brush at you if you don't get out of here and be on your way."

"Well, we'll see how you do today on your own so I'll know what I should plan on for tomorrow," he stammered, dreading his announcement.

"Tomorrow?" Her black eyes stared up at him.

"So I can go to see my friend Hawk get married. He's marrying Gillian Browne tomorrow, Shawna."

She just sat there looking at him. Her thick black eyelashes did not blink nor did she utter a word for a minute.

In a slow, deliberate voice, so soft it was almost a whisper, she spoke. "You will be able to go, Troy." Troy looked at her expressionless face for a second before he turned to leave. He had no inkling of the excruciating pain his words had caused. She'd restrained the desire to scream out her protest that Hawk was making a big mistake.

It was only after Troy went out the door and down the steps that she gave vent to the fury boiling inside her and slammed down the brush she was holding. It landed on the other side of the room.

418

It was not fair, she screamed out to the emptiness of the room. She'd not even had a chance to show Hawk how much more his type of woman she could be. Here she sat, helpless to do anything about it, and there was less than a day left before it would be too late.

She knew that it was not her imagination that she'd seen Hawk's eyes appraising her when he'd carried her in his arms. She'd seen that look before in other men's eyes before she'd come here to Troy's house.

She swung her legs down to touch the floor and tested her injured foot to see if she could stand on it. But it was impossible, and she cussed the fact that she couldn't.

But with a dozen moves of the oak chair to hold onto for support, she managed to move to the point where her brush lay on the floor. Picking it up, she began the whole procedure all over again.

When she was halfway back to the cot, she lost her balance when the old oak chair slightly swayed and she found herself sprawling flat on the floor. She lay there to give way to the sobs of pain so consuming her. "Oh, Hawk—Hawk—you were meant for me, not that girl you're going to marry tomorrow. Oh, Hawk, if only you'd given me a chance, I could have proven that to you."

Shawna knew not how long she lay there and let her tears flow. She knew she had to release all that pain or she felt that she would surely explode.

She was glad that Troy was gone for three hours. At least she had time to gain control of her emotions by the time he'd return.

When she'd cried her river of tears and risen from the floor, she slid across the floor to get back to that miserable cot which seemed to be her prison right now.

As she sat on the cot, she looked around the room for something that would give her more support than the light oak chair had provided. She spied the one with the wooden arms that Troy always sat in during the evening.

After a few minutes of experimenting in it, she found she could do amazing feats of moving around the front door as well as all the way into the kitchen. All she had to do was push with all her force with her good foot and travel backward in the chair.

With an hour's practice, she had managed, tediously slowly, to move around the kitchen and wash up all the dirty dishes. She giggled at herself about the strange moves she had to make to accomplish the most simple task. But what was important to her was that she could do it. It just took a longer time.

But Shawna had had a strange inspiration as she lay there on the floor crying. A vision of her mother had come to her. She'd not seen that vision of Violet for a few weeks now. That lovely face with its classic features came to her so clearly that her mother could have been standing there in the room.

"Only a moment can change our whole lives, Shawna," her mother's soft voice echoed in the quietness of the cabin. But Shawna wanted to cry out that the moments were so very few now before all her dreams would be shattered if Hawk married Gillian Browne.

But then Violet had never lied, so she had to believe this. Maybe a moment would make all the difference!

Chapter Fifty-Seven

It had been an emotional night for Gillian. She and Nancy Foster had spent a lot of time talking about the last two years that she'd lived with them. They had both shed their tears, and Nancy had warmly embraced her and told her how much she was going to be missed after she left with Hawk tomorrow after they were married in the little church a few miles from the ranch.

"You think I won't miss you both? Oh, I shall, but you know I will be coming back to visit you, Mother Foster," Gillian assured her.

"I hope to tell you that you better or I'll feel like spanking you, young lady," Nancy declared with a weak smile on her tear-stained face. Gillian had never seen her give way to emotions as she had tonight. Gillian realized that it was not the mere act of giving birth that made one a mother. It was the unselfish giving of love and caring, as Mother Foster had done for her. She'd been blessed in her life to have had two mothers. It made her all the more determined to be a fine mother to the baby within her.

It would have been her heart's desire that the man she loved with all her heart would have been the one she was marrying tomorrow, for she could not forget that overwhelming, consuming love she'd shared with Steve Lafferty. But Hawk would take care of her and her baby, and she could feel a certain love in her heart for his devotion. Who could say what would happen as the years went by? Maybe her love for Hawk would grow strong. Life was full of surprises, and Gillian was only beginning to realize just how little she knew of life. Now she realized why a worldly-wise, sophisticated Irishman like Steve Lafferty had so easily sweet-talked her into submitting to him. Oh, how simple it had been for him to have his way with her!

To think that she had been so trusting and believed every word he'd said to her. She must have been daft in the head!

What did it matter now, she consoled herself? Tomorrow Hawk would be her husband. She had decided that Steve Lafferty was simply the Prince Charming that all young naive girls dream about. As foolish as that daydream might be, it was a glorious ecstasy that she'd never forget as long as she lived.

But this was the last night she could dwell in this foolish fancy, for tomorrow she must put all thoughts of Steve behind her forever. She must face reality!

She looked around her room and a wave of sadness washed over her. The gown she would be married in hung on the peg and there on the chair was the nosegay Solange had made for her. On another peg hung her traveling ensemble she would wear when she left Maricopa County to travel to Tucson with Hawk.

Reluctantly, she dimmed the lamp on her nightstand. She doubted that she would sleep too much tonight as she lay back on the bed to rest her auburn head on the pillows. She stared out the window at the starlit skies and found herself wondering where and what Lafferty was doing.

She damned him for haunting her thoughts on the night before her wedding. It was Hawk that she should be thinking about this night and not Steve Lafferty!

But how could she stop those thoughts from parading through her mind, she asked herself? She had tried for weeks now to make herself forget Lafferty. It was impossible, it seemed.

As it had been at the Fosters' ranch, it had been an evening of reflecting for Solange, too, with her son to be married tomorrow. Her mood was a strange one and her doting Gaston instinctively sensed it all as the three of them shared their evening meal.

For the last few days, Solange had worked hard preparing for their departure for Canada, as well as for Hawk's wedding, but he knew it was not that she was tired. Not this vivacious lady that he'd discovered Solange Touraine to be! Her mood was a mystery to Gaston, for he knew that she adored the little auburn-haired Gillian with all her heart.

When Hawk excused himself to go for a stroll after supper, Gaston approached her. "Tell me, *chérie*—tell me what is troubling you? I've sensed it all evening. Let me share the burden you seem to be carrying."

Lovingly she turned to stare up at his rugged face. "Oh, Gaston—I would if I could, truly. I can't tell you. Can you believe me? I just don't know. It is there, just so heavy on my heart. I—I just feel that it is not to be. Can you understand me?"

His dark eyes roamed over her lovely, troubled face and he did understand exactly what she was saying to him. How often he'd experienced similar feelings and yet he could not have explained them to anyone who would have asked him.

"I understand, *ma chérie*. Oh, Solange, we are so much alike in our feelings and ways. Ah, it is wonderful to have found a woman I can share so much with as I can with you. Everything will work out right, Solange. Believe me, it will. I know it."

She reached up to plant an affectionate kiss on his lips. "I know, Gaston. I know this, too!"

He urged her to leave her kitchen and go out to sit on the

steps with him. "There is a big full moon out there, so let's go out and enjoy it."

She threw back her head and laughed. "Let's go! I've heard a full moon does strange things to people. Shall we see if that is true?"

Like young lovers, they went out the front door holding hands and gaily laughing. When they were sitting there cozily on the steps, Gaston approached her about when they could make their own departure. "I need to get back, Solange. I've never given myself so much leisure time as I have the last few months. You have proven to be a delightful distraction," he teased her.

She smiled. "Hawk will be married and traveling toward Tucson by this time tomorrow night. Shall we leave bright and early the next morning? I've already made arrangements with Troy to look in over here every so often. Perhaps you've not been aware of how I've been preparing to leave all this last week."

He patted her shoulder and assured her that he surely had realized just how hard she'd worked. "Now, is Little Bear ready to leave?"

She sat up with an indignant look on her lovely face as she informed him, "Do you know what Troy asked me when I talked to him the other day about making a weekly check on my cabin? I couldn't believe him! He asked if I wanted to leave Little Bear here with him. You can imagine what I told him."

Gaston roared with laughter, for he knew exactly what she had told him in no uncertain terms about Little Bear. Nothing would part her from that pup she adored so much. In fact, he'd had to accept that Little Bear shared the foot of their bed, but he did not object to that.

Their lighthearted laughter echoed through the woods as Hawk ambled slowly back toward the cabin. He thought to himself that life seemed to be working out right for both him and his mother. To hear her happy laughter was enough for Hawk to be glad that Gaston had come into her life. God knows, she deserved some happiness. He felt that Gaston was the man who could give her a wonderful life and he knew that the French Canadian loved his mother.

With the full moon shining down so bright tonight, he could see them sitting there on the steps long before they saw him emerging from the woods.

He thought to himself, as he moved closer and closer to them, that someday he would see in Gillian's bright blue eyes the adoration he saw in his mother's eyes when she looked at Gaston. He knew that she liked him but she did not love him. But he was confident that he could change all that with just a little time.

He could not forget the vow he'd made a long time ago to protect and watch out for that pretty little fourteen-year-old girl. He had not even known her name when he made that pledge.

Tomorrow he was honoring it by marrying her. Maybe that could also ease the pain within him that it had been Cochise, his father, who had led the raid on the wagon train and murdered Gillian's parents. Was it fate that had spared Gillian? She could have been taken captive, like his own mother.

He was convinced that he could make her happy and he was certainly going to try once they got to Tucson and he saw what kind of job Warner Barstow had to offer him. Hawk felt that he had the promise of a good future to offer his pretty bride. God knows, he'd work hard to give Gillian all the things she deserved. No, she'd never regret that she'd become his wife, he vowed fervently.

The day had seemed endless for Steve Lafferty. He could almost have felt sorry for the old nag but for the fact that he was so impatient to cover more miles than he was covering by the time the sun was setting. He was not going to be close to Phoenix by the time night fell. The small hamlets were miles apart since he'd left Ocotilla this morning.

By late afternoon, he'd already accepted the reality that he'd not be reaching the Fosters' ranch tonight as he'd hoped to do.

By the time he rolled into Guadalupe he knew he could not push the nag another mile. If he'd been astride the feisty little filly, he could have pushed on.

As he surveyed the small main street of the town, he found it to be a little more promising for finding decent lodgings and a good meal.

He spotted the livery down at the far end of the street and he felt he had better make it there before the old horse collapsed right in the middle of the street. Besides, he figured that he might get lucky and find a horse to replace this old mare who might not make it another ten or twenty miles.

As he pulled into the yard, a man about his age came out and gave him a friendly greeting. "Got yourself a wheel just ready to go off," he said, pointing to the front wheel of the flat-bedded wagon.

Lafferty let out a few cusswords as he leaped off the wagon and went over to the other side. "I see what you mean. Doesn't surprise me. I didn't know if it would make it this far. My name's Lafferty and I'll be staying overnight. Might ask you if you could direct me to a place where I might find lodgings and a good meal. Been on the trail all day and I'm hungry as a wolf."

"Sure can, Mr. Lafferty. Right up the street that you just came down. The Mesa Hotel will provide you with a nice clean room and their dining room serves a pretty tasty meal. I'll tend to your wagon and horse for the night."

"Appreciate that. What's your name?" Lafferty asked, reaching over into the bed of the wagon to get his small bundle of possessions.

"Oh, everyone around here calls me J.J.," the lanky man told him.

"Well, J.J., I thank you for your help so I guess I better see about that room for the night and get some of this dust off before I try the dining room you told me about."

426

When Steve was about to walk away, a boy about twelve came around the corner, leading two magnificent-looking animals with a deep reddish coat that reminded Lafferty of Gillian's rich-colored auburn tresses.

The youth announced to J.J., "Mr. Sharp said to tell you to sell them, J.J."

Lafferty had never had any love for horses, but these animals took his eyes. "God, they're a beautiful pair!"

"Ain't they though," J.J. agreed with him.

"What's this Sharp got to have for them?"

J.J. told him what the pair would cost him. Without flinching, Steve declared, "They're sold! I'll buy the pair."

Lafferty turned to be on his way to the hotel leaving J.J. watching him go up the road. Mr. Sharp was going to be more than pleased with him for making such a quick sale. It would put a few dollars in his pocket, too.

J.J. figured this to be his lucky day. Lafferty was feeling lucky, too, as he made his way to seek out the hotel.

One horse would be for his beautiful Gillian when he carried her away with him from Maricopa County. The other fine beast would be for him to ride, so he could get to the Fosters' ranch at a faster pace.

Something told Lafferty he had no time to waste!

Chapter Fifty-Eight

Steve would not have classed the Mesa Hotel along with the accommodations he'd had at the Old Pueblo Inn, but the sheets were fresh and clean and there were no layers of dust anywhere in the room. He'd enjoyed the luxury of a warm bath and a shave before going downstairs to the dining room.

It was, indeed, a tasty meal he'd enjoyed. It had been a long time since he'd had a delicious serving of bread pudding. Voraciously, he'd eaten the pan-fried chicken with its crisp golden crust, along with the creamy gravy and biscuits.

He'd certainly have to remember to thank JJ. for guiding him to the right place, he thought as he made his way back to his room. His spirits were much higher tonight than they were last night, but he still had a pair of sore knuckles.

By the time he was shedding his clothes and crawling into his bed, he had to figure that his bad luck was now changing. The way would be clear sailing, he felt. Tomorrow, he would hold the woman he loved in his arms. With the fine horses he'd bought he'd travel swiftly the rest of the way. The worst was now behind him.

As he lay in bed, he smiled as he thought about Gillian's deep blue eyes when he presented her with her own horse, a perfect match to his. This long odyssey he'd been on since he'd left Tucson was enough to convince him that he loved Gillian with all his heart and soul. Yet, it still amazed him how one tiny miss had captured his elusive heart so easily.

When he was in the deepest sleep during the night, Steve suddenly woke up. He shook his head to clear the foggy state he was in. He knew he had to be dreaming, but it was Gillian's soft voice he heard, urgently calling out to him. Those blue eyes were as clear as if she was sitting on the edge of his bed. Her soft voice called out to him, "Steve—Steve, please hurry or it will be too late!"

Even though he finally lay back down on the bed, he did not sleep soundly.

The only thing to delay his departure from the hotel was a hasty stop by the dining room for a couple of cups of that great coffee he'd enjoyed last night. But then he made straight for the stable to pick up the pair of horses so he could be on his way.

Before the sun was high in the sky, he was riding his new horse and leading the other one. A devious grin broke on his face as he realized that this Irish sea captain was one hell of a lot better horseman now than he'd been the first time he'd accompanied Gillian on a ride.

Gillian's thick long lashes fluttered as the rays of the morning sun invaded her bedroom window. She stretched her body with a lazy motion and reluctantly flung the sheet away that was covering her body.

Suddenly, her eyes did open wide as she realized that this was her wedding day. Her legs swung over the side of the bed. Instead of getting dressed as she normally would have to go into the kitchen to help Mother Foster, she slipped into her wrapper, leaving her nightgown on.

Nancy was already puttering around her cookstove. She greeted Gillian, "Well, honey, they say that happy is the bride that the sun shines on and that's a bright sun out there this morning."

430

"Oh, I will be happy, Mother Foster," she replied.

"I know you will, honey." Nancy had already promised herself earlier that she would not be a sniveling idiot, but she knew she was going to be on the verge of tears all day. "Once we see you and Hawk on your way, we're going over to the Hills' for a little celebrating. Gregory told John the other day he already had his pit ready and they wanted us to come to share their feast. Don't know whether he's butchering a lamb or a calf."

"Oh, that will be nice, Mother Foster."

"It would be even nicer if you and Hawk could join the celebration, but I know you must get started for Tucson," Nancy said. What she didn't say was that she eagerly accepted the Hills' invitation because she would have found it hard to return to the house and find Gillian gone after the wedding. It was going to seem strange.

"Well, Mother Foster, we'll return here after the wedding so I can change into my riding clothes and out of your wedding gown. Then Hawk has insisted that we must be on our way."

"That's just fine, honey. When we leave the church we'll just go on over to the Hills'. I did tell you that they wanted to come to the wedding, so I invited them. They'll be there. They're real excited about your wedding."

"I'm glad they're coming," Gillian stammered, her thoughts rambling about other things. As she thought about it, she had no friends here in Maricopa County except the Fosters and Solange and Hawk. She'd left all her friends behind when her parents had decided to come to Arizona Territory and only a few days after they'd entered Arizona Territory her parents had been killed by the Apaches. Friends were not easy to make when you lived on an isolated ranch. Miles separated neighbors.

It was not until she'd met Hawk and Solange that she'd made any friends during the two years she'd lived with the Fosters.

She was glad that she and Hawk were going to Tucson because she did not wish to live the rest of her life here in these

431

canyons and mountains. There was a lot of world out there to see and Gillian's young heart yearned to experience more than what she'd done the last two years.

The tales Steve Lafferty had told her about the lands he had traveled to had excited and whetted her curiosity. She was glad that Hawk was taking her to Tucson instead of the two of them remaining here in his mountains or this valley where the Fosters had lived contentedly all these years.

By the time Nancy had their breakfast cooked and Gillian had the table set, John was coming through the door as if he'd known when the meal was ready.

The three of them enjoyed a pleasant time, for it was the last time they'd share a meal for a long time, all of them realized.

John was the first one to get up from the table. "Well, I got to get my chores done so I can get myself all spiffy for your wedding, Gillian honey."

Gillian followed Nancy's move as she pushed away from the table. But as she was gathering up the dishes as she usually did, Nancy quickly insisted that she just go to her room and relax as a bride should do before she had to start dressing for the wedding. "You'll not help me on your wedding day, honey. This is your special day."

"All right, Mother Foster. I'll do as you say." She softly laughed as she gave her a warm, affectionate hug. Nancy had the need to be alone for a while and as she cleaned up her kitchen, she did not try to restrain the tears from flowing. John would be at the barn for a while and with Gillian in her room, she was free to give way to her emotions.

As she stood there washing her dishes, her tears streamed down her cheeks into the dishwater in the pan. When she finished putting her kitchen in order, she lifted her apron to dry her tearstained face. Now she was ready to go to her bedroom and put herself in some kind of order. She'd chosen her deep blue dress to wear to the ceremony. With its white lace collar and cuffs, it was the fanciest frock she owned. Besides, John liked this dress on her.

432

He'd be wearing his dark blue coat and his only pair of pants in the matching shade of dark blue. There'd been few occasions that she or John had gone to dress-up affairs. But that was just another thing the two of them shared; fancy clothes did not interest them.

There in her room Nancy had a stern talk with herself. She and John had enjoyed a very full, happy life before Gillian came into it. She had entered it quite unexpectedly and they'd enjoyed the pleasure of a young girl they'd come to look on as their daughter. But now she was leaving them to seek out a new life for herself so there was no reason that she and John could not live the good life as they always had.

She was not going to mope around after Gillian left, for that would not be fair to John, she vowed.

Silently and cautiously, Solange had slipped out of bed so she wouldn't disturb Gaston's sound sleep. In her bare feet, she'd slipped out of her room with Little Bear trailing behind her. She saw that Hawk was still sleeping as soundly as Gaston, so she did not go into the kitchen as she usually would have the moment she got out of bed. Instead, she slipped out the front door to sit on her step to enjoy a moment of reflecting there in the morning's quiet serenity. She gathered up the generous folds of her batiste nightgown to sit there on the step, and she smiled when she saw the little pup coming to her side to be close to her.

She picked up the fuzzy brown pup and snuggled him up to her cheek. "Oh, my little shadow. I love you!" As if he knew what she was saying to him, he generously began to lick her hand.

Placing him on her lap, she gently stroked him as she watched the sun rising. There could be no more wonderful time of the day. Solange thought how true this new dawning was in the lives of those she loved so dearly. This was the day her son was marrying Gillian and they would be starting their

433

lives together. Soon she would be leaving this cabin where she'd lived for twenty years of her life to go forward to a new life in Canada as Gaston's wife.

She was excited and thrilled as she would have been as a young girl, with wild anticipation churning within her.

From all the tales Gaston had told her about his home in Canada and all the Frenchmen living there, she knew she was gong to enjoy living there.

She knew not how long she sat there on the front step with Little Bear snuggled in her lap, nor did she care. She was enjoying the pleasant interlude.

She did not hear Gaston's footsteps moving so silently behind her as he slipped out the door. He did not intend that she did, for her loveliness entranced him as he observed her sitting there on the steps in her flowing diaphanous nightgown.

Until his head bent down to kiss the top of her head and softly greet her, Solange had no inkling he was so near.

His dark eyes warmly washed over her as he said, "A beautiful new dawn, *ma* Solange."

"A most beautiful day, and Little Bear and I have been out here enjoying it." She smiled affectionately as her eyes gazed up to meet him.

"Then I shall join you." He huskily laughed as he moved his huge body to sink down on the step beside her. They had no need to speak for the next few moments, for their eyes met in understanding and warm smiles were exchanged. Gaston's huge hand reached over to cover hers.

Theirs was a love so deep and devoted and neither of them doubted for a minute that it would be forever!

Chapter Fifty-Nine

Steve Lafferty might not have considered himself a horseman, but he cut a magnificent figure astride the big reddish-brown horse with his firm, muscled legs hugging the animal's sides. He knew that they were making good time even though he was leading the other horse.

As he galloped along, the breeze kept sweeping his sandy hair over one side of his forehead and he was having to constantly brush it to the side.

Each mile they covered fired Lafferty with soaring anticipation of that first sight of his beautiful Gillian. But what would he do if she didn't spark with the same delight when those sapphire blue eyes first saw him? Damned if he'd worry about that until the moment came!

That self-assured, conceited nature of his was convinced that once he took her in his arms she'd want to recapture the flaming rapture that they'd shared. No man could make love to her as he had and stir her with so much ecstasy. His honest little Gilly would have to know this.

Her lips as sweet as wine were made for his kisses and his alone. Her supple body was made for his caresses and no other man's touch could taint her silken flesh.

Just the thought of this made him spur the horse to move faster down the trail. He had no time to waste.

* * *

Gillian sat on her bed in her undergarments, hesitating to slip into the beautiful wedding gown hanging there on the wooden peg. What was she to do about the exquisite sapphire ring Steve had given her that day back at the mission in Tucson? Hawk's ring would be placed on her left hand, but she could not bear the thought of leaving Steve's ring back here with the gowns Helen had given her.

Slowly she removed the ring from her finger and placed it on a finger on her right hand. After all, Hawk could not object to a gift she'd received before they were married. It was the most beautiful ring she'd ever seen and she gazed at it now, thinking of that wonderful day she'd shared with Lafferty when he'd asked her to be his wife.

She urged herself to move over to her dressing table to fix her hair so that she might pin the white flowers in her hair. As she sat on the stool putting the lovely pearl earrings on her ears and the strand of pearls around her neck, she looked in the mirror and questioned why a man would give such an exquisite ring to a lady he wasn't truly in love with. Lafferty had to have felt something for her. She had to have meant more to him than just a passing fancy.

In the next moment she reminded herself that he was obviously a wealthy man if he owned his own clipper ship and traveled all over the world. Perhaps a ring like this was a token he would give to any lady who was pleasuring him for the moment.

Steve Lafferty occupied her thoughts as she pulled the two sides of her auburn hair up to the crown of her head, leaving the back tresses to fall down her back in soft waves. It showed off the lovely earrings, and when she had secured the blossoms in her hair it gave the effect of a lovely crown of white flowers. Gillian was amazed by the beautiful vision she saw reflecting there in her mirror.

A slight commotion just outside her door brought her out of her daydreaming state, for she did not want Mother Foster to come in to find her in her undergarments; her rounding belly

436

would surely be exposed. Hastily, she moved from the stool to put on the wedding gown. When she had it on and once again looked at herself in the mirror, she was truly awestruck by the lovely bride she was going to be. Never had she looked so lovely!

She could not help the thoughts rushing through her mind even though she knew it was wrong. But how could she stop them? In a soft whisper only she could hear, she moaned, "Oh, Steve, if you could see me now you would fall in love with me."

She picked up the delicate nosegay Solange had made for her. Yes indeed, she was going to be a lovely bride for Hawk!

Hawk owned no frock coat or dress coat, so he was going to meet his bride in his only good pair of black wool pants. It was the only purchase he'd made for himself when he was in Tucson. The white shirt he had on was made with loving care and stitched by his mother. It was as fine as any shirt he might have purchased in Tucson. He wore his black felt hat with its tall crown and wide brim. The band was braided strips of leather with the cluster of colorful feathers that represented good luck and good fortune.

In his shirt pocket was the wedding band of his mother's which he was going to place on Gillian's finger.

He was ready to leave his mother's cabin to travel down the mountain to the Fosters' ranch. Solange was in the front room, dressed in a lovely lavender frock that Gaston had brought back with him when he'd returned from Canada. Her hair was styled in a large coil at the back of her head and for this special occasion, she'd fashioned a garland of pink-and-lavender flowers which she encircled around the coil of her hair.

Gaston had raved about her loveliness as he'd joined her there. "You'll be more lovely than the bride, *ma petite*. Oh, Solange, you are so beautiful you take my breath away!"

"Oh, Gaston, you are so very dear and sweet." She sighed, just as Hawk came into the room to join them. She turned to look at him and he looked so very handsome.

She told him that Troy was going to go to the church with them since Shawna was not able to attend the ceremony. Once more she urged Hawk, as she had for the last twenty-four hours, to please not go to the Fosters' ranch to accompany them and Gillian to the church. "It is bad luck, Hawk, for you to see your bride on your wedding day," she'd told him. But for once in his life Hawk could not see any harm in what he wished to do, even though it was against his mother's wishes.

"That's just an old wives' tale, Mother. I can't believe that this would cause any bad luck for me," he'd declared.

As he sauntered into the front room now, Solange gave one last plea to him. "Hawk, are you sure you don't wish to wait until you see your lovely bride at the church?"

"No, Mother—I've already told Gillian I would be there to go with her and the Fosters. Now, don't you worry. Everything is going to be just fine."

He bent down to kiss her cheek and flashed a broad grin in Gaston's direction. He said no more as he turned to walk to the front door.

He flung his full saddlebags over Tache's back. They were much fuller than they had been when he'd left the cabin to go to Tucson on his scouting job, for he figured that he'd not be coming back this way for a while.

Leaping up on the pinto, he spurred him into motion to move down the mountain trail to the valley to meet his bride.

Back in the cabin, Solange looked at Gaston to voice her apprehensions about her son's decision. "I hope he is right."

"It is in his hands, chérie. A man must make his own path in life, n'est-ce pas?"

"Oui, Gaston. It is true!" She reached out to take his hand for the comfort and the strength she knew that she'd find there.

The Fosters had worked hard to decorate the buggy that

would carry them and Gillian to the little church. This would be their special surprise for her when she came out of the house to board the buggy. They'd both spent hours the night before draping the buggy with the colorful streamers and the flowers Nancy had gathered from her garden.

When their handiwork was completed, Nancy gave her husband an affectionate hug and a hearty laugh. "Damned if it don't look downright pretty, John." He had to agree with her and he could see Gillian's eyes when she walked out to board the buggy.

Neither of them were to be disappointed. The three of them emerged from the house just before high noon when John felt they should leave to make it to the church on time. Just before they left, Gillian pointed out to them that Hawk was coming with them to the church. Nancy had shrugged her protest aside. "Now, don't you fret. He'll be riding up before we roll down the drive. It's going to take a little doing just to get you and all that gown on the seat."

So Gillian followed the two of them out of the house. The first thing she saw was the buggy that John had just driven up to the gate and she was overcome with emotion for all the special effort the two of them had gone to so that this would be a wonderful day for her.

"Thank you two! Thank you so very much! The buggy's beautiful. I—I don't think I have to tell you two how much you mean to me and how much I love you," she said with a mist of tears in her blue eyes.

"The feeling is mutual, honey. Now don't you dare cry, for if you do I'll start doing the same thing and if the two of us aren't going to be a mess." Nancy gave out a nervous little laugh.

Gillian laughed, too. John embraced the two of them as they moved down the steps toward the buggy. Gillian looked toward the mountains, but she saw no sign of Hawk.

When they got to the buggy, John assisted Nancy up first so that she could help Gillian with the gown when she boarded the buggy. So full and flowing was the skirt of the gown that it

439

could easily get snagged.

By chance, Hawk had reached the clearing from the woods there on the peak of the mountain where he had a perfect view down below. He caught the first glance of his bride-to-be in her lovely white gown. He thought to himself that this must surely be what angels looked like.

But when he was about to spur Tache into motion, something made him pause. His black eyes spied the sight plowing swiftly through the Fosters' south pastureland. A rider on a huge red horse with another one in tow came galloping toward the wagon.

Hawk was not the only one to see the rider coming so hastily toward them. She froze in the spot where she was standing, making no effort to accept John's hand to help her into the carriage.

When her blue eyes saw that the rider had sandy-colored hair that was blowing wildly as he guided the horse closer and closer toward them, it was no mirage she was seeing. It was Steve Lafferty. Her heart cried out with joy. He had returned to her as he'd promised her that he would. She turned away from the wagon, yanking up the gown so she could run faster to get to the man she loved with all her heart.

Dashing across the pastureland, she looked like a swift graceful gazelle to Hawk, who sat up on the mountain to observe the tender scene below. He knew it was Lafferty who was leaping off the horse and running to catch the breathless auburn-haired beauty up into his arms to lift her up so that their lips might meet in a long, lingering kiss.

He knew immediately there would be no wedding for him today. Lafferty would be the one claiming his bride. But seeing the two of them together, he knew this was how it should be.

"Let's go, Tache," he urged the pinto. He saw no cause to return to the cabin to tell his mother and Gaston what had happened. Let them them go on to the church, he reasoned. They'd just see Lafferty instead of him being married to Gillian. If he'd venture to guess, Hawk would wager that

Solange would say that it was meant to be this way. Perhaps this was true.

Hawk took to the trail that would lead him toward Tucson. As he galloped along he found his thoughts wandering back to his mountains and a pretty black-eyed Shawna. He couldn't deny that he was very affected the day he'd carried her in his arms. Maybe that was who his destiny was linked with. Well, Troy would be telling her that he'd not married Gillian after all!

Steve's strong arms encircled Gillian tightly, pressing her against his broad chest. His sensuous lips refused to release her for the longest time. It was the sweet rapture that Gillian had yearned for so very long. Steve never wanted to release her now that he was finally holding her again and kissing those honeyed lips.

When he did finally loosen his hold on her and his green eyes were staring down on her face, he mumbled in a hesitating voice. "Don't—don't tell me you are married, Gilly! God, don't tell me that! That's a wedding gown you're wearing!"

Still breathless, she murmured, "No, Steve, I'm not married, but I was going to be married today. We were on our way to the church as you rode up."

A slow, delighted grin came on his tanned face. "Damned right you're going to be married today, Gillian Browne, and it's going to be to me. No one will have to be disappointed, for there will be a wedding even though the groom is dusty and dirty. Nothing matters to me, Gillian, but that I make you my wife just as soon as possible."

Gillian stood up on tiptoe so that she might plant a kiss on his cheek as she whispered how very much she loved him. "I never loved anyone as I have loved you, Steve, but I thought you'd forgotten me. I didn't think you were coming back for me."

"Oh, Gillian. I could never forget you. I figured you realized that." His fingers caressed a curling wisp of her hair.

So engrossed they were with each other they had not noticed that Nancy and John were no longer beside the wagon. They'd seen enough to know that there would be no wedding today so they'd gone into the house to wait for the two young lovers.

They watched as the two of them strolled together with Lafferty leading the two horses behind him. They watched as Gillian and Steve looked lovingly at each other.

"Knew I was right, John. Knew it all along that Gillian loved Steve Lafferty!" Nancy declared confidently.

"Well, dear—you usually are right, you know." John grinned.

Gillian glowed with radiance when she entered the room with Steve's arm encircling her waist. Nancy smiled, thinking that this was how a young bride should look on her wedding day. She quickly announced that there was still going to be a wedding.

Lafferty laughed. "A moment's delay for the groom-to-be to at least wash his face and brush his hair so his lady won't be ashamed of him."

A short time later the four of them were departing the house to go to the church where Steve and Gillian would be married.

Chapter Sixty

The initial shock was only for one fleeting moment when Solange saw that it was not Hawk but Steve Lafferty who was there to marry Gillian. She reached over to take Gaston's hand in hers. She smiled and whispered, "Gillian has the man she truly loves. I am so very happy for her." She knew that Hawk must have gone on to Tucson once he found that Lafferty had returned, and she also knew why her son had not informed them that he would not be marrying Gillian. He wanted her to go to the wedding.

Troy sat dwelling in his private thoughts about how elated Shawna would be by the news he would be bringing home.

When the ceremony was over, Nancy had a brief moment with her husband while the young couple were receiving the best wishes of those attending. She urged John, "Don't ask me a lot of questions, John, because there's not enough time for me to answer them. But you strike a deal with that young Irishman that we'll trade him our nice buggy for his fine horse."

"We'll what?" he snapped.

"Ssshh, John! That's right. We got a wagon and, besides, I might start riding again like I used to. It can be our wedding present, John."

He gave out a dejected sigh. "If you say so, Nancy, but I

think you're going to regret this later."

"No, I won't." What she didn't tell him was that she was certain that Gillian was pregnant, but this was not the proper time. She had no business riding a horse such a long distance as they would be traveling. Gillian had not concealed herself as cleverly as she'd thought. Nancy had seen enough to assure her that she was right the day she'd tried on the wedding gown.

After the wedding was over and they'd returned to the ranch, Gillian found herself urging her new husband to accept John's offer when he was a little reluctant. But when she looked up at him lovingly, he was powerless to refuse her. So the swap was made.

Once this was done, the Fosters departed for the Hills' leaving the young newlyweds to themselves so they could soon prepare to make their own departure. Gillian pointed out to Steve, "Besides, it will be much more comfortable and cozy in a buggy than riding separate on horses, don't you think?"

He gave her one of those charming Irish smiles. "You are right, Gilly. Speaking of cozy, I have a great idea." A devilish glint was in his green eyes as he took her by the hand to lead her into her bedroom. After all, they had the whole house to themselves. They could delay their departure for an hour or so. He'd ached with longing far too many nights to deny himself any longer.

Scooping her up in his arms he carried her through the doorway to put her there on the bed. As she lay there looking so tempting and tantalizing, her blue eyes sparked bright. He knew that it was a fire of passion consuming her just as much as it was devouring him.

The aroma of the white flowers tucked in her auburn hair and the sweet fragrance of her intoxicated him. As he looked down he saw the teasing roundness of her breast slightly exposed over the neckline of the gown. God, she was more sensuous than he'd remembered. Had he been gone that long?

His head bent down to take her half-parted lips, inviting him to kiss them. "God, Gilly—if only you knew how often I've dreamed about this moment," he huskily whispered in her ear.

His lips teased each rosy tip of her breast without mercy and she gave out a moan of the sweet agony he was stirring. "Steve! Oh, Steve!" she gasped as she felt his hands moving slowly down the curves of her arching body.

He loved to see the glowing flush of passion on her face as his hands caressed her leisurely. His lips released her lips so that he could whisper the words of love he longed to tell her for so many weeks now.

Usually, his expert hands could remove a gown without any hesitation, but he was finding this one a challenge. Giggling, she assisted him. Impatiently, he rid himself of his clothing and eagerly came back to her.

"I'll swear, Gillian, I thought I had memorized all the divine satiny curves of your body, but you look more voluptuous than you did the last time we were together."

A sly smile came to her face as she knew the reason for her fuller breasts and figure, but she'd tell him that later. Instead, she lightheartedly teased him, "No wonder I lost my heart to you so fast, Steve Lafferty. You and that Irish charm."

He gave out a deep, throaty laugh. "Come here and let me give you a generous dose of that Irish charm." His arms snaked around her to pull her close to him and she felt the powerful force of his manliness pressing against her.

He buried himself between the velvet softness of her thighs. When he finished filling her with all the love consuming him at this moment, she'd never doubt that he loved her beyond all reason.

Gillian felt as if she was being swept away in a whirlwind of passion, so wild and wonderful that it left her breathless. It was a savage passion they gave themselves up to. It was a moment lovers yearn to last forever. They felt themselves whirling and churning, caught in the raging currents of a river carrying them far away. Neither of them cared as long as they clung together.

Then the sweet, serene calm settled over them, but they still held each other as if they were afraid they would be separated again.

Reluctantly, Steve broke their embrace, for he knew that they had a long journey ahead of them. There was nothing more to cause him to linger in Maricopa County. He'd found Gillian and now she was his wife. He had only one need to make him the happiest man in the world and that was to get back to his ship.

Giving her rump an affectionate pat, he playfully urged, "Come on, lazybones, we've got a few miles to put behind us before sunset."

He threw his long legs over the side of the bed and began to get dressed as Gillian moved out of the bed. Picking up the lovely wedding gown that had been so carelessly flung to the floor in their heat of passion, she placed it back on the peg so Nancy Foster would find it when they returned home. She placed Solange's pearls atop the chest.

"Dress for comfort, dear," Steve told her as he was going through the motions of pulling on his boots.

He had not turned around to see that it was a divided riding skirt and loose tunic-styled blouse she was preparing to put on. But it struck her that with them traveling in a buggy she could take the gowns that Helen had given her.

"I've just a few things more to pack, Steve." She started rushing around the room.

"I'll buy you anything you need in Tucson or San Diego before we sail, Gillian." He watched her taking a couple of the frocks he'd seen her wear back in Tucson. Gillian gave way to a pout. He sounded just like Hawk. It seemed very easy for a man to say that you must travel light, she thought to herself as the frocks were put back.

"I'll just put a couple of changes in my bag then," she told him as she sat down at the dressing table to tie her hair back with a ribbon so that it wouldn't blow over her face as they moved across the countryside in the buggy.

Just before they left her bedroom she could not resist

lingering in the doorway to think about the many nights she'd lain in her bed and yearned for Steve to be there by her side and his strong arms to be holding her.

A pleased smile creased her lovely face as she quickened her pace to join her husband in the other room. His green eyes danced over her lovingly. What a fascinating little imp she was, he thought as he watched her place the note she'd written to the Fosters on their kitchen table.

"Now are you ready to leave, Mrs. Lafferty?" He laughed.

"I am, Captain Lafferty," she replied, taking his arm as the two of them jauntily walked out the front door.

Once they were in the buggy and Steve urged the horse into action, he glanced over to see the beautiful smile on her face and he knew she was feeling as happy as he was.

"We're off, my sweet Gilly, to see the world together, and it's going to be glorious future we'll have. I'll take you to all the wonderful places I've already seen and we'll discover new places together for the first time."

"Oh, Steve, you make it sound so exciting and wonderful." Secretly, she wondered how he would feel when she told him that she carried his child. A child might hamper all his marvelous plans for them.

"It will be, believe me." While she was having her private musings, he was having his own. When was she going to tell him "her little secret," for he knew the minute he started making love to her that she was pregnant. He knew that lovely body too intimately not to have realized that.

The next few hours he waited patiently for her to tell him that they were to have a child, but she said not a word. He questioned why she was not eager to announce such happy news as this to him.

By the time the sun was setting and a blue-purple haze was settling over the countryside, the town of Guadalupe was right ahead. He noticed that she was rubbing her back as though she was weary. "We'll stop for the night in the town ahead, honey. Guess it was a good deal I made with Foster that we take his buggy for the horses."

"I—I think so, Steve," she agreed.

What was it that was holding her back from telling him about the baby, Steve's curious nature demanded to know? Being a man of impulse and direct action, he decided to ease her qualms and satisfy his curiosity at the same time.

He reached over to take her dainty hand in his. She could not possibly have doubted the adoration in his emerald green eyes as they locked in with hers. There was such a depth of emotion on his face and in his deep voice as he told her, "You know what I want more than anything, Gilly? I want my son or daughter to be born in Ireland where I was born. So you just tell me how long we have to roam around the world so I can get you there in time."

He saw her blue eyes spark and her long lashes begin to flutter nervously from the shock of his remarks. He could not suppress a devious grin coming on his tanned face as he watched her as she tried to speak but could not find her tongue.

When she finally did speak she could not resist smiling. "You knew, Steve Lafferty! How naive I still am! I should have known better by now. You're a wicked man!"

"But only with you, my pet!" he told her, reaching over to kiss her cheek.

"I shall see that you keep that promise, Captain Lafferty."

"I never meant anything so much. I vow my love for you is endless and forever."

Gillian had no doubt of his vow this October day as she had in the past. She knew that he loved her with the same undying love she felt for him.

Her daydreams had not been fantasy. They had come true!